Praise for *The Broken Teaglass*

A *New York Times* Notable Crime Book of the Year

"[A] beautifully written, engaging mystery, with a very satisfying focus on language, libraries, and the kind of people, like me, who find genuine pleasure in reading a thesaurus or paging through a dictionary."

—DOROTHY ALLISON

"Unique and endearing...a delight: a droll and poignant comedy of manners full of witty insights and oddball characters, as well as a mystery with a one-of-a-kind unfolding."

—*The Wall Street Journal*

"*Charming* and *witty* are not the usual adjectives used to describe a mystery novel, but in the case of Emily Arsenault's debut, all expectations and definitions must be relinquished. Not since A. S. Byatt's *Possession* have I come across such a fascinating secret history as the one hidden within the pages of *The Broken Teaglass,* and the ones we all carry inside us."

—CHRISTOPHER BARZAK

"Winningly unique...one for readers who revel in words."

—*The Boston Globe*

"[An] oddly endearing coming-of-age story."

—*The New York Times Book Review*

THE BROKEN TEAGLASS

THE BROKEN TEAGLASS

A Novel

Emily Arsenault

Bantam Books Trade Paperbacks
New York

2011 Bantam Books Trade Paperback Edition

Copyright © 2009 by Emily Arsenault

Published in the United States by Bantam Books,
an imprint of The Random House Publishing Group,
a division of Random House, Inc., New York.

BANTAM BOOKS and the rooster colophon are
registered trademarks of Random House, Inc.

Originally published in hardcover in the United States by Delacorte Press,
an imprint of The Random House Publishing Group,
a division of Random House, Inc., in 2009.

LIBRARY OF CONGRESS CATALOGING-IN-PUBLICATION DATA
Arsenault, Emily.
The broken teaglass / Emily Arsenault.
p.   cm.
ISBN 978-0-553-38653-0 (trade pbk.)
1. Lexicographers—Fiction. 2. Massachusetts—Fiction. I. Title.
PS3601.R745B76 2009
813'.6—dc22   2008039167

Printed in the United States of America

www.bantamdell.com

2 4 6 8 9 7 5 3 1

Book design by Glen M. Edelstein

For Ross

THE BROKEN TEAGLASS

PROLOGUE

I lifted my head when I heard her knocking. Too much gin, Billy boy.

The door rattled under her sharp little fists.

"Billy! What the hell is going on?"

The slip of paper in front of me came into focus. There was a little drool where I'd laid my head on it.

softbound

But maybe someone picked it up before the police got there, during the cold dawn of that first next day. Sometime at sunup, long after the gurgling had stopped behind the trees, but before the body was found. Someone might have been jogging, tripped over this *softbound* scrap of history, and taken it home, thinking they might just read it. Or it was kicked away—kicked along the path by some kids shortcutting their way to school. Or carried away by a stray mutt and chewed to a slobbery pulp. Somehow shoved beyond the parameters of what would be the crime scene. In any and all versions, it's out of my hands. After everything, could this be all that it was meant to be? That I would have something to carry with me that day? Did all that history lead me to nothing more than an odd good-luck charm? And now that it's gone, what will I carry with me, from this thing to the next?

Dolores Beekmim
The Broken Teaglass
Robinson Press
14 October 1985

This one was my favorite of all of them, I decided.

"Billy!" Mona yelled again.

It asked the right question. *What will I carry with me?*

"Billy." Mona had lowered her voice, as if she knew I was right behind the door. "You're being absurd. Open this goddamn door."

"Just a second," I mumbled, getting up as she punctuated her command with a kick.

I hid the gin bottle, but there wasn't time to hide anything else.

All I could do now was open the goddamn door.

Subject: FYS (For Your Sanity)
12 August 2002
Billy:
Attached is a letter I wrote my first month here. You can steal it or write your own version. Save it onto your computer. Trust me. You don't want to keep writing this letter over and over again.
Mona

Dear _____:
I am writing in response to your query about how a word gets into one of our dictionaries. I am happy to answer your questions.

The process begins with what we call "research reading." On a typical day in our office, each editor spends about an hour reading magazines, newspapers, or books in search of new words, new uses of old words, or any other notable uses. When an editor finds a notable word or phrase, he or she will underline it and then circle a few sentences of its surrounding context. The circled material is eventually typed up onto small individual slips, which we call *citations*. Each citation features a single word in its context—enough information to give editors a sense of the intended meaning of the word. We currently have over ten million citations filed in our office.

When it is time to create a new edition of one of our dictionaries, the editors review each citation and determine what needs to be updated. When a new word or use has accumulated a significant number of citations from a variety of publications, our editors study those citations to determine the word's meaning. If the word appears to have established a consistent meaning, editors draft a definition.

During the final edit of our books, our copy editors and editor in chief make the final decisions as to which drafted definitions will make the final cut.

I hope this answer is helpful to you. Feel free to write again if you have additional questions.

Sincerely,

Mona Minot

Samuelson Company Editorial Department

CHAPTER ONE

How did a guy like me end up in a place like this?

Excellent question. It's the very question that ran through my mind on my first day on the job, and for many weeks hence. How the hell did I get a job at the offices of Samuelson Company, the oldest and most revered name in American dictionaries? In the end, this might strike you as the greater mystery—greater than the one I'd later find in the company's dusty files: How does a clod like me end up in training to be a lexicographer?

Now that you've paused to look up *lexicographer,* are you impressed? Are you imagining lexicographers as a council of cloaked, wizened men rubbing their snowy-white beards while they consult their dusty folios? I'm afraid you might have to adjust your thinking just a little. Imagine instead a guy right out of college—a guy who says *yup,* and watches too much Conan O'Brien. Imagine this guy sitting in a cubicle, shuffling through little bits of magazine articles, hoping for words like *boink* and *tatas* to cross his desk and spice up his afternoons.

Don't get me wrong. When I first got the job, I was pretty excited. I'd been starting to doubt my employability, since I'd majored in philosophy. Admittedly, I'd applied for publishing jobs on a whim, having heard some English majors talk about it. No one at the big New York companies bit at my résumé, but someone at Samuelson must have liked all the A's on my transcript in heady-seeming topics like Kant and Kierkegaard, and they called me just in time—just as I was starting to thumb through pamphlets about the Peace Corps and teaching English in Japan. My interview was with one Dan Wood, a pale, bearded middle-aged guy who didn't really seem to know how to conduct an interview. He mostly just described the defining process quietly, peering at me occasionally as if trying to gauge my reaction. I guess I didn't make any funny faces, because two days later Dan called me to offer the job.

Claxton, Massachusetts, was a far cry from Manhattan, but I wasn't in a position to complain. In fact, I was pretty pleased with myself. The shitty location at least allowed me to get a nice big apartment—on the second floor of a run-down Victorian house near downtown Claxton. Once I'd moved all my stuff out of my parents' house and bought a few cheap pieces of furniture on credit, I had a week left to prepare for my first day on the job. I bought a couple of corduroy sport jackets with elbow patches. I wondered what kind of sharp-witted young ladies I'd meet at the office, and what topics we might discuss by the company coffee machine. I read and reread Strunk and White's *Elements of Style*. I worried about sounding like an ignoramus.

Dan Wood met me downstairs on the first day, and led me up to the editorial office and its expanse of cubicles. After parking me at my new cubicle, he set a dictionary in front of me.

"I'd like you to read the front matter." He lowered his voice as if the request embarrassed him. "That's the section at the beginning of the book. The front matter explains most of the conventions of how our dictionaries are organized. Why senses and variants are ordered as they are, what sort of abbreviations are used, and so on. It's a tradition for our brand-new editors—reading the front matter on the first day."

He paused, watching me open my dictionary to the first page.

"Alrighty," I said. I was trying to convey some of the enthusiasm I hadn't had an opportunity to display in the interview. "Great."

The corners of Dan's mouth twitched a little. "Yes. You might find parts of it surprisingly engaging."

I nodded, feeling somehow I'd already said too much.

Dan gave an encouraging little nod before disappearing into his office.

The front matter wasn't so bad. There were, admittedly, a few things about the basic arrangement of a dictionary that I'd never considered before. That different senses of words are arranged from oldest use to newest use, for example. Or that when there are two equally accepted spelling variations on a single word, they are simply listed alphabetically.

Dan appeared again about an hour into my reading, this time holding a giant blue-bound book. The unabridged edition. Its wide spine barely fit in Dan's long fingers. The way he slapped it into my hands reminded me of someone palming a basketball.

"The front matter in this one repeats a great deal of the same information." Dan sighed heavily before continuing. "But it's also much more comprehensive, as the book itself is more comprehensive. You see?"

I nodded.

"Unless you're some kind of speed reader," he said, "this will take you the rest of the day."

When he left, I looked at the clock. It was nine forty-five. I loosened my tie and started in on the section about "Guide Words," those little words at the top of a dictionary page that tell you what's on that page. "Variants" was fairly interesting, as were "Inflected Forms" and the very long section on "Etymology." But it started to get a little stodgy at "Capitalization." I wanted to look at the clock again, but knew it would only depress me. "Synonyms" was no better, and I tried to skip ahead to something more interesting. "Guide to Pronunciation," perhaps?

I decided some refreshment might revive my enthusiasm. I poked around in the maze of cubicles for a few minutes, trying to look good-natured but academic. A nice petite middle-aged lady came up to me eventually, introduced herself as Grace, showed me to the water cooler, and disappeared. But there were no paper cups. Back at my desk, I started to read about the different pronunciation symbols in the dictionary. The slashes and hyphens and vowels ceased to have any meaning after about twenty minutes.

I sat up straight and stretched before starting a section on schwas. The schwa—the upside-down e—essentially stands for a grunt. A nondescript *uh* sound. A fun, if undignified, role in language study. This was a pronunciation symbol I could relate to. Standing on its head and grunting. Like me the first time I tried tequila, when I was sixteen. It was the same night that the whole varsity team drank beer out of one another's shoes—the night after our first game of the season. We probably never could've imagined that one of us would end up in an office like this, poring over a dictionary, thinking of that night. I didn't miss those days, but there was an odd satisfaction in conjuring those guys here, in this scholarly little institution. I stared into the pronunciation symbols and thought of Todd Kurtz lying flat on his back, trying to get his basset hound to drink White Russians out of his open mouth.

But that was a long time ago, and now I had to focus on umlauts and accent marks. I stared resolutely at the page.

A loud buzz sounded from somewhere. A phone was ringing in the cubicle next to mine.

I heard a chair squeak, and then an older man's voice:

"Hello? Okay . . . all right, Sheila. I'll put you out of your misery. You're welcome. Which line? Okay."

The man clicked a couple of buttons.

"Good morning, Editorial. I'm one of the editors here. I'm told you have a question about one of our definitions?"

A slight pause.

"Okay. I'm looking it up. You're talking about the noun entry for 'boil,' correct?"

Another pause.

"Okay. Okay. Well, I don't remember our exact definition for 'pimple,' but there is certainly a difference. 'Pimple' is generally applied to smaller inflammations, and the application is perhaps a little broader as well."

The man's voice was louder now than when he was talking to "Sheila," but maintained a sort of good-natured monotone.

"No. No. There's no *size* limit for calling something a boil. At least from a lexicographical point of view. If you were to consult a physician's manual, on the other hand—"

A long pause, then a quiet sucking-in of breath.

"Ohhh. I see. That does sound unpleasant. Is it painful?

". . . Uh-huh. Well, I'm a dictionary editor, sir. I think maybe you should call a physician. In fact, I hope you do.

". . . I understand. But our college dictionary isn't meant to be a diagnostic manual.

". . . Right. But even if *you* aren't sure of the right word for it, a trained physician only needs to *look* at it, and he should be able to tell you exactly what you should be calling it. And with a doctor, there's also the possible advantage of treatment.

"... Yes. Yes, sir. That's what I'm saying. That's what I think you should do. I'm sorry I can't be more helpful.... Sure. No problem. Let us know how it goes. If you like.

"... All right, then. Good luck to you. Take care."

The chair squeaked again as the guy hung up the phone. No more sounds came from that cubicle for the rest of the morning.

After lunch, Dan took me into his tiny book-lined office.

"I hope you're not finding the front-matter tradition too much of a trial." He rolled up the sleeves of his Oxford shirt as he spoke, still avoiding my eyes.

"Nope," I said, and immediately felt dumb and caveman-like. *Nope. Yup. Duh.* To avoid looking at him, I stared at the twisted little cactus on Dan's desk.

"Pretty interesting, actually," I lied.

"You have a green thumb?" Dan asked.

"What?"

"Are you interested in plants?"

"Uh ... not really. No more than average, I guess—"

"Because I don't know what keeps this thing alive. I've had it for at least four years. I haven't any idea how to care for a cactus. But still it grows here on my desk."

"Do you water it?"

"Very sparingly."

"That sounds about right," I said, perhaps too enthusiastically. "For a cactus."

Dan handed me a sheet of paper that had *Training Schedule* typed at the top.

"You'll be happy to know you won't be doing this every day. Tomorrow your real training begins."

I nodded.

"It's not meant to be an endurance test, even if it might feel that way. Quite simply, front matter can train you more succinctly than most training sessions can."

I nodded again.

"As the schedule specifies, I'll be doing most of your sessions. Here in this office. Just knock on my door at the scheduled times. For the other sessions—like cross-reference with Frank, or thesauri with Grace—they'll come to you. Do you have any questions about the process? Or anything you've read today?"

When I said no, Dan told me I needed to be introduced to Mr. Needham, the editor in chief. Dan led me to Mr. Needham's office and smiled wanly as he held the door for me. He didn't go in with me.

Mr. Needham's office was pretty Spartan. Unlike some of the cubicles I'd seen earlier in the day, his space contained none of the usual comforting reminders of a slightly rosier existence outside of this office—pictures of smiling children, Nerf basketball hoop, dish of toffee candies. Even on Dan's desk there was at least a framed snapshot of himself holding a large trout, in addition to that sad little cactus. The only sign of nonacademic humanity in Mr. Needham's office was a shiny new roll of Tums resting on the corner of his blotter.

Mr. Needham himself looked a little time-worn, sagging slightly behind his glossy wooden desk. He seemed to be scowling at me, but I tried not to take it personally. Maybe he'd eaten something too spicy for lunch—hence the Tums. A thin layer of gray hair was pulled from one side of his bald head to the other. I wondered if *comb-over* was in the dictionary yet. His clothes, conversely, were crisp and classy: a black sport coat without a trace of lint or cat hair and a tastefully splashy tie that reminded me vaguely of a Gauguin painting. Maybe a gift from a theatrical granddaughter.

"Hello and welcome." His voice had a gargling quality to it.

"Thank you, sir," I said.

"You can sit down."

"Thanks."

"Reading the front matter today, eh?"

"Yes."

"How are you finding it?"

I searched his face for a hint of a smile. Finding none, I found it difficult to suppress my own.

"Informative," I said quietly.

"It's a lot to absorb. But it's important. If everyone who owned a dictionary actually read that information, actually learned how to use a dictionary properly, our jobs would be much easier. Has Wood told you about correspondence?"

It took me a moment to remember that "Wood" was Dan.

"No . . . I don't think so."

"So many letters we have to answer. Most people's questions would be answered if they just *read the information that we provide*. Right there in the front of the book."

"Huh."

"But you'll see that soon enough, I'm sure."

He shifted some papers on his desk and produced a familiar-looking document. My college transcript.

"Philosophy. Hmm. Wood likes philosophy students. I'm not certain why. I don't believe he ever studied much philosophy himself. I used to read some now and then, back when I was getting my doctorate. I enjoyed Hegel a great deal."

"Did you?" I wasn't sure how to take this. I'm pretty certain no one actually enjoys Hegel.

"Mmm...a German minor? Very good. But whatever academic background one has, whether you've got a bachelor's in philosophy or a PhD in linguistics," Needham said, leaned back in his chair, and stuck out his lower lip, "you are about to embark on a difficult journey. The work we do here is not easy. It's an intellectual job, but that doesn't make it an *easy* job. Quite the contrary."

I nodded solemnly.

"We have to be very precise. Very thorough. People count on us to do it right."

"Yes, sir," I said carefully, thinking of boils and pimples and still trying not to smile.

"No, it's not an easy job," he said. He sighed, shook his head, and gazed out the window as if contemplating the many casualties of the great dictionary cause. A moment later he sat back up.

"I encourage you to take a look at some of the histories that have been written about our company over the years. The best one, in my opinion, is *Keeper of the Word: Daniel Samuelson and the Creation of the Great American Lexicon.* There's a copy in the editors' library. I'm sure Pat would be happy to locate it for you."

I didn't know who Pat was, but I nodded.

"You're in good hands with Wood. He took over the trainings five years ago. He's likely to be the next editor in chief, you know."

He creaked back in his chair again.

"But I don't know when that will be. Time will tell. I

wanted to see her through the next unabridged, but Lord knows . . .

"But I'm keeping you from your work. Back to that front matter! One of our most time-honored traditions."

He stuck out his hand and I shook it.

"Have a good afternoon," he said, gripping my hand firmly. His fingers were chill.

"You too," I said, and left him.

I made my way back to my cubicle, where I gazed at pronunciation symbols for the rest of the afternoon. At four o'clock, Dan Wood stopped by my desk and told me I could go.

Maybe it was a sort of omen that my first encounter with Tom was on that very first day of work. He was sitting on the front porch when I got out of my car and trudged toward the house. In my week of living there, I'd never seen him before. He was bald but for a few long clumps of hair growing out of the sides and back of his head, all pulled into a thin ponytail at the back. His body matched his hair—stringy, skinny, and formless in his lawn chair.

"Hello, Billy." His lips labored to keep a cigarette in his mouth as he spoke.

"Hi," I said, pausing before stepping onto the porch.

"You look tired, Billy."

I hesitated. His deliberate, repeated use of my name was a little *Twilight Zone,* but he probably meant it to be friendly.

"I am," I replied. "First day on the job."

"At Samuelson. My brother told me."

"Your brother?"

"Jimmy's my brother. I'm Tom. Jimmy told me about you."

Jimmy was the guy who lived downstairs with his wife, Barbara. They were both about fifty and very friendly, at least so far. Jimmy drank a lot and didn't seem to have a job. Barbara left each morning on the bus, dressed in a skirt and blouse, with her white-blonde hair pulled up into a clip. But I hadn't yet asked where she worked.

"They bust your ass down there at Samuelson?"

"Not exactly. It was kind of a weird and quiet day, actually. They had me read the beginning part of the dictionary, where it explains how it's organized."

"All day? That's what you did all day?"

"Yeah. It was pretty boring."

"Yeah. I've heard some bizarre shit goes down at that place."

"Bizarre shit?"

Tom shrugged. He removed the cigarette from his mouth and took a long sip out of his Black Label beer. "Just check out their definition of 'civil liberty' sometime, and maybe you'll notice something funny going on."

"Really?"

"Or maybe it's 'libertarian.' I can't quite remember. Bottom line, though—those dictionary guys gotta have their hands in everything. Think they're so clever."

I stared at Tom. It had never occurred to me that there might be a townie/lexicographer rift in Claxton.

"Most of the people who work there think they're such hot shit," Tom continued.

"I don't think I'm hot shit," I said, sitting down on the step. I was hoping Jimmy would come out. Jimmy wasn't as creepy as this guy. He'd helped me get my mattress up the stairs the day I'd moved in, and we'd had a couple of good chats since then.

"Maybe not yet. But wait till you've worked there awhile.

You'll get to tell people you're a *lexicographer*, that you write fuckin' dictionary definitions—"

"Yeah. Wait till then. I'll have the chicks just falling all over me when I start saying that stuff."

Tom puffed on his cigarette and studied me through narrowed eyes.

"You want a beer?" he asked, after a time.

I considered whether a cold one would be worth hanging for a few more minutes with this crackpot.

"Sure," I answered.

"Jimmy!" Tom yelled through the screen door. "Bring Billy a beer, would ya? And I could use another too!"

Tom put his beer can on the step. "Don't get me wrong. I'm sure it'll be very educational for you. Just don't let those fuckers throw you to the wolves."

Jimmy appeared, red-faced, with three Black Labels. He looked like he'd just been sleeping. He had lines on his cheek, maybe from pressing against a rough blanket or a folded sheet.

"Billy boy," he said. "Nice tie."

"Where did you go to college?" Tom demanded.

"Don't mind Tommy," said Jimmy. "He's just jealous. He's always wanted to work at that place. He just didn't have the grades."

"Not true," said Tom. "I had a 3.6 GPA. At least I *went* to college."

"Yeah, I know. And dropping out one semester before graduation's a *real* sign of intelligence. If I had the education you had, I sure as hell wouldn't be sitting *here*. Who's the one letting it go to waste?"

Tom maneuvered his cigarette to one side of his mouth.

"Education is not a means to an end," he announced. "Education is valuable in and of itself."

"I'll drink to that," I said, lifting my Black Label. The brothers drank without bothering to clink with me.

"Great. Me and the two geniuses," Jimmy snorted. "How was your first day, Billy?"

"Tolerable, I guess. I was lucky to get this job. I should probably look at it that way."

"I hear you," said Jimmy.

We gulped our beers in silence. After I finished mine, I went upstairs and sprawled out on my futon.

The phone rang later, while I was warming up a canned minestrone.

"Hello?"

"Billy. It's Mom."

"Oh. Hi."

"You sound tired."

"I just said hi. I'm not tired."

"I was hoping you'd call and tell us about the new job."

"I figured I'd wait for something interesting to happen first."

"You're joking. It must be a *fas*cinating place. You must be meeting some interesting people, at least."

"My boss seems nice."

"Well, that's a good sign. Not everyone's lucky enough to have an understanding boss. I mean, I sure don't."

"Yeah."

"So are they teaching you how to define words yet?"

"I'll be doing some practice words next week."

"Do your coworkers seem smart?"

"I haven't seen anyone chewing their own leg off yet."

"What?"

"What's Dad up to?"

My mother sighed. "Tempering chocolate."

"What's the occasion?" I asked.

"The Gardners are coming over for dinner. Your father feels the need to serve his mousse with the little molded chocolate moons and stars stuck into it."

"Dessert is thirty percent presentation, you know."

"*Please.* I'm going to put him on for you."

"No, really. It's fine. I know what a delicate process it is, the tempering of chocolate."

"Yeah, well," she said. "Father-son relations are delicate too. Your first day at your first real job. You should chat."

I heard her calling him, and then:

"William."

"Yes, Dad."

"I wish you were here to share this excellent dinner we'll be having with the Gardners."

"Me too." As soon as I said it I realized, pathetically, that I meant it. "I'm having a can of soup for dinner."

"I hope you're having dessert, then. This mousse I'm making here is pretty delicious. I've already had several test-helpings."

"I'm sure you have."

"Eat dessert first. That's what I say."

"Absolutely," I said. "Because you never know."

"You never do."

"Nope," I said, finding myself strangely eager to let this exchange of platitudes go on indefinitely. To occupy this alternate space where my father and I conquer life's problems with a couple of clichés and an upraised rolling pin.

"How's the job?" Dad wanted to know.

"I'm not sure yet. It's kinda quiet. I don't really know what I'm doing yet."

"Well. That's fine. Just don't quit in the first six months. That's a résumé killer."

"I won't be quitting anytime soon, I don't think. I don't know if I'll find it inspiring, exactly, but it seems a harmless enough way to support oneself. For the time being."

A long pause followed.

"Dad?" I said into the phone.

"This is becoming a little unwieldy," Dad said finally. "The white chocolate stripes are particularly difficult, William. I'm going to put your mother back on."

"No problem."

My mother ended the conversation by telling me how proud they both were of me, and congratulating me on my entrance into the *real* world, which made me flinch. After we hung up, I sat at my little kitchen table and spooned thin tomatoey water into my mouth. I wondered what brainless version of myself had picked this can of soup off the supermarket shelf and deluded himself that it would satisfy him. I vowed to look at a few cookbooks before I went to the store next time.

As I slurped the last of the soup, I stared across the kitchen floor at the two boxes of books I'd left by the stove. I probably didn't have enough shelves for them all, and the idea of unpacking them exhausted me. But those books and my TV were my only means across this endless evening, and I wasn't ready to turn on the TV yet. TV was desperation. TV was a last resort—the inadequate piece of driftwood that you grab just before you drown anyway. If I needed television to survive my first night in the real world, there was little hope for me.

I sat on the floor and opened the first box. *The Shining. The Colossal Compendium of Jokes, Puns, and Riddles.* A couple

of John Grishams. These were older books than I'd antici-
pated. I couldn't remember packing them. My mother had
probably sneaked a couple of boxes into my U-Haul to give
herself more closet space. Beneath the bestsellers were a few
more joke books. I pulled one out and flipped through its
yellowed pages.

Closing it, I leaned back against the oven and thought
again of my mother's use of the term *real world*. I'd seen
some real world in my time, and Samuelson Company didn't
bear much resemblance to it.

CHAPTER TWO

Dear Mr. Mason,

I'm afraid I can't tell you which spelling, *Judgment Day* or *Judgement Day,* is more appropriate for the tattoo you plan to receive. I can tell you that *judgment* is the more common spelling variant here in the U.S. The decision of what to include in one's tattoo, however, is a highly personal one, and I think you should use whichever spelling pleases you. . . .

Dear Mr. Ferguson,

Of course I am happy to put an end to this dispute between you and your wife. There is nothing wrong with your wife's statement "These chicken legs are *moister* than the ones we had last week." Although *moister* is not a commonly used word, it is a perfectly acceptable word, following the conventions of standard word construction. . . .

This was the reading material Dan left on my desk in the middle of my second week of training. Answering customer letters was soon going to be one of my duties, and these examples were supposed give me a feel for how it's done.

Dear Mr. Lawrence,

Congratulations on your successful parole hearing and your early release. It is refreshing to know that you are continuing your linguistic studies outside of the state penitentiary. I am happy to answer your questions.

Indeed, *cunt* is a surprisingly old and well-established word in the English language. . . .

These letters at least made livelier reading material than the usual mimeographed training packets with cryptic titles like "The Philosophy of Defining" *(The job of a lexicographer is to define words, not things. . . .)* and "What Is Lexical?" *(Generic nouns belong in the dictionary proper; names of specific people, places, and historical events do not. . . .)* Usually Dan and I would chat about the packets twice a day in his office. My favorite thus far was "Self-explanatory: A Primer" *(A two-word term is considered self-explanatory, and therefore nonlexical, if its definition can be surmised from the definitions of the two words from which it is formed. . . .)*

Dear Brittany,

Thank you for sharing your coinage, *Funday,* with us. Although *Funday* is a very nice word, I'm afraid we can't put it in the dictionary at this time. It actually takes a long time for any word to make its way into the dictionary. . . .

The last letter on the pile was written by Dan himself:

Dear Ms. Fine,

We are flattered that you considered using our definition of *love* as a reading for your wedding. I'm sorry you were ultimately disappointed with our work.

It's important that I clarify one point, however. At

Samuelson, we do not aim to define the limits of emotional experiences such as *love, hate, faith, friendship,* etc. We aim only to define what these words mean in standard English discourse. That is, what is generally meant by a speaker or writer when he utters or writes these words. If our definition is, as you say, "unromantic," it's because lexicography is, by nature, an unromantic exercise. Precise, clear, and thorough definition is the main objective—and the only objective. A definition could not possibly capture the sensations, the depth, or the variations of something like love as it is experienced by everyone lucky enough to encounter it. And isn't it best that even the most precise of words cannot capture such things?

Best wishes for your upcoming wedding.

Sincerely,

Dan Wood

Samuelson Editorial Department

What a cheeseball, I thought, coming to the end of it. But I liked Dan's approach better than the thinly veiled condescension of some of the others. Dan popped his head into my cubicle just as I was putting the letters aside.

"Ready to try your hand?" he asked.

"I guess . . . I was just admiring this one about the wedding reading."

"Yes, that's one of my recent favorites. I decided to give you a bit of a doozy for your first letter."

He handed me a ragged piece of lined paper with an envelope clipped to it.

Dear Ms. Minot,

Thank you for your response to my last inquiry. While I do not agree with your conclusions about the word *sobriquet,* it is interesting to hear what uses Samuelson has in its citation file, and I appreciate your taking the time to share those examples with me.

Your response leads me to another question. I recently consulted the Samuelson definition of *editrix,* and found *editrices* and *editrixes* given as possible plural forms. The entry for *dominatrix,* on the other hand, gives only *dominatrices* for the plural form. My question for you, Ms. Minot, is if this inconsistency is an error. How can the *-xes* ending be correct for one of the words and not the other? As both an editrix and a lexicographer, I suppose you are uniquely qualified to satisfy my curiosity. I trust I will receive a prompt and satisfactory reply.

Cordially,

Jared Houston

Student

"This is really the worst kind of correspondent," said Dan. "The gadfly. People who don't want to stop writing to us, want to catch us in an error, or just show us how clever they are. Usually these people have a lot of time on their hands.

"Normally this letter would go to Mona, since it's addressed to her. But Mr. Houston . . ." He paused. "*Student*. Whoever he is, he's been bothering Mona for a few months now. And this subtle pairing of 'dominatrix' and 'editrix'— frankly, I find that a little frightening, and I think Mona agrees. It usually helps when another person answers instead. The guy might realize that she doesn't have time for a pen pal. Sometimes we just have to stop answering, unfortunately."

"Who's Mona?" I asked.

"Oh—you haven't met yet? Mona's our most recent hire before you. Last year. Her cubicle is on the other side of the floor, closer to the citation files."

"Does she know about this letter?"

"Yes. I showed it to her. Mona's quite happy not to have to answer it. But you might want to go introduce yourself and ask her about Mr. Houston. She could probably tell you a few stories. Mona's had some bad luck with correspondence."

"Okay."

"And don't be afraid to raid the cit files if you feel you need to. To write your correspondence."

"Okay," I said.

The cit files. We'd talked a great deal about them, but I hadn't as yet been granted permission to look inside them. The editorial office took up the entire second floor of the Samuelson building. Around the perimeter of the floor were the cubicles, but in the middle of the room were the five rows of cabinets with little wooden drawers—like a giant set of old-fashioned card catalogues. Some of the little cards in there were rumored to go back over a hundred years, to the early days of the company. Editors were always getting up from their cubicles, opening drawers, pulling out stacks of cards to consult, poring over the citations. I'd begun to wonder when I'd get to paw around in there myself. Now that I was official, I felt a little twinge of self-distrust, like when you look over a railing and imagine yourself jumping. As if I might have an inexplicable impulse to flick a lighter into one of the files, reducing entire word histories to ash.

Dan thumped the side of my cubicle as if patting someone on the back. "And just—well, just do the best you can with it."

I read the letter a few more times and then decided to take a little walk and find Mona Minot, its original recipient.

When I reached the corner of the office that Dan had described, I circled around the two sets of cubicles there, trying to guess which person was Mona.

"Can I help you find something?"

I turned. A pale, tired-looking woman was standing at the copier, stuffing paper into it in small handfuls. Her high penciled-in eyebrows and stiff movements made me think of Japanese Kabuki theater.

"Hi—I'm, uh—looking for Mona?"

"Oh. Well, I'm Anna, by the way." She walked over and gave me a weak handshake. "I should have introduced myself earlier."

"I'm Billy," I said.

"I know." Anna arched one of her razor-thin eyebrows. "Dan sent a memo around."

"Okay. It's nice to meet you, Anna."

"Thank you. Mona is there, in the farthest corner," Anna said, pointing. "The petite one, with the dark hair."

The cubicle where she was pointing was occupied by a tiny person perched at the edge of her swivel chair. Her tailored blouse and upswept hair gave the impression of a child dressed up as a businesswoman. She had about a dozen little piles of citations fanned across her desk, and she was staring at them through thick-framed glasses—those dark, angular frames people wear when they're trying to look fashionably nerdy.

"Hi," I said, looking into her cubicle. She had a poster of Humphrey Bogart hanging behind her. Next to her computer was a photograph of her with an older woman who was probably her mother. They were both wearing white.

"Hey," she said. She stared at the citations for a moment longer before turning to look up at me. Then she noticed the letter in my hand.

"Brilliant," she said under her breath. "That's *brilliant*."

"What?"

"He didn't tell me he was gonna give that letter to the newbie."

"Who? Dan?"

"Yeah." She lowered her voice. "That is such *shit*."

She grabbed the letter from my hand. I left the hand extended for a handshake.

"I'm Billy."

"Yeah, hi," she muttered, shaking my hand absently. "I'm Mona. You know, he's really a sweet man, but he has no idea how to make a person feel comfortable around this place. Did he make you read front matter all day the first day?"

"Yeah."

"Yeah. Such *shit*. This place is hilarious. That must be why I'm still here. For the laughs. Of course he hasn't introduced you to anyone else, I'll bet."

I shrugged. "Mr. Needham."

"That doesn't really count. You'll never talk to Needham again. They keep him around to maintain a sort of Dickensian feel to the place, but only the senior editors ever really have a reason to talk to him. I mean, have you started to meet some *real* people yet? I guess it's been lonely so far, when your only human contact is those little sessions with Dan, stuffed together in his office."

"It's all right. Dan's actually pretty cool," I said.

"Yeah, I guess. Maybe in the same way a tumbleweed is kind of cool," she replied, tidying her citation piles.

An odd characterization. I wondered if it had something to do with Dan's doomed cactus.

Mona whispered, "So you've met Anna. She's the art editor. Draws all the little pictures. And she's the first African-American art editor in Samuelson history."

A smirk twisted up the sides of her little pink mouth as she watched my reaction.

"African-American?" I said.

"Just look up 'Afro,' " she whispered, pushing her desk dictionary toward me. I did. Next to the definition was a drawing of a woman with a thick Afro of solid black ink.

"Yeah?" I said.

"Look closer," Mona whispered. "You're a dictionary editor now. You need to develop a keener eye for details."

The woman in the picture had a white face—naturally, since she was outlined in black on white paper. But her nose was straight and sharp. Her eyebrows were thin and neat over slightly drooping eyes.

"Holy *shit,*" I said, remembering to whisper only the second word.

"Shhhh," Mona said. "Control yourself."

"That's just *wrong,*" I whispered.

"I think it's brilliant," Mona said. "Putting yourself in the dictionary where it's least expected. A hiding place right in front of everyone's face. Now, probably everyone here's got a secret fantasy of doing that sort of thing. To write their old high school bully's name into the definition for 'asshole,' or put a picture of themselves at 'awesome,' or something. But of course you'd never get away with it. But just adding a touch of yourself, smiling from a little hiding spot—"

"A touch? It's kind of . . . ghastly, actually."

Mona hit me on the arm, swinging unexpectedly hard. "*Ghastly.* Don't take it so seriously. It doesn't hurt anyone. It doesn't alter the meaning or compromise the definition. And we all need to find little ways to keep ourselves happy around here."

I watched Anna as she continued to work the copy machine. She looked fairly content.

"Anna's very sweet," Mona added, whispering. "Don't hold it against her."

"Do the boss editors know?"

She shrugged. "I'm not exactly in the inner circle yet. Probably they noticed a long time ago. I'm told it's not the only trick picture she's done. Clifford's the one who showed it to me."

"Who's Clifford?" I asked.

"He sits right near you. Heavyset guy, in his forties, curly blond hair?"

"Don't think I've met him."

"Well, maybe someday he'll circle around to your side of the island and you'll get to see him. You'll hear him first, probably. Clifford's pretty vocal, as far as editors go. But he's nice, once you get to know him. Very normal. Maybe the most normal editor here. Second to Grace, of course."

"I've met Grace. She introduced herself on my first day."

"Of course she did. See? The most normal. Just a regular old nice person. And always good for gossip when you're desperate to get away from your desk for a little conversation."

Mona paused.

"So . . . ," I said. "What about you? What did you study before you came here?"

"Classics. Greek and Latin. I went to Middlebrook."

"Oh?"

Hmm. Middlebrook. The expensive women's college about thirty minutes outside of Claxton, where rich girls went in wearing cashmere and emerged months later with short haircuts and septum rings and T-shirts that said *Subvert the Dominant Paradigm*. I tried not to wonder if Mona had ever kissed another girl. It just didn't seem like the right thought for a young wordsmith to be having.

"You from around here originally?" I asked.

"No. Ohio. But I'm keeping you from your letter. I should stop talking your ear off and let you get back to it."

"Gee, thanks."

"Do you want any advice for answering that thing?"

"Yes," I admitted.

"First of all, you should explain to him that in general both are accepted plural forms of '-trix' words. But you might want to just tell him a little about what kind of evidence we have in the file for 'editrix' and 'dominatrix,' too. Just to shut him up. Just look in the file at 'dominatrix' and 'editrix' if you need something to beef up the letter. Have you had a chance to poke around in the cit file on your own yet?"

"No . . . I've only seen the citations that Dan's given me to look at."

Mona pushed her chair back and stood up.

"Come on, then. You know you can look in there and take stuff out whenever you want, right?"

She led me into one of the rows of little wooden file drawers, pulled out one of the narrow drawers, and heaved it onto the top of the cabinet. Then she started flipping through the tightly packed citations.

"You know, correspondence is the one task that really gives you an excuse to fool around in the cit file. So often, with other stuff, you can just use the database. Dan told you that they've got the most recent cits all computerized, right?"

"Yeah . . . since 1994, right?"

"Yeah. Maybe someday they'll get around to computerizing all the millions of old cits too. Seems like that'd be a smart idea, don't you think? What if the place goes up in flames someday, you know?"

"Yeah."

"Here." She held up a thin pile of citations. "That's what we have for 'editrix.' Not much. That might actually be why both plurals are listed. Both are standard plurals for that ending. But it's not really widespread enough to even have established a more commonly used plural. You know what I mean?"

"I think so," I said.

She started flipping through the cits. "You'll probably find at least a couple varied plurals for 'editrix' in the cits. . . . Let's see now . . . If it's in the dictionary, some editors at some point had cits to back it up. Everything's in the dictionary for a reason. Jared Houston just doesn't ever quite believe that. . . . Here we are . . . here's a plural."

She held one out to me. I took it and read it.

> **editrix**
>
> Mrs. Hopkins was one of the only *editrixes* at the journal, but she was one of the most valuable members on staff. She had a unique ability to spot and foster young writing talent. Male colleagues patronizingly referred to her style as "the motherly touch."

It was from a news magazine.

"I guess I could quote that one," I said.

"And another." Mona handed me another slip. "The other plural form. Perfect."

I read the slip.

> **editrix**
>
> She warmed that water with her hatred. She sighed plagues into that water. I didn't care. In this chill and inhuman place I

was obedient and invisible to everything. I needed that tea to remember I was alive, warm-blooded. I always carried the tea slowly up the stairs and to my desk. I drank it with careful relish. No spilling on the citations. No slurping, no satisfied Aaaah! Such noises would echo through the cubicles and start an uncomfortable collective shifting of the editors and *editrices* in their seats. So I always sipped quietly.

The citation was from a book called *The Broken Teaglass,* written by someone named Dolores Beekmim, and published in 1985.

"This one's kind of...weird, though," I said slowly. "Should I be quoting something like this? There's something a little off here."

"Whadya mean?" Mona took it and read it.

"Kind of sounds like..." I looked at Mona, hoping she would say what I was thinking, so I wouldn't have to risk sounding stupid. "But maybe not. I mean, a citation can be a lot of things, you know? There are officers' citations, in police departments, and—"

Mona was silent for a moment.

" 'No spilling on the citations'?" she said, wrinkling her nose. She read it again.

"I think this takes place...here," she said.

"Yeah...that's kind of what it sounded like."

"Or maybe at some other dictionary company office. But there's, like, only one or two other dictionary companies in the country."

"Yeah, I know."

"I didn't know there was a book like this." Mona seemed tickled. For the first time since I'd approached her desk, her smile seemed real. "A novel about Samuelson. Isn't that amazing? Can I hold on to this for now?"

"Sure. Doesn't seem like a very objective thing to be quoting, so I'll look for something else."

"Right." Mona looked distracted. She was watching Dan make his way to the men's room. "Look through the rest of those cits. Then look through the ones for 'dominatrix.' "

"Yeah. All right. Sounds like fun."

"Don't spend too much time on it." Mona lowered her voice. "Dan probably just gave it to you so the guy doesn't get any funny ideas about us being friends. The content of the answer probably won't matter so much as the fact that a different editor's name is signed on the bottom."

"Dan didn't quite say it like that."

"Of course he didn't. But that's what he meant."

Dan finally started my "research reading" training on the following morning. I'd been looking forward to it since Dan told me that all editors—even lowly editorial assistants like myself—got to choose most of their own newspapers and magazines for the task. The idea that I could get paid to read *Rolling Stone* and *Time* really jazzed me. He started me off with a little packet of photocopied articles to practice on. I peeked at the titles of his selections while he spoke: *"Reality TV? Not!" "Learning to Say No." "Lesbian Celluloid: Classic Screen Dykes." "Uncle Sam Goody Wants YOU: Materialism as the New Patriotism?"*

"As you can see, I've tried to give you a good variety. Nothing too heavy for your first few times around. You're likely to find some pretty informal writing in some of these. But remember that you're not just looking for new words. The easiest thing to spot is new words, especially slang words. But we also read for slight variations in how older words are being used. Or general usage issues. Or abbreviations. Anything that looks like it could be useful. You'll find more to underline as time goes on. You'll become more free to underline whatever strikes you."

"Should I look things up as I go?" I asked.

"To begin, you can do that, if you wish. It might give you a feel for what we've already got in our books. But typically, you won't be doing that. It goes too slow that way, and it's unnecessary. Citations are there to help us to determine if our definitions are still accurate and up-to-date, not just to determine what we're missing."

Dan cleared his throat.

"It's really one of the more fun parts of the job," he continued. "Aside from defining, of course. You ought to know, though. It's addictive behavior. We've got this one retired editor who still marks everything he reads. A pretty sad case. He comes in every once in a while to drop off his handwritten cits. Takes them off the TV and radio too. Half of his cits are quoted from late-night talk radio."

"Are you serious?"

"I don't think I could make that up." Dan shook his head. "I shouldn't speak of it so lightly, actually. That could easily be my own fate, I suppose."

I glanced down at his hands as he handed me a stapled list. No wedding ring. I don't know why I'd assumed he was married.

"Take a look at this list of periodicals," he told me. "We subscribe to all of these, and you should feel free to add something if there's a magazine you think would make a good addition. Some periodicals are read by a few editors, some only by one. People tend to catch different things. You have any idea what you'd like to read?"

"*Rolling Stone?*" I said.

"Sure," he said, circling it. "Two other editors read that, but I'll put you on the list."

"*Time*?"

"I'm afraid you'll have to get in line for that. Three people already read it. I just kicked someone else off it and put Mona on for a while. She asked for that about six months ago."

I noticed that *Motorcyclist* didn't have any initials next to it.

"Anyone read that?" I said, pointing.

"No, actually. The editor who read that retired a few months ago. His subscriptions have been piling up. I'd be quite happy to give you that one."

"Sure, put me down for *Motorcyclist,* then."

"And can I start sending motorcycle terms to you? Are you a motorcyclist?"

"Um. No, I'm not. It just caught my eye. I'm just interested in it as a, uh, layman."

"I see," Dan murmured. "Well. We'll start with those. You can think about what other magazines you'd like and tell me over the next few weeks."

I suppressed a groan when I saw Tom sitting on the porch as I drove up. Almost every day when I came home, he was there. He'd blow smoke rings and nod as he questioned me about the secrets of the dictionary trade. When he was satisfied with my answers, he usually offered me a drink.

"There he is," he said as I climbed the porch steps. "Billy the Kid."

"I don't feel like a kid. Not after a day at that office."

"Mmm." Tom nodded. "You know, you've got circles under your eyes. You worn out?"

"Yeah. A little tired."

"What did they have you do today?"

"I read a bunch of magazines."

He snorted. "Yeah, right. Sounds like a tough day. Did I tell you yet that I applied to work there once?"

"No."

"Yeah. Well, I did. But they didn't want anything to do with me. Didn't even call me for an interview."

"I wouldn't take it personally," I said. "They probably were just being sticklers. Probably didn't call you because you don't have your degree."

"I don't need to be consoled, man. It's all shit."

"It is," I agreed.

Tom was staring out into the street.

"Shit," he said again, slowly.

"What's the matter?" I asked.

"It's shit," he said. "What superficial things separate an educated man from an ignorant one. In the eyes of conventional society, anyway."

He closed his eyes.

"Shit," he said again, apparently relishing the word. Then he started reciting, " 'For some time he has been aware of shit, elaborately crusted along the sides of this ceramic tunnel he's in: shit nothing can flush away, mixed with hardwater minerals into a deliberate brown barnacling of his route, patterns thick with meaning. . . . ' You know Thomas Pynchon? *Gravity's Rainbow*?"

"No, not really. Heard of Pynchon, but I never read any of his books."

"That's a part that really hits home. Some days don't you just feel like you've gone headfirst into the crapper?"

"I've had a few of those, yeah."

"Ah." Tom opened his eyes briefly, and smiled. " 'Patterns thick with meaning, Burma-Shave signs of the toilet world, icky and sticky, cryptic and glyptic . . . ' Billy. You really should read him. . . . Hey. You know what 'glyptic' means?"

I looked at the ground. I couldn't quite place what the root *glyp* might mean.

"I have a lot to learn," I admitted.

"Don't sweat it. No one expects you to be Daniel Samuelson. They don't make 'em like Daniel Samuelson anymore. I hope they're teaching you a little company history at the office."

The city bus pulled up to the corner and Barbara struggled out of its doors, carrying about four white plastic grocery bags on each arm. She rearranged her bags and tugged at her skirt before heading toward the house. Tom kept talking as she approached.

"People don't generally appreciate what a hardworking man Daniel Samuelson actually was," he went on. "Imagine writing a whole dictionary in just a few years. Now they've got a full staff doing the same thing. The same thing *one man* did back then. Hey, Barb."

"Hello." Barbara stopped in front of the steps and tried to blow a wisp of hair out of her eyes.

"You want help with those bags?" I asked. She smiled, then handed me a bulging plastic sack full of cans.

"Either of you know when Daniel Samuelson started his illustrious company?" Tom asked.

Barbara rolled her eyes. I opened my mouth to answer, but Tom interrupted.

"Eighteen seventy-eight. See that?" He shook his head. "Barb here's lived in Claxton her whole life and she doesn't know a hell of a lot about Mr. Samuelson. It's a shame. That company was here before most of our families even got off the boat. But see, many Claxtonites don't even know about Samuelson. It's actually a little-known fact that some of the country's finest dictionaries are produced right here in our fair shithole of a city."

Tom looked at Barbara and then at me. "You want a shot of something?"

"Please, Tom," said Barbara, opening the screen door. "Not on the porch."

"Tequila okay? That's all I got," Tom said, getting up.

"I'm good," I said.

"You sure?"

"Yeah."

As soon as I closed my front door, however, I was sorry I had turned down the tequila shot. The pouring, drinking, and subsequent light-headed conversation would've filled up a good thirty minutes far better than I could on my own.

I threw down my junk mail.

"What the hell do I do now?" I whispered.

On my kitchen table, *101 Damn Good Jokes* lay facedown, open, with its spine cracked. When I saw the book, I felt chastened. What was wrong with me lately—treating time as if it were something that simply needed to be filled?

I opened the refrigerator and considered its contents. Chicken breasts. Celery. Broccoli. Zucchini. Heavy cream, even. What was that for? I couldn't remember. I figured a stir fry was ambitious enough. I sat down and picked up my book. I would read it until I was hungry enough to start chopping.

• • •

There was an unusually tight and shiny quality to Mona's hairdo when she stopped by my desk a few days later. As if she'd gotten up that morning and decided to really look the part of lexicographer. Ready for grammatical and personal perfection, with not a single loose hair in the way. But there was a mischievous little quirk to her face that offset the stark quality of her straight part, gray blouse, and black skirt—Mona smiled sideways, with one eyetooth showing.

"Good morning." She leaned into my cubicle, whispering. I could smell her soap. It wasn't a floral scent, but something wholesome and robust, like Ivory or Irish Spring.

"If you say so," I whispered back. "Morning, afternoon, night—it's all running together lately. I wake up in this chair sometimes and wonder what day it is."

"You'll get used to it," Mona said. "Although some of the senior editors *still* fall asleep at their desks. Guess what?"

"What?"

"That 'editrix' cit we found? It's even fishier than I thought."

"Really?" I suppressed a yawn. "How's that?"

"No *Broken Teaglass* in the editors' library. No listing of it on any of the library websites I checked. I tried a couple of used-book-shop websites, and Amazon. Nothing. I even called this giant used-book store in Portland, where my cousin works. They didn't have any *Broken Teaglass*. And no one's ever heard of Robinson Press. It's like it never existed."

"I'm sure it *existed*. Maybe it was just a vanity press or something. Maybe *The Broken Teaglass* was just some crappy book that happened to fall into some editor's hands. And then he research-read it for shits and giggles."

Mona closed her eyes. "Please. I hate that expression."

"Alrighty," I said.

"Anyway. Do you really think such a book—about dictionary editors—would just fall into some dictionary editor's hands, and then that dictionary editor would blindly research-read it like anything else?"

"I didn't say it necessarily happened that way, exactly."

"Then how do you think it happened?"

"I don't know," I said. "I just started working here a couple of weeks ago. There are probably a million ways that this could've happened that I'm not smart enough to know about."

"Yeah, well," she persisted. "I was looking forward to reading this book, whatever it is. And it looks like it's just . . . imaginary."

"Maybe you should ask some of the older editors about it. Someone's probably heard of it. Maybe even one of them is the one who research-read it in the first place."

"Yeah. I guess I'll do that. I probably should have thought of that before."

"Tell me what you find out."

I was doing my best to feign interest. I liked Mona. She was sort of cute and vaguely amusing. I wanted to give her an excuse to come back to my desk.

About a month into training, after about fifty practice definitions, I was ready to start defining for real. About half of the staff—fifteen or so regular editors and three of the science editors—had just started working on *New Words Supplement,* and I got to join them early on in the project. The *Supplement* was a small paperback companion book to the unabridged dictionary. Samuelson published a new *Supplement* every ten years or so. The idea was that people could buy this to use alongside their unabridged dictionary, rather than buying a whole new, expensive unabridged. According

to Dan, the *Supplement* was a good place to get one's defining feet wet, since very few people actually bought it.

I joined the *Supplement* staff pretty near the beginning of
the project, when they were halfway through the "B" words.
After that they were going to do the "A" words, then "C"
words, then onward. Turns out dictionary editors rarely start
with "A." Who knew? It's because supposedly reviewers
usually just lazily look up "A" words when they're assessing
the quality of a reference book, and you don't want reviewers looking only at the work produced while your lexicographers are still a little rusty. *And starting with "A" is just
generally considered lexicographical hubris,* Dan informed me on
my first official day of defining. *Not to mention bad luck.*

Defining filled my solitary days. I flipped through citations for words like *bear* and *béarnaise sauce* and determined
they needed no additional definitions. I looked through the
cits for *beat one's meat* and drafted a definition—a simple and
elegant cross-reference to *masturbate.*

I didn't see much of Mona. She gave me barely dis-
cernible smiles when we glided past each other in the office,
but that was all. My only significant social encounters were
with pitying older editors: There was Grace, who liked to
stop by my desk for small talk about the Red Sox and the
new car her husband was thinking of buying and—after I
mentioned that I liked to cook—recipes. Dan also offered a
dry, hesitant friendliness during our training sessions in his
office. And then there was Mr. Phillips.

The first day I saw him, he was hunched over the coffee
machine, humming a Sinatra tune and scribbling something
on the back of an envelope with a red galley pencil. I waited
silently behind him with my empty mug.

I peered over the guy's shoulder. He was shading in some
block letters he had drawn on the envelope.

"Do be do be do," he muttered as he scribbled. Then, unexpectedly, he said, "You must be the new one."

"That's me."

"Your name again?"

"Billy."

"Billy. That's right. Grace told me. Not Bill. *Billy*. I'm... uh... Mr. Phillips. John Phillips. Editor emeritus. Retired about three years back."

"Nice to meet you."

"You look like you could use a doughnut."

"I do?"

Mr. Phillips jutted his skinny hip to one side, revealing a box of doughnuts on the table behind him.

"Take one, Billy. There are a couple chocolate ones in there. And a jelly. I got it for Anna, actually, but she'll eat a glazed if you really want jelly. She likes glazed too."

"You brought these doughnuts?"

"Yeah. And the coffee. The *real* coffee. Jamaica Blue Mountain," he said.

"Impressive," I said. My old girlfriend used to like Jamaica Blue Mountain. It cost something like thirty dollars a pound. Mr. Phillips finished his shading and propped the envelope next to the doughnut box. It said ENJOY! in thick block letters.

"Well, it's called Blue Mountain *blend,*" Mr. Phillips admitted. "But it's still a pretty good brew. Better than what they've got here on a regular day."

"Breaking in the new blood, John?" someone asked from behind me. The voice was familiar. Clifford, who sat near me. He was short and a little overweight, with blond hair curling over his receding hairline. I'd never actually seen him before, only listened to him answer the phone.

"Yep. How've you been, Cliff?" Mr. Phillips asked.

"Same old, same old," Clifford replied. But he looked like he wanted to say something else to Mr. Phillips.

"Guess I'll get back to work," I said.

"Take a doughnut," urged Mr. Phillips. "Take two."

"No, thanks—"

"C'mon, champ. What's your pleasure? Chocolate? Cruller? Boston cream? I think I had them put a few of those in there too."

His rasping voice grew louder with each variety of doughnut that he named, and was now nearly a roar. I grabbed a cake doughnut and a napkin.

"Now you're talkin'. Old-fashioned plain doughnut. Heh-heh," Mr. Phillips chuckled.

"What's so funny, John?" Clifford asked.

"Where'd they find *you,* Billy?" Mr. Phillips asked. "Strapping young fellow. And with a name like *Billy.* Bet you'll suck that doughnut down in no time flat."

Cliff shook his head without looking at me and then poured himself a cup of coffee.

"Nice meeting you, Mr. Phillips," I said, fleeing the coffee station. "Thanks for the doughnut."

"Any time, champ."

I didn't sleep much that night. For the third night in a row, I lay awake past one o'clock. My bedroom's floral wallpaper made me feel oddly old and infirm. *Bean poles* and *bean sprouts* and *bean threads* snaked around in my head. Some animal—probably a cat—kept making a painful sneezing-crying sound from somewhere behind the house. It would stop occasionally and I'd start to drift off—and then it would begin again.

At about 2 a.m., I dragged a sleeping bag out to my living

room and sacked out there instead. The old octagonal Victorian room had huge, curtainless front windows. I pulled up all the blinds so all of the headlights could roll over me as the night traffic shushed by. Crashing on my futon, I felt like an overnight visitor in my own apartment. It was this sensation that tricked me into sleep.

CHAPTER THREE

"Guess what?" Mona demanded, sticking her little head into my cubicle, forgoing hello. As if we'd spoken just the day before. As if we were buddies.

"What?" I said. It seemed her hairstyle had loosened a little in the past month. There was something softer about it, and less slick. Her face didn't seem pulled so tight. I wondered if this had happened gradually or all at once.

"I found another one," she said.

She shoved a citation under my nose. I took it from her.

blow-dryer

I switched off the stove and picked up the phone. By the time Scout answered, I'd lost it. I was crying. He wanted to know what was the matter, nearly yelling the question after I couldn't answer his first couple of tries. I couldn't form sentences, or even meaningful one-word answers. He hung up. A few minutes later, he was there, at my door. His cheeks were red from rushing there in the cold. His hair, usually so carefully styled with a round brush and *blow-dryer,* was tousled in all directions. He had never looked so cute. He had never looked so powerless. I wanted to hug him, for strength, and then push him back out the door. I was glad to have him there, but suddenly acutely aware that he couldn't save me from anything. He followed me into the kitchen and watched me pour tea water from the pot to the sink. He wanted to know if I was all right. I said no. No, I said again. I'm crazy. You wouldn't believe how crazy I've become.

Dolores Beekmim
The Broken Teaglass
Robinson Press
14 October 1985
23

"This one is more bizarre than the first," said Mona.

"How's that?" I asked. "It's funny, cuz I'd forgotten all about—"

"The subject matter, for one. Obviously. Also, most cits are about three sentences. The sentence the word is in and then just enough of what's around it to give you a little context. Look how long this one is. What the hell?"

"Yeah, it's odd," I said. "But I've seen longer ones."

"Usually you make a long cit for a *reason*. What kind of idiot cites practically a whole page of text just for a word like 'blow-dryer'?"

I thought of Dan cringing at my first couple of attempts at research-reading.

"Maybe it was a poor, lowly editorial assistant who didn't know what he was doing?"

"I don't think so, Billy. Look. You want to know what else is weird about these cits? They both have an exact date on them. *The Broken Teaglass* is supposed to be a *book*. Books don't give an exact day of publication. Usually you just get the year."

"Pretty weird," I agreed. "So you think a typist is messing around, sticking bogus stuff in the citation files?"

"Maybe not a typist. Maybe anyone. But yes, that's what I'm thinking."

"Why would anyone do that?"

"I don't know."

"Maybe they just really wanted 'blow-dryer' to make it into the dictionary," I suggested.

"Right. And there's no more covert way to pad the evidence for a word than to make up citations with dictionary editors as characters."

"This one doesn't have dictionary editors as characters."

"How do you know? The narrator in this citation's probably the same as the one in the first."

"Unless it's a short story collection."

Mona shook her head, frowning.

"How'd you find this?" I asked.

"It was in one of my sets of cits for the *Supplement*."

"Wow. That's creepy."

"Yeah. There must be a lot of these around, is what I'm thinking."

"Mona." I lowered my voice.

"Yes?"

"Do you want to maybe talk about this after work today? We could get a beer or something."

"I don't drink beer."

"Coffee, then."

"Okay. How about Friendly's on Carpenter Street?"

The suggestion surprised me. I hadn't been to a Friendly's since I was a kid.

"Cool," I said.

• • •

"I think I'm going to get ice cream." Mona was studying the menu through her squarish glasses. "What about you?"

"Just coffee, I think."

"That's too bad. I don't like to get ice cream by myself."

"Why not? You shouldn't feel guilty. You don't look like someone who needs to worry about calories."

Mona sighed. "So charming, Billy. No wonder Anna's already in love with you. 'That new boy is such a gentleman. So *personable*.' "

"She said that? I just say hello."

"That's all it takes at Samuelson. But anyway. What I meant about ice cream is that it's a communal kind of pleasure, don't you think? Everybody piles into the station wagon when Dad's in a good mood after work . . . drive out to the Dairy Queen and get cones together. It's really not about the ice cream per se."

"Is that how it is in your family?"

"Well, no. Not exactly. But you get the idea. Ice cream is celebratory. It's a special occasion. Eating it by yourself is a little like drinking by yourself. It's base."

"Maybe I'll get some ice cream, then. If that's how you feel about it. Are we celebrating something?"

"No." Mona pulled two citations out of her bag: *editrix* and *blow-dryer*. "We're investigating. Someone's fucking around in the cit file."

"Or maybe someone *was* fucking around in the cit file. In the mid–eighties."

"Sure. The cits are both dated 1985. But everything else on them is bogus. The date's probably bogus too."

"So if they're made up, what do you think's the point? What's it about?"

"Maybe a personal vendetta between editors? A bizarre

psychological game of some kind? All those silent types we have at Samuelson—there's gotta be a sociopath or two among us. Or at least a few passive-aggressive types."

A waitress took our orders. Mona asked for a sundae with hot fudge, peanut butter sauce, two different kinds of ice cream, and "no cherry." I got a dish of rainbow sherbet.

Mona scoffed at my order. "Rainbow sherbet, Billy? Are you some kind of pansy?"

"No, I'm just not very hungry."

"Right. Whatever. So we both agree that the first cit definitely sounds like it's happening at a dictionary's editorial office. Probably ours. Now, in the second one, there's something very dramatic happening. She's sobbing, making a desperate phone call. Did you *read* this thing?"

"Yes, I did."

" *'He couldn't save me from anything.'* What did she want to be rescued from?"

"That's one thing I already hate about defining. You only get to read little bits of things. You never get to hear what happens next."

"This might be a vendetta. Or a trick. But maybe it's a cry for help."

"I hope not," I said. "I can't think of anything more boring."

Mona put down the white slip and rested her pointy chin in her hand.

"This might not seem interesting now," she said. "But trust me. Stuff like this doesn't come up every day at Samuelson. Spend a few weeks triple-proofreading dictionary copy for typesetter's colon errors, and then you'll understand how interesting this really is. You're definitely gonna thank me for involving you in this. Someday."

"I'm thanking you already. Thank you for letting me in

on the second wacky cit. It was truly the most interesting thing that happened to me all day, although I did get 'ass-wipe' in my stack of citations today, so I shouldn't complain. Not that there were enough cits to justify bothering with a definition. But—" I saw Mona's mouth open to say something, but I didn't let her. "*But.* These *Teaglass* things, they're two cits in—what? Ten million? Why do you care so much?"

"You know how you said you don't like reading just the little pieces of articles we get in the cits? It sucks, always just getting to read a few sentences and thinking, *Now* that *sounds interesting*. In the beginning, I used to write down the names and dates of articles with the intention of going to the public library sometime and looking them up. But I never did. You get used to it. You learn to be able to find something intriguing for a second, and then let it go."

"It doesn't seem like you've quite learned how to do that yet."

"Well, I was about to say that these cits are different. This is the one story I want to finish. *This* story is driving me crazy. Because I know it's not just hacked out of some magazine. There's no way to go to the library and look it up. It's *because* there's no clear way to find the rest that I care. And it's so obviously written by someone who works at Samuelson. You can tell. This person is tired of that office, with all of its intellectual, socially inept automatons. Sick of all the silent judgment, and *sticking* it to the place. Don't you think that's intriguing?"

"Yeah," I said. "Sticking it to the dictionary man."

"And then the next cit is about some personal story. Maybe about the same person, who knows? But don't you want to know? Maybe two editors are communicating. Maybe—"

The waitress approached with Mona's large sundae and my sherbet.

"Is he gonna help you with that?" the waitress asked as she placed the sundae on the table. Mona seemed to bliss out for a moment, fixing her gaze on the cherry-less white peak in front of her.

"Nope," I said, answering for Mona. "It's all hers."

"I don't know about that. Where's she gonna put it all?" The waitress examined Mona and chuckled at her own joke. "You guys need anything else?"

"No, I think we're all set," I said.

Mona was silent.

"What a snatch," Mona said as soon as the waitress was out of earshot.

"She was just trying to be friendly."

"Waitrons should never refer to the size of their customers. Large or small."

Mona began working her way through the mound of whipped cream in silence. I puzzled over her use of the word *waitron,* which came out of her mouth without a trace of irony. Perhaps a vestige of her PC girls' school education. A weird accompaniment to her first designation for our waitress.

After a few bites of chocolate ice cream, Mona said, "Maybe 'snatch' was a little harsh."

"Maybe."

"Anyway. The bottom line is I'm a sucker for a juicy story, and this looks like it might be one. And if we've seen two in just a couple of months, there must be more."

"Interesting logic. Those two could just as easily be the only two that exist."

"Right. But c'mon. I don't think so. And I want to figure out how to find more of them."

"Well, that's simple. You go to the first file drawer. You start at 'aardvark,' and just start flippin' your way through—"

"That's ridiculous. I have a lot of free time at the office, but not *that* kind of free time."

"You tried the editors' library. And Amazon. And, what else? Library of Congress? Where else are you going to look now but in the cit file?"

"Yes, but there must be a way to do it intelligently. I think the only way to do that is to look closer at *these two cits.*" Mona waved the cits dramatically as she spoke.

"It looks to me like you've already been spending a little too much time looking at those things."

"What I'm getting at . . . if you will listen carefully . . . is that you can't refer to citations and the painfully quiet office and not expect anyone to ever notice, can you? On some level, whoever's doing this *wants* the cits to be noticed."

"Okay. Maybe. Probably."

"All right." Mona licked her lips, and said, softly, "And then what?"

"What do you mean, 'and then what'?"

"*What,*" she said ominously, "does this person expect to happen next?"

"I don't know. Get fired, maybe."

"No. You're getting ahead of yourself. When an editor first notices a fishy cit, what . . . *what* . . . does the bogus cit writer expect the editor to do about it?"

"Get irritated. Maybe be annoyed that he can't figure out who the scoundrel is, poisoning the sacred cit file with some dumb game. If he's—or she's—a really die-hard dictionary person, I guess, maybe he'd even report it to the boss."

"And if not?"

"Maybe he'd expect that editor to do just what you're doing. Try and find more of the citations so they can be in on whatever the joke is."

"Right. So if this is a subversive kind of thing, like a private joke between editors, don't you think the person who wrote this stuff would want to give another editor a way to find more than just one passing cit?"

"A way to find more phony cits?"

"Yeah."

"I don't know. Maybe it's just supposed to be a casual thing. A one-time ha-ha passing across your desk. A little clean fun between dictionary nerds."

"But why so cryptic, then? You might be right, but I'm hoping you're not. That's why I want you to take these cits."

"What the hell am I supposed to do with them?"

"Just *look* at them. I think maybe the cits themselves somehow can tell us how to find more. Look. These two cits are weird. We've already talked about that. They're too long. A book with an exact day's publication date, and a nonexistent publisher? Whoever wrote them wasn't trying to make them seem like real cits. But I can't figure out what exactly we're supposed to see in the cits. Maybe it's something I'm just not seeing. So I want you to try to figure it out. Maybe all it needs is a pair of fresh eyes."

I looked down at the cits on the table. "You want me to take these from you? Are you sure about that?"

"I've made copies. Besides, I've read them so many times, I've got them memorized. Take another look at them and think about it. What else do they have in common that I haven't thought of?"

"I don't know if this is such a great idea. You might have tons of free time for this kind of thing, but I'm still pretty slow with the defining."

"Just look at them, Billy. A few minutes here and there, maybe at home."

"And I just *got* this job—"

"We're not doing anything wrong. *We* didn't write the

cits. And Dan doesn't—Dan wouldn't care. Dan doesn't care what the hell we do as long as we produce a reasonable amount of work in the seven working hours we're there each day. Did you know that Raymond Shelling spends a couple hours a week browsing bottles of vintage wine on eBay?"

"He's the tall bald guy who's always reading *Wine and Spirits*?"

"Yeah. And he's a real efficient definer. So no one gives a crap what's in that thermos of his. Just do your work, avoid any public mental breakdowns, and no one at Samuelson cares whatever else you've got going on. Certainly not Dan."

I sighed. "All right. What do you have so far?"

Mona steepled her hands and leaned forward. "They're both nouns, for one. That's not much, obviously. Also, both cits are a little long, but have nothing else marked, just the one noun. I noticed that other words *could* have been marked. I might have marked the extended use of 'warm-blooded' in the first cit, and I definitely would have marked 'lost it' in the second cit. So I looked up those words. I thought there might be something there. But nothing. It was a long shot, anyway."

"You went looking for more cits that said *'Broken Teaglass'*?"

"Yeah."

"The title might have some kind of significance," I said.

"Well, if there is, maybe you can figure it out. Really, I don't expect us to figure it out *now*. When you're at your desk the rest of this week, contemplating the weave of the cubicle wall fabric, just pull yourself away for a while and give these cits a little thought."

"Okay. Sure thing. But a newbie like me probably isn't

going to crack the code. It might be some highly elevated lexicographical trick."

Mona laughed and licked happily at her final spoonful of hot fudge. "There's no such thing, Billy. Lexicography is a drone's work. There are no tricks. Are you ready to go?"

So it's probably fairly obvious that I was humoring Mona at first. I thought she was kind of cute with her little sleuthing project.

The morning after our ice cream date, I read over the suspect cits a couple of times. *I wanted to hug him, for strength, and then push him back out the door.* Yuck. Talk about melodrama. I suspected Mona was suspending disbelief for the sake of entertaining herself. If she could do it, I probably could too.

Content aside, Mona was right that the *blow-dryer* cit was particularly peculiar for its length. So many sentences marked just for a word like *blow-dryer*? I wasn't sure how long blow-dryers had been around, but it seemed to me that by 1985 people would be so used to the device and the term that editors wouldn't be noting it anymore.

Editrix, on the other hand—I'd probably mark that word if I saw it in a magazine. Such a weird word. The kind of word someone would use only to sound odd or old-fashioned, maybe to perplex his audience. And *-trix* wasn't exactly an everyday kind of suffix. Maybe it was a fairly new suffix that had never quite taken. Why would anyone use it, when *-ess* could be used much less conspicuously? Would anyone ever say "waitrix" or "actrix"? I looked up *-trix* and *-ess.* They were both pretty old. Both Latin, and *-ess* went back to Greek. So much for my suspicion that *-trix* was some snappy new variation on *-ess.* I felt silly for even pondering the idea. Mona Minot probably already knew all about the origins of -*trix* and the like from her very expensive classical education.

"Office poll."

I looked up, instinctively shielding the two suspect cits with my hand. George, the young pronunciation editor, was standing over me. I'd seen him skulking around the office before. The wide flatness of his face made me think of a steamrolled character in an old cartoon. Usually he wore a sport jacket over some incongruous T-shirt. Today it was a navy blazer over a yellow T-shirt with a large reproduction of a Mr. Goodbar wrapper on it. In one hand he was holding up a pink slip of paper that said BRUSCHETTA on it. In the other he held a little notepad.

"What's this?" I asked.

George let his eyes fall closed for a second.

"You're supposed to just say the word," he said.

"What?"

"Just pronounce it for me."

"Okay. Uh. Brew-shetta?"

George started to make a mark on his pad, but then stopped and lifted his eyes.

"Is that a *guess*?"

"Yes."

"If you don't have a clue, you're supposed to say 'Pass.' "

"What if you think you know, but you're not sure?"

"Then you say it," he replied, in a tone that made me feel as if he'd just flicked me off like a booger. He was gone before I could thank him for his clarification.

"Office poll," I heard him say to Cliff.

"Brew-scetta," Cliff said.

"Office poll," George continued at another cubicle.

"Brew-shetta," a confident male voice replied.

I put away the *editrix* and *blow-dryer* cits. Clearly idiots like me had no business wasting time around a place like this. I took out the next cits in my box for the *Supplement*. A suffix, *-aster*. I'd never heard of it before. I'd had enough of suffixes for the morning. I stuck it back in the box and pulled out the next batch of cits. *Asterisk.* Grand. I was beginning to feel nostalgic for *asswipe*.

Ten after ten was when the ten-minute break time started. At 10:09, Mona peered into my cubicle, resting her little pink chin on the cubicle wall.

"Having fun?" she asked.

"Yeah—I mean, not exactly." I closed my motorcycle magazine. "I've been reading this magazine for thirty minutes and all I've underlined is 'rice rocket,' which is apparently an un-PC term for sports bikes from Japan. And honestly, I don't think 'rice rocket' is ever going to make it into the dictionary."

"Just underline it and move on with your life, Billy. You're thinking about it too much. Whether or not it'll make it in later isn't the point. You want to take a walk for the coffee break?"

"Sure."

Once we were outside, cutting across Samuelson's front lawn, she said, "I don't suppose you've come up with any brilliant ideas about those cits yet."

"Nope." I paused to suck in the crisp fall air. It annoyed me that this beautiful day was occurring right outside of the Samuelson office, just out of reach from my cubicle. "I'll come running if I do."

"Good. I'm looking forward to it."

"So what are you working on right now?"

"Nothing. Taking a morning break from defining. They gave me some proofreading to do on the update of that kids' thesaurus. Mindless."

"Huh. I haven't gotten anything like that yet."

"Oh, you will."

"So . . . what's up with that George guy?"

"What do you mean?"

"What's this 'bruschetta' office poll?"

"Oh, George does that once in a while. He'll probably do it a lot more now that we're working on the *Supplement*."

"Shouldn't he be able to determine how things are pronounced on his own? I mean, based on the evidence?"

"It's just, sort of, for his own clarification," Mona said. "Especially if it's some new foreign borrowing, like a food word. He wants to see how your average educated Americans are saying it. Here he has a roomful of relatively educated people at his disposal."

"All right. But what if we're all saying it wrong?"

"If we're all saying it, it's probably not wrong, exactly. Just Americanized. If no one is saying the real foreign pronunciation, it's probably not going to enter the language that way."

"That just doesn't sound like a very reliable method."

"Well, you know, George doesn't have as much citation evidence as we do for his work. Usually the only person who ever thinks to take regular pronunciation citations is the pronunciation editor. Have you seen the pronunciation cit file? Only a few drawers. He has to use a variety of sources to make his decisions. There are probably some tough calls. I think he usually uses the office poll to decide whether to take a variant seriously. Like, say he's got some evidence that people are starting to say *fajita* like 'fa-jee-ta.' Of course it seems completely dumb to someone like him.

But maybe he'll do an office poll. If ten out of thirty or so educated people are saying 'fa-jee-ta,' maybe there's something to it. Maybe it's becoming an accepted variant."

"Is that a real example?" I asked.

"Of course not. I don't think anyone in the office would say 'fa-jee-ta,' do you? I just heard some girl say it at Taco Bell the other day. Which is what made me think of it."

"You eat at Taco Bell?"

"Yes. I'm tired after work a lot. And I'm not much of a cook, I'm afraid."

"You shouldn't eat too much fast food. It fogs the brain."

"Fogs the brain?"

"Well—it fogs *my* brain, I think, but probably you don't need to worry. I'm just a little bit of a food snob, that's all."

We walked on in silence for a few minutes, heading down a street behind the Samuelson parking lot. A woman started yelling something incomprehensible at us from the third-floor window frame of what appeared to be a gutted house.

"What?" I yelled back.

"Just keep walking, Billy," Mona said.

"Think again!" the woman called. She undid and then re-fastened her graying blonde ponytail with an elastic band.

"Sorry?" I yelled. As soon as I'd said it, I realized she wasn't talking to either of us.

"Not the kind of woman you want around your kids," the woman shouted. "Not if you want them to turn out *right*!"

"Oh," I called, quickening my pace to catch up with Mona.

"You didn't want to stop and hear the whole story behind that one?" I asked her.

"Did *you*?" Mona replied.

"Not by myself," I said.

Mona put her hands in her skirt pockets as she walked.

"Yeah, this is kind of an odd little neighborhood. A dictionary publisher parked himself here in Claxton in the 1800s, and come hell or high water, the dictionary's gonna stay here in this neighborhood. No matter what depressing socioeconomic phenomena have grown up around it."

"It really doesn't seem so bad," I said. "No worse than the neighborhood I live in. I think it's cool. This place has history *and* a little hardened modern-day reality to it."

"Can I ask you a personal question, Billy?"

"Sure."

"Do you still, um, have both of your parents? And are they still married?"

"Yes . . . and yes. Why?"

"I can usually guess these things, based on little impressions. You can kind of tell these things about people, if they give the right signals."

"You had a sort of sixth sense that my parents are still kicking, and still married?"

"Not a sixth sense. Just a hunch. Based on certain psychological vibes."

"What about birth order? Can you guess that too?"

"I'm not as interested in that one. And I'm not as good at it. But I think you're the youngest."

"Very impressive. But how many siblings do I have?"

We were approaching the Samuelson walkway. Mona stopped walking, put a finger over her lips, and studied my shoes, then my knees, then my chest. While she tapped her finger and considered her answer, I looked at the Samuelson building. It still jazzed me to approach the place on foot. Coming from the gray, depressed outer neighborhood, it was always surprising to come upon this building, with its manicured lawn and little front garden. The squat brick structure looked like a venerable old elementary school. An etching of the company building appeared on the front pages of some of Samuelson's older dictionaries, and the outer appearance of the place hadn't changed much since then. Coming in the front door, I always felt like I was entering that old drawing. The back entrance, with its parking lot and Dumpster, had never seemed as romantic.

"Two older sisters," Mona said carefully.

"Wrong. But close. One older sister."

"Okay. Well, that's interesting. Is she much older than you?"

"Two years."

"What does she do?"

"She's a grad student. But she identifies herself as a poet. That's what she wants to be when she grows up, I guess. She's already gotten some things published in a couple of obscure literary magazines."

"Really? What kind of stuff does she write?"

"Long poems. Sort of historical stuff. I don't know how to describe it. It's been a couple of years since she's showed me anything. Rumor has it she's working on a series of poems about the Hartford witch trials of the 1660s. My parents mentioned she was doing some research on that."

"Wow," Mona said. "A research-poet. Sounds pretty classy. I don't even have any full siblings myself. All half-siblings and step-siblings."

As Mona talked she led me up the Samuelson steps.

"Hmm," I said. "Can I ask *you* a personal question?"

"Sure."

"Do you floss regularly?"

"Oh dear. That *is* personal."

"Well?"

"I wish I were better about that. I tend not to do it."

"Interesting," I said, nodding.

"Why do you ask?"

"There's a fundamental difference between flossers and nonflossers," I said.

"And what's that?"

I hesitated before answering.

"Flossers don't really think they're ever going to die," I said, holding the door for her.

"Really?" she said. "Wow. It sounds like I gave the right answer, then."

I'd have preferred we didn't end the conversation there, with my morbid dental hygiene theory just hanging in the air. But before I could say more, she gave me a little wave and headed back to her cubicle, where she could think about how creepy I was for the remainder of the morning.

Back at my desk, I pushed all of my cits aside and took out my dictionary. *Blow-dryer.* I considered the word again as I flipped to its page in the book. What was so special about *blow-dryer?*

The definition was just a cross-reference to *hair dryer.* Simple enough. I flipped to *editrix.* A female editor. I pored over these definitions for a few minutes. They really didn't seem to have any obvious connection. I wondered if the same person who wrote the citations could have also written these specific definitions. It didn't seem possible, though. *Editrix* seemed like an old-fashioned word. It had probably been around for a while. I looked at the date next to the definition. 1950. Surprising, I thought. I'd have thought it a nineteenth-century sort of thing. And who knows when it had actually entered the dictionary? If the first known use was in 1950, it probably hadn't been defined and entered in a Samuelson book until at least the mid-1960s. At least.

Maybe not until the 1980s. I'd have to look back at old editions of the Samuelson books to know for sure. Maybe someone was just playing around with the random lot of words they had defined themselves. I flipped back to *blow-dryer* and looked at the first usage date.

1950.

"Crikey," I whispered. Clifford's chair creaked, registering that he'd heard me.

I slammed my dictionary shut and ran to Mona's cubicle.

CHAPTER FOUR

Access time. Advantaged. Airglow. Alphanumeric. **These** were the first words on the list Mona printed out from the digital dictionary. All words first used in 1950. All she had to do was type *1950* into the Date search field, and in a few seconds, we had a list. My favorites on the list were *head-shrinker, LSD,* and *X* (as in the movie rating). As we huddled together in the downstairs editors' library, I suggested to Mona that we try looking up those words first.

"Be my guest," she said. "But I plan on going about this in an orderly fashion. I say we split the list into parts and check off words as we go. But if you want to reserve a few particular words for the titillation factor, don't let me stop you."

"Yeah, okay. Maybe I'd like 'corn chip' too," I said, looking at the list. "But maybe I'm just being greedy."

"Whatever." She gazed at the list, then asked, "What are you doing Friday night?"

"That's tomorrow night."

"Yes."

"What are you proposing? Taco Bell?"

"We get a pizza. And some beer, maybe. And we knock off a few solid piles of cits at my place."

"You're gonna bring cits home? Is that allowed?"

"No one's ever forbidden it, actually. And we'll put them right back on Monday. I'm always taking big piles of cits from the files to answer letters and stuff. Sometimes they stay at my cubicle for weeks. Nobody cares. Nobody notices."

"And you're buying beer? I thought you didn't like beer."

"I don't. I'm bribing you."

"Well, that sounds good. But what do *you* drink?"

Mona paused. "I don't need to drink. Someone's got to hold this operation together."

"Come on, now. What do you like to drink? Satisfy my curiosity. Wine coolers? Berry-flavored ciders?"

"No," Mona snapped, looking insulted. "Mixed drinks. Cosmopolitans. Whiskey sours. Rum and Coke. But Coke will be sufficient this time."

"All right. I'm buying the Coke, then. Which cits do you want to take?"

"How about you start with 'access time' through 'cable knit.' I'll start with 'maître d' ' through . . . let's see . . . through 'noseguard.' "

"That's gonna be a lot of cits. Am I supposed to carry a big sack of them out on Friday afternoon?"

"Bring a backpack Friday. And just take as many as you can without it looking too weird. You might also try to look through some of the words before you leave work. What kind of beer do you like?"

"Hmm. Corona, if you feel like classing it up. But lately I've discovered I have a taste for Black Label. If you're looking to save a buck or two."

"It's all the same to me, Billy. Really, which do you want?"

"What the hell. Black Label."

Mona rolled her eyes. "That's what my dad drinks with his hunting buddies. And I think you may be the only Black Label–guzzling lexicographer on God's great earth."

"I don't *guzzle*."

"We'll just see about that. I'm going back up to work."

"Congratulations," I said.

I was thinking of the pile of cits on my desk for *astern*. Sitting next to it was a letter questioning the political propriety of the term *little people*. The writer of the letter felt the term was really no better than *midget, dwarf,* or *munchkin*. The writer gave no indication whether he was a "little person" himself.

"I'm just gonna hang around here for a few more minutes, and look at the old books," I confessed.

Mona gave me a skeptical smile as she left.

"I thought you were gonna spend all night there in your car," Tom said. He and Jimmy were watching me come up the walk. "What's going on?"

"I was listening to a song. I wanted to finish it."

"What song?" Tom asked.

" 'No Woman No Cry.' "

"Hmm," he mumbled. I lingered by my door, expecting him to supply his opinion about Bob Marley. He didn't.

"Plans tonight?" I asked.

"Yeah," Tom replied. "Watching an investigative documentary about the October Surprise. Feel free to join me, if that interests you."

"Actually, I kind of have a date tonight."

"Ahh," said Jimmy. "Congratulations. Where you bringing the lucky lady?"

"Well, we're just gonna hang out at her place. We're investigating a little work-related problem together. A dictionary puzzle."

"Pray tell," said Tom. "This sounds interesting."

"Maybe after tonight," I said. "It's all a little unclear still."

"C'mon," Tom insisted. "I love word games."

"It's not a *game*—"

"Then what is it?"

Jimmy snorted. "Tommy. Quit bothering him about the stupid *words*. If you have to bother him, ask him about the *girl*."

Tom sniffed. "That doesn't interest me so much."

"Yeah, right," said Jimmy. "She must be smart, huh, Billy? Since she works with you there at Samuelson?"

"Yeah, she's pretty smart. Listen, I wish I could chat with you longer, but I've got to get ready and then run to the liquor store. I've gotta get a flask of rum."

Jimmy hooted. "You need a little something to nip on during your date? Is the girl that ugly?"

"No, she just likes rum and Coke."

"That's one of my wife's favorite drinks." Tom nodded knowingly.

"Is it?" I said, absently. Then: "Wait. Tom, dude, you've got a wife?"

"Yep."

"You're joking."

"It's not something to joke about. Not a laughing matter, my marriage."

"You're hanging out at her place with a bottle of booze? On a first date?" Jimmy shook his head. "I wish I was part of your generation, Billy boy. Good luck."

Mona's place was classier than mine. It took me a while to find it—a set of old stone buildings called Somers'

Mill. I wasn't used to this tree-lined side of the city, where most of the storefronts were occupied and no one was walking around with an open beer can.

I rang her buzzer, and she appeared almost immediately.

"Hi. Oh my God, Billy. I found one. I found another one."

"You started without me?" I followed her up the stairwell.

"I started last night. But who cares? It's working!"

"What's working?"

"Nineteen fifty!"

Her apartment was on the third floor. She led me into a small but immaculate kitchen. Off the kitchen, I could see a large old-fashioned pantry. Boxed macaroni and cheese, rice pilaf packets, and ramen noodles were arranged in an elaborate pyramid.

I handed her the paper bag with the Coke and rum in it, but she set it on the kitchen table without looking in it.

"You want to see what I found?" she asked.

"Aren't you going to give me the grand tour first?"

"C'mon. Sit down."

She sat down with me at her kitchen table and pushed a little white paper toward me. "So read it."

I did:

maven

When the papers went crazy, I knew everything might very well explode. Still, I resigned myself to the stern presence of my fellow word *mavens*. There was at least an odd comfort in submitting to the long silence of the day. Reliable and insistent, it served as a kind of protector. I was reading a book about drug slang, underlining the word "stash," and you came to my desk. When you saw what I was reading, you said, Now you're talking. You said that junk slang was your favorite, and wanted to know if there was a chapter on junk. Then you asked if I'd finished that other book yet. No, I whispered. I was unraveling fast. Was it a trick question? What exactly had been in that article that I hadn't had time to read? Was there something suspect near the corpse? Were you smiling, Red, because of something you knew?

Dolores Beekmim
The Broken Teaglass
Robinson Press
14 October 1985
32

I read it over a couple of times. Mona went to the refrigerator, got out a beer, and quietly placed it next to my hand.

"That's yours," she said. "You can drink it, if you're so inclined."

"I think that's a good idea. Now that we're dealing with a corpse and all." I snapped open the can.

"I *know*." Mona sounded pretty thrilled. "Isn't it great?"

"Great? Well, I don't know about *great,* but—"

"You know what I think is interesting about this one?"

I took a long sip.

"What?" I said.

"Don't you find the mention of the corpse a little casual? I mean, it's mentioned almost like an afterthought."

"I wouldn't say that—"

"Come on. Corpse? Mixed up in some conversation about junkie slang? I think this is supposed to be amusing."

"Amusing?"

"You know, like British humor."

"British humor?"

"Yes." Mona was growing irritated. "Like someone un-covering the corpse you buried is just a *bother*. Just a dreadful *bother*."

"I don't read it like that," I disagreed.

"You want to know what I think this is, Billy?"

"What?"

"With all the washed-up English master's degrees that pass through Samuelson, there's got to be a half dozen wannabe novelists floating around the editorial office at any one time, right?"

"I guess."

"Yeah. A *corpse*? With some telltale clue next to it? I think someone decided to write a pulp mystery novel and have it take place at Samuelson."

"Okay. And that's interesting to you? What's so great about that? A bored editor writing a trashy novel?"

"Well, obviously with this 1950 thing there's got to be some kind of additional inside game to it."

"Mona, do you want a drink? I brought you some stuff." I showed her the little bottle of rum. "Where do you keep your glasses?"

Mona hopped up again.

"I'll take care of it," she said. "I prefer to mix my own drink, thank you."

"Well, make it a strong one."

"Why's that?"

"Because I have a theory for you. And it might be a little much for you."

"Lay it on me," challenged Mona. She poured a little trickle of rum onto the bottom of a drinking glass.

"Maybe . . . Maybe it's not a *story*. Maybe . . . maybe you should put more rum in that?"

"I'm not a hulking frat boy like you. I'm a lightweight."

"I'm not a frat boy," I said, considering whether I should be offended by *hulking* as well.

"Sorry."

"But anyway. Suit yourself. I was saying. Maybe it's real. Maybe they're talking about a real corpse."

Mona gulped her drink and shook her head.

"Wouldn't that be cool, huh?" she said. "But no. Some of our fellow dictionary people are somewhat lacking in street smarts, but I don't think any of them are dumb enough to kill someone and then write down little clues to drop in the cit file like little Hansel and Gretel breadcrumbs. I could be wrong."

"Okay. Of course it probably wasn't a *murderer* who wrote these cits. But maybe there was something shady going down. Maybe someone was secretly writing about what they knew."

Mona took the cit from me.

"You know, I hadn't even considered that possibility. Call me naive. I guess I just like to think of lexicographers as essentially a gentle people. Shall we?"

She motioned me into the living room, small and empty but for a simple but expensive-looking black couch, a little wooden coffee table, and a tall, skinny bookcase. A single framed Ansel Adams poster hung behind the couch. On the table there were two pairs of shoeboxes. *Unchecked* was written in blue marker on two of the boxes, and *Done* written in red marker on the other two. Two of the boxes already had banded batches of cits lined up inside.

"I made a pair of boxes for you," she said sheepishly.

"I see that," I said. It was both disturbing and flattering, the mental image of Mona sitting down at her kitchen table, carefully fashioning me a set of makeshift "In" and "Out" boxes for my maximum productivity at her place. Probably

she was doing her careful colored lettering just as I was se-
lecting her bottle of rum.

"Got your cits in your bag?" she asked.

"Yup."

Mona sat cross-legged on the floor. She picked up a stack
of cits from her little coffee table and removed the rubber
band.

"I just flip through like this, see? You barely have to look
at the bottom right-hand corner to see if it's got *'Broken
Teaglass'* written on it. See, a word like 'melon baller' goes by
really fast. Not many cits for 'melon baller.' Kind of a shame,
don't you think? Anyway. No *Broken Teaglass* cits. I just band
them back up, put them in the 'Done' box, and check off
'melon baller' right here."

She pointed at the stapled printout of 1950 words, on
which she had begun a neat row of check marks, and put a
star next to *maven*.

"This won't just help us keep track, it might also help us
see if there's a pattern to which words have *Teaglass* cits."

"That's a good idea." I sat on the couch and dumped a
bunch of citations from my backpack into my "Unchecked"
box. "Especially since I probably won't be doing this in al-
phabetical order."

Mona looked like she was considering saying something
else to me. Instead, she just swallowed some more rum and
Coke. I picked up a thin pile of citations for *American pit bull
terrier,* and started to flip through them.

One of them was from an article entitled "Fourth of July
Tragedy," from some women's magazine. It seemed to be
from an article about a kid attacked by a dog at a picnic.

"I can't think of much worse of a nightmare than to see
your kid mauled by a dog," I said.

"Don't *read*, Billy. We'll never get anywhere if you're going to read everything."

I flipped through the rest of the pile, put a rubber band around it, and chucked it in my empty "Done" box. Mona pushed the list and pen toward me without looking up from her cits.

Ffft. Ffft. Ffft. She shuffled through her citations like a banker counting cash. I watched her for a moment before reaching for my next stack of cits.

"So this is it for the evening?" I asked. "Just plowing through these cits as fast as we can?"

Mona looked up. "We'll take a break for pizza. I'll call the pizza place after we get through a few piles."

"You don't want to even . . . put on some tunes or some-thing?"

"That's a good idea. Get through a couple more piles and I'll bring my CD player in here."

We didn't find anything in the first half hour. When Mona decided we'd earned it, she went into the kitchen to order the pizza. I took the liberty of making her another drink.

"Thank you," she said as she sat back down. She took a big gulp of her cocktail. If she noticed that it was significantly stronger than her last one, she didn't mention it.

We worked silently until her buzzer rang. She ran down-stairs for the pizza, and I got up from the couch and wandered over to her bookcase. The top shelf was full of Norton literature anthologies and classics. Propped in front of these books was a picture of Mona at her graduation, surrounded by what had to be her family—an attractive woman, taller than Mona, but with her hair pulled back in a style similar to Mona's, a shorter man with gray hair and glasses, a little girl, and two young men who looked a little older than Mona. On the second shelf was another photograph. This one was of Mona looking a little younger and sitting on a picnic table with a man with an overgrown mustache. Mona was wearing cutoff shorts whose length almost qualified them as Daisy Dukes. I wondered if Mona's legs were still that skinny under all the gray and black clothing.

Behind the photographs was a flat hardcover book: *The Hindenburg.* Next to that was a paperback titled *When We Were All in Bed.* There was kind of a kinky ring to that title, so I pulled the book out of the shelf and looked at the cover. *When We Were All in Bed: Accounts of the Chicago Fire of 1871.* Maybe not so kinky. Next to that was *A Night to Remember* by Walter Lord, which I remembered reading in high school. It was about the *Titanic.*

Mona came creaking back up the stairs. The large pizza box in her arms dwarfed her.

"Let's eat," she said. "I'm hungry."

"You want something to drink with your pizza?" I asked her.

"Yes. That'd be great, thanks."

Mona sipped away at another rum and Coke as we ate our pizza at the kitchen table. I drank another beer.

"Is that your family with you in that graduation picture on your bookcase?" I asked.

"Yeah. That's my mom and my stepdad. With my stepbrothers and my half sister. The guy in the other picture is my father. In case you were wondering."

"Yeah, I kind of was," I said.

"It doesn't ever seem right to put up a picture of one side of my family where I'm not going to put up another."

"Shouldn't it be enough just to have an equal *total* number of pictures of each side in the house?"

"No." She shook her head. "The people you put in your living room are the ones you're proud of. The people you put in your bedroom are the ones you have the most intimate, emotional relationships with. I don't want to compartmentalize my family like that."

I decided to change the subject. "Gotten any good letters at work lately?" I asked.

"Oh. Yeah." She slammed down her glass and laughed. "Didn't I tell you about the 'poon' letter?"

"No, I think I would have remembered that if you did."

"Yeah, so I get this letter. Dan apparently read it and had it sent straight to me. I don't know what the hell goes through his mind sometimes. *Genitally fixated correspondent? I'll put Minot right on it!* Anyway. The writer wants to know all about the word 'poon.' And 'poontang,' too. Guy wants to know if it has an Asian origin. He says he figures it does since it sounds sort of Chinese. You know, 'tang'?"

"So what did you write?"

"Nothing. I decided to try and squeeze a little chivalry out of old Dan. I went into his office and said, 'Do you *really* want me to answer some pervert's letter about a word like "poontang"?' "

"You said that to *Dan*?"

"Why not? It's not exactly appropriate for me to be answering that sort of thing. Especially now that we've got you around. At least *you* might enjoy researching something like that."

"Maybe too much," I admitted.

"Anyway. Dan looks at me sort of funny and says—get this—'I'm sorry, is it a slang term? I'm not familiar with it.' "

I shook my head. "Whoa."

"I know. So I tell him what 'poontang' is—"

"Hold on. How exactly did you say it?"

"Well, I just said 'female reproductive organ.' "

"Nice."

"And he turns red and says, 'Give me the letter. Sorry. I'll handle this.' Then he grabs the letter from me and goes back to his citations."

"Poor Dan," I said. "Some aspects of this job are a little too sleazy for someone like him."

"Yeah. But what kind of guy goes his whole life without knowing what 'poontang' is?"

"Maybe a guy who spends his whole life with his head in a bunch of dictionaries?"

She smiled her sideways smile. "He is a gentleman, though. There's just something old-fashioned and honorable about him."

"Yeah," I agreed. "With the pale face, and the graying black hair, and the long, thin body . . . he kind of reminds me of an aging vampire who never really had any bite."

"A vampire? I wouldn't say so. Vampires don't have beards, for one."

"Well, that's why I said an *aging* vampire. I mean, he has the look of a dapper old Dracula who never had the heart to suck anyone's blood."

"You've given this a great deal of thought, I can see," Mona said, yawning. "Have you ever actually read *Dracula*?"

"No," I admitted. "You?"

"About two thirds of it, then I stopped," Mona said, looking bored. "It's no *Frankenstein*."

"Should we get back to work?" I asked.

"Maybe," Mona said, and sighed. She slumped in her chair and let her arms hang down at her sides.

"Someone's a little tipsy," I teased.

"Just like someone else wanted," she retorted in a sing-song voice that mimicked mine.

We dragged ourselves back onto the couch. Mona scrunched into a little ball and ruffled through her citations at a much slower pace than before.

"You can't leave," she said firmly, "till we find something."

"But we don't know for sure if there's anything else."

"I'm just sayin'." She was slurring just a bit.

I looked through citations for *auxotroph, baby oil,* and *access time*. Nothing. When I looked up at Mona again, her eyes were closed.

"Wake up, Mona," I called to her. "It's still early."

"I don't know about you," she said, without opening her eyes, "but this job takes a lot out of me somehow. By the end of the week, I just crash. I get so tired."

"I try to get some sleep at my desk."

"Mmm. I've noticed."

"Mona?"

"Yes?"

"Why is this *Teaglass* stuff so important to you? I mean, for real."

"Aw, shit, Billy," she sighed. She nestled her head against the back of the couch.

"C'mon," I prodded. "I really want to know."

"I just want to be in on it, that's all. I want to be a *real* member of this exclusive little dictionary club. Not just one of the *babies*."

"I think everyone there already really respects you."

"Give me a break. You have no idea."

"No idea *what*?"

Mona snuggled her head deeper into the couch cushion.

"These are hard questions," she murmured. "Maybe you should ask me on Monday."

"Never mind," I said.

Mona dozed off and I kept flipping through the citations. Soon she was breathing loudly in her sleep, snoring almost, and the sound of it nearly put me to sleep as well. I almost missed it when a *Broken Teaglass* cit fluttered by in my fingers:

> ### advantaged
>
> How did I get here? Even the stories I've asked you to tell, Red, were only another way for me to ask that question. Now I suppose the question might mean something else? If here means this office, this very physical place, well, my story's not so different from that of others who work here. I was a good student. I like books. Languages aren't difficult for me. I graduated with the highest honors, but had no serious grad school plans. My *advantaged* background and education led me here somehow, and I was dropped rather unwittingly into this most bizarre job.
>
> Dolores Beekmim
> *The Broken Teaglass*
> Robinson Press
> 14 October 1985
> 1

I considered whether I should wake up Mona and show the cit to her. She'd probably be pretty excited when she saw it. It confirmed her theory that someone was messing around on purpose—that someone wanted editors to notice his or her work. Probably *her* work. *Someone in the office.* I thought again of the *maven* cit and felt my pulse quicken. The little surprising bit about the corpse in the previous cit didn't seem so amusing anymore. Now that I was alone with

Mona in this quiet, creepy apartment, listening to her murmuring softly in her sleep, the whole affair struck me as eerie. Not just the corpse, but the way this newest cit seemed to be addressing someone so intimately. Somebody named Red? We were either terrible voyeurs or we'd fallen for some colossal joke.

Suddenly I remembered Tom, on that first day, when I met him on our front porch. What had he said? *I've heard some bizarre shit goes down at that place.* Since when had the voice of the downstairs freak become a part of my conscience? The last thing I needed was to have this floating, wiry-haired head of Tom directing my way in this world. The Black Labels were probably starting to affect me in deep and unhealthy ways.

I decided it was time to leave. I went to the kitchen to look for something to write on. There was a stack of papers and other junk on one corner of the table: bills, a Chinese take-out menu, *TV Guide,* a few napkins. I took a napkin to the living room and scribbled on it: *Mona, Look what I found! I guess that means I can take off now. We'll talk Monday. Pleasant dreams. B.*

I looked around for something with which to anchor the note and the cit to the table, where she'd see them. It was then that I noticed there was no television in the room. Then why the subscription to *TV Guide?* Was Mona doing a little research-reading at home? I used *The Hindenburg* as a paperweight.

Mona smiled in her sleep, stretched her legs onto my spot on the couch, and twisted away from me. Still a little spooked by the *advantaged* cit and the creaky, abandoned feel of the apartment building, I wondered if it was unwise of me to leave her alone and unconscious, with the door unlocked and a bunch of incriminating dictionary material scattered around her. Maybe, I thought, I should at least wake her up before I go. But that seemed a little too intimate an act—shaking her awake, whispering goodbye, speaking to her while she was still half in dreams.

On my way out, I peered into her bedroom. It was just as spare and neat as her living room. There was a narrow bed with a fluffy white comforter. A bookshelf full of paperbacks. An antique-looking dresser. No TV. Strange bird, that Mona Minot.

"Huh," I said aloud. On my way out, as I passed the kitchen table again, I picked up the *TV Guide* and looked at the address sticker.

Mona Rasmussen, it said, and then Mona's address.

I put the *TV Guide* down.

Bizarre shit! cried the floating head of Tom in my brain, this time with a cigarette hanging from his lips. But far more bizarre than Mona's two last names—which shouldn't have been all that surprising, considering what Mona had just told me about her family—was my own unexpected impulse to snoop, and my own jumpy mood. I slipped out the door and tried not to squeak the old floorboards too much as I crept down the stairs.

CHAPTER FIVE

Next came the void of Saturday. I slept late. I watched a little TV. I tried not to be too disappointed that the first social encounter of my young professional life ended with the girl falling asleep.

The contents of my refrigerator were grim—eggs, mayonnaise, and some rubbery old carrot sticks—so I at least made it to the grocery store. Once there, I was inspired by the bright plum tomatoes that were displayed on a sale table in the front of the produce section. They reminded me of this great sauce my mother used to whip up from scratch. I'd watched her make it enough times to see that it was largely improvised. Tomatoes, basil, a little wine, and then cream at the end. But the main ingredient was roasted garlic, which she'd bake as a whole bulb and then squeeze into the sizzling tomatoes. I think this sauce was an imitation of something she'd had at a restaurant once.

Mine would be an imitation of her imitation. She'd usually put in some julienned zucchini and yellow squash, so I added that to my cart. Her sauce didn't have any meat in it, but I figured I'd add some chicken breast just to make it a little heartier. On the way home, I stopped at a package store for a cheap bottle of wine.

I started cooking early in the evening, tasting it every so often, adjusting the salt and the wine and the cream until the balance was just as I'd remembered. I covered it, put a giant pot of water on for the pasta, and then went to the living room to catch a little TV. One of my favorite movies was on—*The Usual Suspects.* There was about a half hour left of the movie, and I got caught up in the ending. I just wanted to see the detective drop his coffee cup at the end, and figured the pasta water could boil a few extra minutes before I put the penne in.

The problem, I discovered upon returning to the kitchen, was that I'd turned on the wrong burner to boil. The cream in the sauce had scorched, forming a brownish crust around the edge of the pan. I poked at the sauce with a wooden spoon. It was burnt at the bottom too. I stared into the pan. The limp curls of overdone zucchini spelled something like *even food fails you.* I gripped the handle and flung the pan sideways.

As the metal clunked against the wall, I heard a pathetic wail that must have been mine. Then I slapped the heels of my hands into my eyes. I kept them there for a moment, not yet ready to look at what I had just done. Taking a deep breath, I let my palms slide down my cheeks.

The pan and wooden spoon were on the floor, and a clump of burnt tomato-cream-garlic sauce had slid down the wall by the oven, leaving a greasy reddish trail on the off-white wall. I threw the pan back on the stovetop. As I watched the remains of the sauce settle into the baseboard, it occurred to me that it wasn't quite as burnt as it had appeared in the pan. A small part of it probably could have been saved.

I didn't feel like cleaning it up. I turned off the burners, the TV, and the lights. And went to bed.

• • •

I got up early on Sunday morning and drove down the block for a Dunkin' Donuts coffee. When I returned, Jimmy was out smoking on the porch. He pointed his cigarette at the empty lawn chair beside him.

"Take a load off, Billy boy."

I sat down and sipped my coffee, which was too sweet.

"How was your date Friday?" Jimmy wanted to know.

"Weird," I admitted. "I guess it wasn't really a date."

"Are you gonna go out with her again?"

"It wasn't exactly going out. I don't know if we'll hang out again."

"Wasn't *really* a date. Wasn't *exactly* going out. Doesn't sound like you know what you're doing."

Jimmy mashed his cigarette into the ashtray in his lap. Then he leaned over the porch railing and emptied the ashtray into the hedges.

"Where's Tom?" I asked.

He lit another cigarette before answering. "His wife wants him back. For today."

"What does that mean?"

Jimmy sighed. He shifted in his chair. "Don't worry about it. He'll be back. You know Tommy doesn't actually live here, don't you?"

"I wasn't sure what the arrangement was."

He gazed at me and smiled a little. "Arrangement? Yeah. Tommy stays here when his wife kicks him out. Sometimes she kicks him out for pretty long stretches of time."

"Huh," I said.

Jimmy turned away from me to blow smoke rings.

"You go to church?" he asked me, after a few smoke rings. He was looking across the street again.

"No. I tried a few different churches in college, actually, but—"

"But?" he prompted me.

"But none of them fit right."

He nodded. "The best fit's probably the church you were raised with."

"I wasn't raised with any church. We never went to one."

"Sometimes I think I should start going again. Raised Catholic."

"You and Tom are Catholic?"

"Yep."

"Does Tom go to church?"

"No. He used to memorize whole passages of the Bible just to show off, but he doesn't have a religious bone in his whole body. Only one he worships is himself."

"Huh. Does Barbara ever go?"

"Naw, Billy. Barb's Buddhist."

I snorted, thinking he was joking. He took a long drag and didn't look at me. He was serious. I tried to follow the line of his gaze. I decided he was probably looking at the plastic Mary statue standing in the little yard across the street.

"Huh," I said again.

I didn't see Mona until the following Wednesday. I looked up from my citations to find her standing by my desk. There was a satisfied smile on her face.

"Long time no—"

She put a warning finger to her lips, then slid a citation onto my desk. Another *Teaglass* cit. Before I had a chance to read it, however, she slid another one on top of it. The first was for the word *paperbound,* the next for *plus*.

"What the hell, Mona?"

Mona rolled her eyes. Clifford started tapping on his keys in the next-door cubicle.

"Is this what you've been doing all week?" I whispered. "Aren't you afraid you're going to lose your job?"

"I'm a pretty good multitasker." She kept her voice low. "Don't worry about me. Besides, I should be scolding *you*."

"Me?"

"You left all your cits at my house. It's been days and you haven't even asked about them. They're in my desk. So it doesn't look like you're holding up your end of this deal."

"I didn't know we were in a hurry." She was taking this *Teaglass* stuff pretty seriously.

"Dan's coming," Mona said, gazing over my head. I turned to see Dan's tall form weaving its way between the cubicles.

Mona leaned into my cubicle.

"Your place next time," she said softly. "Friday?"

I nodded.

Dan smiled when he reached my desk.

"Hello," he said, and then, after a slight pause, "you two."

He put his hand gently on top of the cubicle wall, and then swayed a little on his feet. The gesture was oddly like a curtsy.

"Sorry to interrupt. Mona, if you'll excuse us, I need to grab Billy for a few minutes."

"Okay," Mona said. She gave him a tight smile and took off without looking at me.

"I wanted to go over a batch of definitions with you," he said. "Give you a little feedback."

I stood and followed him dutifully into his office.

"All right then," Dan said, sighing as he closed the door. "I apologize for not doing this sooner. I've been a little tied up.

I meant to go over some of your work with you right after your first or second batch."

"No problem." I sat in the chair next to his desk.

"Yes. It seems that way. Looks like you're moving along fine on your own. And overall, you're doing a good job."

He settled into his chair and opened a bulging manila folder. Inside were my first definitions, along with all of the citations I'd used to write them.

"Just a couple of issues," he said, showing me my definition for *Bellini*. I had written *an alcoholic beverage made from champagne and peach nectar*.

"It's a small thing, but space is so precious, you should be careful of superfluous words. You could change 'beverage' to 'cocktail,' if you wanted the headword to be more specific. Then you wouldn't need 'alcoholic.' "

I nodded.

Dan hesitated, and then said, "This reminds me of a little tradition a colleague and I used to have. When one of us would define a new kind of wine, or sometimes an interesting-sounding drink, at the end of the week we'd make an effort to try it out."

"Do you still do that?"

"No. That was years ago. I was about your age."

"How about foods? I've already defined some interesting foods. Often the cits are from recipes."

"I've done it on occasion. But there are so many foods to define. We didn't try all the recipes, no." Dan picked up a new batch of cits from the folder and slipped off its rubber band. "Moving along to 'beauty queen' . . ."

He showed me my definition slip, where I had written *a contestant in a beauty pageant* esp: *a beautiful one*. I had known, when I had written it, that it wouldn't quite fly. Now I felt a stab of embarrassment at submitting it anyway.

"Something isn't quite right here," Dan said. "You're trying to say that a beauty queen is a contestant in a beauty pageant, but you think that a more specific type of contestant is generally implied?"

"Yeah. Basically."

"Aren't most beauty pageant contestants beautiful? Isn't that usually assumed?"

"You ever seen a beauty pageant? I mean, a local one? Like . . . uh . . ." I felt my voice lowering to a mumble, "Miss Tolland County?"

"Excuse me?" Dan said.

I realized then that he wasn't really listening. He wasn't looking at me, but gazing down at the cit by my hand. My adrenaline shot up when I saw it said *paperbound* at the top, and *The Broken Teaglass* on the bottom. I'd absently carried Mona's cits into Dan's office with me and set them on Dan's desk as we'd talked.

"Well. I was just thinking that the . . . the impetus to enter a beauty pageant doesn't exactly, uh, coincide with physical beauty." My thumb twitched uncontrollably at the corner of the cit. "In my experience."

Dan cleared his throat politely behind his hand, then kept his fingers curled gingerly over his mouth. He looked at me over his fist and didn't say anything, so I continued my idiotic soliloquy.

"The girls who enter those things aren't always beautiful, is what I'm trying to say. Maybe it's a low-self-esteem thing? I'm not sure. But some of them are, well, let's say, not attractive by conventional standards."

I crawled my hand over the *paperbound* cit as Dan gave me a thin smile.

"But would you call such women *beauty queens*? That's the only question you should concern yourself with," he said.

"Exactly!" I said, too enthusiastically. "Would you?"

"No," Dan said slowly, flitting his eyes toward his tiny office window. He put his thumb under his chin and rubbed his beard absently.

I crumpled the *paperbound* and *plus* cits into my lap and took a breath. I waited for further criticism, but he didn't say anything more.

"That's why I thought I needed to be a little more specific," I said, after a while.

"But, Billy . . ." Dan finally returned his gaze to me. "What do the *cits* say?"

After several weeks of defining, I was already starting to see the awkward logic of my earliest efforts. But I still wanted to explain my reasoning.

"The word usually means a beauty pageant contestant . . . but always a beautiful one," I began. "That's sort of implied. *Or* more general, like that song . . . You know . . . 'When I was seventeen, I thought love was meant for beauty queens,' or something like that, right? The idea there is just 'beautiful women,' don't you think?"

"Or perhaps beauty contest *winners*," he said, raising one eyebrow. "Then you wouldn't need to specify that they're beautiful ones, I wouldn't think. But I see what you're saying now. There is the pageant sense and then something of an extended sense. But your definition is a little awkward. I think you should look at it again. It could probably be finessed a little more tightly."

"All right," I agreed.

"Good. Let's see. 'Beatnik.' " Dan flipped through another pile of citations, and then chuckled. "Excellent job. You were correct to update the old definition. The old one *did* seem slightly editorialized. Use of the word 'arty' isn't exactly neutral. Perhaps the original definer in the sixties or seventies couldn't help getting a little dig in. It happens. I suppose no one had noticed that recently or no one's bothered to change it. Once something's in, sometimes it just doesn't get noticed anymore." He gave a regretful little shrug before continuing. "It's interesting that you suggested this change, though. Most new editors are afraid to question anything in our older editions."

"Huh," I said. I wasn't sure how I was supposed to respond to this observation. I wasn't certain it was a compliment, so I didn't thank him for it.

Dan didn't seem to know what to say next, either. He tapped the little pile of *beatnik* cits on the table to align the edges. Then he clipped them together and handed me the folder.

"I'll let you look at the rest yourself at your desk. There are only a few other suggestions."

After I returned to my desk, I discovered that there was actually only one other suggestion. On my definition slip for *beat one's meat,* Dan had written, *There aren't really enough cits to justify defining this. But that's okay—when in doubt, define it.*

C'est la vie. It was worth a try. Who could pass up the chance at being the guy who gets to say he put *beat my meat* into the American lexicon? I folded the slip and stuck it in my pocket. A memento of my effort.

Then I uncrumpled Mona's cits and read them.

paperbound

Only you, Red. Only you acknowledged the mishap. You mentioned it offhand when you came to give me yet another *paperbound* book from your home collection: *Beyond the 38th Parallel.* I didn't confess it then but will confess it now. I hadn't even read the last book you gave me. You told me it wasn't exactly an academic piece of work. Just some pretty good firsthand accounts. Diaries. Letters. I thanked you for it and you winked. Just don't spill anything on it, you said, and then sauntered off to the secretary's desk for your midmorning flirtation.

Dolores Beekmim
The Broken Teaglass
Robinson Press
14 October 1985
9

plus

In the meantime, we ate an awful lot of pies. Three a week at one point. We always sipped tea with it, and he always seemed to find topics for engaging, if somewhat one-sided, conversation. He told me about his grandfather's dementia. The poor old man was now confusing the details of his own life with those he had read in some biographies of Charles Lindbergh. He told me about his old Latin teacher who chain-smoked and who, one day, soon after retiring, put on a flowered sundress *plus* a wig, then hanged himself in his study. Maybe he was trying to convince me that he had a stomach for strange stories? Was it the pie or the silence that eased these stories out of him?

Dolores Beekmim
The Broken Teaglass
Robinson Press
14 October 1985
41

Red again. Borrowed books seemed to keep coming up as well, although that detail was less interesting. And then *plus*. Everything in that one seemed a little random, like it could be from a different narrative. Pie? And who was the "he"

with the bizarre stories? The fact that one of the stories involved a Latin teacher made me suspect that *plus,* despite its
random quality, still dealt with the dictionary crowd. It
seemed a Samuelson kind of detail, characters with training
in classical languages. I also wondered about *plus.* Surely that
wasn't a 1950 word. I double-checked our list, then the dictionary. The word had been in the English language since
the sixteenth century. As an adjective, and then later as a
noun. Use as a conjunction, though, had started in 1950. I
looked back at the cit. A conjunction. A somewhat awkward
one, actually. Someone was being very careful, it seemed, to
keep the 1950 pattern. I'd chat with Mona about this later.

I played around with my *beauty queen* definition for a
while, then checked my email. Nothing. I looked at the
clock. Two hours and twenty minutes until I could go home.
Way too early to take out a magazine and start research-
reading for the remainder of the afternoon. I logged on to
the Internet again and did a Google search on *beauty queen.*
"Asian Beauty Queens XXX" came up, along with some
similar sites. Great idea. Just what I needed right now.

I logged off the Internet and stared at my sorry definition.
Reverse the order, I decided, after a while. That's it. Start
general. Then add the specific sense. I took out a fresh definition slip. "beauty queen *n* :" I wrote carefully, then chewed
the end of my pen for a moment: "a beautiful woman: *specif:*
one who participates in a beauty pageant."

An improvement, at least. I was pretty proud of myself. I
made the other changes Dan had suggested and dropped the
folder of cits into my out-box. Then I picked up my next
pile of cits. *Calibrate.* I looked at the clock. One hour and
fifty-four minutes to go.

CHAPTER SIX

The whole dinner was designed around the Bellinis: cod with a lemon butter sauce, herbed rice, zucchini. All a little light for an October meal, but perfect to go along with champagne and peach juice. I'd even called my dad for advice on his famous fruit tart for dessert. *Real vanilla bean, that's the only advice you need,* he'd said. *But I don't know if you can swing that on your salary.*

I had swung anyway. When Mona knocked, I was dabbing the tart with its final touch: a glaze made from apricot jam. I quickly put away the paintbrush I'd been using for glazing. It hadn't dawned on me until that moment that the whole spread—with its delicate flavors and fairly elaborate preparations—might look a little gay.

"Some long-haired freak let me into your stairwell," Mona murmured to me when I opened the door.

"That's just Tom," I said. "He's not so bad."

"That guy's your neighbor?"

"One of them."

"Well, be careful with that. That guy reminds me of some people I knew back home that I wish I could forget. You ever seen *Deliverance*?" Mona handed me a plastic grocery bag. "I brought dessert. I hope you like Chips Ahoy." She wandered into the kitchen. "This place isn't so bad. You made it sound like you were living in some dump. Hey. What's that? Did someone get shot in here?"

She was looking at the tomato-cream sauce stain. I hadn't cleaned it up right away. Once I'd gotten around to it, I couldn't get the greasy orange tinge out of the wall.

"Oh, that." I took a bottle of champagne out of the refrigerator. "I'm not sure what to make of that."

"Hmm. Gross. Could be anything." She made a face. "What are we celebrating?"

I explained to her about my *Bellini* definition, and Dan's drink-defining tradition.

"Really?" Mona looked surprised. "That doesn't sound like Dan to me."

But when the time came, she drank down three Bellinis and really seemed to enjoy them. By seven o'clock, we were lingering over dinner and she was telling me about a college friend who had a fetish for postal uniforms. She hadn't mentioned the citations once. Our citation boxes were still sitting untouched by my front door.

"Didn't you have a boyfriend in college?" I said, changing the subject.

"Not really. Only very briefly. When did I say I had a boyfriend?"

"I thought I remembered that you did. Maybe I'm mistaken."

"Oh. Well, I dated this one guy for a couple of months junior year. That's all. It's difficult to meet guys when you go to a women's college, you know? Anyway. Once it started getting more serious, I lost interest."

"Why? What was wrong with the guy?"

"Nothing. He just didn't have it."

"Have what?"

"I don't know. How do I explain?" Mona pulled her navy cashmere cuffs over her wrists and tilted closer to me. "Those were really delicious, those Bellinis. I think I had one too many."

"You want another one?" I asked.

"We finished the champagne on the last one."

"I know. But I thought maybe a Black Label and peach juice cocktail would satisfy you at this stage of the intoxication process."

Mona yawned and smiled.

"Make it just a Black Label, then," she said.

"I thought you didn't like beer."

"I make exceptions."

I got her the beer from the fridge, along with one for myself.

"See," she said, taking the beer from my hands, "I used to have this Greek professor in college. He was my ideal man."

"You dated a professor?" Somehow it didn't surprise me.

"No. *No.* I didn't say *dated*. I had a major crush on him. For a couple of years. He didn't know it, of course. Although he always gave me A's on everything."

"Naturally."

"He was my advisor too."

"Was that a coincidence?" I asked.

Mona raised her eyebrows as she swallowed some beer.

"I guess not," I said.

She leaned forward again and clasped her hands together. "I would think a lot about cooking his breakfast. I would be sitting there in my dorm room, translating Horace, and I would just wonder what it would be like to fix Dr. Grant bacon and eggs. Or to ruffle his ridiculous, moppy hair in the morning. Iron his shirt. The guy was so disheveled, I don't think anyone ever ironed a single shirt for him. Hand him his briefcase. Maybe have a couple of his babies."

"How do you go from handing him his briefcase to having his babies?"

"Oh, you know what I mean," Mona said. She narrowed her eyes, examining the back of her beer can. "I thought a lot about what it would be like to be his wife. And I mean 'wife' in the most traditional sense possible. And there were a lot of days when I was pretty sure nothing would make me happier."

"Are you yanking my chain, Mona?"

"*No.* I'm serious. Maybe it was just his accent." She glanced up from her beer. "He was from Liverpool."

"Well then," I said. "That's understandable. Everyone would like to marry a Beatle."

"Or maybe it was just that I was so bored, there at that girls' school. But I'm pretty sure that on some level I was really in love with the guy."

"Huh."

"So sometime around the middle of junior year I decided it was time to wise up and start looking for a distraction. That's when I dated that other guy for a while. His name was Alan."

"And you're still in love with the professor? Dr. Grant?"

"No. Of course not. I got over him. But Alan just didn't have it. This is what I'm trying to explain. I never thought about making Alan's breakfast. Not once. In fact, I'm pretty sure I would resent having to make his breakfast, if that was ever necessary. I took that as a sign. Alan wasn't for me. It was just the same in high school. No one impressed me much, or compelled me to say or do truly stupid things."

"So you didn't have a high school boyfriend."

"No," Mona answered. "I dated, but I always ended up hating them after two or three dates."

"Why?"

"It wasn't their fault, really. I always just kind of wanted a *real* man."

"A *real* man," I repeated. It was a little unsettling, picturing the teenage Mona scoping for a *real* man. Still, I couldn't help but wonder if I qualified.

"Yeah. A *real* man. That's what I'm looking for. Still. What about you? Any college girlfriends?"

"I was with this girl for about six months sophomore year. Ella."

"That's all?"

"What do you mean, 'that's all'?"

"I always imagine people at coed colleges having a pretty steady stream of significant others."

"No, it wasn't always like that. Not for me, anyway."

"So how did you and Ella meet?"

"In a philosophy class."

"What was the class?"

"Existentialism."

"Very romantic."

"Yeah."

Mona took a tentative sip of beer and wrinkled her nose at the taste. "So . . . what was the deal with Ella?" she wanted to know. "What happened after the six months?"

"Well . . . For one, she was stoned most of the time. It got old."

"Oh." Mona looked primly startled by this revelation, which was sort of cute. "Old . . . in what sense?"

"Well, as I said, she was a pothead. It was sort of fun, at first, that she liked to party so much. But it started to become obvious, after the early excitement wore off, that we didn't have much in common."

"Hmm. That's funny. I don't know many female potheads. I mean, I knew plenty of women who smoked pot at Middlebrook, but none enough for me to call them potheads."

"Well, they definitely exist. Maybe not at Middlebrook College, but they're out there. Trust me. And Ella was definitely one of them."

It was true about Ella and pot, but I felt unkind summing her up that way. As if the many lazy hours with her—lying on her dorm room bed, watching her goldfish, anticipating the Tater Tots that might or might not be served on our next trip to the dining hall—hadn't been enjoyable. But it was she, after all, who'd ended it. *You don't even know how to* pretend, *Billy,* she'd kept saying, when she was breaking up with me.

"Too bad you didn't stick with her." Mona held her beer can in front of her face, probably contemplating whether she should continue drinking it. "You guys could have had a nice existentialist wedding ceremony."

"Oh. Well, Ella wasn't a philosophy major. She was a psych major."

"So, why'd *you* pick philosophy?"

"You know, it's not so different from your classics major. Difficult, old texts. Not much practical application. Just a good intellectual challenge."

She peered skeptically over her beer can. "Yeah, but... there must have been a reason you picked philosophy specifically."

"Well, the reason changed over time. At first, like most freshmen who study it, I thought I was gonna learn all about life's deep questions. But after a few classes, I actually found that I was pretty good at it. I liked writing the papers. The papers were easy. I liked picking arguments apart. Once you realize that no argument is perfect, that every argument can be torn down somehow . . . you're golden on philosophy papers."

"But what about building arguments up?"

"Well. True, that's important too. But that's not quite as fun." My advisor was always pointing this out—that I was much better at one than the other.

"So when you were studying philosophy, what did you think you might . . . you know, do with it later?"

"Well, I know philosophy is like the cliché of impractical majors, but it's not really that much more impractical than English or history or classics. And philosophy majors actually tend to do well in law school, they say."

Mona put down her beer can. "Are you planning to go to law school?"

"No." I laughed a little. "I actually did think about that idea for, like, a minute. Last year."

"And?"

"And I think law school's not really for people like me. It's a lot of money, a lot of work. It takes a certain . . . confidence."

"But you've got confidence, Billy. At least, it seems like you do."

"I don't mean personal confidence. Not confidence in *yourself* so much. I mean confidence that . . ." I groped for the right words. I didn't know exactly how to put this. *Confidence that life owes you something* was probably the best way to put it. But it seemed too snide a thing to say out loud.

"Confidence that it'll pay off. I mean, it's not only expensive, and lots of work. When you get out, you've got your loan to pay off. You've got to take the best-paying entry-level job you can find, and hope to pay it back. So it's more like a five- or six-year commitment than a three-year one. Who has that kind of confidence? Who's crazy enough to take all of that on and just assume that, five or six years later, you're gonna be in a situation that makes it feel worth it?"

"It takes a certain amount of faith, is that what you're saying?" Mona offered.

Faith. Of course, that had been the right word all along. But I tended to shy away from this word in casual conversation. There was something soft and mushy about it. It always felt like marshmallow in my mouth.

"Faith. Sure," I said. "I guess."

"Hmm." Mona studied me with her champagne smile. I couldn't tell if she found my answers interesting or just amusing. Either way, it probably wasn't smart to go down this road with a girl on a Bellini buzz.

"Should we have some dessert?" I asked.

"I'm kind of stuffed," she said, stretching. "How about after some citations?"

Minutes later I found myself watching Mona pore carefully over a stack of citations in her lap. She sat on my futon Indian-style, in a peculiarly symmetrical fashion—knees and elbows pointy, arranged in equivalent angles. *Ffft ffft ffft,* went her cits. She suddenly didn't seem tipsy anymore. She apparently had a remarkably quick metabolism for alcohol. I couldn't quite reconcile this Mona with the one who'd just been telling me about wanting to have her professor's babies. As I'd prepared our dinner earlier that evening, I'd daydreamed we'd somehow end up fooling around on my futon. Now the prospect seemed pretty remote. It would take some serious conversational gymnastics to bring her around to a tender mood, and I wasn't sure I had the aptitude for it.

I joined Mona on the futon, and started in on my "D" cits. *Death row* was my first.

" 'Death row' has only been around since 1950?" I said.
Mona shrugged without looking up.

"Go figure," she said.

"Nothing useful in 'deep-fryer,' " I announced a few
minutes later. "Disappointing."

Demythologize. I flipped a few cits, and there was the old
Teaglass again:

demythologize

A wounded, resentful version of my face—but blue-white and
open-eyed and dead—started glancing back at me in mirrors
and watching me when I was failing to sleep. In time, the
image began to resemble a dead-prom-queen costume,
sometimes dripping black blood from a heavily lipsticked
mouth, or wearing a ripped ruffled dress. Eventually, it became
more cinematic, bearing little resemblance to me, easier to shut
off, like a bad movie on TV. Almost comical on occasion.
Almost. Dead prom queen on intimate terms. Dead prom
queen *demythologized.* Not frightening so much as unsettling,
constant, and familiar. An unwanted pet you feed out of
obligation. Weeks later, the dead prom queen lingered only
out of habit.

Dolores Beekmim
The Broken Teaglass
Robinson Press
14 October 1985
36

"We have a winner," I said, and handed it to Mona.

A curtain of her brown hair fell between us as she bent
over it eagerly.

"Now, what exactly do you think we have here?" she asked, pulling her hair back.

"A bad dream?" I said.

" 'Dead prom queen on intimate terms'?" Mona grimaced as she tried unsuccessfully to knot her hair on top of her head. "Am I supposed to laugh or throw myself out a window?"

I read it again, and then said, "I think it's somebody struggling."

"Struggling with what?"

"I'm not sure. Maybe with their, uh, personal demons?"

"Whatever *that* ever means," said Mona darkly.

"You know something I've noticed? All the citations have low page numbers. Like, this one is supposedly from page 36 of the book *The Broken Teaglass*. We've found seven citations and I don't think there's been any page number over 100."

"Must be a short book," Mona remarked.

She bent over her citations again. I turned on the TV so we wouldn't have to work in silence.

"It'll make the cits fly by," I said, ignoring Mona's disapproving look.

She scoffed and snorted through a cop show and accused me of letting it distract me. But when a news magazine show came on next, she set her citations down and gazed at the screen. They were doing a story on abusive prison wardens.

"Awesome," she said. "Finally something I can sink my teeth into."

"You serious?" I asked.

Mona shrugged and nodded at the same time.

In the middle of the show, when they were talking about

some superfluously performed strip searches in a Midwestern women's penitentiary, I heard her gasp.

"That actually shocks you, Mona? You need to get out more."

She shook her head. She reached for the remote and shut off the TV.

"Hey," I said. "They're just about to show some sweet hidden camera footage. You don't want to watch?"

"I found another one," she said, her voice tight. "Number 49."

"Let me see."

Mona pulled away from me, hogging the slip in her hand, reading it twice, three times.

"Well, shit," she said, handing it to me.

subtext

Whatever I'll carry, this is what I leave—the explanation, the story I would tell. You told me once that your own stories have no moral, no *subtext*. There is no obligatory response of awe, admiration, gratitude, or pity. That your presence at a certain place and moment was coincidental, and that you're no better or worse than anyone for it. Does telling the story, then, make it not so much yours? Not so much your private and singular possession, but a shared object of all who hear it? Something others can hear—or even tell—as suits their particular ear? You've said you wish to share history, not possess it. But can it really ever be that way, Red? When the blood is on our hands alone?

Dolores Beekmim
The Broken Teaglass
Robinson Press
14 October 1985
49

"What do you think?" I asked.

"I think," Mona said slowly, "that I would really, really like to know who the hell this Red guy is."

"Me too," I said.

"I'd like to know whose blood is on his hands. Is he called Red because there's blood on his hands? Because he's the one responsible for the corpse?"

"Hmm . . . ," I said, rubbing my chin. "I wouldn't draw that conclusion yet."

"This company has *issues*," Mona said, slamming her finger down on the cit to emphasize her observation.

I put my feet up on my cardboard-box coffee table and waited for her to continue.

"It's just a cold, crazy, dysfunctional New England family," she mused, perching herself at the very edge of the futon.

"Hey. Watch yourself, Ohio. What do you know about New England families?"

"I've been working there longer than you, Billy. I know a lot about it."

"A year at Samuelson, give or take? That's nothing. I've *lived* the weird New England family."

"Oh. *Excuse* me. I forgot where you grew up. I suppose you think this is perfectly normal. A couple of unexplained corpses in the family history. A few blood-spattered hands. No need to actually discuss it, or even acknowledge it. Not in spoken words, at least."

"I had no idea you were harboring this kind of resentment, Mona. Maybe I should get you another Black Label."

"No, thanks. But does anyone ever want to admit there's a problem? Is anyone willing to sacrifice a little of their cold, quiet reserve and talk about it? *No.*"

"What're you talking about? Where are you getting this? The Nathaniel Hawthorne guide to tortured family relations?

I'm afraid my family didn't get a copy. But then, my family's from Connecticut. Not exactly hard-core New England."

She curled her lip at me. "Right. Suburban Connecticut families are *real* fuckin' functional. I should know. Middlebrook College is crawling with their bitter female spawn."

"Are you trying to say, Mona, that you didn't feel you fit in?"

She ignored the question. "I'd like to look at that corpse cit again, I think. In light of this. Where is it?"

"I don't know. I thought you had it."

"Shit. It's at my apartment. We need to start keeping copies at both of our places."

Mona tapped the side of her head, sighed, and wandered over to my living room window. She pulled up the blinds and peered outside. Then she started fiddling with the drawstring cord, wrapping it around her tiny wrist. She didn't say anything for a few minutes.

"What's the matter?" I asked. "You freaking out?"

"No. I'm just thinking."

"Alrighty."

I read the *subtext* cit again. Mona was right—the blood in that last line was pretty sinister. But the words that preceded it hinted that it shouldn't necessarily be taken at face value. With all this discussion of stories and subtext, wasn't it possible we were supposed to read the blood—and maybe the corpse—as a symbol, or a tease? Between the blood and the dead prom queen, I got the distinct feeling that our "Dolores" had a talent for inserting disturbing images in place of actual facts. And her choice of the word *subtext* probably wasn't a coincidence.

Mona unwrapped the cord from her wrist. She leaned forward until her forehead was pressed against the glass. She was silent for a few moments, then she said, "Seems like a peaceful neighborhood."

"Some of the time."

"I've lived here well over a year, but I feel like I don't know this city at all."

I didn't know how to respond.

"I've lived in this part of the country for over five years," Mona said, "and I still don't think I get it."

"What's there to get?"

"Well, first of all, people big-talk like they're so used to the harsh winters and the heavy snow. But then nobody buys snow tires. I mean, what's that about?"

"Not sure," I said, shrugging. "Have you been wondering this for long?"

"And some of the people," she continued, "can be hard nuts to crack, I think."

"There are people like that everywhere," I said.

Mona smiled into the window.

"Right," she said to the glass. "There's something I should probably tell you, Billy, just to be fair."

"What's that?"

"Remember 'blow-dryer'?"

"Of course."

"That cit didn't just fall magically into my lap right after we talked about that first 'editrix' cit."

"Okay," I replied. "How did you find it, then?"

"I looked for it."

"But how did you know where to start?"

"I didn't."

"So what're you saying? You just started at the beginning of the file? Started at 'A' and flipped your way through till you found something?"

"I started in the middle of 'B,' actually. It's kind of bad luck to start with 'A.' Dan's told you that, right?"

"Yeah."

"You were that desperate to find another?"

Mona hesitated. "Not at first. Not until I showed the 'ed-itrix' cit to Dan."

"You showed it to *Dan*? Why didn't you tell me?"

"You were a little...reluctant to get involved. I didn't want to make you even more nervous. But don't you remember that you were actually the one to suggest it? I showed you 'editrix' and you suggested showing it to a senior editor. Since maybe they'd have read the *Teaglass* book, or have some insight on it."

"I forgot about that. I didn't think you'd take my suggestion."

"Since you were just trying to get me off your back at the time."

"I guess I wasn't quite thinking of Dan when I suggested it. Maybe Grace. Maybe somebody like that." I rubbed my eyes. I couldn't quite get my head around it. How could the seemingly calculating Mona have made such a rash move? "What did Dan say about it?"

"His reaction was kind of weird," she answered.

"Okay." I put my hands out, inviting further explanation. Mona was still turned toward the window, but I'm pretty sure she could see my reflection in the glass. I wondered if I should tell her about Dan catching sight of the cits while we talked about *beauty queen*.

"He took the cit from me and read it," she explained. "He just sat there reading it, maybe a few times. Then he said to me, 'I'll come by your desk later. I'm a little busy for this right now.' Sort of cold, the way he said it. Now, no one would ever call Dan warm and fuzzy. But he's not *cold* like that. And the odd thing about it was that it was eight-thirty in the morning and he was just research-reading a fly-fishing magazine. He wasn't busy. Then he comes by my desk after lunch. And guess what he says?"

Mona finally turned around and looked at me. She didn't wait for me to answer. "He hands it back to me. And he says," she lowered her voice in imitation of Dan's usual under-the-breath delivery, " 'Citations can come from almost anywhere. Most of the citations come from published works or established periodicals, but every once in a while, you come across something strange.' I just stared at him. Then he finished his speech, the same old speech he does the second day of training. About how citations can come from jar labels or flyers off the street or overheard conversations. Some weird stuff ends up in the cit file, and that's why you can't take any one cit too seriously."

"Sounds reasonable."

"But I've been working there for over a *year*. Dan knows I know all of that. He didn't even acknowledge what was weird about it. That it seemed to be written by someone at Samuelson. I go to his desk asking if he'd heard of this *Teaglass* book and he comes back to me with a response like *that*?"

I thought about Dan's reaction for a moment. On one hand, it sounded a little odd. You'd think Dan would be concerned about someone jeopardizing the integrity of the cit file, cramming their own little thought nuggets into it, tainting the purity of a century of research. On the other hand, I could see him considering one random cit—even if planted by a sadly disturbed editor—not worth his attention.

"And," she persisted, sitting tentatively on the futon, "why the hell did he need to wait a few hours to give me an empty response like that?"

"You think he was consulting his coven in the meantime, on how to deal with you?"

"Billy."

"Sorry. I'm with you. I think it's interesting. Did he let you keep the cit?"

"Yeah. He didn't take it back."

"Did he seem nervous?"

"No. Only . . . circumspect."

"As always," I pointed out.

"I guess, but I'd say more so than usual, in this instance."

"Do you think he's somehow responsible for the cits?"

Mona's eyes looked bleary as she decided how to respond to this question.

"I don't know," she answered, sounding a little angry. She got up and moved languidly toward the window again. "Anyway. *That's* what really got me interested."

I watched as she stood by the window, gazing at the streetlamp outside.

"I see," I said. I wondered why she didn't seem to want to look at me.

I wished she would get away from the window, where she was starting to look like a little waif trapped in an attic. I considered standing up and going to her, but wasn't sure how she'd interpret it. This definitely wasn't a date—I'd figured that out by now. At her place last time, it wasn't so much that she'd fallen asleep before anything romantic could happen. The bottom line was, nothing like that was ever *going* to happen. I wished she'd made this clearer somehow, but it was probably just as well. She wasn't really my type. Not for anything long term, anyway.

"Maybe we should do more on Samuelson's nickel," I said. "Do a little searching at our desks. Might go faster that way."

Mona didn't reply. Instead she slapped the blinds down and wandered back to the futon. "I guess."

"We've found some pretty intense stuff here," I told her. "Maybe we ought to call it a night."

After I heard her Jetta pull away, I remembered the untouched fruit tart in the refrigerator.

Damn, I whispered. All that work for nothing. I imagined myself eating a slice for breakfast the next morning, alone in the cold fish-fry stink of my kitchen. Cursing again, I took my sleeping bag out of my bedroom closet and threw it back on my futon. I reached under the futon and pulled out *The Colossal Compendium of Jokes, Puns, and Riddles.*

My pencil was stuck in the *Psychiatry* section, where I'd left off.

> Patient: My wife thinks I'm crazy because I like sausages.
> Doctor: That's ridiculous. I like sausages too.
> Patient: Really? You should come see my collection sometime.

It wasn't laugh-out-loud funny, but I'd penciled a plus next to it for the unexpected quality of the punch line.

> How many psychiatrists does it take to change a lightbulb?
> One. But the lightbulb has to want to change.

Had anyone laughed at that in the past twenty years? I put a minus next to it so I wouldn't read it again.

> I went to a psychiatrist because I was a little cracked. I stopped going because I was broke.

Decent. Check.

I kept reading until I reached the end of the section. Nothing new. *Think you're a dog? Get off the couch! I'm a wigwam, I'm a teepee. But I need the eggs.* The usual. Good stuff, but I'd read them all before. I turned the page. The next section was *Rabbis,* then *Rednecks.*

I tossed the book on the floor. This was getting to be a pathetic habit. And I wasn't near ready to settle in for the night. I needed to get the hell out of this apartment. I went into my bedroom closet, where I'd stashed a box of old tapes. Among them was my *Traveling Music,* a mix tape of driving songs I'd made just after high school. When I picked it up and examined it, I discovered that it was actually *Traveling Music 2.* Disappointing, but I slipped it into my pocket anyway and grabbed my jacket.

Once in my car, I discovered that the tape wasn't rewound. When I stuck it in, it was in the middle of a Tom Petty song. Four years ago I had stopped this tape right there, and now, squealing away from my apartment at full speed, I didn't feel I'd come very far since then.

Instead of heading down Claxton's main drag through downtown, I pointed my car in the opposite direction, toward the neighboring town of Sanford. After about ten minutes with my foot on the gas, the road grew a little darker, and the residences a little scarcer. I took a right onto a random side road and coasted along that for a while. I passed a little gas station, but trees started to dominate the roadside. I turned on my brights and turned up the music.

Maybe I'd get hopelessly lost. Maybe I'd see some gossamer figure emerge from the shadows. A dead prom queen, perhaps? Or maybe I'd hit a dog and vow to be a better man as a result. Any of it would be better than the slow death of my apartment. The poorly lit kitchen. The pantry, with its persistent scent of rotting potato. The sinking futon cushion. The overheard mirth of people downstairs who by all conventional expectations shouldn't be any happier than me.

By this point the Grateful Dead had rolled around on the mix tape. I eased my foot up on the pedal. I couldn't really get into revving my engine to the Dead. I took the next few curves a little gentler, and ended up in a small town center, very old-fashioned, with a gazebo and storefronts. Everything appeared to be closed. If there'd been a little local bar, maybe I'd have gone inside. But there was no such bar. This was a place where nothing was likely to happen.

When the Ramones came on, I picked up speed again. I screamed up the road so I could take the next turn fast. And the next. *Take it as it comes. Keep your wits about you. Don't think, just drive.* A school flashed by on the left. I made a U-turn and pulled into its long driveway. *Forget that you're a random creep in a random town hanging out in a middle school parking lot in the dead of night. Forget that cops in small towns check these places pretty frequently for random creeps.*

I circled the lot a few times, picking up speed again. I tried a little fishtailing, then did a wide, unsatisfying donut. Then I positioned myself at the very end of the lot, facing forward. I decided to see how much power this old Grand Am really had in it. And then I could see how well these brakes worked. I pressed my foot down on the accelerator, slammed the car forward, then hit the brakes hard. The jolt snapped me forward just a little. The short squeal of the brakes was about as gratifying as a single sip of beer, or a peck on the cheek from a flirty girl. Just enough to make you realize how much more it's going to take to satiate you.

From this side of the lot, I could see that there was another full parking lot nearby, separated by not much more than a grassy little knoll. The building on the other side was

likely a high school. If I hit that knoll just right I could probably get some air under this car. I could jump the hill and
land on the other side.

The same Beastie Boys song would be playing when I hit
the pavement, but would it sound different on the other
side? Would I feel lucky over there? Or brave? Would I drive
home satisfied?

I stared at the hill. I could definitely do it. That little hill
seemed made for it, almost.

I could do it.

If I had any excuse anymore.

But I didn't.

CHAPTER SEVEN

Mona and I decided to devote a few hours of the following week to *independent* (Mona's emphasis) snooping for relevant 1950 cits. Since our Friday night meetings were proving distracted and unproductive affairs, we agreed to meet only once we'd completed checking all the words on the list.

As I started to tick words off my list, I found myself starting to look forward to that part of each afternoon when I'd go pawing through the cit files. My one little slice of deviance each day. My daily dose of unpredictability. But I didn't feel I had the luxury of devoting more than a half hour a day to the search. I moved slowly through my list. One week turned into two. The first time I found another *Teaglass* cit, I resisted the temptation to run it over to Mona. I was complying with her suggestion that we simply compile everything and read it in one big *mind-blowing* (again, Mona's wording, and Mona's optimism) revelation session when the list was done.

For that couple of weeks, we didn't have much reason to talk to each other. And my work, though still difficult, became so systematic and familiar that I hardly ever had reason to consult with Dan or anyone else. Days would pass before I'd realize, while making dinner or watching evening television, that I hadn't actually spoken to another human being all day. The pleasant cool of early autumn was quickly turning into a more biting cold, so Jimmy and Tom never sat outside on the porch anymore.

"How've you been, buddy?"

Why is it that fairly well-developed musculature and a sportsmanlike demeanor make you everybody's buddy?

"Great, Mr. Phillips," I lied to the old man.

"Made sure to get some more of those old-fashioned-style doughnuts for you."

"You really shouldn't go to any extra trouble for me, sir."

" 'Sir,' " Mr. Phillips chuckled. "You kill me, Billy. No false reverence necessary for these white hairs. Really."

"It's not false," I said.

"I'm not gonna have to beg you to take a doughnut this time, am I?"

"No, I'll gladly eat one."

"Take two," Mr. Phillips insisted.

"Alrighty," I said, piling three into my napkin.

He watched me delightedly.

"Ahaaa. Now you're talkin'. Doughnuts are brain food. You're learning fast, I see."

He slapped me on the shoulder as I turned to walk away.

"Thanks," I said.

"No coffee, Billy?"

"Naw. A strapping, growing boy like me? Maybe you should bring a quart of milk next time."

Mr. Phillips started to laugh, but the laughter quickly turned into a coughing fit as I walked away. I could still hear him hacking up doughnut crumbs when I stopped walking about halfway to my cubicle.

"Holy crap," I said aloud.

One of the science editors, whose name I could never remember, looked up from his computer screen and cocked his head reprovingly. I thought of whispering "Sorry," but decided against it. Then I hurried the rest of the way back to my little hovel.

As I sat chewing my doughnuts, I made no attempt to appear busy. I was too excited to pretend. Instead I stared into my blank computer screen and contemplated this windfall—this unexpected new evidence. Or was it evidence? Was it anything? Maybe I was being too much of a Hardy Boy about this whole thing.

Now you're talkin'.

Not a particularly rare or unusual turn of phrase. But was it just that phrase? Wasn't there something vaguely familiar about Mr. Phillips's manner, now that he'd caught my attention? *Now you're talkin'.* The junk slang. The cit with the corpse. *When you saw what I was reading you said, Now you're talking. You said that junk slang was your favorite. . . .*

Maybe it wasn't a *clue.* Nothing so dramatic as that. Maybe just a hunch. The question was how to follow the instinct— see if it could be turned into a certainty. Mr. Phillips had mentioned that he'd retired a few years ago—and I had the feeling he'd worked at Samuelson for quite a while before that. Being here in 1985 wouldn't be a stretch for him. Hell—he could easily have been here in 1965, judging by his age. Mona had likely had many more encounters with the man than I had. I wondered what she'd think. We were both fast approaching the ends of our halves of the 1950 lists, but this new development was definitely grounds for an early huddle.

After my last bite of doughnut, I folded up the napkin carefully and went to her cubicle. She wasn't there, but her computer was on, and she had citation piles of varying sizes scattered across her desk. She had apparently been sorting out the senses of some complex word when she got up in the middle of it, maybe to clear her head. I looked closer at the cits. They were all for *come*. Poor Mona. I'd thought only senior editors had to deal with words like that one, but it looked like she'd gotten unlucky.

I sat down on Mona's chair, waiting for her to return. I discovered that her swivel chair was much looser and could swivel much more quickly than my own. I whirled around once, then eyed the ladies' room door a few yards away. No one came out. Then I thought of the editors' library downstairs. Mona had mentioned she liked to hide in there sometimes when she couldn't stand her desk anymore. She'd go and look up random pieces of information—whatever came to mind, whatever could keep her looking like she was actually researching something.

As I approached the little room downstairs, I knew I'd been right. I could hear Mona's voice coming from one of the back rows. This room reminded me of the consolidated stacks in my university library, where they stuck the dated theology texts nobody cared about anymore. It had a pungent smell of aging books. Rotting paper and near-limitless knowledge—simultaneously intriguing and foul.

"I never imagined there would be so many slang words for 'snake,' " Mona was saying. "But I guess if you live in the desert, why not?"

"Especially if you sleep outside," someone added. It was Dan.

There was a pause and the rustle of a page being turned. Then Mona gave a quick little laugh.

I moved past the first rows of shelves, toward the back of the room, where they were talking.

"Oh, that's great," Mona continued. "A *bone orchard*. For a cemetery? *Took poor ole Billy out to the bone orchard.*"

She said the last part with a little twang, saying the name Billy like *Bill-AY*. I started a little at the use of my name.

When I got to the back row, they didn't look up. Dan didn't even see me at first. Mona's face was buried in a book that had a drawing of a cactus on its tattered cover, with the title *Cowboy Words*. Dan was standing about a foot from Mona. He was really too far away from her to read what she was reading. In fact, he wasn't looking at the book or at Mona. He was looking downward, it seemed. Smiling at the floor.

"Have you ever read *Lonesome Dove*?" Mona asked him. "I wonder if the author, what was his name? I wonder if he read this book? I always imagine cowboys talking like his characters do. But who knows if it's accurate?"

It was when Dan opened his mouth to respond that he raised his eyes and saw me.

"Hello, Billy," he said, and then Mona looked up too.

"Hi, guys," I said. "I was just looking for a reference on different foods. Someone said there was something like that in here."

"Second row, the side closer to the window, facing us," said Dan. "Not back here. Back here are all the slang-related books we've collected over the years."

I went where Dan had directed me and looked up *bittersweet chocolate* just to look busy.

"Excuse me, you two," Dan said, and tiptoed out of the room.

Soon after, I heard Mona close her book and put it back on the shelf.

She approached me in my row.

"When I said 'Billy,' I think I was thinking of, like, Billy the Kid," she whispered. "Not you."

"Sure," I replied.

"Think you'll be done with your list by tomorrow?" she asked.

"Maybe. Maybe not for two or three days," I said.

After she left, I wondered if she had any clue what I'd seen in her face while she was smiling up at Dan. It was an expression I'd never seen on her before. Like she was suppressing a fit of giggles. Like she had a wisecrack in mind but wasn't sure if she should say it.

Back at my desk, I tried to define it, this strange thing I'd seen in Mona. If I had to pare it down to a few words for a concise definition, what would I call it? *Playful interest*? No, that was an oversimplified characterization. *Flirtatious interest*? No, that was unfair. Mona never seemed flirtatious at work, and this was no exception. *Sardonic girlishness*? No. Absurd. And unfair again. I scribbled a few words onto a blank definition card, until I found the right combination: *Self-conscious delight*. I threw down my pencil. *Good luck with that, Mona,* I thought.

Clifford's phone buzzed, and I heard him pick it up.

"Hey, Sheila," he said, a little more quietly than usual. "Whadya got for me...? Brilliant. Sounds like fun. *Rare words?* Not rare citations...? Right. Of course not. What's the name? Boyd? Line six? All right. Thanks. Wish me luck, Sheila."

Clifford hit a couple of buttons.

"Hello, uh, Ms. Boyd? This is Clifford Engels. I'm one of the editors here. Our receptionist tells me you have some new words you want to...uh...share with us?...Oh. So

they're not new? They're not your own coinages? . . . Really.
Really?"

Clifford was silent for a longer stretch.

"Uh-huh. I see. Well, we don't usually purchase words as a
general rule. . . . I understand. I don't doubt—You found
them *where* . . . ? Wow. That was lucky, wasn't it? And they
weren't waterlogged . . . ? Huh. Isn't that something? Now,
strictly out of curiosity, how much are you asking for these
rare words . . . ? Ouch. Yes, I'd say that's pretty steep. . . . Well,
Ms. Boyd, I'm really not in a position to bargain with you on
behalf of Samuelson Company. I can take down your information, though, and pass it along to the company president.
Okay. Okay. That last part was three-nine-five-four? Got
it. . . . Right. But you shouldn't get your hopes up; I don't
think he'll bite on this. . . . Yeah, you know how it is. He's
old school. A little tight-fisted, yeah. Heh-heh . . . Sure, no
problem . . . Yeah, you could try the OED. They might be interested. Who knows? Maybe they're looking to make an investment. Our loss. Great. Good luck. Bye now."

Clifford hung up, and all was silent for about a minute.
Then he picked up his receiver again. He hit a few buttons.

"Sheila. It's Cliff. Listen, if she calls again, could you put
her through to Dan, maybe? Someone with a gentler touch.
I think I baited her. I feel bad, baiting these delusional cases.

". . . Yeah, yeah. It's been one of those days."

A couple of days later, I forced myself to finish searching through my half of the 1950 words. I photocopied the
few cits I had and dropped them wordlessly into Mona's in-
box. She came to my desk an hour later and plopped a copy
of her photocopied cits in front of my nose. She was wearing

a weird filmy black top with loose flared sleeves that fluttered over my desk and swept a couple of citations out of
place.

"Finally," she whispered. "I didn't want to rush you, but
I've had mine done for a *week*."

"Sorry."

"No problem," she said, still whispering. "So when do you
want to have our citational orgy?"

I felt a little manipulated by the word *orgy*, under the circumstances.

"Just say a time." She put both hands on her hips. The
folds of her black sleeves hung down her sides and made her
look like a bat. "Tomorrow night? My place?"

Her place. What did this mean for Mona of the perpetual
schoolgirl crush? Was hanging at our respective places as
sweet and innocent for her as sipping on a lemonade?

I wasn't angry at her. In fact, the whole Dan thing made
her seem so much more human. And it wasn't uncommon
to have a crush on your boss, right? But my more cynical
side kept thinking of her experimental college boyfriend—
the one she dated to get her professor out of her head. And
her ability to suck down champagne cocktails made me
think of a T-shirt I'd seen on a sorority girl once: *Drink 'til
he's cute.* I just wasn't sure where this was all supposed to go.

"I've kind of had a hankering for ice cream," I told her.
"How about Friendly's again?"

Mona smiled and said, "Sounds perfect."

Mona had done me the courtesy of putting the citations she'd uncovered in order. Like most cits from books,
they had page numbers recorded at the very bottom, along

with the other publication information. Mona had started with the earliest page cit and copied them in ascending order on a couple of sheets of paper. There were five of them. As I'd observed earlier, all the page numbers were low—under 100. I decided I'd make a grand final document by cutting up her photocopies, inserting my cits in the right places, and photocopying it again.

I was scissoring away at Mona's photocopies when I felt a presence hovering over me. I closed the scissors.

"Afternoon, Billy," Grace said brightly.

"Hi," I said, laying one hand awkwardly over a photocopied page.

"I'm just passing around this card. For Susan in the typing room. She's having another baby."

"Oh!" I said, taking the pink card and envelope from her outstretched hand. I placed it on top of the scissors.

"We're all just hoping *this* one will be healthy," she said, lowering her voice. "Poor Susan."

"Yeah," I commiserated, clueless.

"So," Grace said, glancing down at the scattered contents of my desk. Despite her age—she'd told me once she'd been editing Samuelson's school dictionaries for twenty-one years—her face was a little like a porcelain doll's: white and delicate, composed, and with a perfect little red mouth. "How're you liking it? Now that you've been here a couple of months? You seem a lot more at home here lately."

"Yeah. It's great," I said.

"Really?"

"Yeah, it's a really interesting place."

"It *does* take some adjusting, though. The office. The quiet. The solitary work. Some days it gets to us, even us diehards."

"Yeah."

"You know, if you ever want to chat, you know where my desk is. I love having visitors. My corner's so *quiet*."

"Yeah," I said again, stupidly.

Grace hesitated for a moment, then said she'd better let me get back to work. I strained for a hint of sarcasm when she said "work," but I don't think I heard one. Naturally, Grace probably wondered what I was doing slicing up photocopies. Could I come up with a reasonable explanation if asked? *Decorating my cubicle,* I decided, and returned to my snipping, looking around every few minutes as I worked. I approached the photocopier with my final product, trying to look confident and casual. I stuck the photocopy and scraps in my backpack and got back to work.

CHAPTER EIGHT

advantaged

How did I get here? Even the stories I've asked you to tell, Red, were only another way for me to ask that question. Now I suppose the question might mean something else? If here means this office, this very physical place, well, my story's not so different from that of others who work here. I was a good student. I like books. Languages aren't difficult for me. I graduated with the highest honors, but had no serious grad school plans. My *advantaged* background and education led me here somehow, and I was dropped rather unwittingly into this most bizarre job.

1

editrix

She warmed that water with her hatred. She sighed plagues into that water. I didn't care. In this chill and inhuman place I was obedient and invisible to everything. I needed that tea to remember I was alive, warm-blooded. I always carried the tea slowly up the stairs and to my desk. I drank it with careful relish. No spilling on the citations. No slurping, no satisfied Aaaah! Such noises would echo through the cubicles and start an uncomfortable collective shifting of the editors and *editrices* in their seats. So I always sipped quietly.

5

schlub

Lexicographers rarely make messes. I had no idea where to find a cloth, dustpan, and broom. Or if any even existed in the building. The secretary went to fetch a custodian, but returned with only a push broom and a plastic bag. Feeling like a *schlub,* I cleaned everything up while everybody watched. I picked up the big pieces first. The jagged spike attached to the base of the glass. Then a large rounded triangle shard. Tried not to make too many unsettling clinking noises with them. Then I swept up the small shards, and slid everything into the bag.

8

paperbound

Only you, Red. Only you acknowledged the mishap. You mentioned it offhand when you came to give me yet another *paperbound* book from your home collection: *Beyond the 38th Parallel.* I didn't confess it then but will confess it now. I hadn't even read the last book you gave me. You told me it wasn't exactly an academic piece of work. Just some pretty good firsthand accounts. Diaries. Letters. I thanked you for it and you winked. Just don't spill anything on it, you said, and then sauntered off to the secretary's desk for your midmorning flirtation.

9

unscripted

Scout drove me to work the next morning. We talked about the usual things. After he parked the car, he asked me what happened to my wrist. Vegetables, I said. It was a short and *unscripted* version of a story I had half-prepared earlier, for this very purpose. Something to do with chopping vegetables, I had thought, would have a touch of realism. I got out of Scout's car to ease the transition from that conversational topic to another. The work day went without incident. No policeman came.

21

blow-dryer

I switched off the stove and picked up the phone. By the time Scout answered, I'd lost it. I was crying. He wanted to know what was the matter, nearly yelling the question after I couldn't answer his first couple of tries. I couldn't form sentences, or even meaningful one-word answers. He hung up. A few minutes later, he was there, at my door. His cheeks were red from rushing there in the cold. His hair, usually so carefully styled with a round brush and *blow-dryer,* was tousled in all directions. He had never looked so cute. He had never looked so powerless. I wanted to hug him, for strength, and then push him back out the door. I was glad to have him there, but suddenly acutely aware that he couldn't save me from anything. He followed me into the kitchen and watched me pour tea water from the pot to the sink. He wanted to know if I was all right. I said no. No, I said again. I'm crazy. You wouldn't believe how crazy I've become.

23

headshrinker

He offered me one of my own kitchen chairs. Even upon seeing his reserved and intellectual girlfriend in such serious need of a *headshrinker,* he didn't lose his composure or his gentlemanly way. What is it? he wanted to know. His calm was impressive, and it made the misplaced absurdity of the story all the more clear. That story and this calm couldn't exist together in the same room.

24

callithump

We passed the next week or two in the usual way. Weekend hikes, book talk, disgust at the verb use of *impact* and the like. And he was still the smarter of the two of us, in all ways but one. There was just one thing now, it seemed, that I knew about the world that he didn't. It wasn't a specific piece of information, or some esoteric knowledge. It wasn't even a story. It was only when the thing exploded later, into a fire-eating *callithumping* fat lady freak tent cinema-circus, that I began to understand the thing as a story. When they figured out who Derek Brownlow was, and what it meant.

28

maven

When the papers went crazy, I knew everything might very well explode. Still, I resigned myself to the stern presence of my fellow word *mavens*. There was at least an odd comfort in submitting to the long silence of the day. Reliable and insistent, it served as a kind of protector. I was reading a book about drug slang, underlining the word "stash," and you came to my desk. When you saw what I was reading, you said, Now you're talking. You said that junk slang was your favorite, and wanted to know if there was a chapter on junk. Then you asked if I'd finished that other book yet. No, I whispered. I was unraveling fast. Was it a trick question? What exactly had been in that article that I hadn't had time to read? Was there something suspect near the corpse? Were you smiling, Red, because of something you knew?

32

demythologize

A wounded, resentful version of my face—but blue-white and open-eyed and dead—started glancing back at me in mirrors and watching me when I was failing to sleep. In time, the image began to resemble a dead-prom-queen costume, sometimes dripping black blood from a heavily lipsticked mouth, or wearing a ripped ruffled dress. Eventually, it became more cinematic, bearing little resemblance to me, easier to shut off, like a bad movie on TV. Almost comical on occasion. Almost. Dead prom queen on intimate terms. Dead prom queen *demythologized.* Not frightening so much as unsettling, constant, and familiar. An unwanted pet you feed out of obligation. Weeks later, the dead prom queen lingered only out of habit.

36

hot ticket

Next to the fear, though, came a twisted sense of power. I was the star of this little show, and the less I said—the longer I stayed quiet—the more they loved me. In fragile, soundless, faceless form, I was a real *hot ticket.* And if it was silence they loved, I could string them along for as long as I wanted. They would spoil me forever, crown me with a glass tiara that could erase from my head the impulse to calculate the value of one life for another, or one life for several, or the tenuous value of life in general.

37

plus

In the meantime, we ate an awful lot of pies. Three a week at one point. We always sipped tea with it, and he always seemed to find topics for engaging, if somewhat one-sided, conversation. He told me about his grandfather's dementia.

The poor old man was now confusing the details of his own life with those he had read in some biographies of Charles Lindbergh. He told me about his old Latin teacher who chain-smoked and who, one day, soon after retiring, put on a flowered sundress *plus* a wig, then hanged himself in his study. Maybe he was trying to convince me that he had a stomach for strange stories? Was it the pie or the silence that eased these stories out of him?

41

larger-than-life

But still I didn't speak. How could it ever work with such a story between us? But even once was too many times to speak it. *Larger-than-life,* that story. Larger than anything. Perhaps neither of us would be capable of climbing from the depths of that story? Weeks passed still, and I didn't tell it. I began to know I never would. Were the pies, then, a sort of peace offering—an attempt to implant a pleasant memory of myself, to sweeten his mind in favor of me in the inevitable event of my betrayal?

43

subtext

Whatever I'll carry, this is what I leave—the explanation, the story I would tell. You told me once that your own stories have no moral, no *subtext*. There is no obligatory response of awe, admiration, gratitude, or pity. That your presence at a certain place and moment was coincidental, and that you're no better or worse than anyone for it. Does telling the story, then, make it not so much yours? Not so much your private and singular possession, but a shared object of all who hear it? Something others can hear—or even tell—as suits their particular ear?

You've said you wish to share history, not possess it. But can it really ever be that way, Red? When the blood is on our hands alone?

49

Mona seemed grateful for my work. She shuffled happily through the pages after the waitress had taken our orders—my clam chowder and Mona's chocolate and caramel sundae.

"Whatever else we have here," she said, "I think this narrator has depressive illness. Did you notice all the suicidal material?"

"Mmm," I said reluctantly. "I can see how you might read some of the cits that way. But overall, I don't think that's the main point—suicide threats. Do you?"

Mona tapped *demythologize* and ordered, "Look at this one. When you consider the cuts on her wrist along with this? C'mon. Adolescent death worship. I can spot it a mile away."

"A woman of many talents," I marveled. "What makes you say 'adolescent,' anyway? We don't know how old she is. And she's at least old enough to be working at Samuelson."

"She's probably our age," Mona said firmly. "Look at the first cit. It seems like she hasn't been there for long."

"You still consider yourself an adolescent?" I asked.

She shrugged. "Not *me*, no. But twenty-three's not out of the woods, for some people. I have a couple of old friends back home who still live with their parents and get falling-down drunk on weekends."

"You're twenty-three?"

"Yeah. And you're twenty-two, right? A spring chicken."

"I just turned twenty-four," I said.

She raised an eyebrow at me. "Really?"

"Yup," I said. "Don't look surprised. Don't I seem to you like someone who usually takes the slow road?"

"I'm not sure if there's a diplomatic answer to that question."

"Don't worry about it. I didn't say there was anything wrong with the slow road."

Mona looked at me carefully.

"Okay," she said blankly. Then she looked back at the cits.

"I have to admit," I said. "That prom queen cit is actually one of my favorites."

"Ew," replied Mona. "Why?"

"I think it gives us a special insight into her emotional state."

"How's that?"

"The dead prom queen is *her,* of course. It's her, but dead. She calls it the dead prom queen to make light of it, I think. But she sees it as something close to her, death. It's not death *worship,* I don't think. It's just become a part of her everyday life, thinking about death."

Mona gave me a bored look.

"And you don't see that as a sign of depressive illness?" she asked.

"No."

"Hmm." She looked doubtful. "Then how do you explain the cut on her wrist, in the 'unscripted' cit?"

"I don't know. But suicidal tendencies isn't the only possibility."

"I disagree. It sounds like she made some feeble suicide attempt. Or maybe she just cut herself. Deliberately, to get attention. I seriously knew girls in high school who did shit like that."

"So did I," I said. "But we're talking about the eighties. Did people do that in the eighties?"

"Probably you're right about that," Mona sighed. "Probably not. Our generation is *sick*."

"I think the important question in the 'unscripted' cit is, who is Scout? And why is she deceiving him?"

"But we know who Scout is," Mona said.

"We do?"

"Well, yeah. At least, we know he's her boyfriend."

The waitress approached and plunked our orders in front of us. After Mona had inhaled all of her whipped cream and began scraping her spoon into the swirls of caramel and chocolate, she said, "We know Scout's her boyfriend from 'blow-dryer' and 'headshrinker.' "

I looked at both cits. "The 'he' in 'blow-dryer' isn't necessarily the same person as the 'he' in 'headshrinker.' "

"It's a no-brainer," Mona insisted. "It's the same guy. One cit directly follows the other. Did you notice the numbers? Twenty-four and twenty-five? You know what those numbers are?"

"Page numbers," I said, making a smiley face on my soup with oyster crackers.

"No," Mona said. "They're not page numbers because there's no real book *The Broken Teaglass*. I believe the cits are numbered. Twenty-five follows twenty-four. Simple as that. It sure sounds like 'headshrinker' is the continuation of what's happening in 'blow-dryer.' Nothing in between. They're not *page* numbers. Someone wanted to make it possible to put the story back in order. With ease."

"With *relative* ease," I said. I drowned the oyster cracker smiley face with my spoon. "We're at a dead end and it doesn't look like we have even half of them."

"Still. You get what I'm saying," she said, before slipping a gob of chocolate sauce into her mouth. She squinted at the photocopy.

" 'His reserved and intellectual girlfriend,' " she read. "She thinks a lot of herself, doesn't she?"

"I wouldn't say that. She's referring to *his* perspective. That's what he thinks she is. Shy and smart."

"And what's the big story that's hanging over them, anyway? In this and other cits, she keeps talking about *the story*. Why doesn't she just tell it, already?"

"I think that's what she's trying to do here," I said.

"Well, then she should quit pussyfooting around. We did all this work. I was hoping for a little instant gratification. What the hell happened to the corpse? Are we gonna get a little dead body action again soon?"

I dug in my soup, looking for pieces of clam.

"We know quite a bit, I think," I pointed out. "We know she worked at Samuelson. We know she had a boyfriend, and it seems he worked there too. We know that she was trying to keep something from him. Something that might have had to do with a cut on her wrist. Maybe she tried to kill herself for some reason, but maybe not."

Mona nodded, adding, "We also know that there's some guy named Red involved. A boyfriend on the sly, maybe? Someone Scout doesn't know about. Red sounds like a player. And she seems to be communicating directly with him about something."

"Red likes flirting," I said slowly, watching for her reaction to the character of Red. "And talking about heroin junkies."

"And there's a corpse," Mona put in eagerly. "The proverbial corpse."

"Proverbial?" I repeated.

She shrugged. "Usage is an art," she said. "Language is fluid."

"Any theories about the corpse?" I asked.

Mona dug into her sundae glass, and slurped up a few last spoonfuls before answering.

"Naturally," she said, "we should entertain the possibility that the cut is related to the corpse. Maybe she battled someone in a switchblade fight and won. There you've got your corpse and your slashed wrist."

"But is that theory realistic for a lexicographer? A *reserved, intellectual* lexicographer?"

"No," Mona admitted. "I'm just saying we should entertain something of the kind. As it seems fairly obvious. But I stand by my suicidal theory. It's not such a crazy theory, you know. Maybe she saw something terrifying. A dead body. A murder. Or she *knows* something about a fatal incident, or at least a crime. And maybe that's what's making her lose her head."

I nodded, conceding that this wasn't a half-bad theory.

"So what about Scout?" I asked.

"Scout's not involved." Mona waved her hand confidently. "Scout's a tool. *Red's* involved. But of course, those two aren't as important as the other guy. We can't forget about the other guy."

"Derek Brownlow."

"Right. This seems like our best piece of information. A full name. And a full name that's apparently been in the papers. This gives us another place to look."

"Maybe. But Red and Scout seem like nicknames."

"But that doesn't mean that Derek Brownlow is too."

"So you're thinking we should—"

"Hit the library, yes."

"Hit the microfiches."

"Well, yeah. I guess. I'm kind of hoping I'll be able to do a keyword search, but I guess it all depends on how far back this thing goes, and what kind of files they keep on the local papers."

"This is really turning out to be delightful, Mona. A microfiche search, of all things. We're like the Bloodhound Gang."

"Didn't I tell you you'd be thanking me? Why don't you let me take care of the library stuff for now? I'll make the first library run. You keep looking in the citations."

"But we're at a dead end," I protested. "Where am I supposed to look?"

"That's true," she said. "But let's think about this. Nineteen fifty is smack in the middle of the century. What could that be? Maybe somebody's doing every decade? Or every fifty years? I mean, should we look up 1900 words next?"

"It could be anything. It could be the year of her Chinese animal. Like, maybe she's doing every monkey year, or every dragon year, or whatever 1950 is."

"If that's what it turns out to be, Billy, I'll buy you a box of Cuban cigars. But I suppose Chinese zodiac years are as good an avenue as any."

"Maybe every five years?" I suggested. "Multiples of five might be important, since there's 1985 there on all the cits."

"I say we try 1940 and 1960," Mona decided. "It just seems the most promising. New decade years. We try those first."

"It'll be a lot of work just to determine if we're completely off base," I said, still reluctant. "Even in 1950, we only found a few cits in all those, what, 250 words?"

"What are you suggesting? That we go with the Chinese zodiac first, then try 1940 and 1960?"

"No," I mumbled. "1940 and 1960 it is."

"I'll do my share, plus I'll see what I can find in some library searches of Derek Brownlow. We'll print out the lists on Monday," Mona said. "Which year do you want?"

On my way home, I thought about this Red guy. If Mona had noticed that there was something familiar about him, she hadn't mentioned it. For Mona, all the blood in this story was literal, and all the slashes deep. So a version of the story that included doughnut man was likely to disappoint. But for me, it made the story more intriguing. Even if it was all real—the corpse and the dead prom queen and the bloodied hands—a version with the Sinatra-humming old Phillips might at least have some redemption in it.

I liked that idea. I decided I'd pursue it on my own for a little while.

CHAPTER NINE

It was all a matter of approach. Grace liked to talk. And she liked to talk about her fellow dictionary people. But she did so in such a soft-spoken, matter-of-fact way that it hardly seemed like gossip. Getting her to talk would simply require a similar finesse.

I waited a couple of days to make my move, mulling over various opening lines, avenues of conversation, sideways turns that would lead to Mr. Phillips. Still, as I stood near the water cooler on the decided day and hour of my approach, I wondered if it was unwise to go on this mission alone. I stepped a few feet away from the cooler so I could watch Grace at her desk.

She was absently stroking the curls over her ear with her left hand, and holding a citation in her right. She scrutinized it for a moment, then picked up another. There was a silver watch on her wrist that seemed to keep catching on her hair, but she didn't seem to notice. Something about her reminded me of Mona. Maybe it was her size—although she didn't seem so deviously tiny as Mona. She seemed a little healthier, perhaps, and less elfin. Maybe it was the similar ease with which she seemed to work. Grace's ease, however, came with a calm that Mona definitely didn't possess. But Mona might very well be this woman someday.

Fancying her just an old Mona made it easier to take a final deep breath, step up to her cubicle, and start shooting the shit.

"Hi, Grace," I said as I approached.

"Good morning," she said, smiling pleasantly as she put down the cit she'd been holding. "How've you been?"

"Pretty good. I got to go through the cits for 'damaged goods' this morning."

"You defined it?"

"No. Unfortunately, it's already been defined."

"Too bad. That would've been a fun one for you. The first words are memorable," she said, pulling a single long hair out of one of the chunky metal links of her watch. "It all becomes unremarkable pretty fast, I have to tell you. For better or for worse. Just a part of the routine. You find yourself defining some sleaze word and you don't bat an eye. Or you'll be with friends and you'll hear someone say a word you defined, and you don't even think of mentioning it to them."

"That's when you know it's lost its novelty?"

"Or just when you know everyone's sick of hearing you talk about it." Grace laughed.

"My family hasn't reached that point yet," I told her. "My mother's still full of questions when she calls."

"That'll change. Trust me. Maybe even by the end of Thanksgiving weekend. You going to see your family for the holiday?"

"Yeah."

"They live near here?"

"Yeah. Connecticut."

"That's nice," she said. "Mona has to fly out to see hers. Says she'll probably be taking that whole week. Flight's cheaper that way."

"Oh?" This was news to me. Odd that Mona had told Grace, and that Grace thought it interesting enough to mention to me.

"Last year we took the same flight out to Cleveland, would you believe that? Her family lives in the same area as my brother-in-law. My husband and I go out there every other year."

"Wow," I said, feigning interest.

"I don't know who was the most nervous of the three of us. It wasn't too long after September eleventh, see?"

"Uh-huh."

"Mona doesn't seem to care much for flying," Grace continued.

Shit, I thought. This conversation was definitely going in the wrong direction.

"So, Billy," Grace said, maybe sensing my disinterest. "Are you enjoying living in Claxton?"

"It's all right. I've got a nice cheap apartment. But it's not exactly a happening city, though."

"No, certainly not. What do you do for fun, then? Go to the mall?"

"It's about come to that, sadly."

"Aren't any of your college friends still around?"

"Not really. An old buddy of mine's up near Boston. I keep meaning to go up and see him there, but ... anyway, Mona and I have hung out a couple of times."

"It's really a shame there aren't more young editors here. They only hire one or two each year. And of course, not everybody stays."

At this point, I was trying pretty desperately to think up a good segue. Time was ticking away. Grace was hurling conversational curveballs at me, and I couldn't seem to whack them away quickly and skillfully enough. Most cubicleside chats I'd observed lasted three or four minutes, max. A few more minutes at her desk and I'd be a work-shirking parasite.

"I don't need young people around to keep me entertained," I ventured.

Grace looked at me as one might look at a child who has just accidentally Super-Glued his nostril shut.

"Just take Mr. Phillips," I said hurriedly, plowing recklessly forward. "What a blast that guy is."

"That's for sure," Grace said. "It's been a lot quieter around here since he retired. I miss him. But it's nice that he comes around once in a while to keep our spirits up. Even if it's just as much to keep *his* spirits up."

"When did he retire?" I asked.

"Three or four years ago. He'd been here almost *forty* years."

"Forty?"

Grace nodded. "Just imagine," she said.

I preferred not to. But I paused for a reverential moment before saying, "Did he by any chance have a nickname around here?"

Grace looked quizzical. "Not that I know of . . . why?"

"I just thought I heard Mr. Needham call him Red the other day."

"Hmm," Grace murmured, gazing sideways into her cubicle, thinking. "He's had gray hair for almost as long as I've known him. But early on, he did have some red hair. He was definitely a redhead, back in the day. So it's definitely plausible. But . . . no one's ever called him that that I know of, and . . ."

She touched her hair again thoughtfully, then lowered her

voice and said, "And Mr. Needham and Mr. Phillips have never exactly been on a, um, nickname basis."

"Oh," I whispered. Oops. As the eldest and crustiest member of the current staff, Mr. Needham had seemed to me the likeliest bud of the even older and crustier Mr. Phillips. "Well, I could be wrong," I said, trying to sound casual. "Maybe I heard wrong. I'm just into nicknames."

"Really? Why's that?"

"I dunno. No real reason. On my old football team, in high school, we always had nicknames for everybody."

Not true. But believable, and somehow an appropriate thing to say, given my uniquely dopey image around the office.

Grace smiled politely. "And what was yours?" she asked.

"Homer," I said. This part was true. I was the only member of the high school varsity team who actually read the books assigned to us in English classes. I usually summarized them in the locker room so the other guys could pass the pop quizzes. Selections of *The Iliad* were the first thing we had to read that year.

Grace twisted a finger into one of her graying blonde curls.

"After the Simpsons?" she asked, her blue eyes drifting up toward my forehead, then quickly darting back to my gaze.

"That or the Greek poet," I admitted. "I was never sure which."

CHAPTER TEN

A few days later, I felt a hard slap on the back. When I turned around, there was Mr. Phillips, hanging over my cubicle with a cake doughnut in each hand.

"Hello, Homer," he said. "Brought you a little treat. Do you know about this Krispy Kreme racket? Do you think I should switch to Krispy Kreme?"

"I don't know." I took one of the doughnuts. "I've never had a Krispy Kreme, but I hear good things. The ones you bring are pretty good, though."

"Heard you were asking about me," Mr. Phillips said, flashing me a disarmingly toothy grin.

"Uh . . . oh?" I quickly bit into the doughnut so I wouldn't have to say more.

"Howdya know my nickname?" he growled, rather abruptly. Maybe he was trying to catch me off guard.

"Howdya know *mine*?" I shot back. But I knew very well how.

"Ah," said Mr. Phillips. "But you've been here, what, three months? You should know by now. Grace's the teat of information on which we *all* suck. Not just you young pups."

My face burned, either for myself or the old man. I heard Clifford snickering in the neighboring cubicle.

"Listen," I whispered.

Mr. Phillips leaned forward intently and handed me the second doughnut.

"What?" he said.

"I've been thinking," I said. "You always treat us here at the office. But does anyone ever treat you?"

"It's my pleasure, Homer."

"Please don't call me that."

"All right, champ."

"I'd like to buy you a cup of Jamaica Blue Mountain," I said. "*Real* Jamaica Blue Mountain."

"That's really not necessary, champ."

"But I want to. There's a place just outside Claxton, on the edge of East Claxton, where they're sure to have it. It looks like a real classy place."

"Naw. It's not necessary."

I needed to take a different tack. "I don't have anyone to go with me. I've been wanting to try it."

Mr. Phillips faked a look of dejection. "You're a terrible liar, Homer. I'm sure little Mona'd go with you. Is it on the bus route?"

"Uhh . . . I don't know. It's on that long street with all the restaurants."

"That's a little ways from the bus route," Mr. Phillips remarked mournfully.

"If I gave you a ride, would you go? Don't you live right near here? I could pick you up right after work."

"Now, that'd be nice," he said.

"Yeah," I agreed.

"When?" he said.

"How about tomorrow? Right after work?"

"Now you're talkin'. You know where Collins Hill Village

is? The big old folks' halfway house off Collins Road? I'm in number forty-seven."

"I'll find it," I promised him.

Mr. Phillips's hands were sticky with honey.

"God," he said, sucking his middle finger. "I'd heard of this stuff. I think I may have even seen some cits for it once. But I had no idea how good it is."

"This one's not as good as my father's, though," I said. "He makes some excellent baklava. The trick is just a little bit of citrus rind in with the honey sauce."

"Your father's a domestic type?"

"Pastry chef, actually," I explained.

"Well, that's lucky. So were you a fat little kid growing up?"

"No. He wasn't a pastry chef until a few years ago. And I guess 'baker' is a more accurate term for what he does, since the place he works for isn't very fancy. It's his second career."

"Ah. What was his first one, then?"

"Oral surgeon."

"That's a good one, Billy."

"I'm serious."

Mr. Phillips picked up a couple of scattered walnuts from the tabletop with his sticky finger.

"It's still a good one," he said. "It just goes to show you. You have to find what you like to do. You like Samuelson so far?"

"Sure," I said.

"What do you like about it?"

"It's real. It's . . . basic."

"Basic?" Mr. Phillips looked at me skeptically.

"Yeah. I mean, at least there's nothing morally question-able about it, like, say, marketing pharmaceuticals. It's the *dictionary*. There's something old-fashioned about it. Every-body I tell about this job *gets* it. Or at least, people are inter-ested in getting it."

I watched Mr. Phillips gulp the last of his Jamaica Blue Mountain. Now that I had him to myself, I wasn't certain what I needed to ask him, and how. Casual mentions of the "morally questionable" weren't likely to get the guy chatting about fifteen-year-old corpses.

"But, Billy. You're not falling into *that* trap, are you? This job is so much more than *telling* people about it."

"I didn't mean it like—"

"It's a privilege, being a Samuelson man." In the coffee bar behind us, a guy with dreadlocks was steaming milk with the usual *squeeee* sound, which seemed to distract Mr. Phillips. The left side of his face twitched slightly whenever the noise intensified. "So much history there. And the idea that your work ends up in so many households, so many schools. The Samuelson dictionary is like a Bible to some people. And they rely on it without ever once thinking about who actu-ally wrote it. But that's the *beauty* of it."

Mr. Phillips and Mr. Needham certainly seemed to be cut from the same cloth. Could it really be true, as Grace had implied, that the two men disliked each other?

"Do you want another cup of coffee?"

"Better not. So, do you like words?"

I thought about this question warily. It was something people seemed to ask me a lot now that I worked at Samuelson. At the bank, for example, when I was depositing my Samuelson paycheck. Sometimes it came in the form of a statement. *Oh, you're working* there? *You must love words!* But I don't like or dislike words. I use words, yes. I am indeed grateful for the vast variety of words available to me in the English language, even if I haven't mastered all of the Latinate constructions that show up on the GRE. And it's mildly interesting to me that *embarrass* comes from a combination of words that used to mean "in a noose." But the progression from "in a noose" to "in a difficult situation" to "in a state of self-consciousness" seems a fairly natural one. *Fascinating. Words are fascinating!* some might respond. But is it really so fascinating? After hearing a few of these little word histories, don't you kind of feel like you've heard them all?

"I'm not exactly an etymology buff," I admitted. "Not like some of the other folks—"

"I didn't ask if you loved etymology," Mr. Phillips interrupted. "Obviously you're not an etymologist. You don't have a great deal of formal linguistic training, like Needham or George. You're a *definer*. Definers concern themselves primarily with usage. Current usage. The living words. You know, I've always been pretty interested in etymology myself. But it's capturing the *current* use of words, right as they're continuing to change—that's the real dynamic work. That's the work that keeps you young."

"Hmm."

"And it's more entertaining too. Listening to how people stretch the language. You know, I've always thought we should be a little more open-minded about our regular sources for the cit file. The only thing we all read regularly is reputable magazines and newspapers. *The Economist. The Atlantic.*" Mr. Phillips wrinkled his nose. "*Newsweek.* But with those you get a pretty narrow picture of how the language is being used, don't you think?"

"I think the idea is that published writers know what they're doing. They're the ones who stretch the language intelligently."

"Bullshit." His left lip twitched as the barista started the steamer again. "Published writers are self-conscious as hell. They don't stretch the language in a *practical* way. Only to be arty and impressive. Now, I'm not suggesting we fill up the files with cits from high school newspapers, but I'd just like to see a more balanced evidence base. If we really want to call ourselves descriptivists here, and not prescriptivists—you know the difference, right?"

"Yeah."

Dan had described the difference on my second day of training. A prescriptivist prescribes the rules of grammar, the rules of language. Tells you what's correct and what's not. Samuelson did not identify its books as prescriptivist. Instead, it liked to think itself an objective observer of the language. Changes in language were to be described accurately; the users of the books could make their own decisions about how to use the language based on that objective information. *We like to think of ourselves essentially as descriptivists,* Dan had told me. *Even if some of us around here have a prescriptivist axe or two to grind.* He followed that statement with a cryptic little chuckle.

"Yes. See, we're not truly descriptivists yet," Mr. Phillips grumbled. He'd worked himself into a bit of a temper. "We're far too snobbish to call ourselves descriptivists. And you know what? It's primarily the *spoken* word that interests me. All those hours spent each day research-reading? I know it's useful. It really is. But what about research-*listening*? There's really not enough of that going on. Cits quoted from the radio and TV, and from everyday conversation."

"But there are. I've seen a few."

"Exactly. You've seen a *few*. Probably mostly mine. I always tried to balance my research between written and spoken uses."

"How'd you do that? Did you listen to the radio at work?"

"Eventually. Once technology allowed me to do so. By the time I had a Walkman, I'd been working at Samuelson for years. At one time I suggested to Ed Needham that *all* the editors spend some time researching with audio media. Supply editors with radios, I told Ed. Allow others to watch TV. Spend a couple hours out eavesdropping at restaurants or bowling alleys. Just during the slow times at the office, you see?"

"That'd be awesome. I'd be game for an assignment like that."

"A little too awesome, I'm afraid." Mr. Phillips shook his head. "The idea that a lexicographer could *leave* the office for an hour or two, or have a little fun on the job—it's all a little too unconventional for Ed. Actually, 'absurd' was the word he used when I suggested it."

"Maybe he was just worried about how it would look if people found out," I suggested. "Lexicographers as spies, or something like that."

"Ridiculous."

"Well, *I* think it's a good idea," I said.

"Yes. Well, I've always made a pretty good habit of it myself. Outside the office, on the weekends, I was always putting an ear out for more evidence. And now all the time. Now that I have a great deal of free time. You know, Billy, the young people living in this city don't really use the same language that we read in those books and magazines at Samuelson. Isn't their language just as relevant to us? The young generally outgrow a great deal of their slang. But they're still the ones who will evolve—or devolve—the language into its next phase."

"Sure. I guess you're right."

"Of course I am. That's why I listen. And take note. But

I'm talking too much, huh? I didn't let you answer my question. You enjoying it?"

I sipped the cold dregs of my coffee and tried to think of an honest response.

"I'm . . . still trying to decide if I belong there, I think," I said, after a while.

"Well, there's no place like it." Mr. Phillips didn't seem to notice my pregnant pause. "Don't you for one moment think, if you decide to leave, you'll find someplace like it in New York or something. What other companies possess our kind of history? And how many people in this world do you think get to spend their whole day with words?"

"My mother," I said slowly, "is a perfusionist. She spends her whole day with transplanted organs and bodily fluids. Not many people get to spend their day that way, either."

Mr. Phillips screwed up his face. "Well, good for her. That sounds like an admirable job."

"I'm just saying that just because not many people get to do it doesn't necessarily make it good."

"It sounds like you have two very talented parents."

I pounced on this clear, if somewhat awkward, opening for a new conversational direction.

"You know, it was kind of weird growing up. Coming to the dinner table each night knowing that both of your parents had to change out of bloody clothes before coming home to you."

"Bloody clothes?"

"And wash blood off their hands every day."

Mr. Phillips rolled his eyes. "I'm sure your parents wore rubber gloves," he said.

"Still. It's macabre. I'm not sure how I feel about it."

He let out a wet, snorting laugh. "It paid for your college

education, I'm sure. What does it matter how you feel about it?"

I felt myself turning red. He still had total control of this conversation. I was getting nowhere.

"That's one of my favorites from your generation, Billy. 'I'm not sure how I feel about that.' I hear that all the time. As if how one *feels* needs to be determined with great exactitude. Even better, as if your progress on the feelings front needs to be *announced*."

"Okay, okay," I said. "Never mind. I was just thinking about, you know, the implications of our career choices—"

"All right," Mr. Phillips said, shaking his head. "I'll quit hassling you about the job. What are you reading these days?"

"Reading? Like books?"

"Exactly. Like books."

"To be honest, I haven't been able to concentrate on books much since I started at Samuelson. I get lazy after work. I've probably read only two or three books."

"What were they?"

"Let me see," I stalled. Once you discounted the joke books, I'd actually read only one book. "I read this book by Paul Theroux. *The Mosquito Coast*. I got it for a dollar at a used-book store."

"I see," Mr. Phillips said thoughtfully. "That's not an Orpah book."

"Orpah?"

"You know. Oprah. I like to call her Orpah. I indulge myself. A little prescriptivism. I admit it." He chuckled.

"Oh. Well. No. I'm afraid it's not an Oprah book, *The Mosquito Coast*."

"You ever read Orpah books?"

"Not that I know of," I answered. "You? You follow that?"

"Ah. Not exactly. I get a lot of my books at the Salvation Army. It's senior half-price day on Wednesdays, and I always check to see if there are new books. Someone keeps coming in every so often and dropping off brand-new Orpah selections. I suppose they just buy them new as soon as she picks them, read them, and get rid of them. So just out of curiosity a few months ago, I gave a couple of them a read."

"What did you think?"

"Could be worse. I wanted to see what the fuss was about. And that Toni Morrison's an elegant lady, don't you think?"

"Sure," I agreed.

"Not as elegant as Nina Simone, though. I like Nina Simone."

"Uhh," I said. I imagined something embarrassing being said on the near horizon, perhaps the word *Negress* being used, unless I did something to steer the conversation elsewhere.

"So are you still reading the Oprahs?" I asked.

"On occasion. It's useful to read what everyone's reading, I think. It's like eavesdropping on the bus. Keeps one . . . in touch. You can work at an academic, isolated place like Samuelson, but that doesn't mean you have to keep *yourself* isolated. Right?"

Mr. Phillips waited for my answer. The eagerness of his expression made me a little sad. Sure, my attempts at manipulating the conversation had failed completely. But the ulterior motive behind my invitation now seemed absurd. Wrongheaded, even. I liked this old guy. I'd determined that much. And I wasn't going to be able to determine much else unless I resolved to be a little more direct.

"Right," I said. "Are you sure you don't want another cup of coffee?"

The cappuccino maker behind us started whirring, and the short white stubble on Mr. Phillips's left jowl began to quiver again. I had to look over his shoulder to keep from laughing. A big-haired woman in a snug pantsuit was leaning on the coffee bar, dialing a cell phone. I focused my eyes on her as I tried to force my smile down.

"Positive." Mr. Phillips pushed his empty coffee mug into the center of the table and folded his arms. "Now, Billy. Let's get down to business. You never said how you knew my nickname. And I'm not letting you off the hook. No one's called me that in at least twenty years."

"It's a long story—"

"I'm in no hurry, Homer. I'm sure you've figured that out by now."

"I learned about it in the cit file," I said, watching his face.

He chewed his lip. "Did I sign an editorial comment slip 'Red'?"

"Nope," I said.

"Then how the hell did you learn about it in the cit file?"

"You really don't know?"

"You're being very cryptic, champ. It doesn't really suit you."

"I found some weird cits that seem to have been written in-house. And they mention someone named Red."

"I don't follow. They were written in-house, but they're not editors' comment slips?"

"No. It's strange. They're written like a book. It's called *The Broken Teaglass*. Somebody seems to have snuck a story into the cit file, and you're, like, a character in it."

I studied his face. It remained perplexed.

"Maybe I should just show them to you," I said.

Mr. Phillips raised his eyebrows. "All right. That sounds like a good idea."

"Maybe we should come here again?"

"All right, Billy. When?"

"How about right after the Thanksgiving weekend?"

"Now you're talkin'," Mr. Phillips said. "Sounds juicy. I can't wait."

CHAPTER ELEVEN

When I got to Mona's cubicle, she was putting on her coat.

"I've got something to tell you," I whispered.

"Unless it's something about an Orange Alert, I don't want to hear it right now."

"Huh?"

"Good thing you stopped by. I was about to buzz by your desk to say goodbye, but I'm kinda in a hurry here. I've got only about twenty minutes to get to my apartment for my bag and on the road to the airport. I meant to put my bag in my car this morning, but I forgot. Dan was nice enough to let me go early today and—"

"I forgot you were flying out this afternoon."

"I have to stop by the newsstand and get some crosswords too. I can't really do anything besides crosswords on the plane. Crosswords and catalogues and mantras. Most reading just makes me nervous. Almost everything I read on a plane seems to have some thread in it that leads me pretty naturally to thinking about terrorists. Like, once, there was this airline catalogue and one of the things you could buy were these soft imported towels made of Turkish cotton, and I started thinking—"

"Shhhh," I hissed, wondering how many editors had heard her. "Are you okay? Lemme walk you to the door."

"I hate flying," Mona confessed, once we were in the stairwell.

"Look," I said, "I just wanted you to know. Mr. Phillips is Red."

Mona grimaced and adjusted the strap of her leather bag. "That doesn't sound quite right to me. How do you figure that one?"

"There was this thing Red said in the cits that reminded me of something Mr. Phillips says sometimes. Have you ever noticed that sometimes he says 'Now you're talkin'?"

"Umm . . . this sounds like more than I have time for. Talk to me about it if my plane doesn't explode, okay?"

"All right," I said. As she turned her face toward the front glass door, I saw there were weary circles under her eyes. "Wait. Just one thing."

"What?"

I started to reach for her shoulder but stopped myself. Probably Sheila, the front desk secretary, was watching us. "I can't tell you that your plane won't explode. But—"

"Christ. *What?*"

"But when you're up there just remember that this is one of those rare moments in your life"—Mona's mouth began to open so I talked faster,—"when everything else goes away and all you have to remember is just *survive this.*"

Mona frowned. She drew a long breath into her nostrils.

"Good Lord," she said. "You philosophy majors."

"It's not philosophy, actually. It has nothing to do with philosophy."

"What is it, then?" She was examining the contents of the front pocket of her bag. Her movements became frantic for a moment, and then relaxed as she produced a folded square of paper, presumably her itinerary.

She scanned its contents. When she looked at me again, I could tell that she didn't quite remember what I'd just said, and didn't quite care. Her face showed the familiar strain of someone pretending to be there.

"It was just advice," I said, opening the door for her. "And therefore pretty much useless. Good luck, all right?"

The morning before Thanksgiving, I found an email waiting for me.

Subject: Alive, Drunk
Billy—
Sorry if my behavior was disturbing yesterday. The flight to Cleveland was awful, of course, but all is well now. I'm pretty sure we hit a very small air pocket, but the pilot didn't say anything about it, so I'm not sure. My mother and I had Mexican tonight, and some giant margaritas. We just got home, and she's trying to get me to watch some terrible chick movie with her, so I'm trying to look busy at the computer. Anyway, I just wanted you to know I'm interested in your Phillips theory. Nothing's turned up in the microfiches yet, but I plan on giving it another go as soon as I get home. I'm halfway through October 1985.
Have a great Thanksgiving.
—Mona

I closed the email and sat back in my chair. I pictured Mona and her mother with a margarita pitcher between them. Mona dwarfed by her giant salted glass, sitting by a taller, more streamlined version of herself. A version that sipped instead of gulped. Both with their hair up. Both laughing.

There were no margaritas at my family's Thanksgiving, but I probably could have used one.

It started out well. My mother didn't make us all talk about what we were thankful for—for which I was, paradoxically, thankful. She was a little frazzled after burning a batch of rolls, and seemed to forget the whole gratitude bit. Nobody reminded her, and we spent the better part of the meal talking about movies. Later, as we picked at the last morsels on our plates, my mother and my sister Jen were full of questions about Samuelson—about what words I'd defined, and which of my definitions would likely "make it" into a real dictionary. I relished their squawks of disapproval when I confessed that I'd drafted a definition for *feminazi*.

"You should have rejected it on principle," my mother insisted.

"I'm not allowed to do that," I said. "There was too much evidence for it. I didn't say I *liked* defining it. But I'm afraid the word's here to stay."

Jen shook her head. "I'm not so sure. Are people still going to use that word ten or twenty years from now?"

"Looks that way."

"No thanks to you. By putting that in, you guys are legitimizing it, and *encouraging* people to use it."

"We don't see it that way. It's not Samuelson's fault that some people treat a dictionary definition as a permission slip. We can't pretend that words we don't like don't exist."

Funny that of all the things I'd said in this conversation, it was my use of the word "we" for Samuelson Company that my father seemed to pick up on. And then he asked the inevitable question: "Do you think you'll stay at Samuelson long?"

"It's hard to say. It's a decent job."

"Do you enjoy being there?" he wanted to know.

"It has its moments. And I'm lucky to be there for now. That's how I've been thinking of it."

"Well, long term—can you see yourself there in, say, five years?" my mother asked.

"Five years." I laughed. "Don't scare me."

"So, maybe not, then?"

"You've said it's awfully quiet there at the Samuelson office," my mother reminded me. "Do you think eventually you'll want something a little more . . . social?"

"Sure. Maybe eventually."

"I've always thought you'd be a good salesman, actually," Jen offered.

"Gee, thanks." I ran the tines of my fork through the remains of my mashed potatoes.

"I don't mean like a sleazy salesman," Jen explained. "I mean, a salesman who sells something important."

My mother shot her a forbidding look.

"What?" Jen said. "I mean it as a compliment. People seem to trust you, Billy. I mean, sometimes I'm not quite sure *why*—"

"Yeah, well," I interrupted. "Okay. Maybe I can sell dictionaries door to door. Better yet—how about Bibles?"

I shouldn't have said that. It was supposed to be sarcasm, but no one was amused. My parents had tolerated my philosophy study, but were always vaguely spooked by my occasional accompanying interest in religion.

"I think that Jen's saying you've got a knack for making

people feel comfortable," my mother explained. "And it might be a waste for you to just sit at a desk by yourself all day—"

"Have you ever thought of teaching, William?" my father wanted to know. "I've actually pictured you in a classroom many times. With, say, seventh graders."

"*Seventh* graders?" Suddenly my stomach was feeling very heavy. "I'd rather sell used cars."

"I was just remembering when you did that Buddies program with your football team. Those younger boys really took to you."

"Yeah. Well. Tossing a ball around with a couple of twelve-year-olds is one thing. Being in a classroom with thirty of them all day is quite another."

"True," my father said reluctantly. "Maybe seventh grade is a little scary. But teaching *something*. Just an idea. I think you'd be great at it."

"Well." I stood to help my mother clear the dishes. "Food for thought, huh?"

That night, Jen went out for coffee with an old friend and I caught up on my television. I'd forgotten what it was like to have a hundred or so cable channels. When I was halfway through my second *Seinfeld,* my father came into the room and handed me a square red envelope.

"We still get a lot of your mail," he said. "I keep an eye out for important pieces, but you might want to fill out a forwarding form at the post office, just in case."

I examined the envelope. It was from my high school's alumni committee.

"Junk mail," I said, but opened it anyway. "A reminder for my five-year reunion. It's Saturday night."

"This Saturday night?" My father sat next to me, wedging a throw pillow behind his back. "That's lucky. You can just stay here an extra night or two. You won't have to make a special trip."

"Umm . . . yeah. It's not exactly a lucky coincidence. They always do it over Thanksgiving weekend. The idea is that people just happen to be home with their families this weekend. Nobody really *wants* to go to the five-year. People just get bored, so they give in and drag themselves over there out of morbid curiosity. That's what Jen said it was like when she went. It didn't sound like she had a very good time."

"You know, I think Jen was actually glad she went. Your sister's not the sort to admit she'd like something so—I don't know—*conventional* as a high school reunion."

"She said nobody's changed enough for it to be worth it yet. Everybody's still trying to act cool."

"And that's not interesting?"

"Sure," I conceded. "Probably it's interesting. If you want to make a psychological study of it."

"I'll bet your old friend Mark would be there. Don't you think? Might be nice to catch up with him. I always liked Mark. Now, where did he end up going to school? Somewhere down south?"

"UNC Chapel Hill." I slipped the invitation back into its envelope. My dad's canned "Gee whiz, son" tone was almost comical. I wondered if my mother had put him up to this conversation.

"So you think you might go?" he asked.

"Maybe I'll go. We'll see how bored I get."

But when I got up Friday morning, I felt like driving. I hit the road to Claxton after breakfast.

CHAPTER TWELVE

It was actually way too cold for a picnic on Tuesday, but Mona and I wanted to talk alone. The creepy Samuelson lunchroom always had a couple of lonely souls in it, looking for a little polite conversation to keep them sane for one more afternoon. No privacy there.

We decided on a little triangle of dead grass two blocks from Samuelson, where there were a couple of park benches and an old skeleton of a swing set. By Claxton's depressed standards, you could probably call this a park. It fit the broadest of Samuelson definitions for the word, anyway. There Mona and I ate our lunches. She spooned yogurt out of a little cup with purple-mittened hands. My own naked hands turned red and raw from holding on to my turkey sandwich in the cold air.

I told Mona about what had tipped me off to Mr. Phillips, and about the conversation that followed. Mona listened in silence. When she finished her yogurt, she took out a giant oatmeal cookie, split it, handed me half, and motioned for me to continue. I finished up by telling her I wanted to include Mr. Phillips—Red—in our subsequent cit search, since he seemed so knowledgeable, so harmless, and so desperate for amusement.

Mona smiled cryptically at this final sentiment. "I don't think Mr. Phillips needs anything from us. He seems to me someone who can amuse himself just fine."

"So you don't want him in on this?"

"No, I didn't say that. I'm a little wary of how it'll play out. Can I ask what made you so sure it was okay to talk to him?"

"I can't say I was *sure*. I was just . . . *eager*."

"You weren't at all scared of where it might lead?"

"Not really." I bit into my cookie half before answering. It was really hard. I wondered if Mona had baked it herself. "Maybe you had to be there, but when I was talking to the guy, I just didn't feel like he was someone to *fear*, exactly."

"I wouldn't be so sure about that. And now he's involved whether we like it or not."

"Oh, come on," I reasoned. I was trying to decide if I should point out that my involving Mr. Phillips made a hell of a lot more sense than her showing Dan those first two cits. "The guy's so lonely and bored. He'll be thrilled just to be in on the game."

"Just because Mr. Phillips is old and lonely doesn't mean he's innocent. He might have had something to hide. And it's not a *game* anymore, Billy." Mona rummaged in her bag. "Look what I found last night in your beloved microfiches."

She handed me two photocopies. "From the *Claxton Daily News*."

Claxton Daily News
OCTOBER 16, 1985
BODY FOUND IN FREEMAN PARK

CLAXTON — An unidentified man was found dead yesterday morning in Freeman Park just a few hundred feet from where his car was parked, according to police.

"A resident found the body near one of the paved park roads while she was walking her dog Thursday morning," said Sgt. John Polaski, who is leading the investigation. "The dog apparently led her a few yards off the path, where she saw the body. She called us immediately. We later found what appears to be the victim's car parked a few hundred feet from the position of his body."

City police, who are working with state police, have identified the man from the wallet in his pocket and documents found in his car. But they declined to name the victim until next of kin have been informed.

"The investigation has just begun, so that's all I can tell you at this time," Polaski said.

The results of an autopsy should be available later this week, he said.

Claxton Daily News
OCTOBER 18, 1985
SCANT DETAILS EMERGE
IN GRUESOME PARK KILLING

CLAXTON — In what is becoming a mysterious murder case, police revealed yesterday that the 43-year-old man found dead this week in Freeman Park was stabbed to death.

"We found a lot of blood at the scene. It could be described as a gruesome killing. And now we're just trying to piece together the events that led to his death," said Sgt. John Polaski of the Claxton Police Department.

The man, Derek George Brownlow of 126 Highland Street in Chesterfield, worked at U-Build-It Hardware Store. He had no family in the area. It appears Brownlow relocated to the area only three months before his death, and police are having difficulty tracing his earlier residence and employers.

"Mr. Brownlow's neighbors and coworkers expressed their

regret at his death, but no one seems to have known him well," Polaski said. "We're hoping that anyone else who knows him will contact us immediately."

Kyle Strand, a coworker from U-Build-It Hardware, described Brownlow as "private" and "smart."

"He was always reading something," Strand said. "On his lunch break, and whenever he had cash register duty. Just a smart, quiet guy."

Brownlow's upstairs neighbor, Vince Poulton, said he didn't speak to him much.

"He received few, if any, visitors, as I recall," Poulton said. He admitted that he had no clue why someone would want to kill Brownlow.

Scant details like these aren't giving police much help in tracking down Brownlow's killer. They are again asking for anyone with information about the deceased to contact them immediately.

This murder brings the annual total in Claxton to 14, which is higher than in previous years.

"Jesus," I said. "Sounds like he was running from the mob. He moved here from nowhere, had no people, and then got whacked. How'd you find this?"

"Naturally I started with October of 1985, since that's what all the cits say. It seems like whoever wrote the cits wanted to make it easy. It took me a couple of visits, but there it was."

"Is this all you found?"

"I looked through a few weeks' worth of newspapers after this article, but the follow-ups didn't say much more. It looks like the investigation just didn't go anywhere. I stopped looking when I hit November. I should probably go back and keep looking, but I don't know if it'll turn up much."

"So maybe it's not an editor writing a story just for laughs."

"Apparently not." Mona frowned. "There's a real dead guy in this thing. After seeing this, do you still trust Old Man Cruller?"

"I don't know," I murmured. The sight of the name Derek Brownlow in the article had sent a chill through me, but I wasn't sure if it made me feel differently about Phillips.

"Well?" Mona prompted. "How do you feel? Still no fear?"

"Maybe some," I admitted.

Mona squeezed her eyes shut and rubbed her temples.

"But I think my curiosity is stronger," I said.

"Okay, fine. Your curiosity is stronger than your fear. But which is *smarter*?"

"You can't really think of it like that. The stronger feeling always wins out, not the smarter one."

"Maybe if you're a caveman, sure."

"Listen, Mona. Think of it like getting on an airplane. You were pretty scared when you left last week. But you got on the plane anyway, right? Why did you do that?"

"Because of Thanksgiving. Because of my family. Because I had to."

"You wouldn't have gotten on if you truly believed it was going to crash. You knew that you'd land, that you'd see your parents on the other end. Because if you didn't truly believe that, how could you have gotten on?"

"I didn't know it wouldn't crash. I didn't believe it wouldn't crash. I *hoped* it wouldn't."

"But that must have been a pretty strong hope. And the hope must have been stronger than the fear. Stronger than you want to admit. Probably stronger than you even realize. Your actions prove it."

"I guess. But when it comes to flying, it usually feels about fifty-fifty, fear to hope."

"Deep down, you know your odds are better than that," I insisted. "That's why you get on."

"So . . ." Mona raised a single skeptical eyebrow. "How do you think your odds are now?"

The cold was getting unbearable. I yanked at my collar and then shoved my hands deep into my pockets. "How do you mean?"

"I mean, how likely is it that keeping your coffee date with Mr. Phillips will be productive and not . . . destructive?"

I hadn't a clue. But since either outcome was likely to be pretty interesting, it looked like my odds were pretty good.

"There's no way of knowing that. All I know is that I'm not scared enough in this case to let it change my course of action. I want to satisfy my curiosity."

Mona shook her head. "Blood on his hands," she said.

"You know, that phrase sounded metaphorical to me from the very beginning."

"It might have sounded metaphorical," she murmured, flicking the photocopy, "before the goddamned corpse turned out to be literal."

"Mona," I said. "This is Doughnut Man we're talking about. Let's get a grip. Listen. I won't mention you, I won't mention the articles. And if it gets ugly, I think I can take him."

Mona rolled her eyes. "Granted, Mr. Phillips is a skinny old man and you're a hefty hunk of manhood. But it's the *situation* we should be wary of. Sure, maybe Mr. Phillips isn't dangerous. But maybe he's connected to someone who *is*. With a real dead body in the mix, who knows what we might be getting into?"

"Maybe it runs all the way to the *top*. Maybe it goes back

to Daniel Samuelson. Maybe this whole dictionary thing is just a front for a century-old WASP mafia."

"Shut the fuck up. I'm serious." Mona glared angrily at the empty swing set.

"Hey," I said, waving my hand in front of her face until she looked at me again. "I know you are. I'm sorry, I couldn't resist. I see what you're saying. It's not Mr. Phillips per se. It's what might happen if we talk to him."

"Exactly. And I don't want you to get in trouble. You're just going to stick yourself out there?"

"I already have. I *mentioned* the cits. If Mr. Phillips is part of some murderous chain of command, I'm already screwed."

"And therefore the next logical step is to get yourself in deeper?"

There was nothing logical about it. But *in deeper* sounded like it could be a trip. The way my life was going lately, I couldn't help but feel that maybe *in deeper* was exactly where I wanted to be. I wasn't sure how to articulate this to Mona without sounding like an asshole.

"Listen," I said. "We've worked hard so far, and we've hit a wall. We've found something—someone—who clearly looks like our best bet for more information. We've started something, and we want to know more. Why not keep going?"

"Because I keep picturing all of the terrible ways this could end."

"Like how?"

"Well. Let's see. There's you getting fired. Or you ending up sleeping with the fishes in the Connecticut River. Or at the very least, Mr. Phillips being dragged away by a cop, shaking a fist and screaming *'And I would've gotten away with it if it weren't for these meddling kids!'* "

I laughed. "I like that, Mona. Keep visualizing that ending."

"I thought you liked Mr. Phillips."

"I do. But it's still a pretty funny image. Listen. I'll be careful. I won't mention you, and I'll call you as soon as I get home and tell you what happened."

"Okay." Mona looked at her watch. "Maybe I just have more of an imagination for disaster than you."

"You think so?" I pulled my collar tight around my neck. I was freezing.

"That's why I'm afraid of flying, actually. I just have this feeling that my life is destined for some kind of disaster. And getting on an airplane is just asking for it."

"You think there's a disaster waiting just for *you*?"

"Sort of. I know that sounds self-centered. But whenever I read about a disaster, like an earthquake or flood, I imagine myself in it. I always think it was meant for me. I keep wondering when my disaster's coming."

"How do you know it hasn't already arrived?"

"Maybe you and I mean different things by 'disaster.' The kind of disaster I'm talking about, you'd know it when you saw it. I'm thinking, like, you're on the tip of the *Titanic* just as it's cracking in half. There's no question. This is it. This is the disaster beyond your wildest imagination. *This* is what life has been saving for you."

Her cheeks were red from the cold. She had a soft gray scarf thrown casually around her neck. With her thin figure all buried under wool and sweaters and tights, she reminded me suddenly of a coed in a liberal arts college brochure. There was something cozy about her. A Salinger Franny before the breakdown. I wondered if she felt as innocent as she seemed. It was pretty naive, this notion of hers—that a disaster needs to announce itself in grand fashion, with a deafening rumble or a crack in the earth. I knew from experience that she was wrong. A disaster can just as easily be a slow, silent rot. A disaster can creep in without much fanfare, and quietly stay.

Maybe she felt I didn't understand her point, because she changed the subject.

"I got a good letter today. Guy wants to know if he should use 'shit' or 'shat' for past tense."

"He should have just looked it up. Either word suffices. Did you tell him so?"

"Billy," Mona sighed. "Listen to yourself. You're really hardening up pretty quick. No, it's not a very intelligent question. But it's a *real-life* issue. How many times did you wonder that yourself, before working here? If we can answer questions like that, well, maybe we're really doing something important."

"If you say so, Mona."

CHAPTER THIRTEEN

maven

When the papers went crazy, I knew everything might very
well explode. Still, I resigned myself to the stern presence of my
fellow word *mavens*. There was at least an odd comfort in
submitting to the long silence of the day. Reliable and insistent,
it served as a kind of protector. I was reading a book about
drug slang, underlining the word "stash," and you came to my
desk. When you saw what I was reading, you said, Now
you're talking. You said that junk slang was your favorite, and
wanted to know if there was a chapter on junk. Then you
asked if I'd finished that other book yet. No, I whispered. I was
unraveling fast. Was it a trick question? What exactly had
been in that article that I hadn't had time to read? Was there
something suspect near the corpse? Were you smiling, Red,
because of something you knew?

32

I started with this one because I figured it was the most
likely to spark a telling reaction.

I watched the old man as he held it close to his eyes.

"Word mavens," he mumbled, then sipped his coffee.

He squinted and read it again.

"I'll be damned," he said finally.

"Does this mean something to you?" I asked, trying not to sound accusatory.

"Maybe. Definitely something familiar here. I can't place it exactly, but . . ."

"What about this thing about the corpse?"

"That's pretty odd. You got me there." He sipped his coffee noisily and looked unconcerned.

"Doesn't this sound like a story about the Samuelson office?"

"Yeah. It's pretty wild. I guess I'm a character in it too."

"You don't find that a little bit . . ." I searched for a word that wouldn't sound accusatory. "Scary?"

He shrugged. "Sure is interesting. But after forty years at the place, I'd be more surprised if such a story *didn't* include me."

"Do you have any idea who might have written it?"

"Nope. Do you?"

"You know a lot more about Samuelson than I do. I was kind of hoping you'd have some ideas."

"Well, Billy," he said. His tone suddenly turned grave. "The place isn't exactly a fortress of mental well-being. You know what I'm saying?"

I nodded dutifully. A few bizarre quirks notwithstanding, no one I'd met at Samuelson seemed all that close to the edge. But I wanted Mr. Phillips to keep talking.

"Offhand," he continued, "I can think of five or ten editors who could have lost it at some point while they were there. Maybe one of 'em started scribbling out a schizoid little story."

"What do you think of this corpse business, then?"

"Let's hope that's just creativity. Or insanity."

I waited for him to say more, but he didn't. He drank his coffee and smacked his lips placidly.

"There's more," I said.

"Then lemme see," he said.

I handed him *subtext,* the one that mentioned blood on Red's hands. He squinted at it for a couple of minutes.

"Well, whadya know?" he said. "I was wrong. Where'd you find these?"

"What do you mean, you were wrong?"

"It wasn't one of the nutcases who wrote this. I'll be *damned*."

He picked up his coffee, but this time he set it down again without slurping.

"Who was it?" I asked, trying to control my voice. *Try not to seem too eager,* Mona had coached me earlier that after-noon.

"What else have you got?" Mr. Phillips asked. "Show me, and I'll tell you for sure."

I handed him the rest. "I'll give you a minute to look at them. I'll be right back."

Mr. Phillips grunted in reply.

Once I was in the men's room, I waited a good five min-utes. This had been Mona's scheme. She'd made copies of all the cits. She wanted me to give Mr. Phillips an opportunity to bolt with the cits and see if he took it.

When I returned, he had all of the cits spread out on the table before him. A few had big soggy brown spots on them.

"I had a little spill. Sorry." He didn't sound sorry.

"So you think you know who wrote these?"

"There was this gal. Real nice young gal. Her name was Mary Beth. Or—Mary Anne, was it? Your age when she worked here. It was years ago. You were probably in diapers then." He rubbed his chin. "Damn. I should have recognized it in that first cit."

"Did you know her well?"

"We chatted quite a bit, for a while. Just a nice young lady. Unfortunately, when I read these now, I wonder if the girl wasn't a little cuckoo. I suppose no one is safe, really . . ."

"But it seems like she addressed these to you. At least some of them. Like this one here—'Were you smiling, Red, because of something you knew?'"

"Yeah. Isn't that something? You think refills are free?" Mr. Phillips gazed distractedly over at the coffee bar.

"Definitely not at a place like this," I said, trying to reestablish eye contact. I couldn't tell if he was evading or just a little bored.

"Even for a senior citizen?"

"*Especially* not for a senior citizen. What makes you think it was the girl you're thinking of?"

"She and I were both interested in history. Had a particular era in common. A common interest." He eyed me with mild amusement. Now it seemed he was scrutinizing me, instead of the reverse.

"Hmm," I said.

"Let's just say I know it's her. Say, Billy—"

"Yup?"

"You're suspicious of me, aren't you?"

"No," I said quickly.

"Yes, you are. You thought I might take out a revolver and shoot you when I read that cit. The blood on my hands and all."

"No," I insisted.

"'Does this cit mean anything to you?'" he said in a dopey, vaguely imitative voice. "Billy, you're a gas."

"Thanks," I said. "I don't think anyone's ever called me that before."

"All right. Never mind. I apologize," Mr. Phillips said. "I'll tell you what I know about these cits. You got any more, by the way? Or is this all?"

"This is all. All the citations here are for words that were first used in 1950," I explained.

"Really?"

Mr. Phillips spread the citations across the table and began reading them again.

"We've started looking in 1940 and 1960."

"I don't think you'll find anything there, Billy," he murmured, still gazing down at the cits. "Who's 'we'?"

"Um..."

Mr. Phillips looked up at me, then harrumphed. "Never mind, then," he said, and went back to the cits.

"Poor girl," he said, after a while. "Try 1951. 1952. 1953."

"Why?"

He handed me the cit for *paperbound*.

"Read this one again," he said.

paperbound

Only you, Red. Only you acknowledged the mishap. You mentioned it offhand when you came to give me yet another *paperbound* book from your home collection: *Beyond the 38th Parallel*. I didn't confess it then but will confess it now. I hadn't even read the last book you gave me. You told me it wasn't exactly an academic piece of work. Just some pretty good firsthand accounts. Diaries. Letters. I thanked you for it and you winked. Just don't spill anything on it, you said, and then sauntered off to the secretary's desk for your midmorning flirtation.

9

"*Beyond the 38th Parallel.* That mean anything to you?" he asked, studying me.

"It's a book," I said.

"Clearly it's a book, Homer. I guess I don't need to ask if you've read it. Obviously you haven't. Anyway. Not a bad book. I don't remember giving that one to her, but I remember that I did lend Mary Anne a book or two, now and then. In any case, does that title mean anything to you?"

"Not really."

"Think. In connection with 1950, I mean. God, you're depressing me, Billy. Thirty-eighth parallel? A little American history? A little world history?"

"Wait a second." I was trying to remember. This certainly sounded like a piece of information I used to know. "I think this is definitely something I learned once, but forgot."

"C'mon, Billy," Mr. Phillips urged, making it impossible to concentrate. "It's astounding what your generation doesn't know."

"You're right," I said, staring ashamedly at the tabletop.

"Well, don't worry about it. There's plenty your generation doesn't know, true. But there's just as much you all know that we didn't."

"You think?"

"Sure. For instance," Mr. Phillips leaned back in his chair, "I'll bet you can't even remember a time when you didn't know what a clitoris was."

I hacked on an improperly swallowed sip of cold coffee, then put down my cup very carefully.

"Korea, son," Mr. Phillips prodded. "The Korean War. The 38th parallel. It's what divides North and South Korea. When the North Koreans crossed it in 1950—"

"Okay, I remember now. The 38th parallel."

"Good. Well, the girl couldn't get enough of it. She was a real Korean War buff."

"So that was what you had in common? You're a war history buff too?"

"Not a buff. A vet. Served in Korea from '51 to '53. Marine Corps."

"Oh," I said. "I see."

"All makes sense now, doesn't it?"

"Not really."

"I told her about a few of my experiences in the war. At lunch breaks sometimes. Once, outside on the steps, I remember us talking about it. It was a nice spring day. She knew my nickname in the service because it probably came up while I was telling her about it."

"Ohhh."

"Glad I could be of service," said Mr. Phillips. "You gonna show me what you find when you look up 1951?"

"Of course," I said. "If you want."

"I do. I'm a little curious, I confess. And who else have you told about this?"

I shifted in my seat.

Red piled all the cits together and pushed them across the table at me.

"Okay. Fine. You wanna play cloak-and-dagger, champ, be my guest. But watch your ass. Cuz I think there are certain parties who get their panties in a snitch when they see other editors having a little bit of fun. If you catch my meaning."

"All right," I said, uncertain if I'd understood him. "Do you have any other advice?"

"No," he said. "But do you want a pastry? I like the look of those brownies."

• ⏐ •

It seemed wise to me to test Mr. Phillips's theory before getting Mona's hopes up. I checked the years of the Korean War—1950 through 1953, just like Mr. Phillips had said. Then I printed out the list of words first used in 1951 and started looking through all of the relevant "A" words. I got about halfway through the A's at the office that day, then decided to band up as many A's and B's as I could without looking suspicious: *après-ski, art house, audiophile, aw-shucks, backup, beef Wellington, beer belly*. In honor of the last word and my renewed investigative effort, I bought myself a six-pack and made a giant pot of chili. After two beers I felt pretty ready to start the old *flip-flip-flip* again. And I wasn't all that surprised when old "Dolores" and her teaglass popped up about a half hour into my search:

aw-shucks

Whatever Scout noticed, if anything, he didn't mention. He talked into all the spaces I'd started to leave blank. This didn't seem natural for either of us, but still, we tried to spend our weekends much as we always had. He made his omelets. I was learning to make pies, a welcome distraction. I've never been good with these things, and at first the crusts would tear or crumble in my hands. But I was determined to make him a decent crust, if only once. Maybe it was the careful way he always scraped the omelet pan clean. Maybe it was the painful, *aw-shucks* way he carried his unusual height, always scrunching forward at the waist, as if to make himself smaller. But probably it was the expression on his face when I talked. Not so much a look of affection, but of interest, of an effort to hear the real meaning of my words, even as they'd grown spare and superficial. For these things I began to regard him as a sincere and obedient boy, deserving of some boyish reward. Pie.

39

The boyfriend again. The poor sucker from the first citations. I was beginning to feel for the guy. The narrator—Dolores? Mary Beth? Mary Anne?—didn't seem to regard him with passion, exactly. *A sincere and obedient boy. Painful, aw-shucks way he carried his unusual height.* Not a great deal of romance in that description.

I started to read the cit once more, but stopped in the middle of the boyfriend's physical description. There was something very familiar about Scout. It made me uneasy to realize this. Suddenly none of it seemed fair—the description or the fact of me reading it. What busybodies Mona and I were, pulling people's secrets out into the open and gawking at them to make the workday pass faster.

I shoved the cits aside and turned on my TV instead of continuing.

All of this weird emotional emphasis on pie made me think back to Thanksgiving weekend. My father had made an extravagant spread of pies, including my very un-Thanksgiving favorite: key lime. There'd been so much pie left over we'd had it with our coffee for breakfast the next morning, right before I left. We'd each had at least two slices of something, except Jen. She'd had a razor-thin slice of pumpkin and then excused herself and left the room.

When she didn't come back, I made like I was going to the bathroom and ducked into her old bedroom, where I found her reading *Washington Square*.

"You're teaching that *again*?"

"I don't have a choice, Billy. I'm just the TA. The professor calls the shots. If it were my class, we'd read Raymond Chandler books and smoke cigars."

"You didn't want any more pie?"

"I had to drink diet shakes for three months to lose seven measly pounds. I'll be damned if I just put them back on over Christmas."

"Huh. Well. The key lime is pretty exceptional. You should at least have a taste."

"I know what it tastes like," Jen said. "Dad makes it for you every holiday. It's a little sad, actually, watching him squeeze all those little limes for you. It's kind of like a Pavlovian thing with him now. *Billy's coming. Must find, purchase, and squeeze twenty key limes.*"

Then she returned to her Henry James, putting a star next to a passage that had already been circled on a previous read.

I sat on Jen's bed. It took me a second to figure out what was unfamiliar about her room. The ugly chartreuse bedspread she'd bought in high school was gone, and had been replaced with a bright floral comforter. Her old *Your Silence Will Not Protect You* poster had been removed from the closet door. The room felt more like a guest room now. I wasn't sure if my mother had done this recently or I just hadn't noticed before.

Jen looked up from her book. "You know, it really makes me wonder. It makes me wonder if I could ever have kids."

"How's that?"

"Mmmm..." Jen threw her book aside and stretched. "For some people, it just never ends. They never stop thinking that their kids' happiness is their responsibility. I mean, even when they're *old*."

"I don't *ask* him to make me key lime pie every time."

"It's like a bird building a nest. It's automatic. Instinctual. It's heartbreaking, actually." Jen's voice was distant, searching. She was probably trying to figure out where she might find a poem in all of this. "I mean, rationally, he knows that you'll be fine if you don't get your favorite. But he just can't bring himself to say, 'Billy will be *okay* without his favorite dessert. And it's winter! Key lime pie doesn't even *fit*. Let's just have a nice warm pecan pie and leave it at that.'"

I didn't say anything.

Her eyes narrowed in on me. "I wish you could see it the way I do. You let them keep doing it."

"Let's not get into it—"

"They don't know how to stop." Her voice sounded a little high.

"Eventually they will."

"Not if you don't give them any reason to."

"C'mon. I've got a job, an apartment—"

"That's not really what I meant by a *reason,* Billy. They need to *feel* like they can stop, there's a *shift* you need to help each other make—"

I turned the TV up, to drown out the memory of my sister's voice. For someone who's supposed to be so brilliant with words, she actually has a tendency to ramble. Sometimes, with her, I think people mistake inability to make a succinct point for thoughtful lyricism. As her brother, I recognize the difference in a way that other people don't.

I opened another beer, but found I no longer had a taste for it.

CHAPTER FOURTEEN

cornball

The Glass Girl. The moniker didn't do much for me at first. I had grown unused to the word "girl" in my feminist women's-college days. But a Glass Woman wouldn't be very intriguing, would she? A woman wielding a shard of glass would just be a crazy, snaggle-toothed bitch. But a Glass Girl could have long, silky hair and a dimple, like the Bad Seed. It was comic relief, this *cornball* superhero. Glass Girl!

30

eek

Scout called after his class, which broke my trance. He talked about a pickup truck driver who had cut him off on his way home, and to whom he had seriously considered giving the finger. And then he wanted to know why I was being so quiet. He asked what was up. I said not much. Why didn't I say more? Why didn't I cry or fall on the floor in fits, screaming Outrage! *Eek!* Blood! Guts! Take me to the police!

18

epiphanic
So I rolled out dough and peeled apples and waited for the pieces to come together in some sensible order. They didn't. There was no *epiphanic* moment in which that man's shit-eating grin suddenly slid into an appropriate slot in my mind like a puzzle piece. No clarity came. Only a different determination of sorts. Eventually.

40

I was pretty proud to present this material to Mona over dinner. Blood. Guts. Middle fingers. Shit-eating grins. This was the kind of stuff Mona relished, I was pretty sure. We were back in business.

"Is the adjective 'shit-eating' in the Samuelson books, you think?" I asked, once she'd finished reading. "How would it be defined?"

"Umm...hmm. Maybe..." Mona squinted in concentration while I collected the dessert dishes. "How about 'expressing a prurient satisfaction'?"

"Excuse me for arguing with a master, but don't you think that's a little pedantic? And it hints at a *sexual* satisfaction that's not really quite accurate."

"Why is it that lexicographical accuracy is most important to you when the word is either sexual or scatological slang?"

I got up from the table and settled on the futon.

"Doesn't that characterize most of us?" I asked.

"Certainly not me," said Mona, following me to the futon. "I'm more one for the zeitgeist kinds of words."

"Like what?"

"Like...'mind fuck.' I'm really hoping that'll make it into

the next edition. I did a NEXIS search for it a couple months ago, found a few cits to add to the pile. We'll see."

"Mona," I gasped in mock surprise. "Stacking the evidence. I'm surprised at you."

She shrugged. "Some words need a little extra push, to make the older editors take them seriously."

"But . . . 'mind fuck'? You're trying to tell me that doesn't have any sexual implications?"

"Sure, a little. But the basic meaning isn't sexual. The idea is having your mind, you know, fucked over."

"And you feel this term says a lot about our times?"

"Sure. Equating an experience of mental instability with raw sex. Like it's somehow desirable and fun. People these days *want* to have their minds monkeyed with. People are bored. People are *sick*. When people say something's a mind fuck, don't you get the feeling they think it's something kind of fun? Like dropping acid?"

"I guess. You ever dropped acid?"

"C'mon. Can you see me doing acid?"

"Stranger things have happened. And it was *your* analogy."

"You know, I had 'drop' for the *Supplement*. What a pain in the ass. You'd never guess how many variations there are on the use of that one stupid word. 'Drop acid.' 'Drop trou.' 'Dropping names.' 'Dropping the ball.' Some phrases get their own definition. Some are probably technically self-explanatory, covered by the definition of 'drop.' It's a fine line. And it seems like things have been added over the years by different editors, some of whom drew the line in a different place than I would."

"That sucks. I thought only people like Dan and Grace and Needham were supposed to get words like that."

"Oh. Well . . ." Mona picked up a pile of cits. " 'Drop's' not exactly a 'make' or a 'have.' It's pretty much regular editor material."

"I heard Dan spent three months going over the cits for 'have' for the last edition."

Mona looked down at her pile of cits. "Probably he did," she said.

"I wonder," I said, "if either of us will ever be diehards like that. If one of us will ever embrace 'have' or 'put.' Have that kind of patience, to do it for months, and feel like it's worth it."

"Shoot me if I ever do," Mona said.

We went back to shuffling cits.

"Hey," she said, after a few minutes. "I meant to ask you about the whole phone thing."

"The phone thing? What's that?"

"Ohmigod. You haven't heard? You're probably getting a phone at your desk."

"What's so great about that?"

"You haven't noticed that only a few people actually have them? And one of those people is Cliff?"

"And I'm getting one because . . . ?"

"You're so laid back and polite they're thinking you should try your hand at appeasing some of the crazies who call. It'll give Cliff a nice break once in a while."

"Who told you this?"

"Cliff. He says he and Dan have been chatting about it."

"No way," I said.

"Yes! Congratulations, buddy!"

"Don't call me buddy. You're far too delighted about this to be my buddy."

"And I can't wait to hear all about it. Mail correspondence is, like, the second circle of hell. But those phone calls—that's the real *depths*. That's right in the mouth of the beast—"

"When did you hear about this?" I interrupted.

"Yesterday."

I went back to my cits in disgust.

"It's not so bad, actually," Mona continued. "Did you hear about the time this old lady called, and wanted us to put 'Lula' in the dictionary, with the definition 'an exceptionally personable and unforgettable housecat'? I mean, that shit is classic! Imagine the stories you'll get to tell your grandchildren."

"Just what I need."

"Besides. It's really a compliment. Dan sees that you've got a gentle way with people. I wish he'd pay *me* that kind of a compliment."

While Mona was talking, the title *Teaglass* caught my eye on one of my cits, and I threw it at her without even reading it.

"Another one," I mumbled. "Interested?"

She dove for it as it fluttered onto the floor. I went to the kitchen to get some sodas.

"Sweet," I heard her say.

"What is it?" I yelled from the kitchen.

"Really hot stuff. Too bad you didn't even bother to read it."

She gave me the cit when I returned with our glasses.

macho

And why didn't I call the police? For one, the police department never seemed an institution that had much to do with me. Dull-witted mustachioed *machos* in coordinated light blue dress shirts. Like a high school football team dressed up before Homecoming Weekend. Big, dumb, brutal boys pretending to be gentlemen. Who are they trying to kid, and what use would I have for them, especially just then? I doubt my sentiment about this point will ever change, at least with respect to my special designation, and their peripheral relationship to it.

19

"This one follows that 'eek' one directly, I think," Mona said.

"Unfortunately, it doesn't say much that's new. She didn't call the police. We already knew that."

"But there's at least some continuity here. We're filling in the pieces. We see that there was a situation in which the police would normally be called, and she's rationalizing why it didn't happen."

"Hmm . . ."

"And she doesn't think much of football players."

"That's perhaps the most important piece, yes," I said, rubbing my chin.

"Does her characterization offend you?"

"Why would it?"

"Didn't you used to play football?"

"Just in high school. And I wouldn't say that defines me. It could've just as easily been another sport. People just sort of assumed I'd try football because of my size, so I did. And I liked it as well as any other sport, so I went with it."

"I ran track myself," Mona said. "I was a sprinter."

"Sounds about right," I said. I could imagine Mona in a bright blue track uniform, hopping forward at the sound of the gun, leaving all the other ponytailed girls in the dust.

Mona hesitated.

"Did you like high school?" she asked.

"Who really *likes* high school?" I countered.

"I know, but...I mean, were you one of those people who was generally happy in high school?"

I thought about her question. No suicide attempts. No drug overdoses. No one sticking my head in a toilet bowl.

"Yeah, sure. I guess so. For most of it, anyway. I always felt like I was inexplicably lucky."

"How's that?"

"Things were fairly easy, that's all. I mean, I didn't like school, exactly. But I didn't find it difficult, and I knew that if I put in a decent effort I'd get more than passable grades. And I looked forward to sports after school. It wasn't a hard life."

Mona shifted in her seat. "What about angst?" she asked.

"What about it?"

"Didn't you have any?"

"Not much. I don't know if this is going to come as a great surprise to you, but I wasn't a very deep man in high school."

"So when you say you felt *lucky* in high school...what does that mean?"

"Well...this is going to sound a little, I dunno, *mundane*...but the best example I can think of is when I was slow-dancing with this girl at the sophomore formal."

"Good Lord. I can already tell this is gonna be good."

"May I continue?"

"Sorry. Please do."

"Thank you. First of all, I had a date. And if you asked me how that happened, I wouldn't really be able to tell you. And I looked up while I was dancing with this girl and I realized that there were lots of kids just hanging out. Sitting at the tables, or standing along the wall. Most of them looking kind of wistful, you know? And I realized *I'm one of the kids who's dancing.* I'm not standing against the wall wishing I had someone to dance with. I couldn't figure out what separated me from those kids, and I didn't think it was fair, whatever it was. And I like to think I didn't consider myself any more deserving. But it was perplexing to me how I'd turned out so lucky. Of course, this all sounds pretty dumb *now*, but—"

"No wonder you became a philosophy major," Mona whispered. "That is *profound*."

"Oh, shut up," I said. "I just mean that I was aware that it wasn't so easy for other kids. Like my sister, for example. She's one of these bigger-boned girls. Nobody really asked her out. This one guy used to always call her Bessie, because she's big and pale and quiet with these big eyes. Like a cow, I guess, was the idea."

"I hope you beat the crap out of him," Mona said.

"I couldn't. He was way older and bigger than me. But Jen usually did all right on her own. Rumor has it she whacked him in the head with a floor hockey stick, when the gym teacher wasn't looking, and that's what got him to stop. I'm not sure I believe it, but I suppose that's the beauty of it. Even if she did it, no teacher would ever believe it. She was usually so obedient and unassuming, teachers always loved her. Jen always got her revenge eventually by being smarter than everyone else. Her senior year she was like the queen of the nerds. She'd write these mean editorials for the school newspaper, and everyone was a little scared of her. Was it like that at your high school, where there's this weird power shift senior year? Everyone starts thinking about the future. The nerds begin their ascendancy."

"But *you* were one of the cool kids?" Mona wanted to know.

"Cool? Not really. I had a lot of friends, I guess. Athletics were a big deal, and I was decent at sports. So I got invited to parties and stuff."

"Okay. Well, let me put it this way. Did you have a superlative?"

"In the yearbook, you mean?"

"Yeah . . . were you, like, Most Athletic? Biggest Flirt? Anything like that?"

"No."

"No?"

"Okay, *fine.* I was voted Most Courteous."

Mona grinned wickedly when I said this.

"And I was nominated for Best All Around," I added. "But some other guy won."

"Shucks," Mona said, snapping her fingers. "Most Courteous is better anyway. It actually means something. I mean, Best All Around? What does that mean, anyway?"

"So what about you, then?" I asked, not wishing to discuss the super-dorky *Most Courteous* any further. "Did you go to a private high school?"

"No. What makes you ask that?"

"I don't know . . . Middlebrook College . . ."

"I see. You think I'm a spoiled brat, don't you? A rich girl from a white-glove girls' school."

I shrugged. "I had wondered about the girls' school thing, that's all."

"Well, I'm not a rich girl. Anything you might see about me that seems moneyed is actually from my stepfather. It's not *me.*"

"I never thought of you as *moneyed,* exactly—"

"Every luxury I've ever had—the expensive college, the plane tickets home for every Thanksgiving, the Honda I drove in high school—"

"Lucky you," I said, impressed.

"Not so lucky, that Honda. But that's another story. All that comes from my stepfather. I was never a rich kid until I was twelve. Then my mother was swept off her feet by a high-powered consultant. She was newly divorced, working at a dry cleaner's. Rob kept coming in with his tailored shirts, and they hit it off. He eventually asked her out. And it changed everything. Double Cinderella, my mother and me."

"What were you before that?"

"Working class. My dad's a welder. He and I would go to the dump together on Saturdays, in his pickup truck. I loved it."

"When did your parents get divorced?"

"When I was eleven. I know it sounds bad to say so, but that was a great year. I really felt like we were taking care of each other, my mother and me. I'd rub her back after work. We'd warm up these frozen pot pies and eat them while we watched game shows. A year later, though, she was married to Rob."

"Is he a good guy?"

"Sure. Rob is very generous with my mother and with me. It's like he's always needed to make a big point of showing that he regards me as his own daughter. He paid for my whole college education."

"That's nice," I said.

"Yeah," Mona agreed. "But it's always made me feel a little . . . mercenary."

"Why?"

"Because I already have a father. A father who could never afford all that ritzy shit."

"You shouldn't feel too bad about it. I'm sure your dad wanted you to get a good education."

"Sure," Mona said. "But it's not so simple."

"What's not so simple?"

"Being two men's daughters. Being a rich girl and a poor man's daughter at the same time."

"And that's why you have two last names."

"I only have one last name. Minot."

"What's Rasmussen, then?"

"When did I tell you about Rasmussen?"

"You didn't. I saw it on your *TV Guide*."

"Oh. I see. I forgot that I was dealing with Hercule Poirot here. The *TV Guide* is a gift from my dad. He renews it every Christmas. And *Cosmo* for my birthday."

"Really? You read *Cosmo*?"

"Believe it or not, yes. Not so much the *TV Guide*, though. I used to read *TV Guide* on the weekends when I would visit him. It was the only reading material my father ever had lying around. He got to thinking I really liked *TV Guide*, I guess. I've had a subscription now since I was fifteen. I've never had the heart to tell him I couldn't care less about the latest Regis Philbin interview or reality-TV update."

"So Rasmussen is your real dad's name."

"Yes."

"How did it change?"

"The usual way. Rob adopted me when I was fourteen."

"Oh."

"So . . ." Mona spread out her hands. "Ask me what you're wondering."

"What am I wondering?"

"Why I was adopted by one guy when I still had a father somewhere else?"

"Doesn't stuff like that happen all the time?"

"Does it? When you're still visiting your real dad once a month?"

"I don't know. How would I know? So you're saying you didn't want to be adopted?"

"No, I'm not saying that. Rob's a great guy. But he wanted to make sure I'd be treated like one of his own kids if he died. He's got a few loose-cannon relatives he thought might contest my place in his will."

"So it's about money," I said.

"Well, not really. Because in the end, Rob was more a father to me than my real dad. But I never meant for that to happen, you see? I never meant for one to replace the other."

"Maybe you're putting it a little harshly. Rob didn't replace your father."

"Um. Well. He sorta did. And when he and my mother asked for my permission on the adoption, I said yes."

Mona slumped back in the futon and folded her arms.

"What would *you* do?" she wanted to know.

"I . . . don't know, actually," I said. "This broken-family stuff's a little foreign to me."

Mona chuckled. "Nice, Billy. Real nice. Let's put it another way. Let's say you were married and had a kid, and the marriage didn't work out. You stay in touch with the kid as best you can, but in the end you grow apart. And then her stepfather wants to adopt her. Wouldn't you be a little hurt by this?"

Mona's brown eyes bored into mine with an intensity that bordered on malice. For an exhilarating second I thought she might lean over and bite me.

"Yeah," I admitted. "I guess I would."

"Thank you," she said, grimly satisfied. "Of course you

would. A manly man like you. You'd want chest-beating rights."

"C'mon," I said. "What makes you all think you can say stuff like that to me? Is a lexicographer with big bones and a letter in football so intimidating that you need to make me feel like a hulking man-child?"

"It wasn't meant as an insult."

"So was your dad upset? When Rob adopted you?"

"I think so. We never actually discussed it in person. My mother got his permission. But he never stopped calling me Mona Rasmussen, and he never stopped sending me stuff under that name."

Mona pulled her legs onto the futon and lay there staring up at my ceiling.

"But you never use the name Rasmussen anymore?"

"No, I don't use the name at all. But I grow tired of Mona Minot. Mona Minot is a rich kid, whether she likes it or not. And a sellout."

"And Mona Rasmussen?"

"Mona Rasmussen misses dump-picking with her dad on Saturdays. Once we found a baby carriage that was practically new. I used it for my dolls."

"Really?"

"And Mona Rasmussen likes Merle Haggard."

"Who's that?"

"You're kidding. You've never heard 'Okie from Muskogee'? About how they never smoke weed in Muskogee, Oklahoma?"

"Nope."

"So . . . I've been meaning to ask." She paused. "Have you smoked much marijuana?"

I hesitated. It was a typical Mona question—a tad more probing than it should be, but nothing I really minded answering. Not really. I had, after all, asked her earlier that evening if she'd done any acid. In both cases, we each had a pretty good idea of what the other's answer was going to be.

I sat there with my mouth open for a second. My silence seemed to surprise her. She gazed at me, cleared her throat, and fumbled for an alternative question.

"Umm . . . how about 'Sing Me Back Home'?" she asked. "Heard that one?"

"Don't think so."

Mona tipped her head back even further off the futon, and sang a different song—one about dying in prison. She had a pretty voice, a little thin, but sweet. I closed my eyes and listened, wondering why, of all the songs to know by heart, she knew this one.

After Mona left, I decided I'd give my bedroom a try. I was growing tired of the sleeping bag setup in my living room. So I lay awake on the bed, thinking of the story I'd almost told Mona:

How are you feeling, William?

Like crap.

That's what I figured. I brought you something.

My father handed me a video, clearly taken from the library. *Little Big Man,* with Dustin Hoffman.

I think you'll like this.

Probably. But not right now, okay? I don't feel like watching a movie right now.

I brought you something else too, William.

A pause. A sheepish look.

Yeah? What?

He reached into his sport coat and pulled out a little baggie with something fuzzy and green in it. For a moment I thought it was a little stuffed animal of some kind, and felt sorry for old Dad, suddenly rendered lame and clueless by my illness.

He shook the bag awkwardly.

It's . . . uh . . . the wacky weed. Some say it really helps. Eases the nausea.

I laughed into my pillow until I found I was crying. When I turned to look at him, he was still standing in the doorway in the same awkward position, with the bag hanging from his hand.

Will you try it? he wanted to know.

I didn't tell him that I had already tried it a couple of times, under very different circumstances. I didn't ask him how a conservative and respected oral surgeon goes about finding a discreet dealer in a suburb like ours.

Only if you'll try it with me, I told my father.

CHAPTER FIFTEEN

The old Victorian's ancient furnace didn't seem to be working the next morning, and I was freezing my ass off. I tried to think of something to motivate me to get out of bed. A trip to the Laundromat? An overambitious cooking project that would leave me with too much food and a bunch of dirty pots?

Ella, my old girlfriend in college, used to keep a bag of Twizzlers in her dresser drawer, across the room from her bed. It was the promise of a mouthful of candy that got her out of bed each morning, she told me. And once she was standing by her dresser, she said, well, she may as well just get dressed. . . . I thought it was cute at first, on the mornings I was with her, watching her gnaw on a little red twist as she selected her underwear and sniffed her sweaters for freshness. After a few times, though, it didn't seem like the healthiest of habits. I could imagine, after a few years and a few disappointments, the red candy easily turning into a bottle of Scotch and the whole scene becoming a little repugnant.

In retrospect, I'd probably been a little hard on Ella. I was starting to think it was a decent idea—having a little something just beyond your bed to lure you up and into the cold morning. The only question was what I could use in place of Twizzlers. I wasn't sure if any candy would really do it for me.

This would be my project for the morning, to find and purchase my own dresser-drawer incentive.

I groaned and rolled out of bed and pulled on jeans and a couple of sweaters. I went downstairs and stepped into the frigid morning air. Cursing, I turned to lock the door behind me. When I heard someone stirring in Jimmy and Barbara's apartment, I hurried down the porch steps. Once I was a few paces down the sidewalk, I slowed my steps.

I walked two blocks to the Mobil station, humming madly into the freezing wind. I was the only other customer there besides a white-haired man in a flannel shirt, rhythmically stirring sugar substitute into a small cup of coffee. I liked the rugged, silent camaraderie of the place.

"You got scratch tickets?" I asked the man behind the counter.

"Yeah. What kind you want?" He tapped on a little plastic display case next to the register. There were about twenty varieties at different prices.

"What are the cheapest?" I asked.

"These ones on this side are a dollar."

I counted my money.

"Thirteen of those, then, I guess."

"Which one? Casino 500? Break the Bank?"

"Um . . . Break the Bank, yeah."

"All thirteen?"

"Yeah."

After paying for the tickets, I walked out, forgetting that I'd wanted a coffee as well. I considered turning back, but didn't.

• • •

"Billy!" Barbara opened her front door as I climbed the porch steps. "That scared me! I was watching from the window. You could've been hit!"

"I was in the crosswalk," I said. "He shouldn't have laid on the horn like that. It's the pedestrian's right-of-way."

"Well, some of the people in this neighborhood don't respect that. You really need to be careful. Do you want to come in? Jimmy and I are having some nice tea, and a crisp. We were thinking of calling you to make sure you hadn't frozen. We just called the landlady about the furnace."

I stepped into the downstairs apartment. The kitchen smelled like cigarette smoke and home cooking. In the next room, Jimmy was watching an infomercial for a rotisserie oven.

Barbara set a mug on the table and stuck a tea bag in it.

"Thanks," I said. "This is really nice."

"I'm just about to start my chanting," she said. "But Jimmy'll join you. Won't you, Jimmy?"

"Yeah," Jimmy said hoarsely over the burble of the television. "We'll both have a couple heaps of that crisp."

Barbara went through the TV room and disappeared into a dark curtained area in the corner. Jimmy joined me at the kitchen table.

"Game's on at three," he said. "You gonna watch it?"

"What game?"

A low moaning came from Barbara's curtained corner, then a resonant gonging sound.

"The Pats game."

"Oh. No, I don't think so. Listen," I said. "Should we turn the TV off? How can Barbara stand that?"

"She's used to it," Jimmy said, pouring our tea. "Says she blocks it out."

"Hey," I said. "Before I forget. I wanted to give you something."

I pulled out my lottery tickets and ripped one off. Handing it to him, I stuck the rest back into my jacket.

Jimmy quirked an eyebrow at me.

"I bought thirteen of them. I didn't realize until I was on my way home that that was the wrong number to buy. I may have jinxed them all by buying thirteen."

"So you figured you'd give me the cursed one."

"I can take it back if you want," I said, dunking my tea bag up and down.

"No, no," he said. "I appreciate it. But you sure you want to give this to me?"

"Why not?"

"What if I win a big pot of cash that could've been yours? Think about it."

I sipped my tea and reached for the sugar.

"We'd both survive," I said.

Some heavy steps on the porch were followed by a clattering on the door. Jimmy shoved his lottery ticket under some newspapers, and Tom came in without waiting for someone to answer. He was carrying an old space heater and a small fire extinguisher.

"Billy boy," he said, dropping the stuff next to the door. "Where've you been hiding yourself?"

"He's got that girlfriend now," Jimmy said.

"She's not a girlfriend." I sighed.

"What? It's not going anywhere?" Jimmy wanted to know.

"Nah."

"Well, maybe you need to take it somewhere, then. Maybe you need to make some moves."

"Yeah, I getcha . . . but . . . she likes older men. That's the thing."

Jimmy served Tom a scoop of crisp. It was a little heavier and more liquid than it should have been, and slid off the spoon with a gross *thluck*.

"So grow a beard," Jimmy suggested. "Wear a tie once in a while. She might like that."

I laughed. "I don't think so, Jimmy. I don't think that would be enough."

"Besides. Take my word for it," he said. "You'll be an older man before you know it. Shit. You'll be an *old* man before you know it."

"That's encouraging," I said.

"Besides," Tom chimed in. "You're a wise old soul, right? Didn't you tell me you were a philosophy major?"

Another soft gong sounded from behind the curtain.

"Yup. That's right."

"Who's your favorite philosopher?" Tom wanted to know.

"Kierkegaard." I didn't even have to think about my answer.

"Oh." Tom looked disappointed. "I prefer the ancients. Why Kierkegaard?"

"Well, for one, I like all the stuff about Regina. And how it keeps coming up, in all different spots in his work. Like he had this one thing that he couldn't get over."

"I don't think I remember the whole story."

"Regina was the girl Kierkegaard was supposed to marry, but he broke it off. He didn't think he could be married *and* devote himself to his religious writings. Some people think he always regretted this decision, at least on some level. Some people think that a lot of his writing is sort of flavored with this regret. His most famous writing is about what real faith is. Have you read *Fear and Trembling*?"

"Long time ago," Tom said.

"On the surface it's about Abraham sacrificing Isaac. And it's all about being willing not only to sacrifice but to *believe*. And a true believer isn't willing to just sacrifice things, but is also somehow able to get them back. On some level, it seems like Kierkegaard wanted to believe God might give Regina back. But he couldn't bring himself to have *that* level of faith."

"See, that just doesn't sound like elegant philosophy to me. Sticking your girlfriend in your argument."

I shrugged. "I guess I like my philosophy to come with a little heart."

"I suppose it doesn't hurt." Tom looked bored. "But I'm more one for a seamless argument."

"No such thing. In religious philosophy, anyway. There always needs to be a jump somewhere."

"The leap of faith," Tom said, snapping his fingers.

"Yeah! You remember your Kierkegaard after all."

"Would you say you're religious? Is that why you like him?"

"Naw," I said. "I just like that idea, that you can be willing to give something up, but still willing to embrace it if it's ever given back to you."

"Like what?"

"Like what?" I parroted. Good question. I remembered discussing this in class once. The younger students couldn't conceptualize this as well as the few older ones. "Well, that depends. It could be anything that God can take away from you. Which means everything, really. You need to be able to give up and reclaim *everything*."

"What the hell does that mean?" Jimmy demanded. "Are you guys listening to yourselves?"

"It means no sour grapes," I said firmly.

Jimmy conceded a nod, but I regretted the oversimplification. It wasn't accurate, and I'd made it sound too easy.

"Or something like that," I added.

CHAPTER SIXTEEN

Mr. Phillips seemed to have adjusted his once-a-month doughnut schedule. He was in the office the following Monday—two weeks earlier than his usual visit.

I was at the cit file, trying to find some information about the history of the word *hornswoggle* for a correspondence, when I heard someone say, on the other side of the file, "No coffee today, John?"

And then Mr. Phillips replying happily, "Not today. Here on business today."

"Oh? What business?"

"Oh, just poking around for a couple of baseball terms. A buddy of mine was asking me about 'chin music' the other day."

"Ohhh. *That* kind of business."

I didn't recognize the other voice. It might have been Anna.

On Wednesday, two days later, I did a double take as I passed the coffee machine. There he was again, leaning casually by the coffee machine, talking to Dan.

"God, I just *miss* this place," he was saying.

Dan was nodding, opening a little plastic creamer with his long, elegant fingers.

The sudden frequency of Mr. Phillips's appearances was not, of course, lost on Mona. She dropped a note in my box:

> Billy,
> Your elderly gentleman friend seems to have come out of retirement. Could it have anything to do with a certain bit of information provided to him by that nice new young editor with the open, optimistic personality and the winning smile??
> M.

Crumpling her note, I went to find Mr. Phillips in the cit stacks.

I arranged to pick him up on Friday.

"Where are we going?" Mr. Phillips asked as he got into my car.

"I thought we'd go somewhere different today," I said. "Know of any good bars downtown?"

"Callahan's," he replied. "Hands down. On the corner of State and Bishop."

"Alrighty," I said.

As I headed in that direction, Mr. Phillips asked me what I'd been working on lately.

"Let's see," I said. "I looked at the cits for 'icky' today. That was mildly interesting, even though there was nothing new to define. And 'icon.' You know, the computer sense? I sent that one to Science."

"That's a shame, Billy. You can't let Science have all the fun. I just went ahead and defined any science terms that interested me."

"I'm sure they didn't like that."

"Yeah, Ed used to howl about that, when he'd catch it.

He'd bounce my definitions back to Science and have them do them over again. Almost always they'd keep what I'd written. See, I'd only do it with terms I knew I could handle. I wouldn't try to define, say, 'ribonuclease.' They can have *those* words to themselves."

After I'd parallel-parked, I started to open my door. But Mr. Phillips didn't move.

"You got any cigarettes?" he asked.

"No. Maybe they sell them inside. Let's go."

"Wait. Before we go in, Billy, I wanted to give you something."

He took an envelope out of his coat pocket and handed it to me.

"Now you just leave poor old Mary Anne's scribblings in the car for now, and worry about her later," he instructed me. "We're gonna enjoy our drink without her."

"Are these—"

"Cits. Ready to go?"

I tucked the envelope under my visor. "Was it Mary Beth or Mary Anne?"

"Pretty sure it was Mary Anne."

"Do you remember her last name?"

"No. But it would be easy enough to find it. Just look in the credits of some of the older Samuelson books. Her name's bound to be in one of them."

Once we got into the place, Mr. Phillips headed straight for a booth in the back. I was a little disappointed. I'd imagined us hanging out at the bar together, maybe doing a couple of shots of whiskey and cursing with the locals.

"What's on tap, dear?" Mr. Phillips was asking the waitress. She was cute, with springy brown curls and freckles. She looked just slightly under age.

"Harp. Guinness. Budweiser," she intoned.

"Gimme a Guinness, then. Please. Billy?"

"I'll have the same. Thanks."

Mr. Phillips propped his elbow on a Sam Adams coaster and scratched his ear. "So. What've you been research-reading lately?" he wanted to know.

"Some cooking magazines. *Rolling Stone.* And *Motorcyclist.*"

"Is that right?"

"Yeah. In fact, I've been thinking of getting a Kawasaki. I figure if I put just a tiny portion of my paycheck aside every month—"

"A motorcycle!" He snorted. "Don't you think you're a little young for your midlife crisis?"

"Yeah," I said. "At my age, you just call it *youth*. I've actually had my eye on this one crotch rocket for a while. I could get a pretty good used one for about eighteen hundred bucks. Can't you just see me zipping into the Samuelson lot on one of those puppies?"

Mr. Phillips shook his head as our waitress slid our beers in front of us.

"What's so funny?" I asked.

"I'm sorry, I'm not laughing at you, champ. I'm laughing at the situation. Marshall, the last guy who research-read that magazine, talked for years about getting a motorcycle."

"What kind?"

"What kind? I don't know. It hardly matters, since it was always a very hypothetical bike. A Harley, probably. But his wife would never let him. We all knew this."

"Well, I don't have a wife."

"If you're smart, then, you'll get your motorcycle before you get a wife."

"Plenty of time. I don't have any prospective wives lined up."

"Not that little Mona?"

"That little Mona? No. She's just a friend."

"You sure about that?"

"Umm . . . Pretty sure."

"Maybe you ought to give that girl a chance. Maybe then you wouldn't need to spend your Friday nights with some old fart from your office."

"Don't say shit like that."

"Why not? Wouldn't you rather be on a date right now?"

"Not necessarily. It bothers me when older people assume that younger people only prefer their own company."

"You're full of it, Homer. Tell me something. You ever actually *been* on a motorcycle?"

"Of course."

"Really?"

"Yeah. There was this guy I knew in college. He was a little older, a part-time student. He let me take a couple of little spins on his Honda." Admittedly, he'd only allowed me one spin, but it was such a long and thrilling ride that it felt like it should count for more. "It was awesome, going that fast. With one of these sport bikes, you get the speed of an Italian sports car at a tiny fraction of the price."

"So you want to go fast. That's what it's about, then?"

"Well, no. I mean, it's not *just* about speed. It's also about how light you feel, and the way you lean into the curves, this way and that. It's just the most smooth, natural thing."

"Huh. Well, in that case, maybe I should try one myself sometime."

"You can take a ride on mine, then."

"Right," said Mr. Phillips. "That's what Marshall always said."

"Well, I really mean it."

"Billy, you know what you remind me of?"

"What's that?"

"Maybe you haven't seen many war movies. So maybe you won't know what I mean."

"I've seen *Full Metal Jacket* quite a few times."

"No, I'm talking older war movies. In those movies there's always a nice young soldier who everybody likes. Works hard. He believes in his fellow soldiers and his cause. And he's willing to make sacrifices."

"This is supposed to be me somehow?"

"But he's shot in the end," said Mr. Phillips, shaking his head. "Almost always shot, in the end."

"Jesus," I said. "Why are you telling me this?"

Mr. Phillips shrugged and sipped his beer.

"I suppose I meant it in a cautionary way," he said.

"How could that be cautionary?" This conversation was starting to annoy me. I much preferred the one about my motorcycle fantasy, which we hadn't quite finished.

"Maybe I should've put it in the form of a piece of advice," Mr. Phillips said with a snicker. *"Don't let yourself get shot in the end."*

"All right, just shut up," I said, plunking my beer down hard.

"What's that, Homer?" Mr. Phillips cupped his ear. Probably he thought he'd heard me wrong.

"As if I have any control over what happens in the end."

"I was just kidding around, champ."

I shrugged, hoping he truly hadn't heard the "shut up." It had slipped out before I'd had time to remember who I was talking to. We both drank our beers. Someone played Fleetwood Mac on the jukebox.

"So," Mr. Phillips said. "Was there something you wanted to talk to me about? Or is this just a social outing?"

"Yeah, well. I was sort of curious about something. I was

noticing this week that you've been spending a lot more time back at the office. Um, is that just a coincidence, or—"

"No. Of course not. I'm just trying to help you out. Took a gander in the file myself, and found those cits for you."

"What year are they from?"

"Nineteen fifty-three. Figured you hadn't worked your way up that far yet. And I figured right. I found a few."

"You looked through all the 1953 words?"

"No. Not yet. I wanted to, but you nabbed me first. I only got through 'H,' but there really wasn't much after 'C.' "

"You find anything good?"

"Yeah. There's some stuff in there, that's for sure. I'm not sure what it means yet, but I think I have a general idea. Something weird happening in that poor girl's head, that's for sure."

"Well, thanks," I said slowly. "I can't wait to read them. But you should let us find the rest. There's no need for you to make special trips to the office. I know it takes you a while to get there on the bus and everything."

"*Special* trips. Hogwash. Samuelson's my second home. Always has been. And you kids sure seem to be taking your time with this. You're still looking through 1951, aren't you?"

I nodded. He was right about us taking our time. Mona and I had agreed—the last time we hung out—to split the remainder of the 1951 list.

"I was curious. Trying to help. Nothing to worry about. It makes Needham nervous when I come around, but there's not much he can do about it. I might be retired, but I'm just as much a part of the family as him. Been there longer."

"But you don't work there anymore," I pointed out.

"When you were at a place forty years, that hardly matters. I trained most of the definers. I trained Dan."

"Really?"

"Yep. Guess that makes me your grandfather."

"Actually, speaking of Dan—"

"Yeah?"

"That girl who we think wrote the cits—" I stopped. I'd been thinking about how familiar her boyfriend seemed, with his height and awkward sincerity. Each time Dan lumbered past my desk, I grew more certain of it. "Any chance she was, you know, seeing Dan?"

"Seeing Dan? You mean dating Dan?"

"Yeah."

"Yep. It seemed like they saw each other quite a little bit, those two. Seemed like they were steadies. But they never acknowledged it. Around Samuelson, some people tend to be a little private. Maybe you've noticed?"

"Sure," I said.

"Yeah, Dan's no exception," Mr. Phillips continued. "Nice fellow, but no exception."

"Nothing wrong with that."

"Nope. Anyway, he never said much about it. To me, anyway. I trained Mary Anne too, by the way. Neither of them said anything about it to me, but you could tell they had something going on. Why do you ask? Something must've come up in the cits."

"Sort of," I admitted.

"You care to educate me?"

"I'll show you next time. I'm pretty sure he's the one she's calling Scout. Just the way she describes him seems...familiar."

"So are you gonna show the cits to Dan, then?" Mr. Phillips wanted to know.

"I don't know...should I? You implied I should keep them to myself."

"Well, I wasn't thinking of Dan when I said that. Dan's got quite a sense of humor, believe it or not. And maybe he could tell you a thing or two about them."

"Maybe," I said. "Maybe sometime. Maybe later on."

Mr. Phillips and I each ordered a second beer, but he started to drowse into his after a few sips. When I suggested heading home, he didn't object.

CHAPTER SEVENTEEN

Back in my apartment, I threw a blanket on the futon, climbed beneath it, and ripped into Mr. Phillips's envelope. He had photocopied three citations onto a sheet of paper:

> **ballpoint**
>
> One day, though, something happened. What so distracted me that day? What was I contemplating? The humbling folly of lexicography? The possible universes that might exist at the very tip of my *ballpoint* pen? Whatever it was, I wasn't tending my tea with the usual care. I elbowed the glass onto the floor. Crash. Splatter. Gasp. Tea everywhere. Not only around my own desk, but onto the feet of a certain sour-faced editor who didn't try to hide his disdain.
>
> 6

> **ball of wax**
>
> I wasn't sure what I owed him. Or admirers of the Glass Girl, left forever hanging from the tip of her pinky finger. To myself? Self-defense is an act that implies you have something valuable to defend. After the instinct, you begin to wonder. What, specifically, was I aiming to save? What, beyond instinct,

makes life worth saving? This isn't a question you answer, of course, but you try to remember to keep asking. It is for the sake of that question that I need to get out of here. What is here? The time and place that nearly finished me? The setting of the story that could swallow up everything that might be mine? To be sure, I'm counting everything as here. This desk, where I wrote Brownlow that letter. The apartment where the dead prom queen resides. This city, these faces, this quiet. The whole *ball of wax*.

45

cut-and-paste

I spent most of those evenings with Scout, often in a deliberate attempt to numb the impulse to ask such questions. Once, when I seduced him into the bedroom and put both of my hands in his dark hair, I imagine his head coming off his body in my hands. His body and mind could just as easily be a *cut-and-paste* job as mine. This made me afraid of both, afraid of myself, afraid of my affection for him. I invited him into my bed to chase away the nightmare. He ended up entering the nightmare instead.

35

I put the photocopy down and called Mona.

As the phone rang, I wondered if she'd be offended at my assumption that she'd be home and unoccupied.

"Hey," I said when she picked up. "It's Billy."

"Hi. How was it boozing up with Phillips?"

"Informative. I mean, at this point, I'm pretty sure we can trust him. He's not keeping anything from me. He's really curious about the whole thing, and he wants to help."

"I don't know if I can believe that."

"Maybe you ought to hang out with us next time. See for yourself."

"Yeah. I'm starting to think that myself, actually. I want a chance at him."

"You're going to need to promise me you'll be gentle with him. He's trying to help. He even dug up some more cits for us. From 1953."

"Really? Anything good?"

"Yeah. I was thinking we could meet for breakfast and you could take a look."

"Sounds good."

After we'd made our plans and hung up, I read the cits again.

What is here? The time and place that nearly finished me? The setting of the story that could swallow up everything that might be mine?

These words stuck with me after I'd gone to bed. I wasn't sure why they nettled me. They didn't say anything new. It wasn't the first time the narration referred to the danger and the power of *the story*. A story, not a confession. Seemed to me there was a big difference between the two.

Just when I'd almost fallen asleep, my brain jerked me awake, dreaming that I was choking on a butterscotch candy. I seem to have this dream often. I'm hanging out in my old bedroom at my parents' house, lying on the bed, killing time reading a *Sports Illustrated* or tossing a Koosh ball around, sucking on a candy. The next thing I know, I'm choking on it. Then I wake up.

"It's the *letter* that interests you?" Mona said. "Quite frankly, I find the decapitation fantasy the more striking element of these cits."

"But a letter shows they had a connection. It shows she knew him."

Mona started to sip her coffee, but then put her cup down. "Ohmigod."

"What?"

"Maybe *not*. Maybe she didn't know him at all. The cit implies she was writing at work. The voice of the cits is someone narrating inside the office."

"So what?"

"She wrote Brownlow a *letter*." She looked at me and said sharply, "From *work*."

I saw where she was going with this.

"Correspondence," I said.

"Yup."

"That makes sense except . . . what could letters about grammar and usage have to do with anything?"

"Maybe they started out corresponding about word stuff, and the relationship deepened."

"And she kept it from Scout?" I suggested. I hadn't yet decided how I'd present Mona with my Scout theory. I didn't know how she would take it. With her schoolgirl weakness for Dan, it was a dicey subject.

"It's as plausible as anything else, I guess," Mona said.

"So are we gonna go down this path now?"

"What do you mean?"

"Are we gonna ransack the correspondence files?"

"How do you propose that?" she demanded. "Aren't they all filed away in Mr. Needham's office?"

"And you're going to let that stop you?"

She looked thoughtful. "The office doors don't lock, do they?"

"Nope. I don't think so."

"But we can't consider . . . I mean . . . how could we?"

"You're probably right." I shrugged. "There's probably no way. And we probably wouldn't find anything anyway."

"But maybe we could come up with some excuse why we needed to look in there."

"Like what?"

"Good question," Mona admitted. "Nothing legitimate comes to mind."

Our waitress brought our orders. I dove into my eggs Benedict while Mona contemplated her Belgian waffles.

"Have you ever read that kids' book *From the Mixed-up Files of Mrs. Basil E. Frankweiler*?" she asked.

"I don't think so."

"No? Well, it's about these kids who decide they want to live in the Metropolitan Museum of Art. They manage to stay in the building past closing by standing on the toilets in the museum bathrooms."

"I'm perfectly willing to stand on a men's room toilet. It sounds more spontaneous and fun than anything else I'll ever do at Samuelson. But how will that get us into Mr. Needham's office?"

"Nobody will stand on any toilets. But one of us will drive the other to work one day. Say you drive me to work. I'll stay after hours and hide in the bathroom. You'll drive home. The parking lot will be empty. The last person to leave won't see any car in the lot. When everybody's good and gone, I come out of the bathroom and go straight to Needham's office. You come by a little later and pick me up. The getaway car."

I stared at her. "Are you serious?"

"Good question," she said. She twisted a lock of hair tightly around her index finger. "Sometimes I look at what we're doing, and think, *What happened to my life?* Is the problem that I never had a life to begin with? And that's what makes me want to start doing shit like this?"

I thought of our conversation on the park bench, when she'd fretted about getting "in deeper." She'd been holding out on me. I really couldn't have come up with a foolhardier plan myself.

"Well, don't look too hard at what we're doing, then. Don't overthink it. It's a pretty insane idea. I'm not denying that. I'm just asking if you're serious."

Mona cocked her head. "I suppose I am."

"Good. How soon can we do it?"

CHAPTER EIGHTEEN

When I arrived at my desk on Monday, Dan was standing over it, scratching his head. I looked around him, into my cubicle. A custodian was on his hands and knees under my desk, pulling a cord down through a freshly drilled hole in the fake wood. On top of the desk was a shiny new white phone.

Dan gave me a guilty smile. It was the same smile that elementary school teachers always gave me when they changed my seat so I could be by the new kid, or the newly mainstreamed Special Ed kid. *Just show him around,* they'd say. Or *just be his friend.* I always got these dubious honors—honors that had more to do with my dunderheaded good nature than any perceived smarts. Dan's new role for me had an uncomfortably similar feel.

"I guess phones aren't a seniority thing around here," I said.

"No," Dan said. "Not exactly. We thought you might like to try to field some phone calls from the public."

Cliff was already at his desk. I heard him shift and start clip-clopping away at his computer keys.

"We thought you would be good at it," Dan said.

"We'll see, I guess."

"You'll learn a lot," Dan assured me.

"Terrific," I said.

"Not about lexicography, perhaps, but about humanity."

A snort escaped Cliff's cubicle.

Dan gave my cubicle a friendly tap before walking away.

Mr. Phillips seemed uncomfortable on Tuesday evening, when we all met for coffee.

"This is a real treat," he said heartily. "I'm glad you're joining us here today, Mona."

"Thanks for having me along," was her reply.

"Good to have some female intuition on this little project," he continued.

"Oh, yeah. I should think." I sensed a little sarcasm in her words. "Considering that female intuition's what started it. Or maybe just lexicographer's intuition?"

"You think there's such a thing?" he asked.

"Certainly. Thanks for doing all that work to find those first 1953 cits, by the way," she said. "That'll save us a lot of time."

"Did you dig up the rest?" Mr. Phillips wanted to know.

"Of 1953? No," Mona answered. "We're about halfway done with 1951."

She reached into her leather bag and pulled out a few photocopied sheets. She'd made copies for each of us.

Mr. Phillips put on his glasses and held one of the pages out in front of his face. He let out a couple of grunts of interest as he read.

"Poor girl," he muttered a couple of times.

Something about the way he said it made me ask:

"You ever been married, Mr. Phillips?"

"Yeah," he muttered. "For a few years. Long time ago. Didn't work out."

"Can I ask . . . What happened?"

"Sure. She left in '78. Left the country. Went to Europe with the feminists."

"What do you mean?" I asked.

Mona sputtered into her latte.

"Just what I said," Mr. Phillips said irritably.

"Went to Europe with the *feminists*?" Mona repeated. "What, just like that? Like they were a traveling band of gypsies or something?"

"You got it, sister," Mr. Phillips muttered. "Your comparison is an apt one, I'm afraid."

Mona gave me a look that clearly said, *I'll let you take this one.*

"Mr. Phillips—" I began.

"You think you'll ever get married, Billy?" he interrupted.

"I don't know," I said.

"You seem like the marrying type," Mr. Phillips persisted. "I can see it. I can just see you on your sit-down mower, earning points so you can have your afternoon off to watch a little baseball."

"Hey," said Mona. "That's kinda harsh, don't you think?"

"Oh, wait," Mr. Phillips said, scratching his head vigorously. "Not his sit-down mower. I forgot. His *motorcycle*."

"Motorcycle?" Mona said. "Now, that doesn't fit at all."

Mr. Phillips nodded at me knowingly. "See?"

"See what?"

"There will be naysayers. Have you told your parents about the motorcycle, son?"

"What motorcycle?" Mona asked.

"No," I said to Mr. Phillips. "Of course not. My mother has probably helped remove donated organs from many a motorcycle accident victim."

"Oh, yes," Mr. Phillips said. "The perfusionist. I almost forgot."

"So she'd probably be pretty dead set against it."

"I'd say she'd have a point if she was."

"You're getting a *motorcycle*?" Mona asked.

"No," I said. "Mr. Phillips and I were just talking man-talk the other day. We're both alpha males, and I was trying to one-up him."

"That's not how I remember it," he said.

"I know someone who was decapitated in a motorcycle accident," Mona said, a little too proudly.

"You still know him?" I asked. "How does that work?"

"Well, I never really *knew* him. He was my friend's cousin."

"So it doesn't bother you, then? The danger of it?" Mr. Phillips asked me.

"It's a consideration, of course. Would it be too much of a cliché to point out that the danger is part of the appeal?"

"It's not that it's a cliché that I find objectionable," Mona said. "It's that it's *dumb*."

"Ahhh, Billy." Mr. Phillips savored my name as if it were a warm sip of his precious Jamaica Blue Mountain. "Billy. Billy boy. Hey—anyone ever call you Willy?"

"No."

"Willy. Old Willy. That reminds me of a little story," Mr. Phillips said.

"Yeah?" I said, hoping to move away from the motorcycle topic. "Maybe you should tell it to us."

Mona shot me a look that I couldn't interpret.

"In Korea, I served with this guy named Willy. Birdless

Willy, we called him. He was a little crazy. And he was missing the middle finger on his right hand."

"How'd he lose it?" I asked.

"It was shot off. He had it shot off in a bar."

"What?" Mona said.

"I'm telling you. Swore he gave a guy the finger once in a
bar and the guy pulled out a piece and just shot it clear off
his hand."

"He was lying to you, Mr. Phillips," Mona said. "Either
that or you got that out of *Blazing Saddles* or something."

"Well, whether or not the backstory was a lie, the guy
didn't have his right-hand bird."

"How'd he shoot his gun, then?" I asked.

"He didn't shoot. He was the company cook. But the real
interesting thing about Willy is he got a second chance at a
middle finger."

Mr. Phillips paused dramatically.

"You see, at Old Baldy, some joker whacked a dead Red's
finger off and brought it back for Willy."

"What's Old Baldy?" I asked.

"That's pretty *sick*," Mona said. "And on a number of
levels."

"Well, honey. War is sick."

"Did he keep the finger?" I asked.

"Now, that's the real interesting part."

"He kept it?" Mona said. "How? Did he salt it like jerky?"

"Hold your horses. No, he didn't salt it. He joked that he
boiled it down in one of our soups and picked out the bones
to keep for himself. Left the fleshy finger bits in the soup.
But I doubt that. We'd have gotten the squirts from that
finger. That finger sure wasn't fresh by the time it got to
Willy."

"God!" Mona said.

"He'd always claim he had the finger bones in his pocket. He'd jangle at his pocket, claiming he was gonna give one of us the finger someday. That is, leave the bones under one of our pillows, or in one of our bowls, or something sneaky like that. He'd say it pretty cryptic, like. So you weren't sure if you were supposed to want the finger or not. Like it could be a curse, or it could be a good-luck charm. He'd say things like 'Who here wants to stay in Korea forever? Well, let's just see who gets this here finger.' "

"That sounds more like a curse to me," I said.

"But some days, he'd say things like 'Maybe I'll just keep this little finger for myself. I kind of like having a finger again. I got my balance again. I got my yin and I got my yang.'"

"He didn't say that," Mona hissed.

"Oh, he did, honey."

"Americans didn't know anything about Asian philosophy in the fifties," Mona insisted.

"We were in *Korea,* for God's sake. We knew a couple of things. And it was a Chinese guy's finger, after all."

Mona cringed.

"So who got the bones?" I asked.

"I don't know. I got my stateside wound before Willy ever gave them to anyone. But I was glad it wasn't me. Something told me those bones—whether or not they really existed—were like the key to Willy's rubber room. Get the bones and you'd find yourself occupying it with him. If he ended up giving them away, I never heard who got them."

"Didn't you keep in touch with any of the guys in your company?"

"When I did, there were always more important things to discuss than Willy's magic finger bones. Anyway, it's important to know when to let a thing end."

"I like how your story ends," I said.

"It doesn't exactly have an ending." Mona looked disappointed.

"Sure it does. It ends with Mr. Phillips getting to go home."

"With a hole in his gut," Mr. Phillips added.

"Can I ask," said Mona, folding her hands primly on the table, "if this is one of the stories that so moved Mary Anne?"

Mr. Phillips raised an eyebrow at Mona, and then turned to me.

"No," he said. "No, I don't think Mary Anne would have appreciated that one."

Mona sighed. "Well then. While we're on the subject of Mary Anne, I have a few questions for you. Nineteen fifty-one brings up some interesting findings."

I took out our two most recent cits:

nebbish

But we are talking about how I got here. And here in a different sense. That story begins, oddly, quaintly, with a cup of tea. Every morning, after his smile disappeared into his corner of the office, there was one other luxury. A cup of tea. A glass of tea, since my drinking glass from home doubled as an unconventional tea vessel. A teaglass, if you will. Teaglass. Is that a word? Every day I'd make a *nebbish* of myself, going down to that pointy, constipated cafeteria woman, and asking, Oliver Twistlike, "May I have some hot water please?"

4

killer

Then you said you thought I'd have finished it by now, that you'd heard I eat books like candy. I wondered from whom you could have heard this. And I thought you were just taunting me, Red, and that you knew very well where the book had gone. Were we now sharing an explosive secret? No, I said, trying to give you a *killer* stare. I wouldn't have you in on it. I said again, No, not yet. And you said all right. I think I saw you hesitate before you walked away. None of the usual wink. Just a defeated posture as you moved on to the pencil sharpener.

33

"Now, let's talk a little about this Mary Anne," Mona began. "Billy told me you said her name was Mary Anne, and I looked at the credits for some of the books that were published around '85. Like the second edition of the kids' dictionary. There's a Mary Anne Wright. Does that sound correct?"

"Sure," Mr. Phillips said. "I don't think there have been any other Mary Annes at Samuelson, so I guess that's her."

"I Googled Mary Anne Wright," Mona confessed. "There are a lot of them out there."

"Can't help you there. Keep in mind, she might be married now anyway."

"Right. Well then. Moving right along... Do you remember this conversation? About this book?"

"No. I lent her a few books, though. So it probably happened."

"Do you remember her acting strange at any point, while she was working at Samuelson?"

"Strange? Can't say as I did. Looks here like she thought I did."

"You think she was capable of killing?"

Mr. Phillips guffawed and looked at me. "Girl's a lot more direct than you, Homer. Who am I to say who's capable of

killing, dear? Mary Anne was a sweet kid. If she killed someone, I'd be mighty surprised. I can tell you that much. You
know, I don't like how all of this is starting to sound. Maybe
you two ought to chat with Dan about this after all."

"Why would we chat with *Dan*?" Mona demanded.

I tried to give Mr. Phillips a subtle little shake of the head,
but he either missed it or ignored it. I'd meant to tell her. I
just hadn't decided *how* yet.

"You didn't tell her?" he asked me. "Why not? You're a
sneaky little sucker, aren't you?"

"Tell me what?" Mona wanted to know.

"Billy, are you a...cunning linguist?" Mr. Phillips
laughed and gave me a quick, jerking wink. "Excuse me,
Mona. Heard that one yet, champ? Cunning linguist?"

"Is this really happening?" Mona asked, turning to me.
"Did he actually just say that? Tell me *what*?"

"Don't get all bent out of shape now." Mr. Phillips sobered
quickly. "I'll tell you. Mary Anne was Dan's girlfriend."

Mona gasped.

"No!" she said. I was so accustomed to her sarcasm that at
first I couldn't believe the genuine depth of her surprise.

"Yup," said Mr. Phillips.

Mona took a moment to compose herself, but then
started firing questions at the old man.

"What kind of relationship did they have? Was it
volatile?"

"Well," Mr. Phillips said, "I wasn't exactly privy to that
kind of, uh—"

"Well, what was she like? Why would he go out with her?"

"She was cute. Pretty. By Samuelson standards."

To my surprise, Mona let that go. "Why'd she leave?" she
asked.

"You know, I don't remember," Mr. Phillips replied. "But

it was rather sudden, I believe. I went to her desk one day and she was gone. She probably gave her notice to Ed and just didn't let the rest of us know."

"What do you think might've happened?"

"I don't know. You know, dictionary work isn't for everybody. Young editors tend to come and go, and we don't ask a lot of questions. There are always more suckers out there willing to come in and help us answer letters from the clink."

I heard a little catch in Mona's breath.

"What did Mary Anne look like?" I asked him.

"She was delicate," Mr. Phillips replied.

"You mean, petite? Like Mona?"

"Naw. She was built like a *real* . . . I mean, she wasn't small. Just girlish. I don't think they make 'em like that anymore."

"Girlish *how*?" Mona insisted. "Pink dresses and eyelet lace?"

"No. It wasn't how she dressed. It was . . . uh . . . physical. She just looked like someone who should have a flower in her hair. A little old-fashioned, even then. Long blonde hair. Strawberry blonde."

The dreamy way he said it made me think Mr. Phillips might be partial to strawberry blondes.

"Did she let you call her *honey*?" Mona sneered.

"What do you think Dan liked about her?" I asked hastily, hoping to ask a more engaging question before Mr. Phillips registered Mona's.

"Jeez," Mr. Phillips said. "I can't really say. There was a lot to like. She did good work. You got the feeling she was smarter than she knew. She was a good definer, but she didn't have a lot of confidence. She was always running her definitions by me, even long after training."

"What did she study?" Mona asked. "I mean, in school, before they hired her?"

"Damned if I know." Our barrage of questions was irritating Mr. Phillips. "I can't remember that kind of thing. You know how many definers I've trained? You're lucky I remember this little girl at all. I think she went to that ritzy girls' school, though. Most of 'em came from there around that time. Same one Grace went to."

"Middlebrook?" said Mona.

"Yep."

"I went there," Mona said.

"Is that right?" Mr. Phillips replied. "That figures. For a time, nearly every female editor came outta that bluestocking factory over there. And most of the men from the Ivies. La-di-da. Now they change it up a little more. Only recently did they start hiring kids out of the state university. That was Dan's innovation. And you're one of the lucky beneficiaries, huh, Billy?"

"Where did Dan go?" Mona asked. "Ivy League?"

"Yep. Yale. Funny thing, though. Did you know he almost went to the Naval Academy? Told me that once, few years ago. Said he changed his mind at the last minute, something like that."

"Why?" Mona demanded.

Mr. Phillips shrugged. "Can't say as I know, kids."

It seemed to me Mona was just asking about Dan to satisfy her own curiosity. I didn't think any of this information would get us any closer to the full story. After glancing at the cits again, I said, "Why 'teaglass,' of all things? It seems like she's trying to stress that somehow. *'A teaglass, if you will. Teaglass. Is that a word?'* "

Mona and Mr. Phillips both replied to me at once.

"I'm way ahead of you, champ," Mr. Phillips said.

"I already tried that weeks ago," Mona said.

They eyed each other suspiciously. Mona stuck her hand out, gesturing for Mr. Phillips to speak first.

"Nothing much in the cit files," he said. "Nothing she wrote, certainly."

"Mostly cits for these Moroccan glasses they use to serve mint tea," Mona added. "Not enough for an entry in a regular dictionary. And a few of the cits had it as two words. 'Tea glass.' Kind of self-explanatory too, right?"

"But 'teacup's' in the dictionary, right?" I asked. "And 'teacup's' self-explanatory, I think. 'Tea.' 'Cup.' 'Teacup.' "

" 'Teacup' is an entirely different story," Mr. Phillips interrupted. "Applying self-explanatory rule is an art, not an exact science. You kids have got to develop a sensitivity for it. Anyway. Regarding Mary Anne—I think she's just got a sense of humor. *'Is that a word?'* She's parroting the dumbest question we ever get at Samuelson. The most common question too. *Is this a word? Is that a word?* Really, anything is a word if you can grunt it out of your mouth and it means something to you. Is that so hard for people to understand? Criminy!"

Mona peered at me as she sipped gingerly at the last of her latte.

I quietly gathered the cits into a neat little pile. I had a feeling this discussion was over.

After our meeting with Mr. Phillips, Mona called me at home for a debriefing. She said she too was now convinced he didn't know any more about the cits than we did. And she'd be waiting for me to pick her up at her apartment at seven-forty the following morning. Our correspondence-file raid would proceed as planned.

CHAPTER NINETEEN

Cliff's phone rang the moment I sat down at my desk the following morning.

"What's that, Sheila?" he said through a yawn. "Of *course* they are. Yup. That's what I'm here for. For senior citizens who play Scrabble at eight-thirty a.m. Dial 'em on through. Line three. Wonderful.

"Hello, Editorial. Yes. Yes, our secretary gave me the background, ma'am.

"... 'Exec.' Yes, that's in our dictionary as a noun. It's not an abbreviation, not in its present usage. It's accepted as a standard noun because—

"... Listen. I don't make the rules, ma'am. Who makes the game? Parker Brothers, correct? Maybe—

"... Believe me. I understand. That 'X' can be a killer. What, is he on a triple-word score? Double? Aw, just let him have it! It's *standard*.

"... It's a noun rather than an abbreviation when people begin to pluralize it like a standard noun and—

"Hello? Ma'am?"

Cliff put his receiver back in place.

"Fine," he muttered.

I gazed at my new phone. No calls for me yet. All week it had remained ominously quiet. Maybe Sheila hadn't gotten the memo yet.

The official getaway car was to arrive for Mona at 8 p.m. We had synchronized our watches, but I left a little early and arrived with two minutes to spare. I parked behind the building and stared up at the dark second-story windows.

I hoped Mona was okay up there in the pitch blackness. She'd insisted upon using a flashlight. About half of Samuelson's employees lived in Claxton. She said she didn't want anyone driving past the office later and noticing that Mr. Needham's office window was lit.

I turned on the radio and considered circling the block. But I didn't want Mona coming down and freaking out to find me missing.

At 8:01 the glass door opened and Mona fluttered down the steps to my car.

"Go! Go!" she yelled, getting in.

"Alrighty," I said.

"Wait. Put something a little more badass on the radio first."

She hit my Scan button.

"Shall I peel out of the lot?"

"Please do."

I stepped on it and cut the wheel. The tires squealed as we cruised out of the lot.

"Real nice, Billy," Mona said, settling on Dire Straits for her getaway song.

"Did you find anything?"

"Yeah. Wow. I feel like I just broke into the Watergate building. I've never done anything like that before. Hey—Jesus. Let's not overdo it. You're driving like a maniac."

"You need to let me have *my* little rebellion. I didn't get to do any toilet-standing, or breaking and entering."

"Where exactly are we headed? You wanna hang out for a little while? I actually got quite a few letters."

"You're kidding. Derek Brownlow letters?"

"Yeah. I don't know what they say yet, of course."

"Wow."

"So are you game?"

I hesitated.

"Your place or mine?" I said.

"What've you got to eat?"

"A frozen pizza. And I think there's some lettuce. Salad dressing."

"I'm down to ramen myself," Mona confessed.

"My place, then," I said.

Mona had looked through the correspondence files from 1980 through 1985. The first letter from Derek Brownlow was dated December 1983. The handwriting was small and neat, with a slight slant to the left.

Dear Sons of Samuelson,

My friends here doubt my explanation of "one fell swoop." "Fell" is clearly defined as "deadly," "savage," or simply "evil." "Swoop," I have explained, is an instance of "swooping" or "sweeping," as in a single swift and precise sweep of a scythe. Hence "one fell swoop."

I recently used the word "fell" to describe an especially

vicious act ("the fell rape and murder of the McCarthy woman") and was met only with perplexed glances.

Is my parsing correct? Is my use of "fell" off the mark?

Gratefully,

Derek Brownlow

"Nothing too unusual," Mona said. "Blowhard looking for confirmation."

"Maybe a touch macabre," I pointed out. "For correspondence."

We examined the response:

Dear Mr. Brownlow,

I'm writing in response to your question about "fell" and "one fell swoop." Your analysis of the phrase is impressive and essentially correct. I do, however, have some additional information about these terms' origins that you might find illuminating.

"Fell" means, as you say, "sinister" or "deadly." A "swoop" might be more accurately described as a "carrying off" as a bird of prey does with its victims. But your connecting of "swooping" and "sweeping" is appropriate. "Swoop" was initially a variant of "sweep" in Middle English, derived from the same Germanic roots. "One fell swoop" was first used by Shakespeare in *Macbeth*.

Your use of the word "fell" is correct, and if anyone questions you on it, you should perhaps direct him to a dictionary. It's not a common word in current English, however, so if clarity is your aim, you might want to consider replacing it with "savage" or "sinister" in casual conversation.

Good luck.

Sincerely,
Daniel Wood
Samuelson Editorial Department

"Looks like young Dan did what he was supposed to," I offered. "Kept it brief, informative."

Mona refilled my soda, looking a little wan.

"What's the matter?" I asked.

"Doesn't it make you a little uneasy? That Dan knew this guy? What does that mean? I had figured she was keeping something secret about this Brownlow guy. But now that doesn't seem possible."

"Well, this one letter doesn't exactly mean Dan knows Brownlow," I said. "Maybe they both wrote to him."

"But there's a lot more," Mona said, flipping through the letters. "And it looks like it was Dan pretty much the whole time."

Dear Daniel,

How delightful to get a response from a namesake of Mr. Samuelson. I wasn't sure if I should hope for a reply and behold! My prayers and questions were answered tenfold!

Now to my next question. Why does the word "carceral" not appear in the standard Samuelson dictionary? I actually use that word often in my regular parlance. In my current situation, I have frequent occasion to use it. Just the other day, I recall remarking on the unappetizing nature of "carceral cuisine."

Thanks in advance for your erudite response.
Cordially,
Derek Brownlow

"So he's writing from jail." Mona shook her head. "That doesn't make any sense. How could Brownlow be in jail and then turn up dead in a Claxton park?"

"It's all in the timing, I guess," I said. "Is there a return address on the letter?"

"No. And we don't keep the envelopes."

"So we don't know where he's writing from. Except that he's writing from some prison or other."

"I guess he got out. Lucky him."

"Really, not so lucky. Maybe he would have been better off if he'd stayed there. It doesn't sound like he met a very pleasant end."

Dear Mr. Brownlow,

"Carceral" has been in the English language since the late 16th century. Just like its more frequently heard relative "incarcerate," it comes from the Latin root "carcer," meaning jail. Likely you already know this.

Indeed, I can imagine that "carceral" has a number of useful applications. But I'm afraid we have little record of actual use of the word. For this reason, its definition appears only in our unabridged dictionary.

We are, however, always collecting new evidence for new editions of our dictionaries. If you happen to come across the use of "carceral" in any of your personal readings, we'd be happy to accept copies of the material for our citation files.

Sincerely,
Daniel Wood
Samuelson Editorial Department

"All right," Mona said. "Still kindly. Typical Dan."
I nodded.

Dear Daniel,

Thanks for your offer to bring me into the dictionary fold. I will read with special care, keeping my eyes open for any uses of "carceral."

Unfortunately, they do not allow us access to a copy machine. Should I come across a noteworthy use of the word, would a handwritten record of my findings suffice?

Yours in lexicography,

Derek

"Okay." Mona shrugged. "A little obsessive here, but nothing we haven't seen before."

"Right," I agreed.

The letters went on for several months in a similar vein, Derek asking usage and etymology questions, and Dan replying succinctly and politely. The last two letters were dated January 1985.

Dear Mr. Brownlow,

Thanks for your recent letter. Due to pressing editorial duties, Mr. Wood is no longer able to respond to correspondence—but I am happy to answer your question.

You were correct to question your cellmate's use of the word "irregardless." Use of that word is generally considered substandard.

Sincerely,

Mary Anne Wright

Samuelson Editorial Department

Dear Miss Right,

Who are you and what happened to Daniel?

I have little patience for strumpets.

DB

The handwriting of the last letter was almost illegible.

"Now, that's a little off," I admitted.

"Poor Derek," Mona said. "Lost his only friend."

"Poor Mary Anne," I added.

"Mr. Needham was not amused," Mona said, pointing to the top of the letter. Mr. Needham had initialed it and scribbled *No Response!*

"I wonder if she secretly responded," I said. "Not that there'd be much reason to."

Mona got up without replying and threw our pizza crusts in the garbage. Instead of sitting back down, she stood there in the middle of my kitchen, plate in hand, staring at me.

"What?" I said.

"Let's put all this stuff away," she said softly.

"Away?"

"Just for the night. Come back to it tomorrow."

"Why?"

"Because . . . it's disturbing. Now that we've found something here, I wonder if I'd prefer to be left in the dark."

"Oh, come on now. We're just getting to the good stuff. Don't back out on me."

"Dan," she said, dropping the end of his name into a sigh. The plate looked so loose in her hand I thought it might crash to the floor. She tried again. "Dan—"

She looked a little pathetic standing there by my overstuffed trash can. I stood up, took the plate from her hand, carried it to the sink, and rinsed it.

"Tell me a little about that," I said, turning off the water. "I've been meaning to ask. Tell me about you and Dan."

A blush crept up Mona's face as it dawned on her what I was asking, and how bluntly I'd chosen to do it.

"Okay," she said. "I will."

I wiped my hands with a dishrag and waited, but she just gazed down at my grimy linoleum floor.

"Should we retire to the sitting room?" I asked, after a while.

"Yeah," she said. "Just let me use your bathroom first."

"Sure," I said.

I flopped onto my futon and waited for Mona to finish in the bathroom. It took her a while. I began to wonder if she'd really had to go or was just in there getting her story straight.

"What is this?" she asked, when she finally came out.

"Oh," I said, looking at the dog-eared paperback in her hand. "That's . . . a joke book."

"But I mean, what are all these little markings? Are you research-reading at home?"

"No . . . they're like . . . ratings, I guess."

"You rate jokes while you're sitting on the toilet? This must be the dirtiest pencil in the world."

"No, not on the toilet. I must have just left it in there when I went to brush my teeth."

"Right, Billy." Mona flipped through the pages. "What's the highest rating? The plus?"

"Double-plus," I admitted.

"I don't see any double-plusses."

"They're rare. Finding a double-plus is like finding a four-leaf clover. You can look for one, but you shouldn't really feel entitled to find one. You can sometimes go through an entire joke book without finding a single double-plus."

"Sounds frustrating."

"It can be sometimes."

"So . . . what would be an example of a double-plus joke?"

"Let me think about that," I said. "I'll get back to you on that. It depends partly on the audience. "

"Funny you should say that. I don't recall you ever telling a joke. Are you a closet comedian?"

"Not really. There's something addictive about reading these. You want to keep going until you find a good one. And when you finally find a good one, you get this rush. You want to find another one. Sometimes I can do it for hours. Hey! I just thought of this. You really should try it the next time you're on an airplane."

"Maybe. I'm not so sure it will work for me like it works for you. It sounds kind of like a personal thing. When did you start reading joke books?"

Mona had put the book aside. It was already mashed into the fold of the futon, by her knee. I gazed at the cover, all spangled with drawings of open, laughing faces. It was an old book—so old I couldn't remember when I hadn't owned it. But I couldn't recall ever really considering the cover before, in all of its abstract glee.

"Weren't we talking about Dan?" I asked.

CHAPTER TWENTY

It started last October, she told me.

"When I say 'It started,' I feel a little ridiculous, because that almost implies that there's something. I mean, something beyond what goes on in my head. And there's really not that kind of 'something,' you know?"

I nodded. Probably it would make sense once she explained a little more.

"Late one night, I think it was a Wednesday. My mother called me up to tell me that my old cat Buzz was sick."

"Buzz?"

"Yeah. I got him when I was eight. He was this great cat. He'd sleep by my head, follow me from room to room." She sighed. "So Buzz was terribly ill. My mother was crying when she called, saying she didn't want to worry me, that she'd already brought him to the vet twice but there was really not a lot they could do. He had some kind of feline virus, he'd stopped eating, and he'd been hiding in a closet for days. He'd cry when anyone tried to touch him.

"Then my stepdad got on the phone. He said he knew of this cat acupuncturist in Cleveland, and he'd be willing to pay for that if I wanted them to try and keep him comfortable until I could get out there and decide what I thought was best. He'd pay for the flight out.

"And I said no, no . . . please, just take him in tomorrow and put him down. It's okay. I understand. My coming would only prolong his suffering.

"I couldn't sleep that night. Because I felt I'd betrayed Buzz. Not by letting him be put to sleep. But because . . . I'd always meant to come back and reclaim him. I'd told myself that once I was settled, I'd bring him back here with me. That's what I always used to say when I was in college. That someday I was going to come and rescue him. From Rob's obnoxious Labrador, and from my half sister Michelle, who's really a sweetie but who always liked to annoy Buzz, putting hats on him or tying ribbons around his neck, stuff like that.

"Buzz and I had an understanding. We always had a good thing going. When I was in elementary school, and my parents would have these terrible fights . . . a few times they'd come home a little drunk, and screaming at each other . . . I really think sometimes they'd drink to be able to stand each other, cuz neither of them drank much after they were divorced . . . but anyway, when they would fight, Buzz and I would hide under the covers together, staring at each other. It was like having a little brother."

"Okay," I said blankly. It sounded like a pretty lonely childhood to me—if her closest companion was a cat with a name like an aging construction worker.

"I'm getting to the Dan part, okay? The point is that I owed something to Buzz. But for years, I'd just been putting him off. When I was in college, and I'd come home and visit, I'd say, 'Just a couple of years, Buzz, and we're outta here.' I'd thought of coming out to get him over Columbus Day weekend. But I'm afraid to fly, and 9/11 had just happened, and I was chicken. And now it was too late. I'd been making false promises for years and now I hadn't even been with him for his last days, or his last moment. I felt terrible all night. It was like I'd screwed him and left him to die alone. I couldn't sleep. I cried all night. Then the next morning I went to work a little bit of a wreck. Exhausted. A little wrinkled. I'd forgotten my lunch.

"That day Dan and I were going over some practice definitions I'd done. One of the words was 'chipotle.' You know, dried jalapeños?"

I shrugged. "I had a fancy sandwich once with a chipotle spread. Wasn't a huge fan."

"I think I was pretty out of it that whole session," Mona continued. "I felt like crap. I looked like it too. After it was over, I couldn't remember much of what he said. I don't know if I was really even distressed about Buzz at that point—just really tired.

"As soon as it was lunchtime, I went outside to get some air and sit on the steps. While I was sitting there, Dan comes out, looking like he's rushing off for some errand. He runs down the steps, and is halfway to his car, and then he turns around. He says, 'No lunch today?' And I just shrugged and said, 'I forgot it.'

"And he nodded, sort of absent-mindedly—you know, the way he does—and then got in his car and drove off. Which was a relief. Because all I really wanted was to be left alone. There's this thing about being my size—being small—whenever you skip a meal or decline a doughnut or something, people notice. They like to theorize. Spotting anorectics—it's like an American pastime."

"Tell me about it," I said. "I get that shit all the time."

She didn't laugh. "Okay. Whatever, Billy. So I sat out there the whole hour. And when Dan came back, he had this greasy bag in his hand. He comes to the steps and hands it to me. 'It's got a chipotle sauce,' he says. And then he says, 'We call this experiential defining.' Then he gives me this sad little smile and goes inside. I looked in the bag. It was a burrito of some kind."

"Cool," I said. "Did you eat it?"

"Yeah. I was pretty hungry. I hadn't had any breakfast."

"How was the chipotle sauce?"

"Actually, I don't think it had a chipotle sauce. I think it was just a regular old burrito. That was the sweetest part about it. I think the guy just saw that I was down and out and wanted to buy me something to eat."

I couldn't help but wonder how Mona could read so much into a burrito when she hadn't even batted an eye at the fancy Bellini dinner I'd made her so many weeks ago.

"That was just the first day I saw it." She hugged her knees to her chest. "That he *sees* so much more than he *says*. I hadn't really noticed before that. I'd just thought of him as some aging old egghead. But if you really watch him, you see that he's always listening to people carefully. And watching them. And not in a creepy way at all.

"And occasionally you'll see him do something like the burrito thing. Something that makes you realize that he's not shy . . . he just saves himself for the right moment, I guess. It's a kind of sadness . . . mixed with this odd sort of . . . *strength*."

The way she talked reminded me of girls talking about Holden Caulfield in English class. An uncomfortable mix of pity and lust.

"So . . . Did you interpret the burrito as a flirtation?"

"Not at all," Mona said. "It woke me up to him. And after that, I kind of approached training differently. I felt like he knew when I wasn't doing my best, so I pushed myself harder. I'd spend a couple of hours on a definition trying to get it perfect. I really wanted his praise, because I knew from him praise *means* something. And it worked. Dan kept giving me harder and harder words. And that's how, for the *Supplement,* he's already giving me words like 'drop' and 'come.' "

"I thought you were just unlucky," I said.

"No, not at all. I don't know why I didn't want to tell you that those words were *given* to me. But I get a kind of charge out of it when he hands me one of those words and says 'Up for a challenge?' "

I was trying not to laugh. It was probably the weirdest turn-on I'd ever heard of. "So it's not, um, lexicographical ambition that drives you?"

"Not really." Mona sounded sheepish. "It's Dan. It's wanting him to . . . I don't know, to keep noticing me, I guess. As pathetic as that sounds."

"Do you think he does?"

"Sort of . . . but probably not in the right way."

"What would be the right way?"

"Oh . . . you know," she said. "Don't make me spell it all out."

"All right," I said.

She was right. Some things were best left unspelled.

The tattered joke book caught my eye just as I was switching off the living room lights before bed. It was still lying on the futon where Mona had left it. I snapped the light off and headed to the bedroom, leaving the book there in the dark.

I knew I probably should have told Mona about the Hodgkin's. She'd asked about high school, she'd asked about pot smoking, and now she'd asked about the jokes. *When did you start reading joke books?* she'd wanted to know. It was a lighthearted question; it wouldn't have been fair, just then, to give her the true answer, to require her to snap into a serious mood, to weigh the conversation down.

I'd skipped over telling her three or four times now. Sometimes I do get lazy like that, I'll admit. It gets old— whipping it out, so to speak. *Cancer. Age eighteen.* People never expect it, and it always blows a big hole in the conversation. Especially with people my age. The reaction is pretty standard. They get quiet and say something apologetic, then forget whatever it was we were talking about before it came up. Then they're afraid of me for a couple days. Don't get me wrong—I get that it makes people uncomfortable. That's why sometimes it's just as well to save everybody their hand-wringing and keep my mouth shut. Mona and I had a good, natural repartee going. I didn't want to screw with that.

CHAPTER TWENTY-ONE

We were up to the K's in our defining. The days before Christmas dragged on. There didn't seem to be much happening in the K's, although I did get to learn about a few interesting "K" terms I'd never encountered before—like *kerygma* and *kerfuffle*. Did dictionary employment give me license to add a word like *kerfuffle* to my regular vocabulary? Was this what adulthood was to mean for me?

Key almost broke me. You would not think *key* a terribly complex word, right? But the cits were endless.

You must sign up for the workshop in advance. That is key.

There were endless cits for this newish predicate adjective. Then there were musical uses, sports uses, a ton of verb uses, and of course all the tiny variations on the basic device that unlocks or releases something. Plus a heroin use for good measure.

How could I start disliking such a thing? Three innocent little letters, signifying something so basic, even charming: a small treasured object, a key. A tiny magical device that opens doors and old hope chests and secret diaries. Ah, and people's hearts! The more I thought about it, the more I grew to hate it. *Key. KEY. KHHHEEEEEY.* I could imagine myself near-catatonic in a padded white room, hoarsely repeating the word, trying to clear the syllable out of my throat like a tenacious bit of phlegm.

Once, while I was engaged in this gloomy reverie, Dan approached my desk with a tabloid newspaper. *Hit by the Ugly Stick: Beauty Queens Need Not Apply,* read the main headline.

"I thought of you when I saw it," he said. "Since we'd talked so extensively about 'beauty queen.'"

As I took the article, I noticed a cutline: *"Not all Johns are looking for the proverbial delicate flower," says Madame Cassandra V.*

I thanked him and told him I looked forward to reading it. He laughed quietly and combed his fingers through his thick black hair. I was almost certain he hadn't read beyond the headline and had no idea what the article was about.

On my third day with *key,* my phone finally buzzed.

I stared at it as it buzzed a second time, and a third. Part of me was terrified at who might be on the other line. Anyone in the world could call me, and with any question. And I, the voice of the dictionary, would be expected to have the answer.

I picked up the receiver. "Hello?"

"Billy," said an unfamiliar female voice. "Dan tells me you're taking phone calls now."

"Yes. I guess so. Is this Sheila, from the front desk?"

"Mmm-hmm. So I've got a guy for you on line five. He has some sentence he wants to run by us. Wants to know if it's grammatically correct, he says."

"Okay," I said.

"Thanks," said Sheila.

Line 5. I tried to remember how to take a line. Nine-star-five? Zero-star-five? It took me a few tries before I got a voice.

"Hello?" a man's voice replied to mine.

"Hello, my name's Billy Webb. I'm one of the editors here at Samuelson. I'm told you have a grammatical question?"

"Yes, sir." The voice sounded small, faraway, and old. "I have a question. I have a sentence. If I read it to you, can you tell me if it's grammatically correct?"

"I'll try," I said. "Go ahead."

" 'She gave so much,' " the voice said, " 'and asked so little.' "

" 'She gave so much and asked so little,' " I repeated. "Is that the whole sentence?"

"Yes." The voice was almost whispering now.

"It sounds fine to me."

"The engraver said it was incorrect. He said it should be 'asked *for* so little.' "

"The engraver?" I asked, with a sinking feeling. "I'm sorry if this is a little forward. But can I ask, sir, what this is about?"

"It's for my wife's tombstone. We were married forty-one years. The girls and I talked a great deal about this. And that's what we agreed upon. 'She gave so much, and asked so little.' Because she really did give so much. And asked for so, so little in return."

"And they told you not to put that on the stone?"

"Yes. The engraver said it's incorrect."

I let the phone hang loosely in my hand for a moment.

"Hello?" the man said hoarsely.

"Yes. Sorry. I'm just thinking. It's fine, the sentence is fine, I just—"

I could have explained to him about descriptivist approaches to lexicography, grammar, and sentence structure. Or about stylistic choices being at the discretion of the writer. About the fluidity of usage.

Instead, I said, "Listen. Considering the situation here, though, I'd just like to run it by one of the bigwigs for you. Just so we can both feel absolutely sure about this."

I took the guy's name and number. Stephen Peterson.

Calling from God knows where. Somewhere in the United States, a little old man was sitting by his phone, waiting for me to give him the go-ahead on his own wife's epitaph.

I wrote *She gave so much, and asked so little* on a slip of paper, and brought it to Dan's office. The door was open.

"Dan," I said. He looked up from his copyediting. "I don't know if you overheard the conversation I just had on the phone. But I'd appreciate it if you would look at this sentence and tell me if you think there's anything wrong with it."

Dan raised his eyebrows, leaned over in his swivel chair, and took the slip out of my hand.

Looking at it, he said, "Billy?"

"I know it's a stupid question. But it's for some guy's wife's gravestone. I didn't want to give him a glib answer."

Dan handed it back to me.

"Big responsibility, I guess," he said, his eyes dancing between sympathy and amusement.

"Yeah."

"It's fine," he said. "But of course . . . I think you knew that."

I lingered there for a moment longer. I had a thousand more questions for him. He could probably answer them all, and still I wouldn't understand the meaning of his half-smile.

"Are you all right?" The kindly way Dan said it gave me a little twinge of sympathy for Mona. It was fairly obvious what drew her to him. Behind the gossamer bit of mystery was most likely a safe and solid place.

"Yeah. I'm fine. Thanks," I mumbled, and hurried back to my desk.

Stephen Peterson answered on the first ring. After I told him again, in a low voice, that the sentence was fine, he thanked me. "God bless you," he said, and hung up. I didn't reach for my cits then. I sat there wondering how many daughters Mrs. Peterson had, and what ambitions she'd probably cast aside to raise them. And if, in the end, Mr. Peterson felt he'd been a good husband. I was still staring into empty space when Mona came to fetch me.

"I know it's freezing today," she whispered. "But didn't we have a cit date or something?"

As we started down the company steps together, I told her about my phone call.

"What the fuck was that tombstone guy thinking?" Mona said, when I was finished. "Telling that family they're wrong?"

"I think if you wanted to get technical about it," I said, "you could say the sentence is vague, like she generally didn't literally *ask* very much. Didn't ask many questions, or whatever."

"I know what the guy *meant*. But what the hell does he think his job is? He's not writing word stumpers for a stupid newspaper. I mean, sure, if you want to be a pain in the ass, you could say that. But their meaning was clear enough. Thoughtful. Simple."

"Yeah. I know."

"That's just so *wrong*," she fumed. "What the hell kind of world are we living in? What kind of fucked-up priorities do people have that you'd tell a little old man just trying to honor his dead wife that he can't put what he wants on her tombstone? Over some little bit of sophistry, no less? Is that what the rules of language are *for*? To keep people from expressing their deepest emotions? To make people feel *stupid*?"

"It's too bad Mr. Phillips is a bit of a chauvinist. Because otherwise, I think you two would really—"

"Is this the kind of thing people use our books for?" Mona's voice had turned shrill. "Is this what we're encouraging here? Do people really think this is what language is all about?"

We approached our barren little park spot, and headed for the bench.

"Language . . . eloquence," Mona insisted, "is supposed to be one of the things that separates us from grunting primates. If you turn it into something you beat your chest over, something that only serves to make you better than someone else, or make you *insensitive* to other human beings—then you may as *well* be a grunting primate."

"Yeah," I said, opening my lunch bag.

"So you got the stuff?" she asked—referring, of course, to the citations.

Between the two of us, we'd uncovered quite a few new ones:

nerd

Everybody looked up. I think I saw a few glares. Maybe I was imagining it. Scout says that in my head I turn this place into a fairy-tale dungeon, exaggerating its darkness and its cold. Interpreting harmless social ineptitude as clammy, crooked-nosed villainy. (Why can't you just call a *nerd* a nerd? he'd say.) Imagining towers and spires on the place. (Is that why you keep your hair so long?)

7

trash man

At the end of the day, the bag was still at my feet. It was moist inside, which made it more embarrassing. It seemed something that definitely should not be in my possession. A bloated, disembodied organ, full of shrapnel. I wasn't sure what to do with it. It didn't seem appropriate to stuff it in my tiny wastepaper basket. The custodian wouldn't be anticipating glass. He might cut himself. I took it with me instead. I'd find a Dumpster on the way home. Or just put it on the curb for the *trash man*, and then forget about it. To fling the bag onto a curb or into a Dumpster would probably give me some satisfaction.

10

ponytail

Besides. The shattering of that glass and the breaking of that anemic silence was enough violence for one day. No more seemed possible. I looked up from your book and there, all of a sudden, was a man. I thought he looked familiar, but from where I couldn't say. The library, perhaps? He had scraggly gray hair, pulled into a *ponytail*. I smiled hello. He was wearing a black concert T-shirt with lightning flash letters. I don't remember the name of the band. It must have been a band I've never heard of.

13

showtime

On the news, that evening's top story was of the dead man found in Freeman Park. Not on the paved path where I had left him, but farther into the wooded area. Stabbed in the neck and bled to death under the evergreens. Derek Brownlow was 42 years old. It was *showtime* now. But oddly, I had a sudden craving for a cup of tea—sweet, milky, and warm. I put on a pot of water and watched it steam and bubble, trying to remember my last cup of tea. The exact temperature, the amount of sugar, how long it had steeped, the strength of the flavor. When I'd had that last sip, I had no idea I wouldn't get another, I'd break my glass, I'd never experience the exact sensation of that cup of tea again. It had been, in retrospect, a particularly delicious cup of tea.

22

opt out

So I opted for silence. Since the only other option was explicit speech, and all the inevitables that would follow: drama, crying, comforting, fingerprints, uncomfortable questions, men in matching blue shirts, photographers outside the police station. I *opted out* of all of that. Because his quiet beckoned me like a warm bed, a soft pillow, a good book, a hot cup of tea.

25

"The glass." There was awe in Mona's voice. "That's why she's so fixated on the glass."

"*Stabbed in the neck?*" I said. "She stabbed him in the *neck* with it?"

Mona lowered her voice almost to a whisper. "Looks that way."

I skimmed the first cit again.

"And it's looking more and more like self-defense," I said. "How so?"

"In 'ponytail' she's taken by surprise by a sleazy-looking guy, and by 'showtime' she's left somebody for dead. And in one of the cits Mr. Phillips found—I think it was 'ball of wax'—she was trying to make some vague point about self-defense. But yet she didn't want to talk to the police. That's the funny thing about it."

"Well, maybe not so funny. Can you ever be totally confident that you're gonna get off on self-defense?"

"Not sure," I said. "I can't claim any expertise on the self-defense plea. Outside of what I've seen on *Law and Order*. Do you think that's all it is? Maybe she's still culpable in some way."

"Maybe," Mona said, absently taking out a yogurt container. "But it makes me sad, the way she's telling this story. You have to wonder...did she tell anyone? Or were these little papers like her confessional? Do you think she was raped or something? It seems so lonely. I mean, can you imagine?"

"It's that final sip of tea that kinda gets me, actually," I said. " *Particularly delicious.*' "

I held the "showtime" cit in my hand and felt my fingers grow raw from the cold.

"It's sort of funny how she puts it," I mused. "What you remember from before. The moment before things went terribly wrong."

Mona stirred her pink yogurt.

"With all due respect," she pointed out, "I think the tea is really the least of the revelations here."

"Is it?"

"Oh, you're just being contrary now. Maybe you don't want to see how very sad this story has become."

"Maybe," I said.

I gobbled my sandwich quickly, wishing I'd remembered mustard. Then I blew on my hands to warm them and tried to think of something to lighten the mood.

"I'm glad she managed to fit 'nerd' into her narrative. Seems appropriate, considering the setting."

Mona smiled just slightly. "Did you know that they don't really know the origin of 'nerd'?"

I shrugged. "Like most teenage slang, seems like."

"Yeah, but 'nerd'...the first print appearance is in a Dr. Scuss book. And I don't think it's entirely clear if that's where it started."

"Did you answer a letter about this?"

"No," Mona said sheepishly. "I looked it up on my first day at Samuelson. I finished the front matter really early, and just spent the rest of the day looking up 'nerd,' 'dork,' 'geek,' 'dweeb'. . . ."

"Trying to identify which one you'd officially become?"

"Something like that." Mona looked down at her purple mittens and pressed her hands together carefully.

"Everything all right?" I asked her.

She nodded. "I wanted to ask you something, actually, Billy. I'd been meaning to ask you . . ."

"Yeah?" I said, prompting her.

"Are you gonna be home in Connecticut for the whole holiday?"

"Christmas Day, you mean?"

"Or Christmas Eve. Either one. I was going to offer to make us a Christmas dinner of some kind."

"Christmas Eve dinner?"

"Christmas Eve or whenever. Post-family Christmas night, perhaps. I'll be by myself the whole holiday. I thought it might be nice to—"

"But you don't know how to cook," I said.

Mona rolled her eyes. "Are you sure that's how you want to respond? To my rather pathetic request for holiday company?"

"You're right," I replied. "That actually sounds really nice. Maybe I could just do Christmas Day with my family. That'd probably be enough."

"Never mind. I don't want to mess up your family plans."

"We actually don't have any plans yet. Our holiday plans are usually silent, assumed. Therefore breakable. I think this could work."

"Really, Billy. It was a stupid idea."

"No, it's not. But why aren't you going home?"

"I can't afford to fly home for both Thanksgiving *and* Christmas," Mona explained, "in vacation time or cash. My stepdad wanted to try and get me a ticket for just two nights, but I said no. I don't like spending other people's money. And I've already decided to go to the movies on Christmas Day. Maybe do a double feature."

"That settles it," I said. "I'll bring dessert."

Mona stood up from the bench.

"You looking forward to your first office Christmas party?" she asked as we approached the Samuelson building.

"When?"

"In just a few days. On the twenty-third. You didn't get the memo?"

"I guess not. Certain parts of this job seem to fly pretty regularly over my head."

"We get half the afternoon off. They decorate the lunch-room and serve wine and fancy hors d'oeuvres."

"Does anyone get plastered?" I asked.

"No. Dimly lit, perhaps. But not plastered. It's all about the respectable appearance of holiday cheer. But if you want to get wasted, Billy, feel free. By all means, put the 'ass' back in 'editorial assistant.' "

"I already have, I think."

Mona shook her head.

"Don't flatter yourself, Billy boy."

CHAPTER TWENTY-TWO

Tom was carrying a hibachi out onto the porch when I got out of my car. He waved and I waved back.

"You're gonna barbecue in this weather?" I asked him.

"Sure. Barb just got her Christmas bonus. Brought home a few nice steaks."

"Good for you guys," I said. "Enjoy it."

"We will."

I hesitated before unlocking my door. "Hey, Tom?"

"What?"

"Jimmy says you've got a pretty good memory—"

"Excellent, in fact," Tom interrupted.

"Okay. Then maybe you can fill me in on something. You've lived in Claxton your whole life, right?"

"Yeah. Shoot."

"Do you remember a murder happening here in the eighties? Of a guy named Brownlow?"

"Brownlow?" Tom ripped open his bag of charcoal, frowning. "Doesn't ring a bell."

"He was murdered in Freeman Park, I believe."

"Oh. You mean the Glass Girl business. Of course."

"Glass Girl?" I croaked.

"Yeah. That was so stupid. I like to think it was some lesbionic feminist vigilante justice group. Then the idiotic local news starts calling 'em 'The Glass Girl.' Lame."

"Vigilante justice?"

"Sure. They figured out the bastard was a sicko."

"What do you mean?"

"Well, that's where the whole Glass Girl theory came from. This sicko had been in jail for beating the crap outta some girl. And there was some other shit he probably did. Some real sicko shit. At first everybody thought he was just some poor sucker who'd gotten knifed or something. Took them a while to figure out about him, but when they did . . . turned out he was a real psycho.

"Figure he had it coming one way or another. But there were inconsistencies in that Glass Girl theory. Didn't sound to me like it could be some teenage girl taking that big guy on. *The Daily* did a great series about five years ago, about the city's cold cases. And there were definitely some big holes in that Glass Girl case."

I fumbled to find the right key, then dropped the whole keychain on the porch.

"Why do you ask?" Tom said. "Glass Girl's pretty old news these days."

I stooped for my keys. "Oh, someone at work just referred to it, that's all. It sounded kind of interesting. When did they actually do that cold case series?"

"Oh, I don't know . . . '98 or so?"

"Huh. Sure sounds interesting."

"Yeah. If it interests you, you should check it out sometime."

"Yeah, maybe I will."

● ● ●

When I got up to my apartment, I sank into a kitchen chair to consider this new take on Mary Anne. Mary Anne as everyone's mystery, not just mine and Mona's.

Why had I begun to think of Mary Anne as ours? Dan had spent his nights with her. Mr. Phillips had sat in the sun with her, telling her war stories. But what was left of her here, the cits, her story—that was *ours,* because we had found it. But now that it was shaping up, it was clear that whoever the story really belonged to, there were certainly people who had a greater claim to it than us.

How strong was Claxton's interest in the story? I wondered. And how accurate was Tom's take on Derek Brownlow? It sounded like Mona hadn't gone far enough in her newspaper search. I decided I'd try to get to the library before it closed for the holidays.

My father called me just as I was pouring bottled vodka sauce on my corkscrew pasta. I told him about my Christmas Eve plans.

"But William," he insisted, "you have to come for Christmas Eve. This is the year."

"The year for what?"

"For the flaming plum pudding. You were so helpful with the Thanksgiving dessert medley. I've decided that the flaming plum pudding would be a satisfying joint project."

"So let's do it Christmas Day."

"No, William. I'm doing a torte and a cookie platter Christmas Day. Flaming plum pudding is definitely Christmas Eve fare. And we'll be using real beef suet. The oldfashioned way. No Crisco substitutions."

"What's beef suet?"

"What are they teaching you there at your new job? *Suet* is fat from around the cow's organs."

"Hot damn, Dad. That sounds right up Mom's alley. *She* can help you this time."

"That's ridiculous. Your mother has no interest in my yuletide culinary experiments."

"Make it with Jen, then," I said. "She'd love it."

"She won't help," Dad said, sounding small and defeated. I thought of old Mr. Stephen Peterson, and felt a little sad. Maybe Jimmy was right. Maybe you turn into an old man quicker than you'd ever expect.

"No," I admitted. "But she'd write a poem about it."

My father sighed exaggeratedly into the phone.

"I can hear it now," I said. " 'The flames. THE FLAMES.' "

"Don't be absurd. Your sister's writing is highly re-strained."

"Do you think Jen ever writes poems about us?"

"I'm not sure," my father answered. "She wrote this strange one about Nixon's daughters a couple of years back. I couldn't help but wonder what that one was really about."

"Hmm. I'll have to check it out sometime, if she's ever willing to dig it up."

"William. Why don't you just bring this girl down to have Christmas with us?"

"That would be a little scary for this stage of the relation-ship. I mean, we're not even *dating*."

"Then why in heaven's name are you spending Christmas Eve with her?"

A fairly logical question. I paused before answering.

"Well?" my father said.

"This girl isn't a girlfriend," I said carefully. "But she's more like . . . a good investment. She's the sort who might grow into me someday. She's the sort who might realize, maybe in a year or two, what kind of potential I have. She might recommend me to a friend."

For a few moments, no more sounds came from my father's end.

"That doesn't sound very promising to me, William," he said finally.

"Well—"

"Not promising enough to disappoint your mother like this."

"How do you know she'll be disappointed? She won't care. As long as I'm there Christmas Day."

"It's really too bad you're going to miss it. Your sister says she has an announcement. Another poetry prize, or something, I think. And what about Christmas morning?" Dad sounded a little peevish.

"How about this," I said. "I have dinner with Mona. Did I mention I'm bringing dessert? I thought you'd at least like that part. Then I drive down home after. I'll probably arrive around midnight. Just like Santa Claus."

"Your mother wouldn't want you driving in the middle of the night."

"I think that's what I'll do. I'll bet the highway will be empty then. Who drives around in the middle of the night Christmas Eve? I'll fly down 91. Be there in an hour. We'll all wake up together, and do the Christmas morning thing."

"I'm not going to tell you what to do, William," my father said. "But if that's what you choose to do, then at the very least, don't drive like a maniac. If you're going to miss the meal anyway, there's no sense *rushing*."

"That's the plan, then. I'll come late Christmas Eve. You'll save the cooking project till the next day?"

"We'll see," he said. "Uh . . . William . . ."

"Yeah?"

"I've been thinking. You'd better do your yearly checkup before long. It's about that time, isn't it?"

"I already did it," I said. "A couple of weeks ago."

"Oh? You went all the way down to Hartford and saw Dr. B.?"

"No," I said. "I went and found a local doctor. Through my very own HMO."

"And everything was . . ."

"Normal. Of course."

"You should have called us. Just to let us know. And I'm sure we could've arranged for a way for you to see Dr. B. Your mother and I would have paid for it if it was a matter of cost . . ."

"Don't worry about it. The guys up here are pretty good. After the crystal elixir and the colonic irrigation, I was feeling a hundred percent."

"Very amusing. So you had a scan, then?"

"*Yes.* But there's nothing to worry about. It'll be five years on the twenty-eighth. I'm even thinking of celebrating a little."

Dad paused before speaking.

"William," he said again.

"What, Dad?"

"If this Mona doesn't already recognize your potential, then she's probably not a very smart girl."

"Oh *God.* I was only joking around about that."

"I suspect that you weren't. And if you really want to wow this girl, can I suggest a flaming dessert? I don't know what would be more impressive than a dessert presented in flaming liquor."

"I'll keep that in mind," I promised. "But I was thinking of doing some kind of soufflé."

I heard my dad take in a breath.

"Well then," he said. "Just remember to look for those soft, curled peaks when beating your whites."

"Will do," I said, chuckling inwardly. I'd mentioned the soufflé just to get him to say it. *Soft, curled peaks.* "See you soon."

Soft, curled peaks. The intensity and calm precision of his pronunciation made me think of the most common phrase from his old repertoire.

A dull, throbbing pain.

My most vivid and consistent memory of my father in my junior high and high school years is of him sitting down nightly at the cleared kitchen table with his cordless phone and a gimlet. Every night he'd call to check on the people whose wisdom teeth he'd pulled that day.

You'll feel a dull, throbbing pain, perhaps through most of the night. Take one of the codeine pills I prescribed. By morning, the worst should be behind you. If the pain gets worse, you should give me a call.

Occasionally there was more: *Which one? The bottom right one? Yes. I thought so. That was the difficult one coming out.*

His tone usually softened if someone seemed to be really suffering. But there was always the ominous warning of the *dull, throbbing pain.*

As I entered high school, I was aware that about 75 percent of the time, the person on the line was one of my schoolmates. But usually I didn't have any idea who he had on the phone. Rarely did I even wonder which bloody maw of which of my classmates he had stared down into that day.

Has the bleeding stopped? Amy, can you put your mother on? I can't understand what you're trying to say.

Naturally, he used only first names most of the time. It didn't occur to me then that he might be growing weary of yanking out people's teeth. He pulled his last tooth when I was about halfway through my treatments. About six months later, we were both ready to go back to school: me to college, he to culinary school. In between, we spent a lot of time at home together. We didn't have many friends, he and I. We experimented with his new Cuisinart mixer. We counted the days.

CHAPTER TWENTY-THREE

The office was shifting uneasily. Everybody wanted to head down to the Christmas party, but no one wanted to be the first to get up.

Mona drummed on the side of my cubicle.

"C'mon down, Billy," she whispered. "Party's starting."

"Go ahead," I said, picking up a new pile. "I'll be right down. I'm just rounding off my last part of 1951."

She nodded and took off. I glanced down at my work. The W's of 1951 had been especially productive:

> **warm spot**
>
> Inevitably, I would have to leave Scout with the rest. I regret this, because if there's one thing for which I have a *warm spot* here, it's him. I wish there were a path that included him, but that's impossible. The day Brownlow chose me was the last day I really occupied this space. He wished to remove me from it, and in a sense, he succeeded. But any losses suffered by either Scout or me are significantly fewer in this version—the one where my elbow slipped and knocked over a glass. This is the best version either of us can probably conceive of, and the only one I care to imagine. Somewhere deep in the layers of remote possibility, there was a version that ended with me

telling him, over tea and pie. Instead of this way. But that version won't ever be.

46

white knight

As we sat at my kitchen table, my mind would often wander from the conversation, and eventually settle me into a familiar image. It wasn't a confused or disturbing one, as those of earlier weeks. It contained nothing rotten, nothing undead. It was me, floating on an inner tube in a lake, with him sitting on a dock nearby. He was reading a book, enjoying the breeze, only occasionally glancing up to smile at me. He didn't seem to notice that I was slowly bobbing away from the dock, but still, I'd just look back at him and wave. The sight of him so content was comforting, but it felt pretty natural, even exhilarating, to drift away. But what was it I wanted to tell him? Bobbing lazily, often I couldn't quite remember, until the last minute, when I was nearly out of hearing distance. By then, I'd need to shout it, if I was ever going to say it at all. It was that he shouldn't ask himself later if he should have reached out and pulled me back. He shouldn't think back and wonder what he might have done differently. He was, in his way, my *white knight*. That I would remember, even if the rest was too hard.

44

Warm spot nagged at me. Mona had wondered if Mary Anne had ever told anyone, and this felt like an answer— probably *no*. Mary Anne longed for a "version" of the story in which she told it to Dan. Maybe her silence was getting to her. Maybe she desperately wished she could tell it. But if they were truly lovers, and if it was truly self-defense—which seemed all but certain now—why *couldn't* she tell him?

I had just a few more to go on the W's. I looked through a couple of piles. Then the lights went out. Someone must have thought the editorial office had completely emptied, and decided to save electricity. Maybe Dan. He struck me as the frugal sort. But there was enough dull winter light from the high windows that I could still squint at the corners of the cits. A cit from the *New Yorker*. One from a book called *Interventions*. *Reader's Digest*. *Glamour*. *The Broken Teaglass*. Another. I held the cit up to the light to read it.

wrap-up

Before the final *wrap-up*, Red, I should explain about your book. But doesn't this just beat all? I have no idea what happened to it, in the end. We both know now that I dropped it sometime during that twelve-second stretch between there and here. But after that? Maybe the police found it. But why, then, wouldn't they mention it in the newspapers? An odd finding, wouldn't you think? Maybe it still sits there now, in a plastic bag at the police department, in a file drawer. A kind of shibboleth to distinguish the real girl from the hoaxes, should anyone ever come forward. The real girl will know the title of the lost history.

47

I threw the cits down and made my way around the cubicles till I found the stairwell.

The cafeteria was barely recognizable. Someone had moved the tables from their usual mess-hall lineup. Now they lined the sides of the room, covered with red paper tablecloths. Each one displayed a different elegant option for consumption: a punch bowl surrounded by plastic glasses, a wine spread, an elaborate tower of fruit. The room was lit solely by little white Christmas lights and a few strategically placed candles. A jazzy version of "Jingle Bells" was playing softly against the subdued chatter of the celebrants.

So here it was again—the holidays. December 28 was almost upon me, and without much warning. I had none of the usual rhythm of the academic semester to remind me what month it was. Aside from the occasional Christmas carol in the grocery store, I'd had few seasonal cues. No Christmas tree, no Christmas cards, no trips to the mall.

Mr. Phillips swept by me, wearing a red ribbed turtleneck sweater. It looked new and youthful. Metrosexual, even.

"Billy's here," he said to no one in particular. "The party can commence."

He was holding a wineglass in his loosely upturned palm. Without waiting for a response from me, he approached one of the typists, a redheaded lady in a brown dress. She laughed gaily at whatever he was saying, which I didn't quite hear.

People were huddled in front of the tables in mostly predictable combinations: little clusters of typists, George and the older etymologist chatting together, a crowd of editors in their thirties knotted in front of the finger desserts. Grace was weaving her way in and out of the groups, carrying around somebody's thickly bundled and impressively tasseled baby.

My eye eventually caught Dan and Mona, who were standing over by the hors d'oeuvres. Dan was examining some phyllo-wrapped concoction with casual interest. After a moment, he pushed the whole thing into his mouth with one deliberate and tortoiselike motion. As he chewed, Mona pointed to an object on her own little plate and said something. He nodded, still chewing, and scanned the contents of the table in front of them. Mona gazed around the room for a moment. When she saw me, she grinned, waved, and made a little *sip sip* motion with her curled hand at her mouth. Since she didn't wave me over, I decided to check out the cheese table.

I sampled a few cheese cubes. None of them tasted exactly like cheddar, but none of them tasted distinctly like any other type of cheese. The variegated colors were maybe just a ruse to give the vague experience of variety. Or maybe the cubes were just too small to give a full taste experience. I started holding the cheese cubes up to examine their colors in the meager light, and to push them into little pyramids on my paper plate. When I had four of the lightest-color cubes, I popped them all in my mouth at once. Definitely mozzarella.

I made my way to the wine table and helped myself to a clear plastic cup half-filled with red wine. It was sweeter than I expected. I didn't feel like drinking the whole cup or bothering with the guilty buzz it might produce. We all had to drive home, after all.

Probably there was more satisfaction to be had upstairs. Upstairs, where for once the citation files stood alone, in the dark. Open for the taking. Promising to fill in all the hungry hollows.

I put the cup in the barrel by the door. As I reached for the door, I heard Mr. Phillips calling, "Hey, Billy . . . Where do you think you're going?" But I knew he was having too much fun to come after me.

I didn't bother to turn any of the upstairs lights on. I preferred the peace of the darkened office. With 1951 finished, I figured Mona and I might want to begin on 1952 after Christmas Eve dinner. With our 1952 list in hand, I wandered into the cit stacks and started extracting the right words. After I found the first fourteen in the file, there was still quite a lot of room in my backpack. The file was very forgiving, so tightly packed with words that you could take giant chunks out and the cits just snapped back into place as if nothing was missing. I took about fifteen more to complete my Santa sack.

Just as I was zipping up my backpack, the office lights came on.

"Were you working in the dark?"

I turned. It was Dan.

"Just taking a break from that party," I explained too quickly, laying a casual hand over my enormous backpack. "I'm not so into these holiday things."

"Me neither," Dan said. There was a slight and unfamiliar lilt to his voice. His face was a little flushed. He'd probably had a few cups of wine. "I came up here to regroup. Something rather perplexing just happened down there."

"Really? Something perplexing?"

"Mildly." He shrugged.

I was about to ask him what it was when he leaned on my cubicle.

"So tell me," he said. "Your middle name's really Homer?"

"No. Who told you that? It was just a nickname at one time."

Dan didn't look surprised. "What's your real middle name, then?"

"Benjamin."

"Really. Mine is Scout."

I hesitated. My heart was racing. "As in the *To Kill a Mockingbird* character?"

"No," Dan replied slowly. "As in Cub. As in Eagle."

I waited for a response to come to me, but none did. I got the distinct feeling that I was disappointing him somehow.

"You have plans for the holiday?" I asked, frantically improvising.

"Yes. My family is having Christmas Eve in Lenox. In the Berkshires."

"Is that where you grew up?"

Dan nodded. "My mother still lives there. And my brother as well."

I could have shared my own plans, but he hadn't asked and likely didn't care. I rummaged in my brain for some other innocuous conversational topic.

"That reminds me of a joke," I said.

"Yes?"

"So a guy is alone for Christmas, so he goes to a diner to treat himself to a little Christmas breakfast. He orders the eggs Benedict. A little while later, the waiter brings his meal in a hubcap. He looks at it and says, 'Hey, man. What's with the hubcap?' And the waiter goes—"

I flung my hand out and lowered my voice to deliver the punch line in a baritone.

" 'There's no plate like chrome for the hollandaise.' "

For a moment, Dan stood in stunned silence. Then he laughed. Not his usual parched chuckle, but a real laugh. I had a feeling it was not the punch line, exactly, that amused him.

"Very good," he said, rubbing his eye. "Well. I don't want to keep you. You have a good holiday, Billy."

CHAPTER TWENTY-FOUR

I headed for the library right after saying goodbye to Dan.

Mona had found that articles about Derek Brownlow trailed off about two weeks after his death, and stopped there. I hadn't thought to ask Tom how long it took the police to learn about Brownlow's background, and he probably wouldn't have remembered anyway. So I started where Mona had left off—the beginning of November 1985.

After about an hour of microfishing, I started to find the events to which Tom had referred:

Claxton Daily News
DECEMBER 12, 1985

KILLER IN OUR MIDST?

*Deceased man had a criminal record
and a history of attacking women*

CLAXTON — Derek George Brownlow, the victim of a gruesome murder in Freeman Park in October, may not have been a victim at all, according to new details released by police yesterday. Brownlow might have died while attempting to abduct a woman, police are now theorizing.

"We found some items in Mr. Brownlow's car and apartment that forced us to reconsider our thinking on his death," said Sgt. John Polaski, who's leading the investigation. "And we've been working with several out-of-state law enforcement agencies to confirm Brownlow's criminal record."

Brownlow, who moved to Claxton just four months ago from Fitchtown, Pennsylvania, served seven months in county prison there in 1983 for assaulting a young woman, whom police said he had been stalking. According to court documents, Brownlow broke her arm and knocked out several of her teeth when he attempted to abduct her outside the office building where she worked.

In Brownlow's Highland Street apartment in Claxton, police found a collection of "disturbing" pornography and evidence that may link Brownlow to other crimes, Sgt. Polaski said.

"Over the last few days, we've been working very closely with law enforcement officials in Mr. Brownlow's last known residence, Wittburg, Pennsylvania. They've been investigating a death there, which occurred in 1979, and evidence we found here may be helpful to them," Sgt. Polaski said during a press conference at police headquarters.

In that case, police are trying to link Brownlow to the murder of an ER nurse whose remains were found in a wooded area only a few yards from the state highway. Evidence indicated the woman had been bound with duct tape before she was stabbed to death. Hospital records indicate the woman had treated Brownlow for minor injuries just months before her death.

Claxton police found two rolls of duct tape in Brownlow's car, Polaski said.

"Knowing that Mr. Brownlow worked for a hardware store, we didn't realize the importance of the rolls of duct tape until we spoke with police in Wittburg," Polaski said.

According to past reports, two witnesses told police that a young girl, probably teenaged, was walking in Freeman Park at dusk. She entered the path just as they were leaving the park. She was described as fair-skinned, average height, with light hair.

"If that young woman saw what occurred or, heaven forbid, was involved, we would hope she would come forward and give us any details of the event," Polaski said. "It would certainly help us in this case, but possibly also in others."

As I neared the end of the article, a freezing sensation crept up my arms. After finishing it, I had to stand up and walk around the library for a few minutes. I paced up and down the current periodicals, scanning the magazine covers. A copy of *Bon Appétit* caught my eye, with a nice-looking shrimp scampi on its cover. But upon reaching for the magazine, I discovered my hand was shaking too hard to turn its pages. A woman in a sparkly pink sweatsuit peered up at me as I fumbled it back onto its shelf.

I sat back down but didn't read the article again. The details were already burned into my memory, and I had trouble determining which was the creepiest of them. Probably the poor dead Pennsylvania nurse. But then there was the duct tape—that was a close second. Also Mary Anne herself, creeping by in the second-to-last paragraph. Surely she was the blonde girl in the park. Mr. Phillips had never said she was pale, but he'd mentioned she was delicate and strawberry blonde. Close enough. It was disconcerting to see her like this—just a glimpse of a girl someone barely saw. Just whispering by, and then gone.

She was so candid and emotional on paper. Why did she choose to make herself a ghost in real life? Could there really be anything at play here but self-defense? Could their encounter have been planned? Maybe they'd developed some connection as a result of Samuelson correspondence? Maybe Brownlow had tried to trap her somehow? Or perhaps Brownlow had done something to her, and she was traumatized into silence. But then, if she wanted to stay silent, why confess at all? Even if only to the cit files?

I made a copy of the article for Mona. I'd be arriving at her place Christmas Eve with this article tucked under one arm and a bottle of red wine under the other. Now all I needed was a gift.

Once, in college, I found myself standing behind a guy at a grocery store who was buying only two items: a dozen pink roses and a box of condoms. There's something to be said for knowing exactly what you want to say with a gift. When it came to my obligatory gift for Mona, I had no such clarity. I wandered the mall for a couple of hours, considering and discarding gift ideas. Some little animal earrings might say, *I think you're cute, but not in a romantic way.* A small framed Edward Hopper print might say, *I recognize your simple but sophisticated tastes.* Body Shop products could have any number of sticky possibilities, such as *I like to imagine you naked in a steaming tub of bubbles.*

I gave up and got her a couple of CDs. I'd noticed she had a pretty meager selection of music that first time I'd gone to her apartment. My final selections were *Johnny Cash's Greatest Hits* and *Buena Vista Social Club.* Something for each Mona.

After seconds on apple-cranberry pie (my father's recipe), we sat together on Mona's fancy black couch. She'd framed one of her windows with a string of twinkly lights, so we got to unwrap each other's gifts in its cozy white glow. Mona was looking pretty festive, with her soft red cardigan and her hair twisted up into a beaded clip. It looked like she might have been wearing eye shadow, but maybe it was just the way the light was hitting her eyelids.

After unwrapping my CDs, Mona thrust a flat, silver-wrapped box into my hands.

"I almost had a T-shirt made up for you that said *Coed Naked Wordsmithing*," she said. "For casual Fridays."

"What stopped you?"

"Eh. That whole 'Coed Naked' thing is pretty old."

"Not for some."

Mona tapped the box. "Well, in any case. You're not getting one. Not from me, anyway. Open it."

Inside the box was a pair of soft black woolen gloves. I wasn't sure how to react to this gift. It seemed a little like the sort of thing my mother would buy for my father in an off year when she couldn't come up with something more creative.

"I wish I was a knitter," Mona said. "Then this present would seem a lot more thoughtful."

"And you'd seem a lot dorkier," I said, picking them up. "They're nice."

Mona watched me for a moment before asking, "Do you know why I got you these?"

"No," I admitted.

"Because I've never seen you wear gloves. Even on our park bench lunches. You always look like you're struggling to hold on to your sandwich."

"That's true."

"Is it a macho thing, or—"

"No," I said. There was no real explanation besides absent-mindedness. As the temperatures dropped, I'd meant to buy a hat and gloves, maybe a scarf. In the strained effort to transform myself into a functioning workaday adult, I hadn't gotten everything in order yet. It was hard enough to get up at six every morning and put the garbage out on Thursdays. Details were often overlooked: flossing, hygienic storage of leftovers, getting my emissions checked. I didn't know whether to regard Mona's observant eye with gratitude or irritation.

Johnny Cash serenaded us. I admired my woolly black hands.

"I have something else for you," I told her. "Not exactly a present, though."

I went to the kitchen and got the article out of my jacket.

"Our mystery's just about solved, I think," I said, handing it to her.

Mona read through the article, punctuating nearly every paragraph with a little gasp.

"Wow," she said, looking up. Her face had gone pale. "Probably Mary Anne did it."

"It sure sounds like it," I said. "But then why didn't she come forward? I mean, if it was self-defense?"

"Lots of reasons, probably. Remember how she said she didn't trust policemen? Maybe she didn't think they'd believe it was self-defense."

"Maybe," I said.

"Can't you just see the headlines? *'Word Nerd Defines "Vigilante Justice."'* I mean, maybe she was terrified of a media circus."

"But if she was just defending herself, then she had nothing to be ashamed of," I pointed out. "Right?"

"I guess we don't really know that for sure, do we?" Mona said softly. "We don't have all the pieces yet. Maybe there's a piece that makes her culpable in some way. Maybe just some small piece that made her doubt she could plead self-defense."

Johnny Cash was crooning a sad song now. I squinted at the square of Christmas lights around Mona's window. *Some small piece*. Seemed reasonable, but I didn't see where such a piece would fit in with everything we already knew. Everything we knew pointed at self-defense.

"But then, maybe she just didn't see it as anyone's business," Mona suggested. "Brownlow was dead. He couldn't hurt anyone else anymore, whether Mary Anne went public or not. What would be the point of confessing?"

"I guess there wouldn't be a *point,* sure. It just seems like what most normal, law-abiding folks would do. Help the police out. Get it off your chest. Put everyone's mind at ease. Then try to move on with your life."

Mona sighed, tossed the article onto the couch next to me, and then started picking nervously at the cuff of her elegant red cardigan. "I don't know. This whole thing is *crazy.*"

We sat in silence. After a few minutes, I started to hear a gentle tearing sound. She was yanking at a knotted thread on the edge of her cuff.

"You shouldn't do that," I said. "You're going to rip a hole in your sleeve. Is that cashmere?"

"Billy." She stopped her fiddling but didn't look at me. "How come you waited all night to show me that article?"

"It just seemed like we should have dinner and presents first. This Brownlow murder isn't a very Christmasy story, you know?"

Mona finally looked up. Her eyes looked dark and grave. I wasn't sure if it was the seriousness of her expression or the dim lighting, but for a moment, she looked much older than usual. "Neither was Ebenezer Scrooge weeping at his own sorry grave. Neither is Jimmy Stewart contemplating suicide."

I folded up the *Claxton Daily* article and slid it onto Mona's coffee table.

"You know what's the least Christmasy thing, really?" This was a subject I could really get into. "That song 'Grandma Got Run Over by a Reindeer.' I heard it on the way home from the mall yesterday."

"I kinda like that song," she protested. "I liked it when I was little, anyway."

"I used to like it too. Until one Christmas Eve when I was about thirteen. It came on the radio while we were sitting around my grandmother's living room. She was like, 'What is this? Is this supposed to be funny? I've never heard anything so asinine.' Then she started ranting about how grandmothers are always treated like some kind of joke. My grandmother was a little like you, actually. It was often a little surprising what would offend her."

I was afraid Mona might be put off by the comparison, but she just grinned.

"But what really depresses me about that song," I continued, "is not the lyrics so much as the fact that it survived my grandmother. She died four years ago, but that stupid song keeps going on. On and on, year in and year out. My grandmother in all of her dignity and intelligence is gone, but that song's still jingling its way into eternity. That stupid song will bury us all."

Mona sat back and closed her eyes.

"Oh wow," she said. "That takes the cake. Pour me another glass of wine."

I picked up our wine bottle and filled her glass.

"Christmasy . . . ," I said, feeling I should somehow lighten

the mood. Her eyes were still closed. "I wonder if that's in the dictionary?"

Mona sighed and opened her eyes.

"Surely it is," she said. "But frankly, does anyone care?"

For that, I leaned over and kissed her on the side of the head, just behind her ear. Her hair was stiff with gel or hair-spray or something.

"Merry Christmas, Mona," I said.

CHAPTER TWENTY-FIVE

Christmas with my family went without incident. Dad's flaming rum pudding was a success, and I drove home the following afternoon. On the eve of my return to work, I stayed up late flipping through 1952 cits, and found:

button-down

I don't remember how long we sat together like that, perched in the middle of the room on wooden chairs like little kids isolated somewhere as punishment. He looked at my hands, took the right one, and ran a finger over the bandaged fingers, saying nothing. He got up after that, kissed me on the mouth, and made an omelet from the sundry contents of my refrigerator. He spent the night in my bed, sleeping in a pair of boxers. He hung up his *button-down* in my closet, ironed and ready for a second day of wear. I slept well that night.

27

Regardless of the fact that I couldn't quite imagine my boss holding a girl like that, kissing a girl on the mouth, I had enough confidence in him to assume he could do both. But I couldn't figure out about Mary Anne and Scout. What was between them? I didn't ever feel I could trust her take on Scout. He never said much. Did they really say so little to each other? Or did she choose to leave most of his words out?

I arrived at Samuelson early the next morning, to put most of the cits back and restock with new ones. I thought I was alone, but when I rounded the corner near the water cooler, I saw Dan. He was looking something up in one of the old unabridged books when I passed him, my hands already full of pilfered cits. He straightened with a slow and graceful movement that reminded me of a quiet surprise in a nature show—a silent hazy veldt, a giraffe lifting its head unexpectedly out of bushes.

"Good morning," he said, blinking at me. I resisted the urge to thrust the cits behind my back.

"Morning," I mumbled. "How was your holiday?"

"Quite good," he said thoughtfully. He looked a little distant, as if thinking back to specific, delectable moments from his Christmas. He turned again to his dictionary without volleying back the requisite holiday pleasantry. As I made my way back to my desk, I remembered that I'd been meaning to ask for the twenty-eighth off. I should've asked him weeks ago. I almost turned back to him, but decided to get my bearings first. This was my second time caught red-handed, pulling an unusual number of cits out of the files. It probably meant little to him, but it was making me nervous.

My phone buzzed later that morning.

"Billy," Sheila said. "Line three. A question about 'venial' and 'venal.' Can you take it? Sounds pretty straightforward."

"Alrighty," I said, clicking over.

"Hello? Editorial." I did my best to chirp.

"Billy," someone rasped on the other end. "It's Phillips."

"What? Where are you calling from?"

"Shh . . . now. Don't say my name, son. Just act natural. I'm calling from home. I wanted to talk to you. Since I don't know your extension, I trotted out the old 'venal' versus 'venial' just as a ruse for Sheila. Grace tells me you're taking the sadder, gentler calls these days. The old folks and the confused children. Cliff's still getting the loonies. For now."

"Is that so?" I sighed.

"So I tried not to sound too nuts. But I disguised my voice. Listen. I don't want to keep you, Homer. I just thought you should know something."

Mr. Phillips paused and breathed heavily.

"It was Needham," he whispered. "In the editors' library. With the lead pipe."

"Sir . . ."

"Seriously, though. I just wanted to let you know that I might have tipped Dan off a little." Mr. Phillips hesitated. "At the Christmas party, I made a few cracks about a 'Splintered Winecup.' "

"Excuse me . . . a *what*?"

"Splintered winecup. Someone's plastic cup had rolled onto the floor, and Dan stepped on it by mistake. I kept calling it 'The Splintered Winecup.' I think the reference went right over Dan's head, but—I know how secretive you two kids have been, and I thought you might just want to know. I'm sorry. I didn't mean to make trouble for you."

"Hmm. I see . . ."

"He really didn't seem to notice. He seemed pretty loosey-goosey after a glass or two of wine. But now that the holiday hoopla is over, see, it just came to mind."

"That's interesting," I said, trying to maintain a customer-service tone. "We'll make a note of that and file it under 'discretion.'"

"What's that?"

"Discretion," I said firmly. "D–I–S–C–R–E–T–I–O–N."

"Are you worried? You shouldn't worry, son. Dan is a kind fellow. The whole Mary Anne business was ages ago. He probably wouldn't be much more than tickled if he knew what you'd been up to. At least—well, maybe 'tickled's' not the right word, but I don't think he'd be—"

"It's difficult to say," I interrupted. "Sometimes it's hard to find the right word. The human heart is perhaps more complex than any language."

"Okay, Homer. I get it. You want to get off now."

"That's what I'm saying, sir."

"Have a good one," Mr. Phillips said.

"You too, sir. Thanks for calling."

The phones were busy that morning.

I flipped through *Teaglass* cits and eavesdropped as Cliff handled an especially difficult call:

"Yes. That's correct," he was saying. "Our latest CD includes an audio feature. You can hear the pronunciation of any word you select, just by clicking on it."

I banded up the last of my "C" words and took out *deep-six*.

"That's correct. Our office is indeed in Massachusetts. But our pronunciation editor is a linguistics expert, and he certainly doesn't work exclusively with regional pronunciations in our area. And when there are significant, widespread *accepted* variants in pronunciation of a single word, both are listed in our dictionary. In those cases, you'd be given both pronunciation options on the audio feature. But none of the words is pronounced with any particular regional twang, I can assure you of that—"

I flipped through *deep-six*, silently thanking Providence for giving this call to Clifford and not to me.

"Actually, sir, the pronunciations were recorded for us by specially hired actors.

". . . To be honest, I don't know where they're from.

". . . I can assure you that they sound nothing like Ted Kennedy."

At that moment, I caught sight of the familiar *Teaglass* heading.

deep-six

He let go. Maybe he was in pain. But more likely he was amused. He grabbed my hair again, and pulled my face into his. I don't remember when I dropped the book. I only remember realizing that my hands were free but for the bag on my wrist. Not very bright, he breathed into my mouth. Just like I thought. I knew you'd be— But he didn't finish, because both of my hands had grabbed the bag, my right hand grasping the base of the broken glass through the plastic, and mashed it into his neck in one quick, upward thrust. Have you ever seen a baby fitting a toy block into a correctly shaped hole? It was just like that. A swift and natural act. But afterwards, mystified, openmouthed surprise. Is it possible this man and I shared a common emotion, in the seconds that followed? We stared at each other, both stunned, him with his hand at the puffy white collar now stuck to his neck, me untangling my left hand from the bag's bloody plastic handle, now dangling beneath his chin. He let go of my hair and stumbled toward the brown car, making gurgles that sounded like Fuck. I watched him stoop and gag for a moment before I ran. I don't really remember running out of the park. I only remember surfacing at the street that runs by the back entrance. And then walking the rest of the way, breathless but comforted by the headlights that were now whizzing by in the dusk. After I got home, I sat at my kitchen table for I don't know how long, doing and thinking nothing. It wasn't until at least an hour passed that I noticed the cuts on my hands and wrist, and not for a while after that I got up and cleaned them and covered them. And it wasn't until the next day that I began to worry about your book. *Beyond the 38th Parallel,* so hastily *deep-sixed* in the park.

17

I stared at it.

"In fact, I'll do a little demonstration for you," Cliff was saying.

His chair creaked and I heard a few clicks.

"Hold on a sec. Here we go. Here's the pronunciation given for 'corps.' You know, c-o-r-p-s, as in Marine Corps? Or Peace Corps?"

A button was pressed. Then a contented-sounding lady enunciated "corps."

"Hear that? Here, I'll turn it up."

Two more taps of keys. "CORPS. CORPS," the woman shouted.

I stood up. Took a breath. Sat back down. Set the cit on my desk and rested my fingers on it.

"See, no 'co-AH.' And here's another one for you."

Tap tap. "CAR. CAR."

"No Boston 'cah,' see? That supposed 'Massachusetts' accent is common really only in a relatively small region in and around the Boston area. Our office isn't in that area. And even if it were, our editors and software development crew would certainly make sure that our products' audio features were accurate and accessible to all users.

"...All right. What else do you want to hear?

"...Sure thing."

More clicks. "GOD. GOD," said a pleasant male voice... "SIR...FAR...DEMOCRAT...YARD."

"Good enough, sir?

"...You're welcome.

"...Yes, it can be ordered online. I believe several chain bookstores carry it as well.

"...Yup. Take care."

Clifford's chair creaked and the phone clicked as he put it back into place.

He typed something else and clicked.

"FOOL," the lady announced into the silent sea of cubicles.

And then the office was quiet again.

I wondered if the whole office could hear the discomfort in the squeak of my chair. Everything Mona and I had learned had pointed toward this, so I wasn't shocked, exactly. Sickened, maybe, by the physical reality of it. The violence intended for Mary Anne, the blood, the glass, and the jugular. All the stuff we'd hungered for in spite of ourselves.

So we were right about the teaglass. She'd killed her attacker with a weapon that destiny had laid in her hands for *just that day*. I wanted to feel awe and relief for the girl. I wanted to fall head over heels for her story. If I could believe this really happened, I could believe in anything. But part of me felt it was all too convenient. An undeniably sick man. A girl with a shard of glass. A heroic ending.

"Office poll."

I looked up, my heart hammering.

George was standing over me holding up a little slip of paper that had *feng shui* scribbled on it.

"Feng SHOE-ee," I said loudly, just to get him out of my face. The faulty pronunciation had a satisfying "shoo-fly" quality to it.

George bristled and stalked away.

I read the cit once more. Then I brought it to Mona.

CHAPTER TWENTY-SIX

We huddled in the editors' library downstairs again.

"So it's true. He grabbed her in the park the same day she broke that glass," Mona said softly. "That's freaky."

"Do you think it's true?" I asked.

"Sure. How else would she have been able to stab him?"

"It just seems pretty...improbable. That she could pull that off."

"Yeah. But it totally confirms the theory that was in the papers. That he was a psycho and he died in a struggle after trying to grab some girl."

"I just want to read all the cits before I can really believe this. I mean, why her? Why then? Why *that day*?"

"She probably asked the same questions," Mona whispered. "I don't think she'll be able to answer them."

"Maybe so," I said. "But I think I'm going to do a marathon session for the rest of the cits. I'm gonna bring as many 1952 words home as I can."

"Whatever floats your boat," she said. "But I think we've got the gist."

"I'm gonna see how many I can dig up in the next few days. I want to have the whole thing. I'm getting tired of just pieces."

"Ah, yes," Mona sighed, and waved the "deep-six" citation. "But we lexicographers so rarely get to have 'the whole
thing,' as you put it. In work and in life."

"Stop. Did I tell you I'm taking the twenty-eighth off?"

"You are? For what?"

"Mental health day, sort of. 'Attending to personal matters,' as they say. I'm using a vacation day."

"You've already cleared it with Dan?"

"No."

"No? Better ask him soon then. The twenty-eighth is the
day after tomorrow, you know. I'd give him a little lead time.
Dan never says no, but he appreciates at least a gesture of
courtesy."

I knocked on Dan's open office door.

"Hello there," he said. "Come on in."

"You have a second?"

"Certainly."

"I wanted to ask you if I could use one of my vacation
days the day after tomorrow. Something personal has come
up."

"Billy," he said, "close the door."

I did.

"Sit down a minute."

Dan spread his palms out in front of him. Mildly, like a
cartoon Jesus.

"First of all—yes. Of course you can use one of your vacation days this week. They're yours to use as you wish."

"Thanks."

"I was hoping you had come to me to speak about a different matter."

"I'm sorry?"

"The *Teaglass* cits . . . ," he began.

It took me a few seconds to compose my face. Dan seemed to be deliberately giving me ample time to do so.

"Can we speak about those for a moment?" he asked.

I nodded, mortified.

"I actually recognized some time ago that you and Mona were uncovering them."

"I'm sorry—" I said hoarsely.

"No need to apologize. It wasn't only your own indiscretions but also Mr. Phillips's." Dan chuckled.

"You didn't do anything wrong," he continued. "It's a pretty extraordinary situation. It's always awkward when someone makes something private public, at the wrong time, or in the wrong place. There's no right way to handle it.

"Now, I imagine this will strike you as highly unorthodox, and I don't usually condone this sort of thing . . . but I'm going to ask that you put all of the citations back where you found them. When you get a chance."

I nodded. Dan leaned forward. Slowly, he pulled a newly sharpened pencil out of the mug on his desk.

"That's where she wanted the story to reside, for whatever reason. I'm sure you agree it's best to respect her wishes. Even if those wishes were wrought mostly from trauma. Now, I don't know how much you've gathered—"

"She was . . . the girl . . . the girl they saw in the park?"

"They?" Dan said. He poised his pencil over his blotter calendar.

"The two witnesses who said they saw a blonde girl. I saw it in the papers."

"I see . . ." He began to draw the pencil lightly back and forth across one of the calendar boxes, barely making a mark. "I didn't realize your interest had reached that level."

"Yeah, well . . ."

"It was really just a horrifying situation," he continued, looking up at me. "It seems to me that a victim of such a random act of violence should be given the freedom to disclose on her own terms. However irrational, I've always felt it best just to leave it—"

"You don't have to say anything else," I said. "Consider it done."

"Am I correct that the only other readers were Mona and Mr. Phillips?"

"Um . . . yeah."

"Fitting," Dan sighed. "As the cits are addressed to Mr. Phillips."

"Maybe this will sound a little forward. But it sort of seems like they're really, in a way, meant for you. Like she just wanted you to know why—"

As soon as I said it I regretted my presumption. I actually had no idea who Mary Anne wanted to know what or why or why not.

"They're addressed to Mr. Phillips," he repeated, a little huskily. "I'm part of the intended audience, but not the actual conversation. . . . She speaks directly to Red. She acknowledges him. But I believe 'Dolores Beekmim' is what's supposed to catch *my* eye. Only I would know about Dolores Beekmim."

"Who *is* Dolores Beekmim?"

"Dolores Beekmim is just a name." Dan started doodling absently on his desk blotter. "It doesn't mean much. It was a cat."

"A cat?"

"Mary Anne's cat. She disliked cats. She wanted a dog, but couldn't have one in her apartment. At my urging, she decided to give a cat a try, just for company. We named the cat together."

"So you've read them all? All of the cits?"

"Well. Some of them. Over the years. So many cits cross my desk, Dolores Beekmim was bound to catch my eye eventually. The first one was quite a shock."

He chuckled stiffly, reddening a little. I glanced down at his sketch. On his blotter, he'd drawn a crude little picture of a pie. Squiggle marks spiraled out of the top of the drawing, denoting steam.

"But there's a certain elegance to a story that's meant to be revealed slowly, in fragments, to give its readers a little pause, a little . . . caution."

He shifted in his seat.

"In any event," he continued, adding one more curl of steam to his pie, "you'll return them to the files."

"Yes."

"While you're at it . . . ," he said, and then didn't continue.

"Yeah?"

He threw down his pencil and rummaged in his desk for a moment, then handed me a cit.

"Will you do me a favor, please, Billy, and return this one as well? It caught my eye a year or two ago, and I held on to it. I've been meaning to return it."

"No problem," I said.

Dan's face tensed. "This isn't a *favor* I'm asking. Do you understand?"

"Yes," I said.

"And I'd appreciate it if you didn't mention this to other editorial staff. I think you can imagine how easily the information could fall into indiscreet hands."

"Do any other staff—"

"I think what I'm saying is clear enough," Dan cut in quietly. "A big part of what makes this job difficult is knowing how to handle silence. Can you handle silence, Billy?"

He stared at me. I clasped my hands in my lap because they were shaking.

"Yes," I answered.

"Good," he said icily.

Dan sighed and finally blinked. I wondered if all the sighs were out of disappointment in his wayward staff or for lost love.

"So you can handle what I'm asking you to do?"

"Yeah," I said.

"Then let's both get back to work. I've an appointment with Needham in five minutes. We've got these geography dictionary edits to discuss. Wars and coups keep happening. Places keep changing their names."

"But, Dan," I squeaked.

"What?"

"Why the Korean War?"

It could be anything. Maybe she liked *M*A*S*H*. It would make about as much solid sense as Dolores Beekmim.

Dan raised a weary eyebrow.

"She considered herself," he said, "oddly tied up in that moment of history."

I waited for him to say more.

"It wasn't an academic interest," he added.

I wasn't sure if he considered that a full explanation, so I didn't move.

"Mary Anne's father nearly died in Korea. Her mother's first fiancé *did* die there, while they were still engaged. Mary Anne felt a personal obligation to understand as many details of that history as possible. Every moment of it, she told me once. As if she could narrow down the specific seconds when it was determined that she would exist and someone else wouldn't."

"But any moment could be like that."

"But none is so concentrated as it is in war," Dan said.

"You think so?"

"She thought so. But she was a little self-involved when it came to the topic. It was an odd obsession of hers. So those years were a natural choice for her. When the time came to tell the story of *this* very fateful moment. Plus it gave her more words to work with than 1985. It was a practical choice, if you look at it that way."

Dan got out of his chair, put a hand on his lower back, and gave a slight stretch.

"And she was a practically minded young woman," he said quietly.

"Well, thanks. Thanks for the explanation." My voice was far too high. "I was just wondering, you know?"

Dan nodded without looking at me and then opened the door.

"No worries," he said, and motioned for me to go ahead of him.

Once I was alone at my desk, I read the cit he'd given me:

billboard

Sometimes I wish he knew better how to ease a particular story out of me. Not because I needed to tell it, but because I wanted to. Not to everyone, but to someone. That distinction was, however, the main problem. After telling once, who could stop telling such a story? And who could find the right face to put on after the telling, or the right words to continue a conversation after that story was used up? Who could carry that story and still have the strength to carry everything else she'd had before she acquired it? Who wouldn't be reduced to the birdsong of that story? Not me. But complete silence didn't suit me, either. I know there was a puritanical day when people were more disciplined about such things. Secrets were real, in the sense that they were not told, and people carried them dutifully to the grave. A real secret doesn't outlive the person who carries it. It becomes ashes and dust and blows away into nothing. It's very simple, how you make a secret disappear from this earth. Do I think I'm so special, then, to want a different end for mine? I suppose so. I want mine to be told. Infinite silence doesn't satisfy me any more than *billboarding* myself for all to see. Can't there be something in between? Can't there be a way to tell it endlessly but still maintain a dignified silence?

42

CHAPTER TWENTY-SEVEN

Mona freaked when I told her about Dan. She was pretty sure Dan was going to fire us both, and wanted to put all the cits back right then and there. But I convinced her that a day or two more with them wasn't going to hurt anything. Dan wouldn't check up on us, I was pretty sure. And there was no sense in putting them all back when we were so close to rounding the story out.

In preparation for the twenty-eighth, I crammed my backpack with 1952 citations and bought a bottle of gin on the way home. When I was nineteen, I'd spent my first anniversary stinking drunk, and every subsequent year had been a fading variation on that theme. This year, a couple of drinks and a decent lunch would probably suffice. It was just a nod to the tradition, after all. At the grocery store, I watched my limes, tonic water, and fancy lunch meat slide down the conveyor belt, and felt like I'd forgotten something. Later, as I carried my treats upstairs, I concluded that I hadn't forgotten anything. The tradition had officially simply grown old. This celebration would, thankfully, be my last.

• • •

December 28 was quiet at first. Mostly sipping and flipping. A cit here or there. Nothing too revealing. I paced myself. My phone rang about noon.

"Hello?"

"Hey, Billy," Mona chirped. "How's your day going?"

"Decent. Did they put a phone at your desk too?"

"No. I'm calling from my cell. I'm at our park bench."

"Oh."

"I'm just calling to tell you that Raymond is going apeshit because he needs to answer a letter about 'top banana' and all the cits have mysteriously disappeared from the file."

"Define 'apeshit.' Someone going apeshit at Samuelson? I'll believe it if I ever see it."

"Okay. Well, it hasn't been pretty, let's just put it that way. You've got the cits there?"

"Yup. I think so. Haven't flipped through them yet, though."

"Well. Just make sure you bring those ones back tomorrow. You might have to say something to Dan. Tell him you didn't get around to finishing your filing before your day off. I don't know if we should just slip them in quietly, or stick them in the wrong spot so it looks like a filing error, but—"

"Don't worry about it. I'll bring them. I'll take care of them."

As I hung up, it occurred to me that this anniversary had indeed turned out to be pretty lame. It was a day like any other day, really. I poured myself a stronger drink than my previous one. A gimlet.

I sat at the kitchen table and kept flipping. I was on my second gimlet when this one fell out:

subliterature

Seems wishful thinking, but I'll try it this one time. Since nearly all the words are set now, all that's left is the telling. Your eyes have told me you wouldn't be shocked by anything. Your hands tell me you would have killed him yourself. Your voice has always calmed me, even when you talked of the grenade in your foxhole. As I write this, I can almost hear you. You do what you have to, honey. What can I say? And now the telling's almost over. Just a few more words, then a few more days, and maybe I'll be free of it. Once the thing is released to a perpetuity of endless words and endless quiet. My own bit of forgotten, irrelevant *subliterature*. Made even smaller, even more forgettable, once hacked to pieces and scattered. Not dust yet, but closer to it. Will it blow away into nothing? Or piece itself into meaningful existence? I will leave that to you— you and your knack for stories. Because this is the only telling this one will ever get from me.

50

I downed my drink as I read the cit a few more times. This cit had a satisfying finality to it—and its number, 50, was the highest I'd seen so far on any of them. But it reminded me of a question that Mona and I had never quite answered: *Why Red? Why was she narrating to Red?*

I had an idea. I stood up quickly and felt like someone had kicked me in the stomach. A day's worth of slow alcohol intake will do that. But after splashing some water on my face, I felt almost good enough to drive.

"Billy!" Mr. Phillips said, opening his door. "Why aren't you at work? They let you out early? You look a little ragged."

"I'm supposed to be attending to personal matters today. Don't tell anyone you saw me."

"Well, come on in. I'd suggest going out for coffee, but I'm afraid someone might see us."

"I just wanted to show you some stuff," I said.

He turned off his radio and led me to a brown plaid couch with sunken cushions. The couch was piled with a bunch of newspapers and magazines, which he swept onto the floor with a single sweep of his skinny arm.

"You want a cup of tea or something?"

"I'm okay, thanks." As he sat beside me, I handed him the articles about Derek Brownlow.

He put on his glasses and read the first. Wordlessly, he flipped to the second.

"I'll be damned," he muttered in the middle of it.

When he put them down, he shook his head. "I don't know if I believe it," he said. "I don't know if she had it in her."

I handed him some of the newer cits, the more revealing ones. He took them but didn't even look at them.

"Do you remember this Glass Girl thing?"

"Yes. Now that you show me those articles. But I never made the connection with the cits. It's been a long time. It was one of those fifteen-minute kinds of things, you know what I mean?"

"Yeah," I said.

"Are you sure you're all right? You look like you could use a glass of water."

"Maybe. I'll get it," I said, getting up slowly. I got him one too. As I watched him sipping, I tried to decide if this apartment depressed me. The ancient plaid couch smelled like hot dogs. The radio was probably older than me. Much of his furniture was covered with newspapers and scattered bits of paper, many of which looked to be handwritten cits. But Mr. Phillips himself was sunny enough.

I put down my glass and handed him "subliterature."

"That's addressed to you, I think," I said. "Like the rest of them."

"Probably," Mr. Phillips admitted.

I didn't say anything.

"I'd like to think I'd have said a little more than that. A little more than"—he looked at the cit again—" 'You do what you have to, honey.' It's sad to read that."

"Why did she want to tell you this story?"

"Sounds like it was a story she really needed to tell."

"Well, that's not enough! Why didn't she tell her boyfriend, then? Why not tell Scout? Or a sympathetic lady friend, like Grace?"

"I'm an extremely sympathetic fellow, Billy. The ladies have always recognized that."

"But why *you*? You must've known her better than you've been admitting."

"Maybe it was never really me she was telling." Mr. Phillips frowned. "Except perhaps in her head. Ever think of that?"

"How well *did* you know her?"

"I trained her, just like Dan trained you. I told her war stories at lunch on the stoop. I've already told you that. I never saw her outside the Samuelson office. I don't even know where she was from, or where she lived when she worked there."

"But you knew enough to say you thought she didn't have it in her," I pointed out.

"Appearances. That was based on *appearances*."

I raised my eyebrows at him, and his face grew red.

"I've shot a few men dead in my life, you know that?" he barked at me.

"No. I'm sorry." I slumped back onto the sour brown cushions.

"But I still don't know if I could've stabbed a guy in the jugular under any circumstance. Excuse me if I have trouble believing that sweet, quiet gal could've done it, either."

I stood up impulsively.

"Tell me the truth," I began. I was dizzy from the head rush, but talked through it. "Did you know what happened to her? *Did you know?* Did you know the newspapers were writing about someone you saw *every day*? That the police thought she was a killer?"

"Sit *down*," he said, out of the side of his mouth. "Quit the dramatics. No, I didn't know. If I had known, this little cit chase of ours would've been an incredible bore."

I sank back into the couch.

"You're being a little insensitive, Homer. You're forgetting that I'm closer to this story than you. Don't you think I'm wondering the same things? I can just *see* her sitting there on the steps. I didn't know her well, but I *remember* her. And when I see her there, and I read what she was trying to say . . . I just wonder." Mr. Phillips shook his head. "I wonder if there was something I was supposed to do, or supposed to see. I can't do anything now. Mary Anne's probably out there somewhere, and I hope she's well. But that girl on the step. She's gone. And there's nothing I can do for her."

"Probably—" I yawned. "Probably there was nothing you were supposed to *do*."

"Not sure about that, Homer."

"I'm sorry," I said, leaning into the side of the couch. "I'm a little out of it. I've been drinking all day."

"That's a good one, Billy. All-American boy-boozer." He laughed and said something else, but I didn't hear it clearly. His voice faded away from me as my eyes closed.

When I woke up, I heard a newspaper rustling. Across from me, Mr. Phillips lowered his *Wall Street Journal*.

"Finally," he said.

I looked at the couch cushion beside me. Mr. Phillips had left my cits and articles there in a neat little pile.

"There's a few new ones in there for you," he said. "I don't know if it matters, at this point. But there are a few more '53 cits. I meant to give them to you the day of the Christmas party."

I glanced out the window. It was dark.

"Damn it," I said. "I'm so sorry. Why didn't you wake me up?"

"Because you were annoying the hell out of me before you passed out. Seemed best to let you sleep it off."

I sighed. "I'm really sorry. I don't know what happened."

"Maybe you oughta go home and get into bed. Do you want me to call you a cab?"

"No, I'm all right. What time is it?"

"Just about eight."

As I began to gather my cits, Mr. Phillips said, "Hey, Billy. Dan tells me you're quite the joker."

"Oh, no," I said, blushing at the memory of the hollandaise joke. "That would be an exaggeration."

"Did you hear about the constipated mathematician?" Mr. Phillips asked.

"No, I don't believe I did."

"He worked it out with a pencil."

"Wonderful. That is truly a new one for me."

"But you're not laughing," Mr. Phillips said.

He'd already picked up his paper again and was grimacing at something in the *Marketplace* section. I wondered how, at his age, one comes to decide what to care about. It dawned on me that even fifteen years ago, when Mary Anne knew him, he was already old.

"She wanted to know how you come back from a war," I said.

"You think so, do you?" Mr. Phillips barely looked up from his paper.

"Yeah. That's why you. That's why you and not Dan."

Mr. Phillips harrumphed, but put down his paper. His face puckered in thought.

"How do you come back from a war?" I asked.

"There's no *how* in it," he said. "You just do. Because you have to. Because what's the alternative, after all?"

I watched him shift in his chair.

"You know, I was thinking about it while you were sleeping," he continued. "I think the problem we're having here is generational. Your generation thinks everything can be worked out if you talk about it enough. Your generation is always looking for answers to all the little questions and never bothering with the big ones. You young folks know nothing about real history. But you love to talk about your own little pasts. Ad nauseam."

"I'll have to work on that," I said.

"It's not your fault. It's the baby boomers that started it. You don't know any better."

"I'm not sure about that."

A light snow was falling when I came out of Mr. Phillips's place. I let the defroster run for a minute and scanned across the Collins Hill complex. Mr. Phillips's was the second apartment out of about eight in his section of the village. Only two other apartments had their lights on. The line of numbered doors reminded me of a motor lodge. I wondered if the clean, efficient anonymity of the place was comforting to its residents. That manufactured sensation of being on your way someplace else. I pulled out of the driveway and headed in the direction of my apartment.

He worked it out with a pencil. Mr. Phillips's punch line came to me suddenly. Laughter rolled up into my chest as I sped down the road. My shoulders shook as I leaned into the steering wheel.

Red light. I stomped on the brake. Everything whirled. I yanked the wheel to the right. When the car stopped spinning, I was right in the middle of the intersection. The road was empty. I'd gotten lucky. If anyone had come through the perpendicular street, I'd have slammed right into them. And here I still was, with my car's nose pointed toward the sidewalk. I sat silent, heart pounding, playing chicken with nobody in particular. I wasn't quite ready to move my old Pontiac from this fated spot. How undignified it would've been to die here. And with the dirty secret of my death forever mine alone—that it was a constipated mathematician who had sealed my fate.

Still I didn't move. Because this wasn't about a tasteless joke. It was about fate. It was December 28, five years out, and I was in the middle of an intersection. In the wrong lane, facing the wrong way. The street was deserted but there was still some danger in it—someone could speed into this intersection at any moment. The light gave my hood a red glow, but everything else on this corner was a holy gray, lit by the subdued streetlamps and nothing else. The Sunoco station two blocks up looked very distant. I kept my foot on the brake. The light above me turned green. It didn't matter. I was so turned around, I didn't know which light was mine. My hands stayed locked on the wheel, and my foot on the brake. This was what I'd been looking for all day. This was where I was supposed to be. Where I could remember how dangerous my life really was. Where no one could tell me otherwise, and nothing could distract me from it.

What had today meant? Shuffling citations. Primly sipping cocktails. Snoring like a drunk on an old man's couch. When had my life become such a gentle disgrace? Days in a cubicle, summarizing every concept known to humanity in the blandest possible terms. Nights trying to forge a path through darkness with lightbulb jokes. For this I had fought and survived?

I hit the gas and accelerated up to the Sunoco station. It wasn't until I was parked next to the gas pump that I realized how badly I was shaking. I turned the car off. I didn't need gas, I just needed to decide what should come next. Drive west? Drive to my apartment? Drive to Mona's and hope for the sort of drop-in love that happens only in movies? I stared into the gas station, where a bearded attendant was stacking cups by a coffee machine. I waited for him to turn around and see me, but it never happened. He finished his work, balled up the plastic bag in his hands, and then disappeared into the back of the store.

Once he was out of sight, I released the breath I'd been holding. Then I rummaged through the tapes on my passenger side and stuck my old traveling music into the tape player. The Allman Brothers. I started the car again. As I approached my house, "Midnight Rider" was still going. I couldn't bring myself to stop the car in the middle of this song. So I kept driving.

I gunned it past the endless two-family houses, the

Salvation Army store, the China Buffet. The end of the song dumped me at the light next to Discount Liquors, which appeared to be open. I turned in and parked in their enormous lot. Half of the population of Claxton could get a hankering for a cocktail on the same night, and there would still be ample parking for all.

Funny I should end up here tonight. Had the constipated mathematician and the Allman Brothers brought me here, or was I headed here the whole time? This was how I'd spent my one-year mark, four years ago. That had been the most significant one. I'd spent a year biting my nails, waiting for the cancer to get me again. Each time I went in for another gallium scan and chest X-ray, I fully expected bad news and never quite believed the good news that always came. I lived like a monk my first semester, burying myself in philosophy as if it were my last chance to understand anything before my body took me hostage again. When it dawned on me that a year had really passed without another sign of the sickness, I was stunned.

On the official one-year mark—December 28—I didn't know if I was relieved or angry. I'd felt I should mark the occasion in some momentous way. Since I was home for the holidays at the time, I couldn't come up with anything much more exciting than sneaking off to a bar in the town next door. My parents were asleep when I got home, but my sister was up, reading on the living room couch. When I told her why I'd been out celebrating, she'd considered me for a moment, then said, "I'm really happy for you. I know what a tough year it's been for you. If you'd said something about what day it was, we could've all done something together."

When I didn't manage much of a response, she continued.

"I kinda wonder, though. Of all the things you could be today, why you chose drunk."

I probably could have called her on her faux-professorial tone, which she'd perfected over the course of the year I'd been sick. Or woken everyone up screaming about how little she understood. But instead I just laughed and staggered to my bedroom to sleep it off.

In fact, there was an answer to her question—*Why drunk?* What my sister didn't know was that I'd actually been a teetotaler the whole first year after the treatments. The reason for this was simple. As a veteran of some serious high school ragers, I associated drinking with nausea. And nausea was one thing I didn't need any more of. But when I contemplated how I'd celebrate my first-year anniversary, I found that I was curious about trying alcohol again. While it might have seemed pathetic to my sister, there was a certain euphoria in reclaiming the simple pleasure of a few stiff drinks. And it had felt like a very special occasion.

Inside Discount Liquors, I wandered the wide, endless white aisles of hooch and tried to decide what I wanted. Failing that, I decided to get everything. I put a new bottle of gin in the cart, along with lime juice, a six-pack of Black Label, rum, two liters of Coke, and an experimental bottle of pear schnapps, which I'd heard was pretty good. If the first year was euphoric, the fifth was going to be a revelation.

No one seemed impressed or alarmed by my purchases. In a liquor store, my selections probably seemed about right for a young man of legal age preparing for a small party at his pad. Besides, the woman behind me in line was buying four bottles of Absolut Citron and two of Southern Comfort. Her story was probably far more troubling than mine.

On my way out of the store, something on the sliding glass door caught my eye. It was a large sticker that they'd used to decorate the glass. "Celebrate *Life!*" it said, in sparkly silver letters. The edges of the sticker were peeling and brown. The very top of the exclamation point had been pulled off, and the "C" was curling in on itself.

I laughed, standing with my blue plastic Discount Liquors cart poised in front of the open glass doors. *Celebrate life!* I intended to. But what did that really mean? And how many of us actually know how to go about it? I stood there puzzling over my own attempts, past and present, until the SoCo and Citron lady came up behind me with her cart. She wanted to get by. I pushed my cart through the doors and we were both on our way.

CHAPTER TWENTY-EIGHT

When I woke up the next morning, my breath tasted like rotten malt and squandered youth. I'd had a couple of beers upon returning home, rummaged through a few piles of cits, then dozed off on the futon. As I watched myself lift my toothbrush in the bathroom mirror, I knew that I wouldn't be making it to work that day.

After leaving an apologetic message on Dan's voice mail, I went to bed for a few more hours. I got up around noon, knocked back a couple of shots of gin, and perused my refrigerator for something to eat. Eggs, milk, cheese, and onions would make a passable omelet. I didn't have any real vegetables, but that hardly mattered. A few more shots and I wouldn't be fit to wield a knife anyhow.

After I chopped the onions, I took a third shot and quickly chased it with milk, which was a mistake. While my onions sizzled, I frantically opened my new Coke bottle and took a big cleansing swig.

When I carried my plated omelet to the kitchen table, I found it covered with cit piles and old photocopies.

"The story that never fucking ends," I murmured, pushing the papers aside to make room for my plate. "Get over yourself, Mary Anne."

When the plate was clean, I was ready for another drink.

I set up my shot glass and gin bottle on the table in ceremonial fashion and wondered if I was doing this for myself or an imagined audience of everyone who had ever failed to empathize. No matter. Once the shot had slid down my throat, it didn't seem an important distinction.

I pulled Mary Anne's mess in front of me, fanning a bunch of cits out across the table. Scanning them, I saw no *Teaglass* cits. I swept them onto the floor and grabbed another pile. I proceeded like this for the better part of an hour. When I finally found another Mary Anne installment, I added it to the *Teaglass* stack.

"Victory drink," I said aloud, and had some schnapps. This did the trick. After a couple more piles of cits, the kitchen started a slow carousel movement.

I dragged myself into the living room and lay on the futon for a while, watching the ceiling spin.

Of all the things you could be today . . .

The phone rang. I reached for it without getting up.

"Yo?" I said into the phone.

"Billy!" It was Mona. "What's going on? I thought you were coming back today."

"I called in."

"What? You're supposed to *be* here."

"What's the matter?" I asked. "Emergency situation at the office? They need me? Words being coined at an alarming rate? Old folks lining up at both doors, demanding to know who the hell hijacked the word 'gay' and gave it to the fairies?"

"Is everything okay? You sound weird."

"I'm *sick,*" I said. "Tomorrow everything will be all right."

"You sure of that? Cuz *I'm* not. You're starting to worry me."

I looked over at the mess on my kitchen table.

"I appreciate that," I said. "But try not to let it ruin your afternoon."

Mona seemed reluctant to go, but my stomach was starting to revolt.

"Bye, Mona," I shouted into the phone, then ran into the bathroom.

I slid onto the floor in front of the toilet.

I'm that guy, I marveled. *That* guy. I'm that stupid guy who finds himself wasted, curled around a toilet. I'm every dumbass freshman I ever helped stagger home from a frat house. Every moron who I stepped over in the dormitory hall. I thought I'd escaped that guy, but here he was. Just as stupid as the rest of them. Probably no smarter for the philosophy or the experience.

Five years ago yesterday, my father drove me home from my last treatment. We stopped at Riverdale Park, which was completely empty of people. No surprise, as it was bitter cold. We smoked a joint together. It was a relief to spend some time away from my parents' living room couch, where I'd spent most of the previous six months.

"Now I guess I just sit tight for five years," I'd said. "And wait. And hope it doesn't come back."

My father kept turning the car on, running the heat full blast, turning it off again.

"You warm enough?" he kept asking.

I said yes, and a little later, told him I'd been thinking. I wasn't going to try and take second-semester classes locally. That I was thinking about taking it easy till September, when I'd finally be leaving for college for real. So I'd have a chance to think some things over. Then I'd start school the following fall. Then maybe I'd try philosophy. Philosophy seemed a worthwhile subject to me now. I didn't know why. It just did.

He nodded, his eyes wide and searching, like he was try-ing to find his reply somewhere in my face. Then he spoke:

"You're going to come through this, and you're going to know who you are. So much better than some people do. I just see it happening for you that way, William. Five years from today, you're going to be finished with college. You're going to be starting your life on your own. You're going to wonder where the time went. You're going to realize you haven't even thought about this for a long time."

I don't remember replying. He'd been wrong, but it was a touching thought.

"You're going to be such a fine young man. You already are. But then, even more. I can just see it. Such a fine, strong young man."

He was embarrassing me.

"As long as I quit it with this reefer," I said, taking the joint from him. It seemed to me he'd had enough.

But my dumb joke had come a little too late. To my as-tonishment, my father had already started to cry, quietly, wiping his eyes and then drying his wet hands on his black upholstery. When he couldn't seem to stop, it was me who ended up driving us the last couple of miles home.

He'd never quite arrived—this brave, fine young man my father had promised. I'd always told myself this fifth anniver-sary would be my last. But then, I'd always imagined I'd be a far different man by now. A man who, by the fifth, would not even notice the date's passing. Who'd have more important things to think about. Who wouldn't be lost anymore.

I remained on my bathroom floor for a good half hour at least, until I heard a light tapping on my door.

"Billy," a low, scratchy voice was insisting. "Do you have a second?"

It was Tom. I got up and pulled the door open.

"Down and out, huh? Taking a sick day?" he said, stepping inside. "I noticed your car was here, and Jimmy said he thought he heard you walking around up here."

"Yeah, well. You're right. I'm taking a sick day."

"What've you got?" he wanted to know. "The flu? Just don't cough in my direction, all right? I'm practically homeless, so I can't afford to be sick."

"I'll try," I said. "You want some tea or something?"

"Sure. Looks like you've been self-medicating with something a little harder," he observed, gesturing at the bottles on the counter. "You think that's the best way to treat a flu? Shit, man."

I began to boil some water and take out some mugs.

"How have the holidays been treating you?" I said, changing the subject.

"Not bad. Jimmy and Barb got me some movie passes. I'm looking forward to using those."

"Nice."

"Not going so good for Barb, though. She's been sick. Maybe you've got whatever she's got."

"Maybe."

"She's been holed up down there for three days. Sick as a dog. In bed, drinking lots of tea. The whole deal. Bet she's going nuts in there, with only Jimmy to keep her company. You know what? I think Jimmy *likes* having Barb all laid up in there. Gives him a sense of purpose. Now, I'm not suggesting any Munchausen-by-proxy shit, anything like that, but —"

"Would you like a cookie or something? Something to go with that tea?"

Tom shook his head while he squeezed his tea bag with

his spoon and his thumb. My stomach didn't like the carnal-ity of this act. I put my hand on my middle and took a few shaky breaths.

Tom didn't notice. "Hey, Billy. I've been meaning to ask you. How are those lottery tickets working out for you? Jimmy mentioned you're on a gambling kick."

"Not exactly. I won five bucks and bought some more tickets with it. But those ones turned out to be losers."

"That's usually how it happens."

"True," I admitted. It was difficult to feign interest in the lottery tickets. I'd managed to do one a day for about three mornings, then scratched the rest on a particularly boring evening.

Tom took a long sucking sip off the surface of his tea.

"I actually came up here because I've got something for you," he said. "I don't know if it still interests you though."

"What?"

"That Glass Girl article I mentioned. I dug it up for you at the library."

I looked down at the headline. *Unsolved Crimes: Claxton's Coldest Cases.*

"Thanks, Tom. This is great. I've been really curious about this."

"I copied the whole series for you. All three articles. I think you'll find the Olsen double-murder/suicide pretty interesting too."

"Alrighty," I said. "Cool. I'll know all of the Claxton lore eventually."

Tom wrinkled his brow as he took a sip of his tea. "Are you sure you're all right up here?" he asked.

"Why wouldn't I be?"

"You just don't seem your usual self."

"Not sure what that means, man," I said.

"That's too bad, Billy. I'm sorry to hear that. Because 'Know thyself' is, like, one of the most important tenets of philosophy."

I laughed.

"*Which* philosophy would that be?" I said. "The school of platitudes?"

"Don't be a punk," Tom said. "It doesn't become you. Neither does inebriation, by the way."

"Thanks for the tip," I said. "Do you have anything else for me today?"

"I don't think so," he replied, a little stiffly. I'd hurt his feelings. "Unless there's something you need?"

"Nope," I said. "I'm sorry, Tom. I didn't mean anything. It's just that philosophy's worthless when you're sick and drunk."

Tom set his cup down, lined up his spoon next to it.

"I disagree," he said, getting up. "But I hope you feel better soon."

"Thanks for the articles." I opened the door for him.

As soon as he was gone, I read the first article:

Claxton Daily News
DECEMBER 1, 1997
Cold Case: "The Glass Girl"
A BOTCHED KIDNAPPING
OR CRIME OF PASSION?

Editor's Note: This is the second in the three-part series about unsolved murder cases in Claxton over the last decade.

CLAXTON — Sometimes a case is more about questions than answers.

As Claxton's only cold case investigator, Lt. Alvin Martino, leafed through the pages of Derek Brownlow's case file on a recent afternoon, all he had were questions.

Why was Brownlow killed?

Was he trying to attack someone who fought back, or was he himself a victim?

Where would someone find a piece of glass in the middle of a park to stab Brownlow in the neck?

And why did no one come forward in what many considered a heroic act?

Brownlow, a hardware store worker with a criminal background, was killed twelve years ago, just a few months after he moved to Claxton. Police found his lifeless body under a tree in Freeman Park.

At first the murder seemed random. But evidence found in Brownlow's home and car—as well as details about his conviction for attacking a woman in Pennsylvania and suspicion that he was involved in two murders there—led police to theorize that he was killed while trying to kidnap someone.

Many in the public and the media attributed the killing to a mysterious young woman they called the "Glass Girl," in reference to the murder weapon, shards of a broken bottle or glass. Witnesses had seen a young woman entering the park around dusk.

"It's a frustrating case," Lt. Martino said during a recent interview in his office at police headquarters. "At first we had a lot of leads. It seemed this fellow got involved in something he couldn't handle. Or maybe that's what we wanted to believe because of his background. Sometimes facts just don't come out."

In his 22 years of reviewing cold cases in Claxton and with the Massachusetts State Police, Martino has helped solve dozens of murders. But rarely, he admits, has he come across a case with so many striking details but so little forensic evidence.

"The weapon had no usable fingerprints. We didn't find any other broken glass in the area, implying it was brought in for the attack," Lt. Martino said. "In searching through the victim's personal effects, we found a lot of evidence, but none of it has proved conclusive, at least so far."

A commonly overlooked detail about the killing, Lt. Martino said, was that Brownlow didn't appear to have bled to death.

"The autopsy indicated that the cuts did not sever the jugular," he said. "The glass was apparently moved as the victim attempted to remove pieces from his neck. The cause of death actually appeared to be choking, probably on his own blood."

A few years before moving to Claxton, Brownlow served seven months in a Pennsylvania prison for attacking a young woman, whom police said he had been stalking. Brownlow broke her arm and knocked out several of her teeth when he tried to abduct her outside the office where she worked.

"I guess he wasn't as good at grabbing women as he'd have liked to be," Martino says and shrugs. "It looks like he botched it a few times."

Brownlow was a suspect in the murder of a nurse in 1979 and the disappearance of a college girl in 1975. In both cases, authorities did not find enough evidence to arrest him, Martino said.

After Brownlow's death, the media spent weeks speculating on the possibility that a mysterious "Glass Girl" heroically killed Brownlow in a thwarted kidnapping attempt. Claxton police questioned several young women from local high schools and the community college in an effort to support the theory. But they found no trace of the woman in question.

"A few young women did come forward claiming to be the 'Glass Girl,' but after questioning them about the details of the case, we concluded that all of them were hoaxes," Lt. Martino said. "The actual 'Glass Girl,' if there was one, elected not to come forward and help us solve this case."

Although Brownlow apparently knew few people in Claxton, it's possible that he was killed in a fight or a crime of passion, he said.

"Frankly, this one has baffled all of us."

I put the article aside and looked at my piles of cits. There couldn't be that many more to go before all fifty were in place. When I counted, I discovered that there were only three more to be found. It wasn't likely those three would answer every question these policemen had. But Mary Anne's tone implied she thought she was answering everything.

I rubbed my eyes hard. I wanted to fill in the holes. I might not have the whole story then, but at least I'd have the satisfaction of having all the words. For once.

I grabbed yet another pile and flipped through it. Then another. And another. I found a *Teaglass* cit. I kept going.

I'm not sure how long I worked. The room spun around me. Cits fell onto the floor. I found another. I folded myself forward and tried to ignore the twisting sensation in my stomach. I didn't wish to spend any more time hanging over the toilet. At this table I could at least get someone's story straight, if not my own.

I'd never been able to tell the story because I didn't know how to end it. Six months of chemo, one year of careful medical maintenance, and now five years ahead. A neat little package, wrapped beautifully, with a ribbon and a little tag on top that says *But he's okay now!* This was the gift everyone wanted from me, and I couldn't give it. I refused to. Because it was the kind of gift you find under a Christmas tree at a bank. Nothing sincere about it. Nothing inside.

More cits. The ache subsided. Another *Teaglass* cit appeared. I threw down the stack I'd been shuffling and grabbed the stack of *Teaglass* cits. I checked the numbers again. They were all there. All fifty. I leaned back in my chair and read them all at once.

CHAPTER TWENTY-NINE

advantaged

How did I get here? Even the stories I've asked you to tell, Red,
were only another way for me to ask that question. Now I
suppose the question might mean something else? If here
means this office, this very physical place, well, my story's not
so different from that of others who work here. I was a good
student. I like books. Languages aren't difficult for me. I
graduated with the highest honors, but had no serious grad
school plans. My *advantaged* background and education led
me here somehow, and I was dropped rather unwittingly into
this most bizarre job.

1

overachiever

I felt unworthy of the place at first, but a year passed and I
grew accustomed to it. Never did I feel quite worthy, but at
least accustomed to feeling unworthy. I felt so insubstantial here
that I thought it a joke, at first, when Scout took an interest. An
overachiever one year my senior in both age and company
experience. In the early days, I wondered why he bothered
with me. Now I'm just grateful, for those and other days.

2

holding pattern

So I had a boyfriend. I'd lucked out. But it still wasn't much like what I'd imagined adulthood should be. But had I really visualized adulthood before this? Who had the time, between papers on Plato and Kant, between summa and magna? And then this semblance of adult life simply happened. I settled in here, learning to accept the hushed, endless days and appreciate Scout's Friday night cooking and odd little kindnesses. I tried not to despair too much in the notion that this *holding pattern* of identical days might eat up life while I waited for weekends.

3

nebbish

But we are talking about how I got here. And here in a different sense. That story begins, oddly, quaintly, with a cup of tea. Every morning, after his smile disappeared into his corner of the office, there was one other luxury. A cup of tea. A glass of tea, since my drinking glass from home doubled as an unconventional tea vessel. A teaglass, if you will. Teaglass. Is that a word? Every day I'd make a *nebbish* of myself, going down to that pointy, constipated cafeteria woman, and asking, Oliver Twistlike, "May I have some hot water please?"

4

editrix

She warmed that water with her hatred. She sighed plagues into that water. I didn't care. In this chill and inhuman place I was obedient and invisible to everything. I needed that tea to remember I was alive, warm-blooded. I always carried the tea slowly up the stairs and to my desk. I drank it with careful relish. No spilling on the citations. No slurping, no satisfied

Aaaah! Such noises would echo through the cubicles and start an uncomfortable collective shifting of the editors and *editrices* in their seats. So I always sipped quietly.

5

ballpoint

One day, though, something happened. What so distracted me that day? What was I contemplating? The humbling folly of lexicography? The possible universes that might exist at the very tip of my *ballpoint* pen? Whatever it was, I wasn't tending my tea with the usual care. I elbowed the glass onto the floor. Crash. Splatter. Gasp. Tea everywhere. Not only around my own desk, but onto the feet of a certain sour-faced editor who didn't try to hide his disdain.

6

nerd

Everybody looked up. I think I saw a few glares. Maybe I was imagining it. Scout says that in my head I turn this place into a fairy-tale dungeon, exaggerating its darkness and its cold. Interpreting harmless social ineptitude as clammy, crooked-nosed villainy. (Why can't you just call a *nerd* a nerd? he'd say.) Imagining towers and spires on the place. (Is that why you keep your hair so long?)

7

schlub

Lexicographers rarely make messes. I had no idea where to find a cloth, dustpan, and broom. Or if any even existed in the building. The secretary went to fetch a custodian, but returned with only a push broom and a plastic bag. Feeling like a *schlub*, I cleaned everything up while everybody watched. I picked up the big pieces first. The jagged spike attached to the base of the glass. Then a large rounded triangle shard. Tried not to make too many unsettling clinking noises with them. Then I swept up the small shards, and slid everything into the bag.

8

paperbound

Only you, Red. Only you acknowledged the mishap. You mentioned it offhand when you came to give me yet another *paperbound* book from your home collection: *Beyond the 38th Parallel.* I didn't confess it then but will confess it now. I hadn't even read the last book you gave me. You told me it wasn't exactly an academic piece of work. Just some pretty good firsthand accounts. Diaries. Letters. I thanked you for it and you winked. Just don't spill anything on it, you said, and then sauntered off to the secretary's desk for your midmorning flirtation.

9

trash man

At the end of the day, the bag was still at my feet. It was moist inside, which made it more embarrassing. It seemed something that definitely should not be in my possession. A bloated, disembodied organ, full of shrapnel. I wasn't sure what to do with it. It didn't seem appropriate to stuff it in my tiny wastepaper basket. The custodian wouldn't be anticipating glass. He might cut himself. I took it with me instead. I'd find a Dumpster on the way home. Or just put it on the curb for the *trash man*, and then forget about it. To fling the bag onto a curb or into a Dumpster would probably give me some satisfaction.

10

riff

Scout had class after work on Thursdays. That was the only
day of the week he didn't drive me home in his diminutive
Chevy. He was multilingual already, but for some reason he
was determined to add German to his impressive repertoire.
On Thursdays, I went to the library and he went to class. I'd
always take the long way home, meandering through the park.
That day, I *riffed* through the pages of your book as I walked.

11

hang-up

The park was abandoned, as was usual for that hour. I
actually had wondered a couple of times if it was dangerous,
wandering the more isolated, tree-hidden road through
the park when the sun was setting. But when you think of
yourself as invisible, the possibility of crime seems fairly
remote. Crime is a concern for women who have jewelry that
might be snatched, or attractive, creamy white necks that invite
slicing. For women who read too many rape scenes in too
many novels, worrying themselves into needless *hang-ups*
about walking alone, looking into the backseat, opening the
front door to men in ski masks. I've never been any of these
women.

12

ponytail

Besides. The shattering of that glass and the breaking of that
anemic silence was enough violence for one day. No more
seemed possible. I looked up from your book and there, all of
a sudden, was a man. I thought he looked familiar, but from
where I couldn't say. The library, perhaps? He had scraggly
gray hair, pulled into a *ponytail*. I smiled hello. He was
wearing a black concert T-shirt with lightning flash letters. I

don't remember the name of the band. It must have been a band I've never heard of.

13

whoopee cushion

And now we're approaching the difficult part, and I'm delaying, wasting time and words. My method is feeling ridiculous already. These words. They fit into my narrative with all the subtlety of a *whoopee cushion* at a ladies' auxiliary tea. You like that one, Red? It feels to me like you would. It feels like what you would think of my work. But I digress. Because here is where everything changes. Here is where I cease and the story begins.

14

off-the-wall

Good book? said the man. I stopped and tried, for a second, to assess the meaning of his question. The meaning of the moment in general. Was this a weird thing, the approach of this man? His asking about a book? Could he even see the cover? He was about the right age to be a Vietnam vet. Maybe he was interested in all manner of Cold War military interventions in Asia. But still, wasn't this encounter maybe a little *off-the-wall*?

15

sonic boom

If I'd had long enough to think about it, would I have realized what this moment was going to be? Too late. He grabbed me hard by my hair. Then I knew what this moment was. Every brain cell screamed the answer, but too late. A *sonic boom* of survival instinct, but too late. He had me locked against his body with the crook of his arm. There was a brown car a few yards up, and he was dragging me to it. I opened my mouth and bit down hard into his arm.

16

deep-six

He let go. Maybe he was in pain. But more likely he was amused. He grabbed my hair again, and pulled my face into his. I don't remember when I dropped the book. I only remember realizing that my hands were free but for the bag on my wrist. Not very bright, he breathed into my mouth. Just like I thought. I knew you'd be— But he didn't finish, because both of my hands had grabbed the bag, my right hand grasping the base of the broken glass through the plastic, and mashed it into his neck in one quick, upward thrust. Have you ever seen a baby fitting a toy block into a correctly shaped hole? It was just like that. A swift and natural act. But afterwards, mystified, openmouthed surprise. Is it possible this man and I shared a common emotion, in the seconds that followed? We stared at each other, both stunned, him with his hand at the puffy white collar now stuck to his neck, me untangling my left hand from the bag's bloody plastic handle, now dangling beneath his chin. He let go of my hair and stumbled toward the brown car, making gurgles that sounded like Fuck. I watched him stoop and gag for a moment before I ran. I don't really remember running out of the park. I only remember surfacing at the street that runs by the back entrance. And then walking the rest of the way, breathless but comforted by the headlights that were now whizzing by in the dusk. After I got home, I sat at my kitchen table for I don't know how long, doing and thinking nothing. It wasn't until at least an hour passed that I noticed the cuts on my hands and wrist, and not for a while after that I got up and cleaned them and covered them. And it wasn't until the next day that I began to worry about your book. *Beyond the 38th Parallel,* so hastily *deep-sixed* in the park.

17

eek

Scout called after his class, which broke my trance. He talked about a pickup truck driver who had cut him off on his way home, and to whom he had seriously considered giving the finger. And then he wanted to know why I was being so quiet. He asked what was up. I said not much. Why didn't I say more? Why didn't I cry or fall on the floor in fits, screaming Outrage! *Eek!* Blood! Guts! Take me to the police!

18

macho

And why didn't I call the police? For one, the police department never seemed an institution that had much to do with me. Dull-witted mustachioed *machos* in coordinated light blue dress shirts. Like a high school football team dressed up before Homecoming Weekend. Big, dumb, brutal boys pretending to be gentlemen. Who are they trying to kid, and what use would I have for them, especially just then? I doubt my sentiment about this point will ever change, at least with respect to my special designation, and their peripheral relationship to it.

19

pj

Alone in my apartment, it seemed best to stay silent, and stay put. I was alone but surrounded by just enough humanity to feel safe. The nameless couple in the apartment on one side, the unemployed Tarot card man on the other. That old woman adjusting her thunderous Craftmatic upstairs. I put on my *pj*s and watched TV all night.

20

unscripted

Scout drove me to work the next morning. We talked about the usual things. After he parked the car, he asked me what happened to my wrist. Vegetables, I said. It was a short and *unscripted* version of a story I had half-prepared earlier, for this very purpose. Something to do with chopping vegetables, I had thought, would have a touch of realism. I got out of Scout's car to ease the transition from that conversation to another. The work day went without incident. No policeman came.

21

showtime

On the news, that evening's top story was of the dead man found in Freeman Park. Not on the paved path where I had left him, but farther into the wooded area. Stabbed in the neck and bled to death under the evergreens. Derek Brownlow was 42 years old. It was *showtime* now. But oddly, I had a sudden craving for a cup of tea—sweet, milky, and warm. I put on a pot of water and watched it steam and bubble, trying to remember my last cup of tea. The exact temperature, the amount of sugar, how long it had steeped, the strength of the flavor. When I'd had that last sip, I had no idea I wouldn't get another, I'd break my glass, I'd never experience the exact sensation of that cup of tea again. It had been, in retrospect, a particularly delicious cup of tea.

22

blow-dryer

I switched off the stove and picked up the phone. By the time Scout answered, I'd lost it. I was crying. He wanted to know what was the matter, nearly yelling the question after I couldn't answer his first couple of tries. I couldn't form sentences, or even meaningful one-word answers. He hung up. A few minutes later, he was there, at my door. His cheeks were red from rushing there in the cold. His hair, usually so carefully styled with a round brush and *blow-dryer*, was tousled in all directions. He had never looked so cute. He had never looked so powerless. I wanted to hug him, for strength, and then push him back out the door. I was glad to have him there, but suddenly acutely aware that he couldn't save me from anything. He followed me into the kitchen and watched me pour tea water from the pot to the sink. He wanted to know if I was all right. I said no. No, I said again. I'm crazy. You wouldn't believe how crazy I've become.

23

headshrinker

He offered me one of my own kitchen chairs. Even upon seeing his reserved and intellectual girlfriend in such serious need of a *headshrinker*, he didn't lose his composure or his gentlemanly way. What is it? he wanted to know. His calm was impressive, and it made the misplaced absurdity of the story all the more clear. That story and this calm couldn't exist together in the same room.

24

opt out

So I opted for silence. Since the only other option was explicit speech, and all the inevitables that would follow: drama, crying, comforting, fingerprints, uncomfortable questions, men in matching blue shirts, photographers outside the police station. I *opted out* of all of that. Because his quiet beckoned me like a warm bed, a soft pillow, a good book, a hot cup of tea.

25

cop out

I said, Momentary despair. Of an existential nature. It's passed. Shut up, he said then, maybe for the first time since I'd known him. He was tired from his class. He pulled up another chair to sit next to me. He asked again what was going on. And I told him that I didn't know what I needed, but it wasn't talk. He insisted that there must be something, something deserving discussion. You were crying on the phone, for God's sake, and you never cry. What was it? What was it? When I replied, it was something like, You need to trust me. It's true, isn't it? I never cry. I'm not a hysterical person like that. You need to trust that there was a good reason, without knowing what it is. You need to trust me when I say I need you here with me tonight, even if you're not going to get a reason. At the time, I didn't feel like I was *copping out* on the truth, or some unspoken requirement of disclosure between girlfriend and boyfriend. I was only asking him for something I needed, on terms I doubted he'd accept, but seemed worth trying. He looked around the kitchen, thinking and patting his hair down with his hand. The refrigerator hummed. He took off his glasses, rubbed his eyes, put them back on. Sounds fair, he said.

26

button-down

I don't remember how long we sat together like that, perched in the middle of the room on wooden chairs like little kids isolated somewhere as punishment. He looked at my hands, took the right one, and ran a finger over the bandaged fingers, saying nothing. He got up after that, kissed me on the mouth, and made an omelet from the sundry contents of my refrigerator. He spent the night in my bed, sleeping in a pair of boxers. He hung up his *button-down* in my closet, ironed and ready for a second day of wear. I slept well that night.

27

callithump

We passed the next week or two in the usual way. Weekend hikes, book talk, disgust at the verb use of *impact* and the like. And he was still the smarter of the two of us, in all ways but one. There was just one thing now, it seemed, that I knew about the world that he didn't. It wasn't a specific piece of information, or some esoteric knowledge. It wasn't even a story. It was only when the thing exploded later, into a fire-eating *callithumping* fat lady freak tent cinema-circus, that I began to understand the thing as a story. When they figured out who Derek Brownlow was, and what it meant.

28

track record

The police had put together Brownlow's *track record*. The very tenuous connection he had to this office was either unknown or ignored. More important, of course, was the girl he'd tried to kidnap near Philadelphia so long ago, for which he'd gone to jail. And worse still: the nurse in Pennsylvania whom no one could quite prove he'd killed. She'd died under the worst possible circumstances, and was found in pieces in a state park. Suddenly those two witness reports of seeing a girl enter the park at dusk seemed important. She looked like a high school girl, they said. They were pretty sure she'd been carrying some books. It didn't take long for the local news to think up an alliterative nickname for the poor girl.

29

cornball

The Glass Girl. The moniker didn't do much for me at first. I had grown unused to the word "girl" in my feminist women's-college days. But a Glass Woman wouldn't be very intriguing, would she? A woman wielding a shard of glass would just be a crazy, snaggle-toothed bitch. But a Glass Girl could have long, silky hair and a dimple, like the Bad Seed. It was comic relief, this *cornball* superhero. Glass Girl!

30

lopper

In a way, I became attached to the absurd alter ego. To think I could indulge in a little amused disdain that night, the first time I saw it all on the news? For a moment or two, before the images began. I won't write about the worst of them, but you can probably guess. Naked. Duct tape. Garden *loppers.* Just like the poor nurse. Before death or after? Anything he wanted. It occurs to me as I write this that I should be crazy. For months I've been waiting for it. I started waiting when that first newscast ended. Instead of shutting off the TV, I sat staring at my bandaged hand as the next show came on. I imagined this hand separated from the rest of my body, oozing something black from where the wrist used to be, white fingers curled and grasping at nothing but the dirt burying them. Wheel. Of. Fortune. Said the people in the studio audience on the TV. People who think it's about cars and leather couches, and whether or not you get them for free.

31

maven

When the papers went crazy, I knew everything might very well explode. Still, I resigned myself to the stern presence of my fellow word *mavens*. There was at least an odd comfort in submitting to the long silence of the day. Reliable and insistent, it served as a kind of protector. I was reading a book about drug slang, underlining the word "stash," and you came to my desk. When you saw what I was reading, you said, Now you're talking. You said that junk slang was your favorite, and wanted to know if there was a chapter on junk. Then you asked if I'd finished that other book yet. No, I whispered. I was unraveling fast. Was it a trick question? What exactly had been in that article that I hadn't had time to read? Was there something suspect near the corpse? Were you smiling, Red, because of something you knew?

32

killer

Then you said you thought I'd have finished it by now, that you'd heard I eat books like candy. I wondered from whom you could have heard this. And I thought you were just taunting me, Red, and that you knew very well where the book had gone. Were we now sharing an explosive secret? No, I said, trying to give you a *killer* stare. I wouldn't have you in on it. I said again, No, not yet. And you said all right. I think I saw you hesitate before you walked away. None of the usual wink. Just a defeated posture as you moved on to the pencil sharpener.

33

aficianada

In those first few days of media interest, I became a sort of *aficianada* of doom. Disembodied appendages can become a study of any discipline you wish. Mathematics: How many pieces could my body be reasonably split into, with standard gardening tools? A few hours at my desk, that one. Science: I found a moldy heel of bread on the top of my refrigerator, turned gray and green in its plastic package. Would similar patches have sprouted on my face, or does human flesh rot differently? History: Red. You've seen far worse than me. How do you get these poor soulless body parts out of your head?

34

cut-and-paste

I spent most of those evenings with Scout, often in a deliberate attempt to numb the impulse to ask such questions. Once, when I seduced him into the bedroom and put both of my hands in his dark hair, I imagine his head coming off his body in my hands. His body and mind could just as easily be a *cut-and-paste* job as mine. This made me afraid of both, afraid of myself, afraid of my affection for him. I invited him into my bed to chase away the nightmare. He ended up entering the nightmare instead.

35

demythologize

A wounded, resentful version of my face—but blue-white and open-eyed and dead—started glancing back at me in mirrors and watching me when I was failing to sleep. In time, the image began to resemble a dead-prom-queen costume, sometimes dripping black blood from a heavily lipsticked mouth, or wearing a ripped ruffled dress. Eventually, it became more cinematic, bearing little resemblance to me, easier to shut off, like a bad movie on TV. Almost comical on occasion. Almost. Dead prom queen on intimate terms. Dead prom queen *demythologized.* Not frightening so much as unsettling, constant, and familiar. An unwanted pet you feed out of obligation. Weeks later, the dead prom queen lingered only out of habit.

36

hot ticket

Next to the fear, though, came a twisted sense of power. I was the star of this little show, and the less I said—the longer I stayed quiet—the more they loved me. In fragile, soundless, faceless form, I was a real *hot ticket*. And if it was silence they loved, I could string them along for as long as I wanted. They would spoil me forever, crown me with a glass tiara that could erase from my head the impulse to calculate the value of one life for another, or one life for several, or the tenuous value of life in general.

37

wind down

But Channel 9 couldn't dance with me forever. The Glass Girl stories *wound down* as police hit a dead end and reporters got bored. I watched this happen with a mix of relief and apprehension. Relief because it seemed I'd be left alone after all. Apprehension because once Channel 9 left me, to whom would I direct all my defenses, and all my knowing silence?

38

aw-shucks

Whatever Scout noticed, if anything, he didn't mention. He talked into all the spaces I'd started to leave blank. This didn't seem natural for either of us, but still, we tried to spend our weekends much as we always had. He made his omelets. I was learning to make pies, a welcome distraction. I've never been good with these things, and at first the crusts would tear or crumble in my hands. But I was determined to make him a decent crust, if only once. Maybe it was the careful way he always scraped the omelet pan clean. Maybe it was the painful, *aw-shucks* way he carried his unusual height, always scrunching forward at the waist, as if to make himself smaller. But probably it was the expression on his face when I talked. Not so much a look of affection, but of interest, of an effort to hear the real meaning of my words, even as they'd grown spare and superficial. For these things I began to regard him as a sincere and obedient boy, deserving of some boyish reward. Pie.

39

epiphanic

So I rolled out dough and peeled apples and waited for the pieces to come together in some sensible order. They didn't. There was no *epiphanic* moment in which that man's shit-eating grin suddenly slid into an appropriate slot in my mind like a puzzle piece. No clarity came. Only a different determination of sorts. Eventually.

40

plus

In the meantime, we ate an awful lot of pies. Three a week at one point. We always sipped tea with it, and he always seemed to find topics for engaging, if somewhat one-sided, conversation. He told me about his grandfather's dementia. The poor old man was now confusing the details of his own life with those he had read in some biographies of Charles Lindbergh. He told me about his old Latin teacher who chain-smoked and who, one day, soon after retiring, put on a flowered sundress *plus* a wig, then hanged himself in his study. Maybe he was trying to convince me that he had a stomach for strange stories? Was it the pie or the silence that eased these stories out of him?

41

billboard

Sometimes I wish he knew better how to ease a particular story out of me. Not because I needed to tell it, but because I wanted to. Not to everyone, but to someone. That distinction was, however, the main problem. After telling once, who could stop telling such a story? And who could find the right face to put on after the telling, or the right words to continue a conversation after that story was used up? Who could carry that story and still have the strength to carry everything else she'd had before she acquired it? Who wouldn't be reduced to the birdsong of that story? Not me. But complete silence didn't suit me, either. I know there was a puritanical day when people were more disciplined about such things. Secrets were real, in the sense that they were not told, and people carried them dutifully to the grave. A real secret doesn't outlive the person who carries it. It becomes ashes and dust and blows away into nothing. It's very simple, how you make a secret disappear from this earth. Do I think I'm so special, then, to want a different end for mine? I suppose so. I want mine to be told. Infinite silence doesn't satisfy me any more than *billboarding* myself for all to see. Can't there be something in between? Can't there be a way to tell it endlessly but still maintain a dignified silence?

42

larger-than-life

But still I didn't speak. How could it ever work with such a story between us? But even once was too many times to speak it. *Larger-than-life*, that story. Larger than anything. Perhaps neither of us would be capable of climbing from the depths of that story? Weeks passed still, and I didn't tell it. I began to know I never would. Were the pies, then, a sort of peace offering— an attempt to implant a pleasant memory of myself, to sweeten his mind in favor of me in the inevitable event of my betrayal?

43

white knight

As we sat at my kitchen table, my mind would often wander from the conversation, and eventually settle me into a familiar image. It wasn't a confused or disturbing one, as those of earlier weeks. It contained nothing rotten, nothing undead. It was me, floating on an inner tube in a lake, with him sitting on a dock nearby. He was reading a book, enjoying the breeze, only occasionally glancing up to smile at me. He didn't seem to notice that I was slowly bobbing away from the dock, but still, I'd just look back at him and wave. The sight of him so content was comforting, but it felt pretty natural, even exhilarating, to drift away. But what was it I wanted to tell him? Bobbing lazily, often I couldn't quite remember, until the last minute, when I was nearly out of hearing distance. By then, I'd need to shout it, if I was ever going to say it at all. It was that he shouldn't ask himself later if he should have reached out and pulled me back. He shouldn't think back and wonder what he might have done differently. He was, in his way, my *white knight.* That I would remember, even if the rest was too hard.

44

ball of wax

I wasn't sure what I owed him. Or admirers of the Glass Girl, left forever hanging from the tip of her pinky finger. To myself? Self-defense is an act that implies you have something valuable to defend. After the instinct, you begin to wonder. What, specifically, was I aiming to save? What, beyond instinct, makes life worth saving? This isn't a question you answer, of course, but you try to remember to keep asking. It is for the sake of that question that I need to get out of here. What is here? The time and place that nearly finished me? The setting of the story that could swallow up everything that might be mine? To be sure, I'm counting everything as here. This desk, where I wrote Brownlow that letter. The apartment where the dead prom queen resides. This city, these faces, this quiet. The whole *ball of wax*.

45

warm spot

Inevitably, I would have to leave Scout with the rest. I regret this, because if there's one thing for which I have a *warm spot* here, it's him. I wish there were a path that included him, but that's impossible. The day Brownlow chose me was the last day I really occupied this space. He wished to remove me from it, and in a sense, he succeeded. But any losses suffered by either Scout or me are significantly fewer in this version—the one where my elbow slipped and knocked over a glass. This is the best version either of us can probably conceive of, and the only one I care to imagine. Somewhere deep in the layers of remote possibility, there was a version that ended with me telling him, over tea and pie. Instead of this way. But that version won't ever be.

46

wrap-up

Before the final *wrap-up*, Red, I should explain about your book. But doesn't this just beat all? I have no idea what happened to it, in the end. We both know now that I dropped it sometime during that twelve-second stretch between there and here. But after that? Maybe the police found it. But why, then, wouldn't they mention it in the newspapers? An odd finding, wouldn't you think? Maybe it still sits there now, in a plastic bag at the police department, in a file drawer. A kind of shibboleth to distinguish the real girl from the hoaxes, should anyone ever come forward. The real girl will know the title of the lost history.

47

softbound

But maybe someone picked it up before the police got there, during the cold dawn of that first next day. Sometime at sunup, long after the gurgling had stopped behind the trees, but before the body was found. Someone might have been jogging, tripped over this *softbound* scrap of history, and taken it home, thinking they might just read it. Or it was kicked away—kicked along the path by some kids shortcutting their way to school. Or carried away by a stray mutt and chewed to a slobbery pulp. Somehow shoved beyond the parameters of what would be the crime scene. In any and all versions, it's out of my hands. After everything, could this be all that it was meant to be? That I would have something to carry with me that day? Did all that history lead me to nothing more than an odd good luck charm? And now that it's gone, what will I carry with me, from this thing to the next?

48

subtext

Whatever I'll carry, this is what I leave—the explanation, the story I would tell. You told me once that your own stories have no moral, no *subtext*. There is no obligatory response of awe, admiration, gratitude, or pity. That your presence at a certain place and moment was coincidental, and that you're no better or worse than anyone for it. Does telling the story, then, make it not so much yours? Not so much your private and singular possession, but a shared object of all who hear it? Something others can hear—or even tell—as suits their particular ear? You've said you wish to share history, not possess it. But can it really ever be that way, Red? When the blood is on our hands alone?

49

subliterature

Seems wishful thinking, but I'll try it this one time. Since nearly all the words are set now, all that's left is the telling. Your eyes have told me you wouldn't be shocked by anything. Your hands tell me you would have killed him yourself. Your voice has always calmed me, even when you talked of the grenade in your foxhole. As I write this, I can almost hear you. You do what you have to, honey. What can I say? And now the telling's almost over. Just a few more words, then a few more days, and maybe I'll be free of it. Once the thing is released to a perpetuity of endless words and endless quiet. My own bit of forgotten, irrelevant *subliterature*. Made even smaller, even more forgettable, once hacked to pieces and scattered. Not dust yet, but closer to it. Will it blow away into nothing? Or piece itself into meaningful existence? I will leave that to you— you and your knack for stories. Because this is the only telling this one will ever get from me.

50

"Yeah, Mary Anne," I mumbled. "Right. As if you don't still tell this story over in your head every day of your life. As if you could ever stop asking what it means."

Even if I didn't entirely believe the finality of her last

paragraph, I appreciated the sentiment. The girl had discipline, I had to give her that. Wrestle it down to fifty paragraphs, call it your "past," then pack it away in a dusty file.

I poured a shot of gin.

"Good work," I said. "Good try."

The citations stared back at me. All I could see was their whiteness. The words blurred in front of my eyes. Anything could have been typed there.

Try was the operative word here. I gazed openmouthed at the shot I'd just poured. Sure, there was some bullshit in this story of hers. But at least she'd tried.

I held the stack in my left hand and tried to flip through the cits with my right. There was a particular cit I wanted to find.

I didn't like the last one so much because I didn't believe in it. What to *do* with the story was not so much what I cared about. Because you never control the story. The story does with you what it will. And each time you try to fight it down to a beginning and end, it dominates you a little more. So she'd gotten it wrong in the end. But there were places in the middle where I thought she'd gotten it right.

I found the cit I liked and laid it in front of me.

"Now we're talkin'," I slurred. But there was no sobriety left in me to read it.

I pushed the gin shot away from me, laid my head on the cit, and passed out.

CHAPTER THIRTY

Mona started knocking just after four. I think it took me about ten minutes to actually reach the door.

"Jesus," she said. "What the hell is wrong with you?"

I stepped aside, letting her into my kitchen.

"I was wondering if I'd have to kick some ass to get in here. I was about to."

"What's up?" I asked.

Mona gazed at my kitchen table. It was a mess of citations and used glasses. A few cits were stuck to the plastic table-cloth where I'd spilled a little Coke. I needn't have bothered to hide the gin bottle—I'd left out the rum and the schnapps bottles, and the room stunk of gin anyhow.

"Let's go to the living room," I said, feeling exposed. "It's a mess in here.

"What's up?" I asked again, leading her to my futon. I flopped down on it, but she remained standing. "I suppose it's just as dreary in here, isn't it?"

"It smells too," she added.

"Yeah, well. Sorry. That's what happens when you drop in on a bachelor on his yearly bender."

"Yearly bender?"

"Last one too. Last one ever."

"That's what they all say," Mona said, and sighed, sitting next to me. "What's a *bender* all about, anyway? Have you ever wondered? I mean, where's that word come from? What distinguishes a bender from just a regular old drinking binge?"

I shrugged and sprawled on the futon again.

"We could ask George," she continued.

"Go right ahead," I said. "I'd rather stew in my own ignorance than stroke that asshole."

"Billy. How uncharacteristically *unkind* of you. And you're mixing your metaphors. Who ever strokes an asshole?"

"You know what I meant. I meant stroke his *ego*."

"You know what?" Mona said, ignoring my clarification. " 'Bender' is like 'shit' and 'shat.' It's not something I wonder about as a lexicographer. It's something I wonder about as a regular old *person*."

"Pretty soon you won't even know the difference."

"That's not a nice thing to say." Mona frowned. "So, are you really drunk?"

"Not sure. I think it's worn off some. And I've got a headache."

She picked up my oldest joke book. It had been wedged halfway into the futon cushion since she'd left it there the night we raided the correspondence files.

"Maybe I ought to find a good one for you," she said. "Maybe that'd cheer this place up."

"Don't bother. I'm offa that shit."

"You've replaced jokes with liquor?"

"No."

"If I were you, I'd just combine them. There's nothing like a good joke after a couple of drinks."

I sat up and faced her. "I want to tell you about the jokes."

"You've already told me. You rate them. Double-plus is

the highest. And you promised to tell me a double-plus sometime."

"No, I mean, I really want to *tell* you about the jokes," I said, leaning closer to her.

Mona moved away from me, just slightly.

"I'm not gonna *do* anything. Jesus," I said. "Just listen. Do you want to hear, or not?"

Mona arranged her lips in a thin, disapproving line. "I guess."

"I'm trying to tell you that there's a story behind the jokes."

Mona nodded.

"It's about . . . distraction," I said slowly.

Mona sighed, but looked me in the eye. "Distraction," she repeated.

"It's about what you do when you can't stand to lie alone in the dark. I started when I was eighteen. I had cancer and my aunt gave me this book called *Laughter: The Best Medicine*."

"You had *cancer*?"

"Just *listen*. I thought she was a fucking dumb old biddy for giving me this stupid book. Like a bunch of dumb jokes would fix anything."

"You had cancer?" she repeated, looking, predictably, like a deer caught in headlights.

"Don't worry about the stupid *cancer*. I'm talking about *jokes*. Okay?"

She nodded uncertainly.

"One night when there was nothing good on TV, when I was feeling nauseous and pissed, and I couldn't concentrate on anything else, I picked it up and read the whole thing cover to cover. The next day I read it again with a pencil, and rated everything."

Mona waited.

"It's distraction. You know what I mean?"

Mona opened her mouth to answer, but didn't say anything for a few seconds.

"When did you have it?" she asked finally. "What kind?"

"They figured out what it was right before graduation. Hodgkin's disease."

"That's so . . . awful, Billy."

The word was inadequate, but that wasn't Mona's fault.

"Has something happened?" she asked gently. "Is that why you're drunk? Has it come back?"

"No," I said. "Just the opposite. It's pretty much gone for good. It's been five years. After five years, your chances of it coming back are much lower. Five years yesterday. December twenty-eighth. I celebrate every year."

Mona thought for another moment.

"So you had, um, chemotherapy?" She looked tentative, as if she might break something by saying the words too loud. "And everything?"

"Uh . . . yeah. Listen. We don't need to . . . you know, it was Hodgkin's disease. Do you know what that is?"

"No."

"Well, it's a kind of lymphoma. But it's not as virulent as the other kinds. If they catch it early, the survival rate's, like, better than ninety percent. So it's not like . . . you know. Basically, if they catch it early, chances are you're gonna live. And I did. Obviously."

Mona regarded me skeptically, and for a moment, I wondered if she thought I was telling a wild drunkard's tale.

"Do you always apologize for that?" she asked.

I closed my eyes and ignored her question. A couple of minutes passed before I decided to talk.

"I kept imagining the varsity team as my pallbearers." I paused for a moment to determine if I'd actually said this out loud. "I could just *see* it so clearly in my head. All in their suits and ties. Every one of them, strong and youthful and just a little bit sad. Me just a withered, lifeless body in a box. And them carrying me like that. They'd put me in the ground and they'd be depressed for a while, but they'd get over it. They'd move on with their lives. Because they'd have to. They'd have parties and girlfriends and jobs. Decades would pass, and I'd just be a sad story they'd tell their kids."

I could hear Mona breathing. I didn't open my eyes.

"And I hated them for it. I *hated* them. So badly that I couldn't look at them, couldn't talk to them. Even the ones who were my *friends. Hated* them. I keep saying that word but it's not ugly enough to describe how I felt. I was scared too. But I think what I felt the strongest was hatred. And that, in itself, scares me."

"Do you still hate them?" Mona asked.

"I don't have any reason to hate them now. I'm still here. I'm one of them." I laughed at this statement without knowing why. "Not that I know any of them now."

"Was it just them? That you hated?"

I finally opened my eyes. Mona was perched very tentatively on the couch, with her hands clasped between her knees. I closed my eyes again and said nothing. A few minutes later, I heard Mona get up, walk to the kitchen, and turn on the faucet. She returned with a glass of water.

"Here," she said. "Better pound a few of these."

After I had a few sips, she said, "I think it'd be healthy for you to get out of the house. There's a place I've been meaning for us to go."

"Okay," I said. "But you'd better drive."

"Brilliant," she replied.

• • •

There was only one other car in the Freeman Park lot.

"We have to park here and walk," Mona told me. "You know you can't drive on the little side roads of the park anymore? You can only walk them now. I wonder if the Brownlow case had something to do with that?"

I stared into the naked cluster of trees.

"It'll be dark soon," I said.

"We'll survive," said Mona. "You ready?"

"Where are we going?"

"The scene of the crime, naturally. And what better time? The sun is setting."

"You know where it is?" I asked.

"Not exactly. But we could probably figure it out, or at least get close. This is the back end of the park. It's not far from here—we know that."

"To what end?" I said.

"I dunno." Mona shrugged. "Closure?"

"I hate that word," I muttered.

"Oh, Billy," she said, opening her door. "Don't hate *words*. Hate the people who misuse them. Let's go."

"I wish she'd given a few more details," Mona said. "This path is longer than I expected. I mean, it could've been anywhere along this stretch of road."

Mona stopped and looked down a small ravine.

"Couldn't have been around here," she said. "Or she would have said something about that stream."

"Are you sure?" I asked, stomping my feet on the brown, flattened snow where the path had been plowed. I looked down at my boot laces. They were tied so tightly, so securely. Like someone's mother had tied them. Already I couldn't remember doing it.

"No," Mona admitted, and began to walk again.

I followed her. It was freezing. The kind of cold you can just imagine dying in. The kind of cold that makes you want to take every living, breathing thing you can find, bring them all home, put them all to bed.

"Mona," I huffed, "what do you think we're gonna find? You think if we find the right spot and kick away a little snow, we'll find a copy of *Beyond the 38th Parallel*?"

"Of course not," Mona said, and then stopped again.

"Maybe around here," she said, and took a noisy breath, maybe hoping to smell something. A bloody residue of some kind.

"Maybe," I agreed. My face was starting to stiffen, and I was trying not to move my lips too much. My hands were also freezing, as I'd forgotten the gloves Mona had given me.

"This isn't at all what it looked like when it happened," she said. "I wish it hadn't snowed so much last week."

She was turning slowly, taking in the path, the trees, the low branches.

"We'll never see it like she did, anyway," I said. But Mona continued to scrutinize the unremarkable scenery.

What did she see in these bare branches? I wondered. Thin, pointed fingers, reaching for empty white air. I shivered. What did she expect to see? What did either of us expect?

Nothing, I decided. I expected nothing. I'd never have come here if Mona hadn't suggested it. I wouldn't come to such a spot, expecting it to echo some life-or-death promise. Expecting it to smell of some bittersweet slaughter.

"Do you think he wonders how it might have been if it had never happened?" Mona asked, still gazing at the trees. I assumed she was talking about Dan.

"Probably sometimes. But he doesn't seem one for idle wondering."

"I think you're wrong," she said. "He'd probably be married now, if she hadn't walked this way that day. He might even have a few kids. Can you imagine—Dan with kids?"

"Yeah, actually," I said. "The day I first met him. I imagined him with a wife and a little white house and a lawn. A boy and a girl. Maybe even a collie."

"Are you joking?"

"No," I said. "That's what I pictured."

"But sometimes one little thing changes everything." Mona sighed. "Or at least, one thing sticks out in your mind as the thing that changed everything, whether or not it's really to blame. Like, I always think about my stepfather and his shirts. I mean, there was another dry cleaner two blocks away. What if he'd gone somewhere else?"

"Then what?" I said, wondering if this conversation was worth freezing to death for.

"Then I never would've been a rich girl. No one would have ever spray-painted *Rich Bitch* on my car in high school. I never would've started wearing all of this J. Crew clothing, or gone to Middlebrook. I wouldn't be here right now talking to you. I wonder all the time who I would've been."

"What do you think?"

"Maybe someone more sincere." Mona slanted her gaze sideways, thinking. "Less intellectually superficial. Maybe I'd have been a nurse. Something like that. Or gotten a degree in public health at the state university. Maybe I would've wanted to help people. Maybe I'd still live in Ohio. Maybe I'd be taking better care of my mother."

"Maybe," I said. "Maybe not."

Mona shrugged. "Maybe I'd have been a slutty cheerleader in high school. That probably would have been more fun than Rich Bitch."

"Tiny girl like you," I said. "They probably would've always had you at the top of the pyramid. I'd like to have seen that."

"You know, that incarnation follows me around. I see her sometimes. Looking at me, chewing her gum, wearing her polyblend pants and her sensible nurse shoes. I think she pities me. She probably hates me too."

"She doesn't exist," I told her. "So quit worrying about her."

As we walked, she continued, "There should be a word for it, for this thing I'm talking about. Seems a common enough experience. It would be a word like 'doppelganger,' but of course, different."

"Well, how would you define it?"

"I've given it some thought, believe it or not. At my desk once. If I had to define it, it would be something like 'the imagined alternative persona of... of an individual who conjectures about his, um... potential identity had critical events or circumstances of his life been altered.' "

"Alternatively," I said, " 'who you might have been if things were different.' "

"Don't you have a little ghost like that of your own?" Mona asked. "That person you might have been had one time or another happened differently?"

My fingers and toes were frozen. I didn't want to go any farther.

"That's not the ghost I'm worried about right now," I admitted.

Mona tipped her head back while she waited for me to continue, blowing big, deliberate puffs of fog out of her mouth.

"Remember I said this year was my last bender?"

"Yeah."

"I want to mean that."

"Why wouldn't you mean it?" She continued to blow fog rings.

"Well, for one, it didn't really have much of a feeling of finality to it." I had to look away from her to explain. I felt like I was pouring my heart out to the Little Match Girl. "And it's hard for me, sometimes . . . to really *mean* anything. You know what I'm saying?"

Mona stopped her puffing. "Maybe."

I looked up at the bare treetops again. It occurred to me that it probably wasn't just "cancer" I'd been avoiding saying all of this time. "It's like . . . you can choose to believe in something, or you can choose to believe in nothing. But both are actually really terrifying, when you think about it. So I just sit on the fence and watch and hope someday one or the other won't scare me to death."

"By believing in *something,* do you mean . . ." Mona looked a little uncomfortable. "Like, God?"

"No," I answered. "By 'something,' I mean *anything.*"

Mona reached out and tugged a piece of bark off a tree. She crumbled the bark to bits and sprinkled them onto the snow.

"Sounds like you need a new plan, Billy."

It wasn't the response I was expecting, and I didn't know how to reply.

"Next year," she said quietly. "December twenty-eighth. You'll spend it with me."

"It's not just about December twenty-eighth."

"I understand that. But let's start there. Next year—no bender. We'll just go to the movies together or something. Or make a big fancy lunch. We'll both play hooky."

"I appreciate the offer," I said. "But I have a feeling we're not going to both be in Claxton anymore a year from now. Samuelson's a cool place, but I'm pretty sure lexicography's not my life's work."

"That doesn't matter. I'm promising you now. If you're somewhere else, I'll meet you there."

"I really don't know where I'll be. Maybe I'll be somewhere far away."

"Wherever it is, it's a date. I can fly anywhere. We rich girls are good like that. My stepdad's got frequent-flier miles coming out of his ears."

"But you're afraid to fly," I reminded her.

Mona stepped closer to me and put her hand on my arm. I couldn't really feel it through my thick coat, but it was the first time I noticed her gloves. They were a shiny black leather, instead of her usual purple mittens. Probably a Christmas gift sent from home. I had no idea they made sleek black gloves for child-sized hands. There was something macabre about this little black hand, but it was surprisingly comforting to have it on me.

"Yeah," she said, gripping my arm a little tighter. "I am."

"Okay," I said. I took her hand in mine and squeezed it just for a second before letting go. "Good plan."

We stood there shivering and stamping our feet for another moment before she announced, "I think we've found all we're gonna find here."

Mona came back up to my apartment for a little while after we left the park.

I gave her the new article and the full stack of cits to read. She spread them out on the table while I started a kettle of hot water for tea.

When she was finished with everything, she asked, "What do you think we should do with this?"

"What are you suggesting?"

"Well, I'm not suggesting that we bring this to the police or anything. But we *are* holding something here that they'd want to know about. I don't know if we can justify just saying nothing, doing nothing."

"I'd say it's more up to Dan than up to us," I said. "I mean, if he's known about them all these years—"

"Do you think he really has? It's possible he was just saving face."

"No. He knew all the content of the cits."

"And it's not really *Dan's* decision anyway."

"No. And he knows that. It's *hers*. That's the whole point. That's why he wanted me to put the stuff back. To leave it where we found it. He knew Mary Anne better than anyone. So he knows best, I guess."

"But it seems such a shame, in a way, to just scatter it again. We said from the beginning that this was clearly someone who wanted to be found out."

"Maybe she just wanted to feel like someone knew besides her. And someone does. Dan does. Red does. Now we do. Maybe that's the whole point. And the only point."

The kettle whistled and I poured us each a mug of tea.

"So that's it?" Mona asked glumly. "We're done?"

"That's it. I suppose."

"So what do we do now?"

I pushed the sugar toward her, along with Tom's spoon.

"Now we sweeten our tea just right," I said. "And drink it all while it's still warm. And I think I still owe you a double-plus joke."

"That's right." She blew on her tea before taking a sip. "Lay it on me."

"Well, I'm not sure if this is your style, but it kind of fits the situation."

"No disclaimers. Just tell it."

"Okay, well, Sherlock Holmes and Dr. Watson are on a camping trip together. In the middle of the night, Sherlock nudges Watson awake and says, 'Watson, look up. What do you see?' Watson replies, 'I see millions of stars.' And Sherlock says, 'And what does that tell you?' Watson sighs deeply and says, 'Well, astronomically, it tells me that there are millions of galaxies, and it's therefore very likely that we are not the only intelligent life in this universe. Astrologically, it tells me that Saturn is in Leo. Theologically, it tells me that God's creation is vast, and we are comparatively insignificant. Meteorologically, it tells me that the sky is very clear and we will probably enjoy a beautiful day tomorrow.' Sherlock is quiet for a moment, and then says, 'Watson, you imbecile. Someone has stolen our tent.' "

Mona smiled. "I've heard that one before," she confessed. "Sorry."

"Okay then," I said. "Have you heard about this new breed of dog that's half Doberman, half collie?"

"No."

"It rips your leg off, then runs for help."

Mona giggled and wiped a dribble of tea from the corner of her mouth.

"I prefer that one," she said.

"You would," I said. But it was nice to see her delighted.

CHAPTER THIRTY-ONE

I was nursing a mild hangover the next morning, but it was nothing bad enough to keep me from propping myself up at my desk, flipping through an occasional cit pile, moving my mouse now and again.

I also managed to put the *Teaglass* cits back into the files. Mona offered to put back the last few stacks of 1953 cits I'd been hoarding at my apartment, including the *top banana* cits. She stuck those in with the *banana* cits in hopes that someone would find them later and chalk it up as a filing error.

As I neared the end of the *Teaglass* cits, this one caught my eye again:

softbound

But maybe someone picked it up before the police got there, during the cold dawn of that first next day. Sometime at sunup, long after the gurgling had stopped behind the trees, but before the body was found. Someone might have been jogging, tripped over this *softbound* scrap of history, and taken it home, thinking they might just read it. Or it was kicked away—kicked along the path by some kids shortcutting their way to school. Or carried away by a stray mutt and chewed to a slobbery pulp. Somehow shoved beyond the parameters of what would be the crime scene. In any and all versions, it's out of my hands. After everything, could this be all that it was meant to be? That I would have something to carry with me that day? Did all that history lead me to nothing more than an odd good luck charm? And now that it's gone, what will I carry with me, from this thing to the next?

48

The missing book was one of the unanswered questions of this story. And there were others. I slid the cit into my pocket. I'd done everything else Dan had asked. But I wasn't ready to give this one up.

I fingered the cit in my pocket all afternoon, and toyed with the idea of knocking on Dan's door. If there was more to the story, he probably wasn't going to volunteer it. But maybe he wouldn't be angry, I thought, if I simply asked for it?

Grace came by. She told me a story about her lost cat who had mysteriously reappeared that very morning. I nodded and watched her bright red mouth move and wondered if I could ask her about her old coworker Mary Anne. But no, I decided. It would be unwise. There was no telling what she already knew. Or who'd find out I was asking.

No, I decided, around three o'clock. Dan was the only one I could ask. And the sun was going down on my opportunity to ever bring it up again. Today I had something to report to him—that I'd done what he'd asked with the cits and their copies. Tomorrow it would be history. I charged toward his door and knocked on the doorframe before I could change my mind.

He seemed in high spirits. "Come in, come in."

I closed the door carefully.

"How's your cactus?" I asked.

"Decent. Alive."

"I put everything back in the files."

Dan blushed a little and nodded.

"And destroyed the copies."

"Good," he said. "Thank you. I appreciate your discretion. I'll talk to Phillips about it, and as for Mona—"

"I'm pretty certain she'll understand."

"Thank you," Dan said again.

"I just . . ." I began.

"What is it?" he asked gently.

"I had a question . . . as I put the cits back a couple of things dawned on me, and I know it's none of my business but—"

"No apology necessary. What did you want to ask?"

"Well, I can't figure out why Brownlow singled out Mary Anne. Why *her*? I mean, we gathered that he corresponded with the company for a while, but it didn't sound like he had enough of a reason to want to punish her specifically for anything."

"Well." Dan paused. "Of course, a sociopath's motives are often difficult to determine. His selection of her probably wouldn't make any more sense to us than his tendency toward depravity. From what I gathered from the newspaper profiles, they suspected him of some pretty perverse crimes against young women. In some cases young women who had wronged him or belittled him in some way, however trivial. What about their brief correspondence set him off has never been clear to me, though. Or how long he'd been watching her. He knew about her weekly walks through the park. We know that much.

"Maybe he came to Claxton specifically for her. It's a frightening prospect. But for all intents and purposes it was a random act. She was really just a name to him, but in his mind perhaps she had done him some terrible wrong. And that's largely what makes the story so disturbing. Its randomness. The randomness of the weapon she used, for one. The fact that someone so quiet, so reserved, so feminine, managed to defend herself against that . . . that . . ."

There was awe in his voice. He shook his head, then he leaned back and folded his arms.

"It's so troubling. From his letters, you'd have imagined a sniveling, bookish type. You'd never have guessed him to be so big, so strikingly robust a figure. And with that long hair, and the beard stubble, he looked like, well, like a Viking of some kind—"

Dan stopped talking. We sat in silence for a couple of minutes. I wondered, at first, if his sudden stoniness was for the realization that Mona and I had messed around in Needham's correspondence file. But that wasn't it, I realized. He was describing someone he'd *seen,* and we both knew it. It was not so much the details of his description, but the way he said it, so matter-of-factly. *You'd never have guessed . . . like, well, like a Viking of some kind.* My heart raced. The air between us was chilly enough to make his little cactus croak. One of us needed to say something, and I decided it would be me.

"You asked me if I can handle silence," I said shakily.

"Yes," Dan said flatly. I couldn't tell what was in his eyes.

"I can," I promised.

Dan's face looked weary but his voice was hard.

"Good," he said. "Then get back to work."

CHAPTER THIRTY-TWO

That night, I dreamt again of choking on butterscotch candy.

I tossed in my bed, thinking of all of Mary Anne's cits, now scattered and buried in the file again. I wished I had certain ones to look at once more. The parts where Scout seemed oblivious. The parts where Scout seemed suspiciously knowing. The shifting "you" of the audience—sometimes a stranger, sometimes an intimate. The parts where the "you" didn't seem to be Red at all—the parts that had—perhaps unconsciously at first—made me think they were somehow intended for Scout.

Then there was the odd reference to Scout as a "white knight"—when he usually came across as mealymouthed. Their kiss in her kitchen. The fact that Scout seemed to come home from his weekly class two nights in a row. Lines came back to me that had seemed a little incongruous upon my first reading, but that I'd ignored for the overall sensation of the story. *I slept well that night. Afraid of my affection for him. I invited him into my bed to chase away the nightmare. He ended up entering the nightmare instead. How could it ever work with such a story between us?*

She'd been sloppy somehow. Inconsistent. There was

something she was trying her melodramatic best not to say. But she lost herself in her narrative a few times. Maybe lost sight of what, exactly, she was trying to tell.

One particular line kept running through my head: *This is the best version either of us can probably conceive of, and the only one I care to imagine.*

I avoided Mona the following morning, and buried myself in citations for *madwoman* and *madwort*.

My phone buzzed.

I picked it up.

"Billy?" someone said softly, hoarsely.

"Come on, man," I mumbled. Not Mr. Phillips. "Not *now*."

"Excuse me?"

I started to sweat under my twice-worn polo shirt. Those two words didn't sound like Mr. Phillips at all. Had I just said that to a customer? An old man with pen poised to write his wife's epitaph? Or a pimply-faced artist checking the grammar on a suicide note?

"I'm sorry . . . ," I said. "Is this . . . ?"

"It's Dan."

"Oh."

"Do you have plans for lunch?"

I hesitated.

"Billy?" Dan said.

"Yes?"

"Yes, you have plans?"

"I mean, no. No plans."

"Okay, then. Let me buy you lunch. There's a little pizza and sub place a couple of blocks away. Best-kept secret in this neighborhood."

Right at noon, I looked up to find Dan towering over my cubicle.

"Ready?" he said.

I got up and followed him.

"Get a twelve-inch," Dan instructed me as we stood by the counter. "I'm buying. I like to watch young people eat."

I nodded and pointed to *Meatball sub* on the menu card.

We sat in an orange booth, beneath a poster for Michelob.

"I apologize if I startled you yesterday. In a way, of course, I startled myself."

I nodded. I had to strain to hear him over the sound of sizzling onions.

"If you'll indulge me, Billy, I wanted to show you something."

He took out a piece of lined yellow paper and pushed it across the table to me. It looked like it had been folded and refolded a number of times—maybe even put through a washing machine.

"I'd thought of just giving this to you at your desk, but I didn't want to startle you again. Giving it to you would imply that I expect something to be done with it, and I don't want that, either. Open it," he said. "And read it."

As I began, he said, "And you needn't take this damned silence business so literally."

I didn't reply, but kept reading:

> In fact, she called him that very night. As soon as he got home from his class. And he drove to her apartment. She was crying. She was certain of this man's intentions but did not know who he was or if he'd died. She was oddly frantic about a book

she'd left there, that might or might not have an incriminating name scribbled into it. He thought for a bit that she was either drunk or had lost her mind, but the cuts on her hands indicated that it was all true. He offered to go to the park himself. To see who and what, if anything, was left. To get a better sense of what had happened after she'd fled.

"Stay here in the apartment and keep the door locked," he told her, feeling oddly bold. As he drove to the park, it struck him that this, what he was doing, was what men do. Men go back and check out the scene after women come home screaming. He'd never felt such a sense of importance.

This is what men do, he thought again as he drove into the dark park road. He turned on his high beams and sucked in his breath. The brown car she'd described was there. It was real.

He left on the headlights as he got out of his car. He didn't see anyone. He certainly didn't see any book. He fumbled around the edge of the pavement for a while, looking behind trees and kicking up leaves.

He was about to return to his car when he heard the crack of a twig, and then a gasp. *This is what real men do.* He followed the sound, but even so, he nearly stumbled over him. A man sagging limply against a tree. He had blood all over his hands and shirt. In the beams of the headlights, the blood looked black. He looked like he was struggling to stay awake, or stay alive—the young man couldn't tell. When he caught sight of the younger man, the injured man tried to speak. His lips moved but no sound emerged. He stared up at the young man with pleading eyes. He had managed to pull out the plastic bag but not all of the glass.

This young man had never seen anything so terrifying before. This sight gave life to her story and all of the pain and violence it implied. It was all of the evil he'd read about in Latin texts and Victorian novels but somehow never truly believed existed. There it was, right there before him, breathing and gurgling.

He picked up the plastic bag and, in a panic, silenced the sounds. He did it much as a child squeezes his eyes shut in a horror movie, or runs for a light in the dark. It was not revenge. It was not mercy. It was not even anger. He just wanted the sounds to stop.

Neither he nor she knew that night who he was. The name came later. His history came later. The news came to them as it did everyone else, in newspaper headlines and the excited innuendo of TV announcers. The recognition of his name was a shock, but an inconsequential one. The real shock was always the raw events of that evening. The scant hows and whys did little to change either his or her feeling about what happened that night.

She was able to face her own role in the death, but not his. His role was not excusable the way hers was. His could not be called self-defense. She probably would have come forward, in the end, if she hadn't decided to protect him. The "confession" she left behind was to protect him.

What she left in the files was a fiction. Or more accurately, half-fiction. She wrote the story out perhaps as she wished it had happened. To make him appear innocent if there was ever a need. She told him about this confession just before she left. She didn't mention the addressee—Red. Why she told it that way was never clear. Maybe it gave her a sense of safety, telling Red. Maybe it was a further measure of protection. Maybe Red seemed the natural audience—accounting for his lost book. Most likely it reflected a longing to really tell—to tell someone, anyone, besides me.

I refolded the paper. I handed it back to Dan. He held it for a moment, then put it back inside his jacket pocket. It occurred to me that he had taken me here because he didn't trust that paper out of his sight. He wanted someone to see it, but he didn't trust anyone enough to possess it. I wondered how many times he had rewritten it.

"I've often thought of filing it under some word or other," he said, softly. "Or several, as she did. But I've never been sure which would be the correct ones."

I was curious why he was telling me this—what he saw in me that made him say more than he needed to. Was it something kind and gentle, or something cynical and ugly?

The cook behind the counter called our number, and Dan got up for our sandwiches. As he set mine in front of me, I realized I didn't have much of an appetite. The sub looked heavy and stunk of overcooked peppers. As I stared at it, I remembered Mona's chipotle burrito. How lonely Dan must have been that day he bought her lunch. And yesterday, after I left his office. And the day of the Christmas party. And for years, stretching back to before I was in college, before I was sick. To think that all the time those seeming eons of my life passed, before I even knew what the word *solitude* meant, he'd been sitting up there on that silent second floor, shuffling little papers, trying to explain the meaning of all and everything to the oblivious and ungrateful masses.

"It was a just thing you did," I told him. "Even if you didn't know it at that exact moment. You probably saved a few girls' lives, in the end."

"I've spent my life putting life's complexities into pat, formulaic little nuggets. I prefer not to do it with my own moral ambiguities." Dan paused and then pointed at my sandwich. "Eat."

I took a bite that I didn't wish to swallow.

He took a bite of his own sandwich.

"Would you like a soda?" he offered. "I forgot about drinks."

I felt my eyes filling with tears. I shook my head vigorously, hoping to hide them. He returned to his own sandwich and, I hoped, took no notice of my discomposure. I tried to take another bite. A slice of meatball fell out of my sandwich. I put the sandwich down.

"You don't need to worry about me," I said. "I won't ever say anything."

"I appreciate that. You needn't keep assuring me."

As I watched him chew and study the Michelob poster, I thought about my last couple of anniversaries, and how each one had fallen a little flatter than the last. I thought of all of my teenage righteousness. The clumsy, experimental spirit that had worn off in my first year of college. The friends I'd rejected for their presumed naïveté. The philosophy I'd thought would make everything clear.

"It isn't our most courageous or most cowardly acts that matter most," I said. "It's what comes after those moments. It's what we do *next* that defines us."

Dan turned from the poster and reached for a napkin.

"What?" he said.

"Nothing," I said. "Just more pat, formulaic nuggets."

CHAPTER THIRTY-THREE

When I called Mr. Phillips and asked him what his favorite dessert was, he said "blueberry grunt" so quickly and firmly that I didn't dare question it. No matter that I wasn't sure what a grunt was, or that when I later looked up the recipe online, I discovered that it wasn't something that could be easily transported from my kitchen to his apartment. Mr. Phillips gave a snort when I called him back and asked him what he was doing the afternoon of New Year's Eve.

"Rereading my Kahlil Gibran, same as last year," he said. "You?"

When I arrived at his place with all of the needed ingredients, he waved off both of my apologies—for my bizarre behavior the other night, and for the blueberries being frozen, not fresh.

He humored me for a few minutes while I showed him a picture I'd cut out of *Motorcyclist*—of the Kawasaki I planned to buy in the spring. It was one of my New Year's resolutions, I told him, to start putting money aside.

"Wait till March at least," he said. "Don't put yourself on that thing until it warms up a little and the ice melts."

Then he handed it back to me without further comment. He seemed more eager to talk about Dan than anything else. About how cool he'd been when Dan called him, and what a worrywart Dan tended to be.

He sat at his little round kitchen table and talked as I poked around in his cabinets and drawers to find the right equipment—a fork, measuring cups, a cast-iron skillet that looked twice as old as me. Then I listened while he talked, letting the berries bubble and mixing up the biscuit dough. Eventually, the smell of blueberries covered up the hot-dog smell of Mr. Phillips's apartment.

"He said he knew he could count on my discretion," Mr. Phillips said, "and that this was really Mary Anne's secret to either tell or to keep. And I said to him, 'Dan, you're like a nephew to me. You can trust me to—'"

" 'Nephew'?" I said, putting the lid on the berries and biscuits. "Why not 'son'?"

"Because we both would've known that's ridiculous. Even 'nephew's' a little bit of a stretch. But I told him poor old Mary Anne's business is nothing to me. If he wants to keep those sad little slips in the file, it doesn't hurt me any. Or anyone else. Except maybe Dan himself."

"How's that?"

"Seems a little pathetic, doesn't it? Him pining away all these years over his little supergirl? Guarding those slips she wrote like a bunch of lost sea scrolls?"

I was afraid my face might say more about Dan than even Mr. Phillips needed to know, so I changed the subject.

"So why do *you* think Mary Anne was so into the Korean War?" I asked. "Dan said something about a family connection, I think. Her father was there, plus her mother's first—"

"A personal connection, yes." Mr. Phillips wrinkled his

nose and thought for a moment. "Something like that. But I like to think it was more than that. Maybe she liked to know about things everybody else tends to forget."

I wasn't sure why my face reddened as I turned back to my biscuits and berries. We were silent for a while, until a little burping noise escaped from under the skillet's cover.

"You hear that?" Mr. Phillips said, cupping his hand around his ear. "That's why they call it a *grunt*."

"I would've thought it'd be from the satisfied grunts you make when you eat it," I said.

"No," Mr. Phillips said. "Wrong again, Homer."

I watched him sit back, close his eyes, and take in a long breath of blueberry-scented air. I wondered what the smell made him think of, and what other questions I'd forgotten to ask.

Mona and I spent that night soaking up a little Claxton culture—a New Year's fireworks display by the river. We parked downtown and walked to the bridge, talking the whole time about Mona's romantic prospects with Dan.

"Did you know I tried to flirt with him a little at the Christmas party?" she asked.

"Really?"

"Yeah. We were talking about our mutual love of dark chocolate. I implied that we should do a taste test sometime. Maybe at that shop next to Cool Beans Coffee in East Claxton."

I stifled a laugh, thinking of Dan coming upstairs in the middle of the Christmas party, flushed and "perplexed." I wondered if his confusion came from Mr. Phillips's behavior or Mona's—or both.

"An implied date," I said, sucking air through my teeth.

"Hmm. That was definitely a risk. And your topic was pretty intense. Dark chocolate is awfully sensual, you know. You might have started a little gentler."

"I had to work with what came up in conversation. We were standing at the dessert table."

"You're definitely resourceful. That's pretty admirable. But I think you need to look at the big picture here, Mona," I said. "I'm going to level with you."

"Okay. Please do."

"*If* Dan were ever to date someone half his age," I assured her, "I think you'd have a pretty decent chance. But would he ever do that? That's the real question."

"Well, what do you think?"

We'd reached the bridge. I followed Mona as she squeezed through the throngs of our fellow Claxtonites, finally settling on a spot by the railing at the far end of the bridge.

"Honestly," I said, "I don't think he ever would. It's that quiet dignity thing. Grabbing at twenty-three-year-old ass just doesn't jibe with quiet dignity. Maybe if he were ever having a nervous breakdown or an identity crisis, you could break him, but would you want him under that circumstance?"

"I suppose not."

"Yeah, see . . . I think the stuff you like about Dan—the gentlemanly manner, the intellect, the quiet respectability— would have to seriously break down for him to consider dating a young employee . . . the Dan you *wanted* wouldn't be the Dan you'd get."

"If he was willing to take the May–December plunge, he wouldn't be the kind of man I want?"

"Exactly," I said. "It's the unfortunate paradox of your situation."

"My life has been a series of unfortunate paradoxes."

Mona sighed and looked across the bridge. "I think the show's about to start."

"Don't talk like that on New Year's," I said. "Maybe this year will present you with a fortunate paradox."

"Maybe," Mona said.

I'd forgotten my gloves. I jammed my hands into my pants pockets and felt a little piece of paper on the right side. It was that one cit I'd kept the day I'd returned the rest. The one that prompted me to knock on Dan's door and ask one last question. As I pulled it out of my pocket, the first rocket exploded, and Mona and I both looked skyward.

It wasn't until after midnight, after the ball had dropped on TV and Mona had left my apartment, that I remembered the thing and checked my pocket again. The slip was gone. Maybe I'd let it slip out of my fingers as I turned my attention to the first crack of the fireworks and the first lights in the sky. I imagined it still lying on the bridge, maybe surrounded by confetti and paper casings from the exploded fireworks.

I wondered if it would be swept up the next morning. Or if it would be left to skitter down the street, into downtown Claxton, or out to one of the residential streets. Maybe it would get kicked around awhile, until it reached someone who'd pick it up and, ignorant of its significance, carry it off into oblivion. Then passed around till it reached the hands of someone who'd never know where it had been and how it had come to be there. Someone who wouldn't know how a word gets into a dictionary, or that in all this swirling humanity, all this endless discourse, only a few occasional bits get caught, taken down, made official. The hands of someone who wouldn't even know what they were holding. Someone who could know, but would never need to.

ACKNOWLEDGMENTS

Thank you to my wonderful agent Laura Langlie and insightful, enthusiastic editor Kate Miciak, and to everyone at Bantam Dell who helped bring this book to life.

Thanks to everyone who read and commented on all or portions of the manuscript: Jessica Grant Bundschuh, Nicole Moore, Becca Bryer-Charette, Danny Arsenault, Megan Gregory, Sara Jones, Cari Strand, Jacob Vaccaro, Leigh Anne Keichline, Arn Albertini, Mason Rabinowitz, and Rachel Schmidt.

I'm also grateful for the support and kindness of the following people: Jane Rastelli, Richard Arsenault, Luke Arsenault, Cyndi Arsenault, Lynella Grant, Kgopoloeng Chabaesele, Lawrence Baepile, and Emily MacFadyen. And reaching a few years back—thanks, Alan Chute.

Many thanks to the lexicographers with whom I was once honored to work—truly a more interesting and eloquent bunch than the one imagined here. Also, apologies for the small liberties taken with the lexicographical process.

And of course, to my dear husband, Ross Grant—thanks for everything you are and everything you believe I can be.

EMILY ARSENAULT has worked as a lexicographer, an English teacher, a children's librarian, and a Peace Corps volunteer. She wrote *The Broken Teaglass* to pass the long, quiet evenings in her mud brick house while living in rural South Africa. She now lives in Shelburne Falls, Massachusetts, with her husband.